The Bar Stories

A Novel After All

▼

Nisa Donnelly

ST. MARTIN'S PRESS   NEW YORK

Previously published stories that are included in this book are the following:

"The Scavenger Hunt" published in *Erotic Interludes*, copyright © October 1986 by Nisa Donnelly. "Table Topics" originally published in *Yoni Magazine*, copyright © January 1988 by Nisa Donnelly. "The Ground Shaking" an earlier version of which was originally published in *Yoni Magazine*, copyright © January 1987 by Nisa Donnelly.

Design by Jaye Zimet

Library of Congress Cataloging-in-Publication Data

    Donnelly, Nisa.
      The bar stories.
      I. Title.
    PS3554.0532B37 1989   813'.54   88-29895
    ISBN 0-312-02544-0

First Edition
10 9 8 7 6 5 4 3 2 1

For Judy, who gave me a rock when I only had one;
Jeanne, who gave me love when I could find none;
My mother, who taught me to find beauty in all things.

Contents

As a matter of fact, tomorrow never happens.
. . . It's all the same day.

—Janis Joplin

Babe's: The Bar

Come close, so close your breath might fog the blue-moon window on the black door, shining like patent leather in the afternoon sun. Go on, look. It's all right there. No one will tell. Let
your eyes widen against the dusk that lies beyond the glass so
you can see it all. Then step—quickly or slowly, however you
please—into the shadows that twirl and dance, into the kaleidoscope of sound and motion, a magic machine that sets promises
of passion and dreams awhirl.

   See them there, just beyond the door? The losers and outcasts, the lonely, the hopeless, the pained who prowl life's alleys on starless nights. Look again and see the oasis, the haven,
the secret shared by the winners, the daring, the holy women,
the passionate, the believers, the lovers who walk proudly
down a sun-filled street hand in hand.

   And know it's the same thing, after all.

Saturday Afternoon

Memoirs of an (Almost) Roller Derby Queen

Babe raps a Lucky—no filter, thank you—against the bar, torches it, and settles back to survey her domain. She likes what she sees, and all of it—from the red vinyl bar stools cracked like lipstick at 3:00 A.M. to the very last bottle of Southern Comfort—is hers. No more haggling with the bosses for a measly raise. No more grubbing for a buck to buy a beer. No more coming in early to clean up somebody else's mess in somebody else's place—watching them live good while she had nothing.

Pulling deep on the cigarette, smoke shoots from her nostrils down past the corners of her hard mouth. Dragon Lady, her enemies call her, a title not altogether undeserved by this woman who once broke a man's arm when she caught him jimmying the lock on the bar's back door. The news had exploded through this neighborhood where *gentle* is just another word for *sucker* or *coward,* and everyone understood: Nobody messes with Babe Daniels or what's hers. And what's hers is defined by the walls of the bar, this bar, her bar.

Steely eyes roam the room, taking their time, drinking it in as if she'd been lost in the desert for a very long time and this, finally, is her oasis. Taking another drag, Babe blows a double smoke ring and watches it hang lazy in the cool, still air. A perfect bar halo, dissolving in the bluing, dusky light. She smiles. The mirror smiles back, reflecting a small woman with huge fast hands, and eyes that probe so deep they might be able to touch even the devil's core.

Over the years, the mirror has looked out on life inside

Babe's bar and the women moving through its recesses and shallows. Lean early days when only shadows crossed the gleaming dance floor, building to a crescendo of nights when a thousand faces, all anxious and eager, bounce and sway, tease and twirl across the mirror's surface. Time passes; only the names change.

Like the mirror, Babe's eyes reflect the years, but now she knows fewer of the names, more of the faces that call her bar home for a night or longer. And with each year gone, Babe's sheared hair grays a little more. A few new laugh lines march to the corners of her eyes and settle into wrinkles. The gray eyes flash less often from passion and rage.

Only the hands grow faster, more sure, as if all her talent has settled in the beefy stretch of flesh between wrist and fingertip. Hands that pull a beer, push a bar rag, scoop up change and light a Lucky without letting a breath or a beat pass. Hands with a heartline as deep and strong as any oak, and ringed with magic. In another lifetime she might have been a wizard, a harpist, a master pickpocket even, so wondrous is the talent in those hands. Instead she chose this bar, this life. Or maybe it chose her.

That is the pattern of Babe's life: a series of fortunate accidents strung together like popbeads. It's how she came to be the relief bartender at Tommy's Hole one rainy October afternoon in 1966.

"You the boss?" she demanded of Tommy Agres, whose eyes were on a losing solitaire spread. He nodded without looking up. "And you're looking for a bartender?" Tommy slowly raised his eyes to Babe. A worn leather jacket dwarfed the young woman before him. Droplets of rain trickled from her short hair onto the collar. Her cheeks glowed from the chill and damp. She grinned, hopeful.

Every year the bartenders seemed to get younger, or maybe he was just feeling the years a little harder. The hustlers who used to line the edges of the dance floor were his kid brothers just the other day; now they could be his sons. If he'd had sons. And the girls. Like this one, trying to look hard beyond her years. Tommy Agres smiled, his once-magnificent face softening.

"How old are you, kid?" He handed her a bar towel.

"Twenty-three," she answered, "as of next month." The eagerness in her face reminded him of a girl he'd known a long time ago.

"You ever been behind a bar?"

"Not the working side, but I was practically raised in a saloon. And I learn real quick. I wouldn't give away drinks unless it was called for, and for sure I wouldn't be hustling your customers." The words spilled out all at once, finally punctuated with a crooked smile.

Tommy chuckled and motioned her to silence, then settled his sharp chin on his palm; his eyes drooped in thought. Cigarette smoke plumed past his rugged face. "How badly do you need a job?" he finally asked without looking up.

"Bad," Babe admitted. "I got a baby and a woman to take care of. We just come down from the beach." Tommy nodded, considering his options. He hadn't planned on a dyke bartender, but some of what she said made sense. He'd had bartenders who cost him more than they brought in some nights. The ones who didn't have their hands in the till had roaming eyes that seemed to fix on the newest hot trick who was always thirsty but never had the price of beer. At least a dyke wouldn't care about that. Besides, there was something about this one that he liked—the way she met his gaze, defiant and hopeful all at once. Opening his eyes, he took a long drag from the cigarette, coughed deeply, and looked closely at Babe.

"Relief bartender don't pay much. Tell you what I can do, though. I need some help with the early mornin' cleanup. You willing to do that too, and it'd pay a hundred bucks a week, plus tips for your bar shift." He turned to her, his eyebrows raised, waiting.

"Sounds okay by me." It was better than she'd imagined.

"Then it's all yours," he said, extending his bony right hand. Babe beamed and shook it until Tommy thought his arm would rattle from its socket. With that, they stepped into the future together, pausing occasionally to watch a little history being made. From her post behind Tommy's bar, Babe saw a strange world: the vice squad's bagman stopping by every Wednesday afternoon for the little white envelope filled with fifty-dollar bills; the beautiful long-haired boys burning their draft cards on the same television newscast that showed other boys, just as beautiful, just as young, wading single file through rice paddies, with both hands raised high, clutching loaded rifles over their heads—tightrope walkers with bayoneted balance poles; the hippies, wearing smiles and rainbows, flooding to San Francisco to be part of the orgy of freedom and love, even after it had turned cold and ugly. Every night the eleven o'clock news showed America burning, the fires set by its own people. And all of it seemed to reach into Tommy's Hole, chipping at the veneer of bravado they wore so carefully and so well.

Their turn was to come unexpectedly one cool June night when Red burst through the door, her eyes bright with excitement. "I just heard it on the radio, a bar full of queens and queers in New York City went up against the vice squad. It's still goin' down. We're finally bustin' heads and kickin' ass!" A hush fell across Tommy's Hole. The men looked from one to another, confused. Then in the midst of the crowd a clenched fist was raised, and another, and another after that until they were all standing together, fists raised in solidarity, in unity, in anger, too, that it had taken so long. A giant whoop rose from the very floor and echoed from the walls. Babe turned to Tommy, who was wiping back a tear. "This time, for us," she mouthed, and grinned.

Nothing perceptible changed after the weekend of the Stonewall Rebellion. The laws would still shackle the patrons at Tommy's Hole and every other bar like it for years. But a hum was rising from deep in the people's hearts, a buzzing that refused to be silenced or disowned. Stonewall, women's liberation, black power, the antiwar movement, all were conspiring to burn away the shadows that haunted the bars' dark secret corners. It was the beginning. Three years later, when Tommy Agres unclipped the bar's keys from his belt and with a stiff bow handed them over to Babe, the new owner, change was rumbling, untethered on the horizon.

"Take good care of the old girl, kid," Tommy said as Babe's fingers closed around the keys.

"I will," she whispered, pushing down a rush of tears and memories of the past six years. To an outsider, theirs might have seemed a strange partnership: an aging gay bar owner and a dyke bartender half his age. But it was a relationship as carefully tended as gardenias in winter. If the regulars didn't know that Tommy rented a flowing white beard and red velvet suit every Christmas Eve to play Santa Claus for Babe's daughter, well, it wasn't their business anyway. Any more than they needed to know how Babe could see the future in Tommy's palm with its strangely shortening lifeline, or that she read the tarot for him every Friday before her shift started. An outsider never could have known that almost from the beginning both Tommy and Babe had understood how their story would end: The child would outgrow Santa, just as Babe would grow into the bar.

Under Tommy's guidance, Babe had become as much a part of the bar as Tommy himself. She'd run the punchboard and the poker games in the back room on Friday nights. She'd made friends with the thugs who owned the jukeboxes, and was a cagy adversary for the vice-squad boys. She'd nursed hangovers and broken hearts with equal skill. She'd kept her early promises to Tommy, and he'd taught her all he could; the rest was up to her.

Clearing his throat, Tommy steered Babe to the front of the crowd. "Ladies"—he nodded stiffly to the cluster of Babe's friends to his right—"and gentlemen." He smiled at his friends on his left. "The next glass we raise tonight will be in Babe's bar. To Babe!"

Forgetting where she was, Babe hugged Tommy, her eyes misting. Stepping back, she took a deep breath, looked at her lover, Sharon, and winked. Clipping the keys to her belt, Babe grinned until the years washed away and she was once again the gangly kid in the Roller Derby team picture that would hang over the cash register before the night was out. The crowd was still laughing and toasting her good fortune, as Babe ran her fingers lovingly over the mahogany finish of the bar as if she were caressing a lover.

"Reckon I got myself a bar," was all she managed before Red popped the champagne and the crowd closed in, whooping and stomping, lapping up the foam that belched from the open bottles.

It had been a good party, maybe even a great party as such things go. At 11:00 P.M., calling themselves La Femme and the Butchettes, Sharon, Andy, Red, and JoJo sang three encores of "My Girl," the only song they'd rehearsed. At 1:00 A.M., Tony, the blond bartender, started his farewell striptease on top of the bar, only to have Red join him. Babe shooed them both down when she saw Red was still in her spit-shined biker boots. By 3:00 A.M., they'd run out of champagne and cold beer, which sent most of the party roaring into the night, leaving only Babe and Tommy, his attorney, the bartender, and a handful of regulars who were too drunk to care what they were drinking.

With a loud groan, Babe settled on the bar stool next to the lawyer, Richard Dunfrey, who turned to her with a sullen stare. She was holding a bottle of twelve-year-old scotch and a pair of glasses. "Never could stand that fizzy crap," she announced, opening the bottle and pouring a pair of hefty slugs. "Over the teeth and past the gums, look out belly, here she comes!" Babe raised her glass in greeting.

"Oh, for a simple skoal." He sniffed, accepting the glass she offered and raised it slowly, an aging soldier attempting a final salute. He took a guarded sip. A smile warmed his sagging jowls. At least the bar's new owner knew her scotch. Babe was looking at him expectantly. "And congratulations." Babe grinned and thumped him soundly between the shoulder blades.

They'd met a few times before, most recently that morning at the final negotiation of the bar's sale. Then, as now, her look reminded him of an overly friendly dog.

"Well, Dick, this was some party, I'd say." She unwrapped a pair of sugar cubes and dropped them in her glass.

He peered closely at this woman who so easily committed the sacrilege of sugaring well-aged scotch. Her black satin brocade vest, the kind worn by Hollywood's riverboat gamblers, shone in the bar light. The black western shirt was formally fastened at her neck, where a silver and turquoise clasp held a black string tie with silver tips. A huge silver belt buckle rode on a tooled leather belt that sat stiffly on crisp black western trousers. When she crossed her legs, mirror-polished hand-tooled boots, resplendent with silver toe guards, gleamed. This, he knew, was a woman dressed to kill; he could only hope that he wouldn't be her prey.

Richard Dunfrey carried an irrational fear of lesbians like Babe and her friends who rode motorcycles, won at pool, cheated at poker, and belched when they drank canned beer. If any one of them had been a man, he'd have gratefully been on his knees in an instant. But they weren't, and that alone made him nervous.

If only women like these would try to better themselves, he mused. With a little work and imagination, she could be a new woman. Yet she talked like a longshoreman, was proud of an erstwhile career with the Roller Derby, and washed down potato chips with sugared scotch. That was the problem with women like her, he decided; they were willing to settle for what life handed them. Even when they did manage to better themselves, they never let anyone forget their beginnings, no matter how humble.

In her gray eyes he could see the plumes of smoke rising from the factory where his father and his brothers spent all their working lives—when they were working, that is. Their faces lined with filth and hopelessness. And his mother, like all the other women, too early gray, too soon old, locked in the day-after-day sameness that provided neither comfort nor relief. They had offered him nothing but more of the same. Only he had escaped, clawing his way out of that New Jersey factory town and never looking back. The fourth son of a mostly out-of-work ironworker, Richard Dunfrey had taken his night-school law degree, changed his name, his accent, his background. And he never looked back or bothered to remember, except on those rare moments when he felt his past stalking him like a ruthless, hungry dog, just waiting for him to drop his guard. But this woman who carried no shame or fear of her past would never understand any of it.

Shaking his head sadly, the lawyer started to rise until he felt Babe's hand on his shoulder, heavily guiding him back onto the stool. "Don't be running off now, Dick. We're just gettin' to know each other." Babe poured him another drink and winked. Richard Dunfrey was nothing if not polite; besides, he wasn't one to turn down good scotch. Resigned, he sank back against the bar.

Only casual tricks and his father ever called him Dick, but at that moment he was too drunk to care. His attention strayed from Babe to the far wall where a young cowboy, who was neither, leaned against the jukebox, more for support than for style.

The lawyer weighed the odds of his rubbery legs carrying him across the twenty-five feet of dance floor to the jukebox, when the cowboy slid in slow motion down the wall. Red and green lights flashed in time to the music across his white jeans and straw hat. Richard Dunfrey sighed, disappointed. Babe's upper lip curled slightly. "Ought to dump his drunken ass in the parking lot," she grumbled, but she'd leave the cowboy there to sleep it off.

"I'm gonna get a better class of customers . . . ones that can hold their liquor." She laughed. "My customers. My bar." She turned the words over proudly, as if they were sacred. "I sure never thought I'd say that." Richard Dunfrey studied her with party-dimmed eyes. Babe had taken a sudden liking to him and, in the way of late-night, late-drunk confessions, was determined to share her life's story with this man, her unwilling confidant.

"Say, I'll bet you two bucks you can't guess how long I've been in the bar business." She slapped two dollars on the bar. "Two years either way. You won't get odds like that at the track."

"All right. Ten years. No, nine. I guess nine years."

Snapping her fingers, she opened her palm in front of him. "Wrong. I was eight years old when I first started in a bar; that was twenty years ago." Babe's words strolled in the easy rambling way that comes from a lifetime of talking to strangers. "Other kids played house, I played bar. Me and Grandaddy lived over Smokey Joe's in Joliet, Illinois. Grandaddy'd been a railroad man, like my old man. After my mom died, my dad dumped me off with Grandaddy, who'd say to me 'Beatrice'— that's my given name, though it's been Babe as long as I can remember—'go on downstairs and fetch me up a bucket of beer.' I'd march into old Smokey Joe's like I owned the place. Then mornings Grandaddy'd take me with him when he washed the place down. He always made me do the johns. God, I hate johns. It was just a hole in the wall across from the railroad depot. Nothing special, just a stopover for the Zephyr on its way to Chi-town. You ever make that trip, Dick?"

Richard Dunfrey was suddenly and deeply saddened that he had never seen Chicago. " 'City of the Big Shoulders,' " he boomed, raising his glass. " 'Hog Butcher for the World.' " Babe laughed, pouring her newfound friend another shot.

"Carl Sandburg'd be real proud of you, old buddy. I think I saw him getting into a taxi once, least it looked like him. But that's another story, and I got a ton of 'em. Just like Grandaddy." A gentle smile softened her hard features; memories warmed by scotch and Patsy Cline, who was walking after midnight through the jukebox and across the dance floor, where a pair of tired drunks swayed to the music.

Babe turned to the attorney, whose eyes were riveted on the end of the bar, first on Tony the bartender, and then on Rock Hudson, who was pursuing Doris Day on the "Late Late Show." "Fate's a funny thing, wouldn't you say, Dick?" Thumping him between the shoulder blades, Babe jarred him back from a sodden fantasy that vaguely involved Tony and Rock and a trampoline.

"It's not been a month since Tommy went to the doc and found out he's got emphysema. God knows I love that man like a brother." She blinked hard, pushing down a threatening tear. " 'Course, for a long time we'd known something was bad wrong with him because of how his lifeline kept changing every time I looked at it."

And how he coughed until he turned blue, thought Richard Dunfrey, who toyed with the idea of handing Babe his handkerchief, then decided against it.

"Well, next thing I know, he gets it in his head to move to Miami and retire with a bunch of other old faggots—pardon my French—and bam! Babe's got herself a bar." She slapped her leg, still marveling at her good fortune.

"It wouldn't be mine, neither, if my old man hadn't cashed it in last year. Heart attack took him—'course he never had much of a heart that I ever saw—while he was on the graveyard shift at the switching yard. Did I say he was a railroad man? So the Illinois Central life insurance paid up with almost ten grand. That was what made the down payment." Richard Dunfrey eyed her curiously. He'd never heard anyone sound so matter of fact about a father's death.

"Condolences," he offered. Babe shrugged.

"My old man gave me two things—the moniker Babe and the money to put it over the door on my own bar. He didn't plan to even give me that much, so I figure there's nothing for anybody to be sorry about."

"What are you planning to do now, Ms. Daniels?" The title *Ms.* had just come into common use and the attorney pronounced it *muzz.* "I mean what plans have you for this veritable tavern on the green?"

"Well, a sign's comin' next week with my name spelled out. A big fancy purple neon. Flashes, too. The women who come down to Babe's will know they're at one first-class club. And don't ask what that sign cost, 'cause, mister, you can't even guess."

"I wouldn't presume to," the attorney muttered, pouring himself another drink and automatically toasting Babe with a nod and cursory smile. Babe grinned, watching the neon flash in her mind.

"And it's been a while, but better days are coming now. I

saw it in the cards. Only real drawback I can see to us moving in upstairs is there's no room for a garden out back. I always promised Sharon on the next move we'd find a place where she could have a real garden." Babe nodded toward the rear of the bar. The attorney choked on Babe's words. He'd seen the ramshackle apartment over the bar—Tommy had even alluded to it as a possible asset when they were discussing negotiations, but Richard Dunfrey hadn't taken him seriously. "Believe me, love, nobody would ever live in that rattrap" had been his exact words.

"You're living upstairs . . . here?" His voice rose in disbelief.

"Not yet, our rent's not up at the other place until the end of the month." Her voice dropped in disappointment. "Too much to do, anyhow. But I've got some talented friends." Babe stretched the words out and punctuated them with a knowing wink. "Red even knows how to lay linoleum."

"Linoleum?" parroted the attorney, trying to imagine why anyone would want to know such a thing.

"It's a real skill, Dick. Not many people willing to do it for the price of a six-pack, either."

"You're truly blessed," the attorney replied, his voice chilled with a sarcasm that Babe ignored. "And when might we look forward to the housewarming?"

"Oh, we won't go to all that trouble, but if you ever feel like dropping on up for a belt, you just ring the buzzer, or if there's a window open, just holler." Babe thumped the bar with her open palm and nodded so he would know this wasn't an empty promise.

"I'll be sure to do that," he answered hollowly.

"The best thing about it, though, is I'll be home more for Tara. God, she's a sweet little kid. I was going to name the club after her. It would've been her legacy. But Sharon wouldn't go for it. Said people'd think we named the kid after a bar." A warm laugh rolled from Babe. "Anyway, with us living upstairs I can check on her when she gets home from school. Make sure she don't watch too much TV; you know how kids are."

The attorney nodded, although he had no idea what children were like. No one in his world of three-piece suits, operas, and occasional forays into the club scene downtown had any children, at least none that he knew of. And how, he wondered, had a woman like Babe Daniels ever produced a child? Certainly, he knew that some lesbians had children—remnants of failed marriages and abandoned husbands, he'd always assumed. But Babe Daniels? He raised his bifocals and peered over them, as if seeing her unaided would somehow reveal an overlooked crack in her exterior. He tried to imagine her in an apron or a wedding gown but came up empty, his heart pouring out to the faceless Mr. Daniels who had been shackled to this woman. "Poor bastard." He sighed.

"Who?" Babe asked, vaguely interested.

"Uh, your ex-husband," the attorney muttered. "I was merely extending my condolences. About your marriage, I mean." Even drunk, he sounded pompous.

"Whooee! That's a good one!" Babe hooted. "I don't have a husband, ex or otherwise!" She looked around for someone to share the joke with, but all the women were long gone, leaving her with a dozen men who wouldn't appreciate the irony. "Hell, I never did have nothing to do with men. I told you I was with the Roller Derby." This she announced with such finality it was obviously meant to settle the question, but the attorney couldn't make the connection.

The ways of lesbians, especially ones like Babe, eluded Richard Dunfrey, who suddenly wondered if it was decent for a pair of them to raise a child. Well, at least it was a girl child; there was some comfort in that, he decided. But where, he wondered, was the child's father? The endless stream of Scotch and champagne was playing tricks on his mind, eroding reason. Surely they couldn't . . . He looked skeptically at Babe. No, he finally decided, they couldn't. Still, he'd seen a movie once on the "Late Late Show" about a tribe of jungle Amazons who'd captured an English gentlemen tourist and kept him in a cage like a common bull. If that was their heritage, who was to say what they were capable of? Confused, he pushed down the idea and drained off the last of the scotch. Intimate thoughts about lesbians and six hours of drinking had left him slightly nauseated.

Rallying slightly, Richard Dunfrey looked around the bar with its tired clientele of aging men and young hustlers and realized he was saying good-bye to Tommy's Hole. He knew better than to think that this proud and slightly drunken woman next to him might leave things the same. Looking at Babe, he could see the future in her eyes. Suddenly overcome by nostalgia, he excused himself and headed toward the men's room. The glory holes would probably be the first to go, he thought sadly, relieving himself. "Damn dyke," he muttered, wondering if she had an attorney.

Left alone for the first time that evening, Babe sucked the sugary syrup from the bottom of her glass. Pouring another drink, she routed the last Lucky from the pack that nestled against her left breast. Flipping back the cover of her old silver Zippo, she sent its wheel spinning until a blue-gold flame erupted against the night. A promise to hold back the demons for a few more hours until dawn. The lighter had been the first present Sharon had ever given her and, like the two of them, it still worked.

Turning the lighter over in her hands, studying the scratches that threatened the elaborate monogram, Babe remembered the night she'd opened the little white box with its crumpled pink bow. "But I ain't got nothin' for you." Her voice had gone husky with embarrassment.

"You gave me my daughter and the best time of my life," Sharon had replied, nuzzling under Babe's arm like a persistent kitten. Her touch had warmed Babe like summer, even though the winter rains were already threatening the leaking roof in the two-room summer cabin they rented for twenty dollars a week from the old man at the bait shop north of Stinson Beach. It was the best they could do since they'd escaped to California without daring to look back.

"Are you ever sorry?" Sharon would ask, sometimes twice a week, sometimes more, during those first months. "You don't have to stay. The baby and I could get along. It would be easier . . . for you." Under the shadow and silence of darkness, the words were as much a dare as a question, and Babe always stiffened against them.

Did Sharon somehow know or guess of Babe's late-night motorcycle rides down the highway, which put miles between herself and the roadhouse where she was the second-shift fry cook, and even more miles between herself and the beach house? How many times had she meant to leave, only to end up walking the beach alone, looking into the black water as if the waves might wash answers or maybe courage onto the shore like the starfish that struggled silent and helpless on the sand? And then, with dawn teasing, Babe would always climb back on the bike, turning its headlight toward home and Sharon.

Once, Babe had imagined herself flying on down the coast, not looking back until she hit the Mexican border patrol. Drunk on boilermakers one night, she'd even made it as far as Monterey, where a Gypsy woman in the back of a rusty station wagon had offered to tell Babe's fortune for spare change and the last of the bourbon. In the drunk of the night, Babe had imagined the woman was Mama Maria, who wove magic and visions beneath the sign PALM READER AND ADVISOR that hung over the door of her storefront across from Smokey Joe's. On nights when Grandaddy lost his way home, Mama Maria would rock Babe on her wide lap, teaching the little girl the ways of the cards, the secrets that lay hidden in the swirls and ridges of fingers and palms. But Mama Maria was a lifetime gone.

A chill wind had risen from the bay, ruffling the night spirits. Waiting for the woman to warm her bones with the Kentucky proof, Babe had looked over the collection of candles, cards, and wands spread out on a frayed purple cloth draped over the car's tailgate. A red and gold silk scarf had covered an untended crystal ball the size of a softball. The scarf had rustled in the stiff breeze and had fallen away. Leaning over the ball, Babe had flicked her lighter, shielding it with her hands to get a better look at the future. Inside the crystal, a motorcycle with a lone rider moved through gray shadowy mists, never stopping, only slowing at the crossroads as if the rider was lost, then moving into the dusky drizzle again. Cold had reached from the heart of the crystal, clutching at Babe, chilling her with the fear of dying—or worse, of living alone. This would be her, Babe had known, if she walked out on Sharon, leaving her to sign the papers that would give Tara away like an unwrapped Christmas present to a pair of smiling strangers. Babe Daniels had freed her last pair of dollar bills, tucked them under the crystal, and without looking back had mounted the bike and roared up the highway the way she'd come, determined to keep right on beating the devil's odds.

Babe wasn't one to question the fates that had pushed Sharon into her life, even if fate had come disguised as Tess, who had slammed Babe into a retaining wall on the team's first night in Kansas City. By the time Babe regained consciousness, she was in traction in a four-bed ward in the county hospital, her fledgling Roller Derby career as shattered as her leg. The doctors pinned the leg together and patched up a few hopes that Babe Daniels might skate again. She knew better. The leg never did heal properly, which left Babe with a distinctive gait that ever after sent her sailing across the floor like a ship listing off-center, as if its cargo had come unsettled.

Before leaving town, Fearless Faye Fletcher, who'd known well the spotlight saved for real Roller Derby queens, stopped by the hospital bearing sympathy, Babe's last check (minus uniform and skate fee), a pint of Canadian Club, a note that the Roller Derby had fifteen hundred dollars on deposit to pay the hospital bills, and a bouquet of half-dead carnations. Faye also confirmed the rumor that Ceil, the leather-tough tryout they'd picked up the week before, had been slotted into Babe's position and her uniform. Babe understood. It wasn't as if she'd ever been a real Roller Derby queen like Faye. The truth was, the fans would never even miss Babe Daniels; she was that unremarkable during her second season.

"Lucky you and Ceil are both the same size," Faye announced, taking a deep swig from the bottle and stuffing the flowers in a urinal she'd found in the closet.

"That's me—lucky," Babe answered, suddenly wishing it had been Faye under Tess's 220 pounds. "You going to show Ceil the ropes?" Babe asked, trying to sound nonchalant, wondering if the new recruit had taken her place in Faye's bed, too. Not that Faye had ever promised anything more than a few laughs. Still a knot filled Babe's throat and hot tears burned the corners of her eyes, threatening to expose her.

"We'll see." Faye ignored the tears, if she even saw them. Sharing the bottle with Babe, Faye settled into a chair to watch "The Edge of Night." The whiskey worked fast and Babe stopped fighting sleep. When she woke up, Faye was gone.

The first day after Faye's visit, Babe cried. The second day, she plotted revenge on Tess. The third day, after deciding that no two of the acoustical ceiling tiles over her bed were alike, she started to count the holes in each one to settle up her two-dollar bet with the day janitor. On the fourth day, Babe was still counting when Sister Timothy Francis materialized at her bedside.

"Miss Daniels?" the young nun asked hopefully, staring blankly at the apparatus that kept Babe's right leg suspended from the ceiling. Sister Mary Agnes hadn't mentioned a broken leg, too.

"Yo. Whatcha need?" Babe answered, pretending to be more irritated than she actually was at losing count. The constant stream of women eager to take care of her both pleased and amazed Babe. Sister Timothy was probably there to check her cast, change the bed, or read to her. Whatever the reason, Babe was grateful for the company.

"I'm Sister Timothy Francis from St. Mary's Home." The young nun searched Babe's face for some glimmer of recognition. There was none.

"You're kidding" was all Babe could manage. Raised without religion, Babe had never met a woman named Timothy and couldn't imagine why this one didn't change her name to something more becoming.

"Uh, no."

"Well, glad to meet you anyway." Babe beamed, wondering if nuns made Lucky runs. Sister Timothy smiled back, hesitantly. Usually her charges were younger, more openly distressed.

"To tell you the truth, I've been racked out here just hoping somebody'd drop by." Babe grunted deeply as she rearranged herself under the sheets. "This is the shits. Pardon my French."

Sister Timothy suppressed a chuckle. Babe reminded her of other girls she'd known and guardedly admired in school: tough, no-nonsense girls who could take on the world. All so very different from what the young nun imagined herself to be. A girl like this wouldn't be bowed by her dilemma; she might not even acknowledge the help the home could offer, Sister Timothy decided. The nun tried a direct approach. "Miss Daniels, your people have made arrangements for you to join us at Saint Mary's." The words sounded stronger than Sister Timothy felt.

Still fascinated by the nun's name, Babe didn't question the reference to "your people." The Roller Derby was paying for her leg and she assumed they'd arranged for this, too. Probably a convalescent home, she decided. At least there she could get up a game of poker with a couple of geezers. And it beat the streets. Babe smiled pleasantly at Sister Timothy and asked, "So when do we move in?" Sister Timothy said a silent prayer of thanksgiving that the assignment was finally going well. Sister Mary Agnes would be pleased.

Unfortunately, Sister Mary Agnes was anything but pleased when Babe Daniels, using a crutch and Sister Timothy to hobble up the twenty-seven steps into Saint Mary's Home, arrived two days later. "Whooee! Good thing I got one good leg or I'd never have made it" was Babe's greeting to the elder sister, who examined her new charge closely. Babe hadn't let the nurses cut her jeans to accommodate the cast, so she'd arrived dressed in practice clothes: gym shorts and a sweatshirt. Shocks of dark cropped hair escaped from a Chicago Cubs baseball cap. At twenty-one, Babe was still slight but well-muscled and solid, her stomach hard and smooth, her breasts tiny and firm. Sister Mary Agnes was visibly concerned.

Babe was studying her own reflection in the elegant brass plaque by the door. Its raised letters read SAINT MARY'S HOME FOR YOUNG WOMEN, with a list of names beneath it. The names, Babe would discover later, belonged to wealthy businessmen who felt that keeping the home open, discreet, and comfortable was in their teen sons' best interest.

"Sister Bernadette will show Miss Daniels to her room. Sister Timothy, come with me, please," intoned the stern-faced nun as she disappeared down the hall, Sister Timothy dutifully trailing behind.

"It's just Babe," she called to the pair of retreating habits. Waiting for Sister Bernadette, Babe gingerly settled on a chair in the parlor. A pair of pregnant teenagers played Monopoly by the far wall. On the sofa, a brunette with carefully teased hair read a copy of *Seventeen,* the magazine propped on her bulging belly. Everywhere there were pregnant girls taking turns stealing glances at Babe, who smiled back a greeting.

"Holy shit!" Babe suddenly intoned, realizing she was about to become the newest resident in what was known, in the vernacular of 1965, as a home for unwed mothers. She tried to suppress a chuckle, but it broke free and exploded deep from her belly. A dozen pairs of questioning eyes shot toward her. "They ought to call this place the Home of the Blessed Virgin," Babe croaked. A titter began at the Monopoly table, then spread to the couch and across the room to the corner where two girls were practicing dancing the swim. The sound rocked through the room, down the hall, past the closed door where Sister Mary Agnes was quizzing Sister Timothy, all the way to chapel and Sister Bernadette. The trio of nuns nearly flew to the parlor to investigate the strange foreign music of girlish laughter.

Babe had been settled in her cubicle for two days before the nuns were able to sort out the strange circumstances of her arrival. It had all started when a pregnant sixteen-year-old, Barbara Daniels, had tearfully convinced her mother to take her home instead of sending her to Saint Mary's as they'd planned. No one had thought to notify the home, so by the time Sister Timothy had arrived to meet her newest charge, Babe was the only B. Daniels in the hospital. Fresh from the university and anxious to please, Sister Timothy had assumed that the remaining B. Daniels was hers.

Sister Mary Agnes shook her head sadly. Babe was already a problem—partly because of the cast, partly because she wasn't a Catholic, but mostly because of her attitude, which the sisters termed "unorthodox." Already she was excused from daily Mass, so Babe and the home's lone Baptist resident sat in the front parlor playing double solitaire. The cast prevented her from attending classes, which were on the third floor, or from doing most of the routine chores with the other girls. So she ended up permanently assigned to the vegetable room, where Sister Joan described her as "trying," owing mostly to Babe's hobby of carving faces into the potatoes she was supposed to be peeling. "Sister Maria finds it, well, unnerving to find little heads floating in her potato pot," Sister Joan reported. Sister Maria was as deaf as she was old, and it was generally agreed her remaining years should not include surprises in her cooking pots.

Only Sister Timothy, whom Babe had quickly dubbed Timmy, argued that Saint Mary's was a residence for young women in trouble and, even under the strictest interpretation, wasn't it their Christian duty to come to the aid of all such young women, even Babe? Against her better judgment, Sister Mary Agnes relented. Babe could stay until her leg healed, but Sister Timothy must speak to her about the potatoes.

So it was that an almost Roller Derby queen took up residence in a seven-by-ten-foot cubicle with a twin bed, a picture of Jesus, a three-drawer bureau with no mirror, and one small window that overlooked a tiny but well-tended rose garden.

Sister Timothy convinced Sister Maria to let Babe take over cooking the potatoes. The kindly old nun, who was tired of cooking potatoes anyway, readily agreed. So Babe resigned herself to spending the most of every day balanced on a high stool, her back propped against the wall, one eye on the pots that bubbled and steamed the creations that came from her potato whittling. She was amazingly accomplished at it, too. On a good day she could turn out the early presidents, a few movie stars, and an assortment of farm animals.

One morning, while she was transforming an especially large potato into Marilyn Monroe, a blonde with piercing blue eyes joined her. "Beatrice, this is Sharon Winston, she's here to help you," Sister Maria shouted. Sister Maria, who refused to wear a hearing aid, shouted at everyone. "Glad to meet you," Babe shouted back, even though she suspected they'd sent Sharon to curtail the whittling.

Sharon smiled shyly, looked down at her stomach that she self-consciously tried to shield with her tiny hands, then into Babe's eyes. Babe's heart plunged to her stomach, then lurched to her throat. She'd seen a sky as wide as the universe in those eyes, which reflected love and beauty, sadness and regret all at once. Babe felt she'd glimpsed a thread of heaven itself and wanted more than anything to be close to this girl. Every evening Babe counted the hours until the next morning when she could be with Sharon again, wade into the beauty of her eyes. One day Sharon wore a Beatles T-shirt, so Babe sang a medley of "I Want to Hold Your Hand" and "Please Please Me" until Sharon giggled. When Babe heard Sharon telling another girl that she liked roses, Babe hobbled into the garden the next night to steal a perfect blossom, the last of the season, which she left in a Coke bottle outside Sharon's door. As Sharon's middle grew, so did Babe's love.

If Sharon knew of Babe's devotion, she never let it show. They rarely talked during their potato shifts or even later when Babe settled across from her in the dining hall. But then Sharon rarely talked to any of the other girls, who translated her simple, shy fear into conceit. This group of frightened, isolated girls, forced into women's choices too soon, lashed out at any among them who were different and defenseless. Circumstance was all they really had in common, and Sharon became an easy target for their rage.

Led by Linda, a vicious girl with long, bleached, carefully styled hair that rose a full five inches from her head, the attacks against Sharon started subtly, almost without notice. A missing geometry assignment, a phone message from a boy who would never call, an unmade bed when Sister Mary Agnes would be sure to pass Sharon's room. Linda engineered it all. From the beginning, she'd hated Sharon, who was so like the girls to whom Linda's mother always compared her. Girls who were always on the honor roll. Girls who had their pictures in the newspaper for winning music contests and college scholarships. Girls who didn't know what was really important. Even at Saint Mary's there was no escaping them. The same nuns who told Linda to wash her face and comb out her hair fawned over Sharon just because she could quote Shakespeare, do geometry, and answer their stupid questions about Saint Peter. Linda's black-rimmed eyes narrowed as Sharon passed awkwardly in the hall.

"What's the matter with those nuns?" Linda would growl. "Can't they see Sharon is just a fat blob? It's a wonder she ever got anybody to do it to her, ugly as she is. Hell, she probably waddled like that even before she got knocked up," Linda would intone, day after day, her voice low and venomous. And the other girls would nod, tittering anxiously in agreement, welcoming an outlet for their own rage at confinement.

The other girls desperately wanted to please Linda, who bragged about her boyfriend in the Marines. He was going to come for her, she said, and they'd escape to California and live in a trailer park near the base. To most of the girls there, Linda's life sounded exotic and exciting, far better than the drab Missouri landscape and whispers in high school corridors that awaited them when they left St. Mary's. Girls in Linda's favor got to borrow her Maybelline eyeshadow and sneak cigarettes with her in the basement. So, like starving cannibals, the girls stalked their prey, forgetting Sharon was one of their own. They shot darts of poison words into Sharon's fragile heart as they relentlessly followed her to the bathroom, loudly criticizing her hair, her clothes, everything about her. And Sharon would huddle quietly in the stall, trying to fight the hot tears, waiting for them to tire of the game and leave. Others would sit near her in the parlor and pointedly tell elephant jokes, sending knowing looks to each other. And Sharon would bury her head in her books, huge tears dropping onto the page.

Fat jokes had always been an inescapable part of Sharon's life, so Linda's abuse was nothing new. But Sharon had desperately hoped to fit in with these girls who all whispered of boyfriends and tragic love affairs torn apart by fate and angry fathers. Once or twice, Sharon had even dropped hints that her baby's father was a blond lifeguard named Alex who had been drafted and promptly killed in Vietnam. None of the girls really believed it, so thinly was the fantasy spun, but it sounded more romantic than the truth that her virginity had become a boring question. That was why, one gray spring weekend when her parents were away, Sharon had invited Rodney Mittsfield into her bedroom. Rodney was the high school band's pudgy first-chair French horn player who suffered from acne and insecurity. He was also Sharon's boyfriend. Sharon never imag-

ined she loved him—only that the experience would turn
her into a sultry, worldly seductress like those who prowled
the paperback novels. Only Rodney had been clumsy and
embarrassed, and Sharon had cried herself to sleep in disappointment. Five months later, Sharon's parents had
checked her into Saint Mary's Home. Rodney, like everyone
else, thought she was spending her senior year at a private
college-preparatory academy in the East. Her mother called
it "an attempt to save face."

Linda's game had worn on for nearly two weeks before
Babe, who mixed little with the other girls, heard of it. One
afternoon, as she waited for Sharon in the vegetable room,
Linda's voice cracked through the open doorway: "Out of my
way, Tubbo!"

"Stop it, Linda. What did I ever do to you? Tell me. I never
did a thing to you." Sharon's voice sounded sad and small,
almost pleading. Babe's head shot up as she listened closely,
her eyes dark as tornado skies.

"You don't have to do nothin', Lardo, you just are. And that
makes me want to puke!" Linda answered, pushing ahead into
the vegetable room where she met Babe's icy glare. Linda
goose-stepped past Babe to hand Sister Maria the list she'd
been sent to deliver. "Thank you, my child," the old nun
shouted to Linda's mockingly shy smile and curtsy. Linda lowered her eyes and took the long way out to avoid Babe.

That night, Babe made it her business to be in the cafeteria
line behind Linda. Babe suspected that if there was a Marine
boyfriend, he was in Vietnam, not California, and either way
she doubted that he'd show up for a sixteen-year-old brat with
blue eyelids. Still, he was the one sure thing that would silence
Linda.

"Once more with that mouth of yours," Babe whispered, her
voice hoarse with rage, "and that boyfriend of yours is gonna
be callin' you baldy." She tugged lightly on Linda's hair to
make her point, then moved out of the line and hobbled from
the cafeteria, leaving the rest of the girls to stare.

"You don't have to stand up for me," Sharon said the next
day after the story had gotten back to her, although she was
silently grateful. Linda had actually passed her in the hall that
morning without comment, and no one had messed up her room
or even come near her schoolbooks.

Babe continued peeling her potato, not looking up. She
hadn't wanted the story to get back to Sharon, to embarrass her

in front of the other girls, but she couldn't let her be hurt, either. More than anything, Babe wanted Sharon to be happy. Babe turned to Sharon, hoping she'd see in her eyes the words that wouldn't come. Instead, Babe sliced through her thumb.

"Shit!" she hollered, sticking her thumb into her mouth, then pulling it free at the taste of blood.

"Let me," Sharon said, taking Babe's hand, holding it tight. "I took first aid in school." Her voice was cool, soothing, calm. The blood slowed to a faint ooze. "See, you won't even need stitches," Sharon announced, wrapping the hand in gauze. After that, the two were inseparable. "Blood sisters," Sharon called them.

"So, what do you want it to be?" Babe finally asked one October afternoon, pointing to Sharon's protruding belly. The baby was due in two months, yet they never talked about it or its father.

"I don't know," Sharon answered, lowering her eyes, as if the very act could make her invisible.

"What do you mean, you don't know? You have to know. There's only two choices. Pick one." Babe was teasing. She didn't believe Sharon never thought about the baby, talked to it, even tried out names for it.

"It doesn't matter," Sharon answered. Her voice was small and the words slow. "It's not like I'll get to keep it. I won't even get to see it after it's born. I'll just sign some papers so a very good family can adopt it and I can go back to my life." The words came stiff and distant, as if she was reciting a class project.

Babe was shocked. In her world two parents were a rare luxury, and she'd assumed the young mothers took their babies home to walk-up apartments and jobs as waitresses or hotel maids, with old ladies down the hall watching the babies for four bits an hour. She couldn't imagine girls giving away the babies they bore without even seeing them. Babe suddenly felt ill. "You can't," she whispered, large tears plopping on her hands as she peeled. "I won't let them make you." When she looked up, Sharon was crying, too.

That night, sitting on the corner of Sharon's bed, watching her lips move while she read aloud from *Sonnets from the Portuguese,* Babe laid her plan. Sharon didn't have to give up the baby. They'd find a place together and take care of the baby themselves. Of course, Babe's only real job had been with the Roller Derby and even if she could skate again, it would be a long time before she was ready for the circuit. Still, she could always get a job doing something else, and if Sharon could find work, too . . . Sharon smiled, her eyes gleaming as she listened to the dream Babe spun, and for a while she even believed it. The hope was enough to carry them past Babe's twenty-second birthday and into Sharon's last month. But dreams quickly born can too easily die. Theirs came crashing in when Sharon's mother came to visit.

"Not give the baby away?" Margaret Winston was incredulous. What was her daughter thinking of? Sharon would finish her education, she argued, just like they'd planned. A nice, married, childless couple would adopt the baby. "Who put such ideas in your head?"

And Sharon had looked at the floor, and answered, "No one, Mother. I guess I wasn't thinking."

When her mother had gone, Sharon turned to the wall and cried as though her heart would break. She was still there when Babe knocked softly at the door after supper for their nightly reading session. Letting herself in, Babe lowered herself on the edge of the bed and gently stroked Sharon's leg. It was the most they'd ever touched. Dusk fell into darkness, but neither one moved. The lights-out warning flashed at nine o'clock. "Nuns sure do believe in locking the barn after the horse is long gone," Babe would always say, and Sharon would laugh. But that night Babe didn't say it and Sharon wouldn't have laughed even if she had. When Babe finally rose awkwardly to go, Sharon rolled away from the wall. Even through the darkness Babe could see her eyes illuminated by the moonlight that chased across the rose garden. "Stay," Sharon whispered.

Babe stood, unsteady, unsure if she'd heard the word or willed it. Then Sharon added "please" and stretched out her hand. Soon, Babe's cast would be off and she could go on with her life. All she had to do was walk through that door and never look back. Instead, she lowered herself slowly to the bed and pulled Sharon to her, changing both their lives.

"It won't be easy to keep a baby," Babe cautioned with all the wisdom of her twenty-two years. "You're eighteen, but who knows what the law says about that, especially with your folks being so against it."

"We'll run away to California," Sharon answered simply. At an age when the improbable seemed easily achievable, she'd

built a few fantasies of her own. She and Babe would run away
to San Francisco, just like Jack Kerouac. Sharon would sit in
outdoor cafés, the baby in a wicker basket at her feet. She
would write poetry while Babe trained for the Olympics.
Sharon smiled sweetly.

Babe sighed. California was a good thousand miles away
and getting there would cost more than even the two of them
had together. And this girl didn't even know there wasn't any
roller skating in the Olympics. "We'll see," Babe answered,
settling back to listen to Sharon read *Gone With the Wind.*

The next week Sister Timothy drove Babe to the county
hospital to have her cast checked. On her way back to the car,
Babe stopped at the cashier's office. "I'd appreciate you giving
me what's remaining on the account for my leg," she told the
woman in the teller's cage. "I'll be leaving here before I can
start my therapy." She was toying with a scrap of paper her
doctor had given her. It had the name of an orthopedic surgeon
in San Francisco. The doctor had assured her great advances
were being made in sports medicine, and perhaps with surgery
Babe could skate again. When she'd asked how much it would
cost, he'd mumbled about special cases and surgeons and waiv-
ers of fees. Babe suspected it would never happen for her but
took the surgeon's name anyway. It was the only thing she
could think of to do.

By the time Babe met Timmy back at the car, she had three
hundred dollars in her wallet. That, plus what was left from
Babe's last check from the Roller Derby and the money
Sharon's grandmother had sent for her birthday would amount
to nearly five hundred dollars. It was more money than Babe
had ever seen in one place before, but still not enough.

"Timmy, if you had two options and one was easy and the
other wasn't, how would you know which one to pick?" Babe
asked suddenly on the ride back to the home. Over the months,
she and Sister Timothy had become friends, but their conversations mostly focused on softball: Sister Timothy had played on
her college team and helped coach the parish girls' team on
Saturday afternoons. Babe's sudden interest in philosophical
questions puzzled the young nun.

"I would ask for guidance through prayer," she answered
guardedly.

"Not me," Babe replied, shaking her head. "I don't know
nothing about that. What if you had to choose between covering

your own ass or putting it on the line for somebody else, even it if meant you might be screwing yourself, what would you do?"

"I would follow my heart," Sister Timothy answered quietly, looking closely at Babe. "Love never fails."

"Maybe not, but it don't pay the rent neither, does it, Timmy?"

" 'For now we see through a glass darkly,' " Sister Timothy recited.

"That's beautiful. What's it mean?"

"To me it means there are often many sides to every question and that the answer may not be apparent at first. However, if you look deeply and love enough, you will find the one answer that is right for you."

Babe smiled, a tear leaking from her eyes. "I may have to ask you to do something for me, Timmy. You can say no, that'd be your right, but can I trust you to not rat out on me?"

"Yes, Babe," Sister Timothy answered solemnly. "No matter what, you can trust me."

Babe reached across and squeezed her friend's hand, surprised by the quiet strength that lay in the long fingers.

A few days later, while Scarlett O'Hara was fighting Yankees from the steps of Tara, Sharon went into labor. They wouldn't let Babe into the delivery room, so over the nuns' protests she settled into an orange Naugahyde settee in the hospital lobby. It was there Sharon's father found her. A large sober banker, pale from Kansas City's feeble winter sun, he began without introduction. "I don't know who you are or what you're trying to pull, Miss Daniels, but if you don't leave my daughter alone, I'll have you arrested."

"On what charges?" demanded Babe, who bristled at the way he called Sharon *my daughter*. Harvey Winston was a man obviously accustomed to protecting his possessions—and his family—from intruders.

"Just get out of town, missy," he blustered, his bloated face ruddy with rage.

"That takes money," Babe answered coolly, rearranging herself on the couch, trying to look hard and casual.

Relieved that she was willing to talk in terms he understood, Harvey Winston opened his wallet and pulled free three fifty-dollar bills. "Take this and go, then." He handed the money over gingerly as if he were dealing with a viper. Babe smiled and folded the bills into her breast pocket. "And I'll need a lift down to the bus station," she added, brazenly pressing her luck.

Sailing through the streets of Kansas City in Harvey Winston's big blue Lincoln, Babe picked out random houses that might belong to this man, the father of the woman she loved, the grandfather of the tiny baby who was still fighting her way into the world. Neither spoke on the long ride to the bus station. "Where will you go?" Harvey Winston finally broke the silence as he helped Babe free her duffel bag from the trunk.

"Florida," she answered, hoisting the bag to her shoulder. "Miami." Watching her hobble into the station, he sighed. It had gone well. His wife would be pleased. Sharon would get over it. It was all working out the way he'd planned.

Inside the station, Babe found a large locker, stoked it with quarters, stowed the duffel bag, and went to find her decoy. Rousing a sleeping drunk from his whiskey-soaked stupor with "How'd you like to make five bucks?" she guided him toward the line under the sign that read TICKETS. "Remember, two one-ways to Frisco." Pressing the money into his trembling hands, she added, just in case, "You cross me, and I'll cut you . . . bad." She patted the jacket pocket that hid an eight-inch switchblade. The bum nodded solemnly.

Tara had already indignantly wailed at her arrival by the time Babe made her way back to the hospital that night. Standing outside Sharon's room in the shadow of an alabaster statue of the Holy Mother, Babe listened to Margaret Winston's voice escalate to a high whine as Sharon continually refused to sign the adoption papers. Pressing her ear to the wall, Babe heard first the nuns, then Sharon's mother. Voices rose and fell, angry, terse. Only after the nuns left did Sharon speak. "Babe Daniels is my friend, Mother, and she's going to help me keep Tara. She loves us."

"Thank you," Babe whispered to the life-size Virgin Mary who smiled a cool alabaster smile.

At her daughter's words, Margaret Winston's voice dropped, turning hard and furious. "Well, if you think that woman's going to help you, you're wrong. Your father paid her off. That's all she ever wanted from you, anyway, Sharon. Your father's money. That's all her kind knows. She's on her way to New York City right now."

New York? Babe turned this over in her mind, then grinned.

These people were as devious as Babe herself. Poor Sharon, she thought, waiting for the nuns to flash the lights signaling the end of visiting hours. Babe checked her watch: nine o'clock on the button. The lights flashed. You could set your watch by those nuns, Babe thought, ducking into the shadows as a nun moved quietly into Sharon's room. A moment later the nun and Mrs. Winston emerged, talking in earnest whispers.

"I know my daughter. She'll do the right thing, Sister. After breakfast tomorrow, her father and I will come and talk to her. He always could reason with that child." She attempted to chuckle, but it came out strained, self-conscious.

Babe waited until she was sure Mrs. Winston and the nun weren't coming back before she slipped silently into Sharon's room.

"I thought you went to New York." Sharon's face was swollen from crying.

"Hush," Babe cooed, gathering Sharon into her. "Not without you, Winston, never without you. Have you seen her?"

"Who?" Sharon raised her face to look at Babe. At that moment she looked younger and more fragile than Babe had ever seen her.

She's just a kid, suddenly flashed across Babe's mind before she pushed the thought away. Instead, she answered, "Tara, of course." They both smiled. This baby was theirs; they'd named her: Tara for a girl, Timmy for a boy.

"They won't let me see her," Sharon said, starting to cry again. "Mother wants me to give it—I mean, her—away."

"Well, she ain't much to see yet," Babe said, ignoring the reference to Sharon's mother.

"How did you see her?" Sharon's eyes widened.

"Changing of the guard, I just took a quick peek—she's the only one up there. Kind of red and wrinkled, squints a lot. Makes a good fist, though." Sharon wiped at her eyes, trying to focus through the tears. "Winston, look at this," Babe said, reaching into her jacket pocket and producing the bus tickets. "Couple more days we'll be ridin' the dog all the way to Frisco, baby. The three of us. Just like we planned."

Sharon tried to smile, but her lower lip trembled. Dreams didn't come true for girls like her. "How?" was all she could manage.

The how was a complicated web that entangled Sister Timothy, who had witnessed only pain and the sorrow of separation in the eight months she'd been at Saint Mary's Home. Love was such a rarity, it seemed only right to help, even at the risk of being defiant. It was Sister Timothy who helped smuggle first Sharon's things, then Sharon, and finally the baby out of the hospital that night; who drove them to the Stockyard Inn, an aptly named, second-rate motel; who bought the keyhole saw that Babe used to free her leg from its cast. By evening, Sister Timothy was asking forgiveness at vespers, and Babe was counting the days until they could escape from the winter storm clouds that masked the horizon. Sister Timothy had said it might be three days before Sharon was well enough to travel. Babe settled down to wait.

The afternoon of their escape, Harvey Winston tried to have a warrant sworn out against Babe on kidnapping charges. Only, the FBI wasn't interested, and the sheriff said his hands were tied because Sharon was eighteen and it was her baby. The stationmaster said he needed more leads than New York or maybe Miami, especially since no one at the bus station could remember anyone fitting their description. Besides, there was a war on and with Christmas only a week away, the station was filled with every form of humanity imaginable crisscrossing the nation.

"Why would a woman and a baby stand out?" asked the stationmaster, who thought they'd have better luck looking for the dyke in a cast. Reluctantly, he consented to check the Florida-bound buses. The answer: "No passengers fitting any of the descriptions were on any of their buses. Maybe Mr. Winston should try the train station?" Harvey Winston set his jaw and started back to his Lincoln; a pair of tears escaped and hung unceremoniously on his jowls. He cried all the way home.

When Sharon was strong enough to travel, Babe checked them out of the Stockyard Inn. Timmy, who was responsible for overseeing the maintenance of the home's Chevrolet station wagon, took it for a tune-up, after making a brief detour to drive the little family to the bus station on the other side of the Kansas line.

"God go with you," Sister Timothy whispered as the bus pulled into the station. Babe pushed tears back, then turned and suddenly hugged the young nun.

"If you ever dump the penguin suit and need a friend, you got one, Timmy," Babe whispered, her voice choked with emotion.

When the Greyhound crossed the California state line, Sharon squeezed Babe's arm.

"Are you happy, Winston?" Babe asked, turning to Sharon's eager smile.

Sharon nodded. "It's more beautiful than I ever imagined," she whispered, careful not to wake the baby.

"California?" Babe asked, watching the warm green roll out like a carpet before them.

"No," Sharon whispered, "freedom."

Kansas City was a memory more than seven years gone when Sharon, Babe, and Tara moved to the apartment over Babe's bar. The attorney had been right, it wasn't much of a place, but in those days, Babe's wasn't much of a bar, either. It squatted on a busy street in a neighborhood remarkable only for its mediocrity. As Tommy's Hole, the bar with its nightly strip shows, hustlers, and back-room action had at least been interesting. As Babe's, it wasn't even that.

If there'd been a way out, Babe would have taken it. Only nobody else wanted the bar. Hers had been the only offer for Tommy's Hole, and that had taken everything Babe and Sharon could scrape together. The bar and Babe were intertwined. Before she'd found Tommy and the bar, Babe had been an itinerant fry cook in an assortment of all-night diners and day help on the charter fishing boats. Before that, she'd been an almost Roller Derby queen. Now she was a bar owner with an empty bar.

As dusk settled heavily across the sidewalk, Babe faithfully flipped the switch that lit her fabulous flashing sign. Some nights, she sat alone on a bar stool just inside the open door, the purple light discoloring her skin with eerie shadows, ghostly memories of other days.

Just as Richard Dunfrey had predicted, the transformation from Tommy's Hole to Babe's had been swift and complete. No one had danced on the bar since Tony the bartender had taken Tommy up on his offer to go to Miami. The hustlers in their tight jeans and open shirts had left soon after, seeking more lucrative sites. Finally only a few of the old-timers dropped by for a quiet nightcap. Some nights in the early days they were Babe's only customers. Slowly they were replaced by women in flannel shirts and leather boots who clustered around the pool table and tipped beers by the dart board. The quiet was giving way.

Babe's brazen neon had burned its own magic on the black
sky, and customers started filling the bar nightly. Sharon no
longer had to get up at dawn to scrub the bathrooms before she
went to work. Babe could finally give notice to the cab company
for which she'd been driving most mornings. By the time she
hired Matty as her first permanent bartender in 1978, Babe
could see good times coming.

If Tommy Agres had ever bothered to look back from his
lounge chair on the beach, where his dying lungs were gasping
out their final days on the planet, he might have been surprised
at the metamorphosis of his shabby little bar into what was
becoming the watering hole and meeting ground for the lesbian
nation—at least its West Coast contingent. Or maybe not. After
all, who'd ever have believed that his dyke bartender could
come up with nine grand in hard cash, not to mention regular
payments? If Babe Daniels could do that—hell, anything was
possible.

Tommy was ten years gone by the time Babe paid off the
mortgage. The nights by then were so fat that even the bar
itself was hidden from the customers crowded three and four
deep against it. It had been like that for as long as any of the
new generation of women could remember. More than sixteen
years of Saturday nights in Babe's bar, of cranking up the
magic machine, of forgetting names and remembering faces,
and watching nights and years move as fast as a phantom roller
coaster across the sky. And through it all, Babe Daniels held
court from her bar-stool throne.

And now another Saturday night was nudging. Babe had
slipped through the back door at three o'clock that afternoon,
though the bar wouldn't open for another hour, carrying a
handful of brave roses whose red petals were fighting thirst.
Stuffing the flowers unceremoniously into an empty wine
carafe, Babe set them by the cash register. Like the afternoon,
the flowers were already fading. The roses had come from a
pale young woman with strange, almost purple eyes who was
selling them as "blessings." Babe had thought a buck a blessing
was too much and offered the girl five dollars for the lot. "Bless
you," the girl had whispered, reaching her hand to Babe, who
eyed her suspiciously and then pulled her hand away.

Rearranging the flowers, Matty smiled, listening to Babe's
story. When she came to the part about the blessing, Babe
paused, waiting for Matty's response.

"So what'd you say?" Matty asked. After ten years with
Babe, her timing was perfect.

"I said, 'Honey, I got me a fine woman at home and a bar
full of others just waiting to spend all their money on me. Any
more blessed than that and I'd be one dead dyke!'" Babe roared.

Matty smiled. By the evening's end Babe would have the
story polished into a gleaming anecdote—more fiction than
truth. Laughing richly at her own wit, Babe had often kept a
roomful of women in stitches for hours. It was a gift she'd
carefully cultivated on slow nights when the hours shuffled
through the door faster than customers. Now on Saturday
nights there was rarely time for stories. It was one of Babe's
small regrets.

Gently lifting a worn leather pouch from her private drawer
under the bar, Babe loosened the string and freed a deck of
tattered tarot cards. Another Saturday was yawning before
her. Babe tuned the wide-screen television to afternoon wres-
tling. The Mad Missouri Stomper, intent on slamming Fancy
Dan's head into the canvas, flew across the screen. "Scum,"
Babe muttered, watching the scene for a moment as her hands
automatically rustled through the cards with the grace of a
seasoned gambler. In another hour the wrestlers would be replaced by rock videos.

Savoring the delicious intimacy of a private moment, Babe
Daniels tapped the cards three times with her left middle finger, the way Mama Maria had taught her a lifetime ago. The
Queen of Swords automatically settled herself home. Babe's
quick hands cast the rest of the night on the bar's glassy surface. Tiny worry lines sprouted between her gray eyes. The Fool
grinned up at her. A vague chill raced down her spine. Gathering up the cards quickly, Babe rapped them sharply against the
bartop as if to punish the intruding imp. She cast the cards
again. Again the Fool smiled back at her. Irritated, Babe
shoved the cards back into their pouch and flicked the television to the afternoon Giants game. She turned down the sound
and cranked up the stereo so the players ran the bases with
Tina Turner singing backup.

"The Fool come to see me. Twice," Babe announced, dropping a pair of sugar cubes into the glass Matty set before her.

"Maybe she wasn't coming to see you," Matty offered.
"Maybe she was just passing through."

Babe snorted. "She's always just passing through. That's

the problem." Babe turned her eyes back to the television, talking more to herself than to Matty. "I been in bars my whole damned life and believe me, fools and trouble travel together."

Matty shrugged. "Nothing you can do about it, I'd say. Just take what they give you."

"That's the story of my life," Babe answered, sinking into her own thoughts.

Her eyes turned flat, flat as the prairieland she once called home, surveying the past in a swoop like a dying crane. Like dreams, only a few memories are worth bothering to remember. Those few were hard and clean, like the pair of yellow diamonds she wears on each middle finger—and just as hard won.

And then Babe Daniels smiled, raising her glass in a casual toast as she braced herself against the Saturday-night hunger one more time.

Eleanor Roosevelt and the Dykeball Losers

With a low moan, Eleanor Roosevelt creaked and wheezed, then backfired once before lurching down the exit, following her shadow. The late afternoon sun hung heavy over San Francisco, threatening to sizzle when it plopped off the horizon into the sea. Kate Solomon smiled broadly. "Almost home, El'nor," she shouted. The aging van's engine banged out a loud SOS. That they'd made it this far was no small feat.

Kate and Eleanor were about to end the vagabonding that had begun more than four months and a whole country ago. Or had it begun six months ago in a doctor's office? Or six weeks after that, when Kate Solomon walked out on her well-ordered life, loaded her cameras, a bulging backpack, two boxes of canned food and soda water, a fifth of vodka, a ten-pound bag of cat food, and a white cat named Berenice Abbott into the back of Eleanor's newly refitted interior? That was when the three of them—Kate, Eleanor Roosevelt, and Berenice Abbott—had started on a trek across the backroads and freeways of America to find the lesbian nation. Babe's was to be the last stop.

Soon, Kate would buy a one-way ticket home on the red-eye to New York and Chris Collins, the network-news weekend anchor who had been with Kate since college. Kate would tuck Berenice Abbott's cat carrier under the seat in front of her, flirt with the stewardess, and let the 747 carry her in its aluminum and plastic womb back across the country. Chris would be waiting at the airport, looking soft and sleepy, unused as she was to being in airports at 6:00 A.M. Kate would walk toward her slowly, deliberately, hoping Chris would believe it was only from sitting too long on an airplane, but knowing she wouldn't. A bright yellow taxi would take them home, back to their sensible, predictable life together. A life with boundaries like a newly painted picket fence. A life with doctors and decisions. The life she'd left four months before, or maybe more. But, oh, the freedom had been wonderful. When the jet roared through the blackness to meet the rising sun, Kate would smile, remembering.

Thinking back, Kate knew it had all started that late-winter afternoon when a pair of doctors had closed the door and looked solemn.

"It's bad news, I assume," Kate had begun, looking into their faces. She'd built her reputation as a photojournalist on an uncanny ability to see beneath the masks her subjects fashioned and so carefully wore. The doctors were old, certainly not in years, but in understanding the workings of pain. It was as if that very knowledge had stripped away any youth that might otherwise have remained.

"The results, I'm afraid, aren't what you'd hoped," the woman doctor had said, checking her notes as if she might find something there that she'd missed before.

What I'd hoped, not what they had hoped; Kate turned the doctor's choice of words over in her mind. Maybe doctors weren't allowed the luxury of hope, maybe all that knowledge precluded something so simple, so naive. Kate had come to them only when there was no one else who could give her answers about the tingling in her fingers, the unpredictable numbness in her arms, the unexplained twitching in her legs, the intolerable headaches that refused to go away. They had listened intently, asked questions, taken tests. She had spent whole afternoons in the medical library, translating their possibilities. And now the nightmare none of them had wanted to imagine was coming true. It was no longer abstract fantasy. For the first time, she wouldn't be just the onlooker with a camera. For the first time, she had to focus on herself, on the legs and arms and hands that she'd overlooked for so long. Slowly. So slowly that it would be almost immeasurable, the changes would come. Slowly. So she would have time to adjust, to learn, to adapt, and to go on. Kate turned her eyes back to the doctors.

"The prognosis, as we explained earlier, is such that . . ." The other doctor was speaking. He was used to dealing with celebrities. His words had ended promising careers before, although usually for athletes and actors. Kate was his first photographer. He liked the way his voice sounded on such occasions: calm, controlled, yet concerned. He imagined he was offering comfort. Kate watched his mouth move, unable to make out the words.

How long it would be until the disease grew stronger than her body, they wouldn't or couldn't say. A year, they agreed, or maybe two if she was careful or lucky or both. "And then they prop me behind a desk for how long . . . until maybe I'm not even able to be there. Until . . ." Her voice trembled, her hands knotted around a wadded tissue. The woman doctor's mouth moved, then the man's. Back and forth. Taking turns. A tennis match of words. Kate was trying to listen, to sort out the words so they would make sense. Trying to memorize the moment. It seemed so important to remember it all, to know the precise moment when they said her life would change. Irrevocably. Forever. But the words jumbled into her thoughts until finally she gave up trying to make sense of them. She was watching a movie, waiting for the subtitles. She was starring in the movie, but everyone was speaking gibberish.

Still numb, Kate left the medical building and started walking. It was late March, chilly but sunny. The streets and shadows of Manhattan swallowed her and her pain. She walked for blocks—miles, probably—that afternoon. For how many years had her cameras recorded the loss, the pain, the silent torment

in the world around her? Presidents and welfare mothers and
singers in rock 'n' roll bands had looked into Kate Solomon's
unblinking third eye, and it had made her famous. Everyone
said she was the photographer who could look into a face and
photograph a soul. Twice that gift had won her Pulitzer nomi-
nations; and twice she'd lost. "Hey, what's the rush? You got
all the time in the world; just wait till the next assignment,"
Wally, the photo editor, had offered each time the list of winners had come up without her name. Now she was running out
of time and no one could promise her a next year, another
chance, an assignment so choice that it would make all the
waiting worthwhile. Only she could do that.

Long shadows had turned to twilight when Kate found herself in front of Abby's gallery. Abby was a third-generation
gallery owner who believed in Kate's talent and handled her
work, booking her shows, selling a few pictures that caught the
eye of casual collectors of contemporary photojournalism.

"Now, *this* is a photograph," Abby had oozed when Kate
had unveiled the Louisiana woman for her show the year
before. Proud black eyes burned unflinchingly at any who
dared to look upon her, the Louisiana woman, Tilla. Kate had
found Tilla—her name was the only sure thing she knew about
the Louisiana woman—behind a neat white house with a wide
porch in a small town that sneered at the passage of time. Kate
and two writers had been documenting poverty in America.
They thought of themselves as crusaders of hope, of change.
They even believed that if the faces of human fallout could
invade the living rooms of America's middle class, something
would change, maybe even improve. They were wrong; the
Louisiana woman knew it all along.

Kate had found Tilla on the last leg of the assignment. For
more than a week, the crew had roamed through the South's
peculiar brand of poverty, working deeper and deeper into the
back country to where a half-dozen people share a two-room
shanty on a dirt road lined with ruts and shacks; where hungry
kids with open sores on their arms stare out from windows
patched with yellowed newspaper; where a mile away white
houses with long porches shaded by honeysuckle and trumpet
vines sit like dowager queens; where southern hospitality—for
some—runs as free as bourbon on a Saturday night.

Abby had been enchanted by Tilla, or at least by her photograph. Confronted with the woman herself, with that unflinch-

ing stare, would Abby have turned away or, like Kate, bought a little salve for her own conscious? Kate wondered.

"So, I've got a buyer for your Louisiana woman," Abby ventured after Kate's unexpected arrival in the gallery five minutes before closing. "Believe me, it's no easy task to sell pictures of the down and out. Nobody wants pictures of the poor folks; they figure it's enough bother to step over the homeless on their way to work. Tits and ass, that's what's selling this year. You got any nudes lying around? They'd go like that." Abby snapped her fingers. Kate chuckled and shook her head.

Later over wine, Kate studied the picture. Looking into Tilla's eyes, she could almost feel that afternoon again. The oppressive heat had seemed to rise out of the earth's very core. The hum of insects had been so persistent the very air had been alive with them. Kate shuddered. "I betrayed her, you know. I didn't know what to do, so I did what was comfortable." Kate was absently leafing through a pile of photographs on the edge of Abby's desk. Abby pushed her glasses up on her nose and leaned back in her chair as if to say, Do tell. Kate Solomon rarely talked about her work, and knowing the inside story about a photograph never hurt a sale. Besides, there was something haunting about the woman in that picture. About the eyes. Always, the eyes. The eyes of a saint or a sinner, but always of a survivor.

"We'd spent the morning in a shantytown," Kate recalled, turning the wine glass back and forth in her hands, watching the red liquid rock slowly like a bloody sunset on the water. "We'd decided to hit the area where they grow sugarcane, and that afternoon I was photographing in uptown nowhere Louisiana. We'd been in there for a couple of days, and the writers were hot to beat it out of town and get to Baton Rouge and a hotel with hot water and room service. I guess I was holding them up, chasing the light. As always. They have beautiful light in Louisiana." Abby nodded, testing the wine.

"Anyway, there was this house, a nice house with a big yellow swing on a porch rimmed in flowers, the kind of a house that nice people live in: church deacons, school-board members, good people. The house was closed: a couple of newspapers on the porch, curtains and shades drawn at the windows, the doors closed on a day when every other door and window in town was open to try and catch a hint of breeze. I guess those nice people were on vacation, at least that's how it looked. Ordinarily, I wouldn't have bothered, but there was something about the light and that house. Behind the house was a garden, well-tended like the house, neat and tidy. And there in the garden was a woman, old, I thought at first, a thousand years old, but big-bellied pregnant." Kate closed her eyes for a moment and when she opened them, Abby was looking at her. She smiled.

"It was Tilla, of course, there on her hands and knees, pulling carrots out of the ground and putting them into a flour sack. When she saw me, she grabbed that sack as if it was full of dollar bills instead of carrots and lettuce and tomatoes." Kate looked intently at Abby, her eyes burning. "Do you know how some tribes believe photographers steal souls? Well, we don't. But sometimes the people we photograph crawl right through the cameras into ours. That's what she did to me when she looked through that camera's lens into me. I wasn't stealing her soul; she was challenging mine. And I was coming up empty. I was ready to turn her into the new poster child of poverty. She looked into the lens, into my eyes, and I saw it all right there: the fear and hate and defiance. But no shame. Dammit, Abby. No, damn me. Damn me for trying to steal her privacy. Her dignity. That's what I was looking for. And I would have taken it, too, if she would have let me." Kate inhaled slowly and moved to the window that overlooked the street below, so crowded with traffic and noise and lights.

"And for the first time in a long time, I said, 'My name's Kate Solomon. I'm a photographer for *The New York Times*. May I take your picture, please?' Just like that. And she said, 'My name is Tilla and I'd be pleasured.' Then without another word, she laid down her sack and smoothed her hair." Kate's fingers ruffled through her own short curly hair. "Did you know that everybody does that—smooths their hair? Not politicians. But everybody else. It's like a reflex. The eyes see a camera and the hands zoom to the hair. Zip-zap!" Kate laughed uncomfortably. Abby smiled. "And we did it. Me and Tilla. I suppose it's short for Matilda?" Kate turned to Abby, who shrugged. "Tilla straightened her shoulders and raised her chin and looked through that camera into my heart. Right there by that garden, I saw it all."

"Too bad you aren't Joan of Arc—it could've been a religious experience," Abby observed dryly. Kate ignored her.

"Abby, she gave me that look like a gift. That look defies any of us to take away her determination to survive despite it all, despite all of us," Kate turned back to Abby, smiling.

"So?" Abby pressed.

"So I put the camera back on my shoulder. I didn't know what else to do. God, I felt guilty as hell. I guess I wanted to rescue her, only I didn't know how or even why. What could I do? Move her up here so she could steal lettuce from dumpsters instead of gardens? Or send her to a trade school? Maybe turn her into a hotel maid or if that didn't work out, another scared, lost woman wandering the streets of the city?" Kate exhaled sharply and turned to the window, her shoulders sagging.

"So who named you Saint Kate?" Abby asked absently, studying her fingernails.

Kate chuckled, harsh and dry. "Abby, you would have been proud of me. I did just what you would have done, the only thing I could think of. I started digging in my jeans pocket for some money to give her. That was my answer to the guilt. But as I started toward her to give her the money, she began backing away, clutching that flour sack. We both knew I couldn't save her or myself. All I could do was hold out a twenty-dollar bill for her to buy off my demons for a little longer. And she took it to buy off the demons that gnawed at her belly every damned day. I knew then, maybe for the first time, that I couldn't change one fucking thing. All I can do is record it. And I'm running out of time for that, too."

"How so?" Abby asked, pouring another glass of wine, wondering why Kate had dropped by.

"Let's just say I'm planning an early retirement, a career change. You can call the pictures limited editions or something; maybe they'll go for more. Or if we're both real lucky, I'll succumb at the peak of my popularity. However, that's fairly unlikely, at least according to my doctors. They think I'll probably just wither." Kate was trying to sound calloused, bitter, but her voice trembled, then faded like a shadow.

Abby blinked, surprised. "I didn't know you were ill," she finally managed. "Is there anything I can do?"

Kate swallowed hard, then turned away from the window. Her voice was calm, almost determined. "Actually, yes. That's why I'm here. I have an idea for a show. It's something I've been putting off for years, but no more. Do you remember what I said I saw in the eyes of the Louisiana woman?" Kate's color, like her voice, was rising in excitement. Abby nodded. "Well, it's not the first time I've seen it. Like this afternoon, I was standing in front of a record store and there was a woman with that same look staring at me. It was there: the will to survive, the daring, the triumph over pain. And pride. So much pride. I looked at her for a long moment before I realized it was me. Then I started thinking about all the women I've known . . . and loved . . . and they have it, too. It's how lesbians look—like you can beat us down but never beat us. Ever since college, I've wanted to photograph those women, all of them, wherever they are. And now I'm going to do it, because if I can do that, if I can sort out who we are, then maybe I'll know . . . . "

"Know what?" Abby asked, stretching in her chair and swallowing the last of the wine and a yawn.

"Who I am," Kate answered, starting across the gallery. "Book me for a December show." She was suddenly smiling, charming. "We can start a new trend: lezzies instead of nudies. Something of substance, more than a flash in the pan." Kate grinned. "Of course, if that doesn't work we could always have nude lezzies flashing in the pan."

Abby chuckled. "You are a wonderful photographer but a terrible wit. Sure, I'll pencil you in for December." She was making a note to herself.

"Don't worry," Kate said, pulling on her gloves, "even the good doctors of gloom and doom give me that long." She raised the grate on the freight elevator and stepped inside.

"Keep in touch!" Abby called as the elevator groaned to life, adding, "Chin up!" It was all she could think of to say.

On the way home, Kate rehearsed what she would say to Chris. Abby had been easy. Even the doctors had been easy. Chris, though, was never easy about anything.

"How-dee!" Kate called in her best Minnie Pearl impression, trying to make the door slam behind her. She and Chris had been living in the fifth-floor co-op apartment for more than a year and they'd never heard a door slam. Silence. Shucking her shoes by the front door, Kate padded in her stocking feet through the apartment on her way to the refrigerator. It was Wednesday so there would be food. Every Wednesday Mrs. Johnson came to clean and do laundry and buy a week's supply of groceries. A few times Kate had come home early while Mrs. Johnson was still there. They'd exchanged uncomfortable pleasantries and Kate had retreated to her room. On Wednesdays the apartment belonged to Mrs. Johnson.

Mrs. Johnson was a compromise of sorts: Chris wanted a housekeeper who would make the apartment feel like home; Kate wanted no part of living with a stranger. Besides she was planning to convert the maid's room to a darkroom. Kate had shouted. Chris had pouted. Kate had tried reason. Chris had tried tears. Finally they'd agreed on Mrs. Johnson, who had once worked for Chris's father.

Chris had grown up in a rambling house filled with an assortment of distant relatives, various hangers-on, and a fairly steady stream of stepmothers and their children, all supported by her novelist father who had a decided bent for women and companionship. The place would have collapsed around them all if it hadn't been for the string of housekeepers who somehow managed to instill a sense of haphazard order. Her father had sold the Connecticut country house of Chris's childhood while she was still in college and had moved into this apartment where he lived alone with Helga, his housekeeper whom he promised to marry. He died before making another trip to the altar, leaving Chris the apartment and Helga with an engagement ring, and not much else. His extravagant lifestyle of four decades had claimed what might otherwise have been a fortune. Chris had been disappointed at not being an heiress, although, as Kate had pointed out, a rent-free apartment in a neighborhood they would never have been able to afford on their own wasn't a bad inheritance.

Chris and Kate had met ten years earlier in the newsroom of their college newspaper. They were talented, idealistic, full of dreams that they wore like scarves. They wanted to change the world and imagined that they would. Doors opened easily for Chris, thanks to her father's fame, and she took Kate along. While their classmates put in their time and waited for the big break that would take them out of the small-town television stations and newspapers, Kate and Chris had already arrived. When Kate sometimes puzzled over their good fortune, Chris would laugh and say, "But don't you see, we're the lucky ones, my darling." Only Kate didn't feel so lucky now.

Halfway through her second helping of Mrs. Johnson's casserole and a PBS special on Ansel Adams, Kate heard Chris's key in the lock. Leaping from the couch where she'd been sprawled a moment before, Kate wiped her mouth on her sleeve and stood facing the door like a guilty child. Chris smiled an automatic greeting, then her perfect face clouded. Kate kissed her stiffly.

"Mrs. Johnson left us a chicken casserole," Kate said, not looking at Chris.

"I had dinner with Sammy. He's interested in me for that new Sunday-morning show, the one I told you . . . " Her voice fell away. "Kate, what's wrong? Why won't you look at me?"

Kate was standing by the window, watching lights that stretched as far as her eyes could see. She suddenly wanted very much to be part of the night where you could see stars through the streetlights. Not here. Never here. Her hands were stuffed in the back pockets of her jeans. "I saw the doctors this afternoon, Chrissy." Her voice was slow, soft, as if she were selecting her words very carefully. "Chrissy, I'm afraid you and F.D.R. were wrong. We've got a whole lot more than fear to worry about now. It's what they . . . what we . . . suspected." She felt Chris behind her even before she raised her eyes to their reflection in the glass.

Chris wrapped her arms around her lover, pulled her close, buried her face in her neck, and rocked her as their tears fell quiet as rain, washing their reflection wavy in the glass.

Later, when the night hung around them like black velvet, Chris stroked Kate's back. It was the same touch she used on the cats. From the nape of Kate's neck, slowly, deliberately, firmly, Chris's hand moved along her lover's spine, following the channel of flesh. Kate arched her back under Chris's touch that lingered on the gentle rise of buttocks. Kate smiled.

Earlier that evening she had cried as Chris made love to her. Her skin had leapt under Chris's hands. Trembling, she had sobbed against Chris's shoulder, clinging to her, sobbing, "Don't let me go. Stay by me." And Chris had held her tightly, wrapping her legs around Kate, locking her in the intertwining of flesh. They'd pushed back the hours as best they could. Finally, though, they'd collapsed against the pillows, damp, spent, their breath shallow and rapid as tears.

"So what now?" Chris asked as her fingers tickled Kate's shoulders, scratching gently, back and forth, feeling the skin warm under her fingers. If she could see Kate's back, it would be pink with tiny white lines. Kate purred against her, sleepy, far away.

"I'm going to do the show." The show was what they had come to call Kate's idea for an exhibit of pictures of lesbians. Chris had never liked the idea of bouncing across the country and liked even less the idea of Kate being gone for months. It had been easier to encourage Kate to set the project aside time and again as she chased fame disguised as news. It was obvious she didn't want to put it off any longer.

"But not the whole country, right?" Chris sounded scared and hopeful, not at all like she sounded when she read the news.

"Uh-huh," Kate disagreed, her voice muffled by the pillow. "I'm gonna ask Wally for a leave. Might as well tell him the truth. He'll have to know eventually. See, I've been thinking about this old VW van John's got stashed in his barn. I'll be a New Age hippie." Kate chuckled, caught up in the excitement of planning a trip, forgetting for the moment why she would be making it.

Kate sensed Chris was crying before she heard her soft sobs. "But who will take care of you? What if you get sick? What if . . ."

"Hush, shhhh," Kate crooned, pulling Chris against her, petting her. "If I get sick, I'll go to a hospital. And I don't need anybody to take care of me. Don't do that to me, Chrissy. Don't make me feel like I'm helpless. Not now. Not ever. Okay?" Chris nodded, her breathing quieted.

"I could go with you. We could close the apartment, or sublet."

"And what about that new show you were so excited about not five hours ago? The network won't hold off on it just because you've decided to go traipsing across the country with your girlfriend. Chris, don't give up your dream because you think you have to take care of me while I go after mine." She switched on the night-light and sat up in bed, looking straight ahead. "Chris, today I really understood déjà vu, when I was sitting in the doctor's office and then at the gallery. Only it wasn't like they say—that you've been there before. Mostly it was like I was taking a picture of it. Like none of it was real, but it was all so familiar, so intimate. I knew it but I didn't. I was part of it, but I wasn't." Kate turned to Chris. Her face was flushed, her eyes flashing, her hands fluttering.

"Do you remember that woman Marta went out with last year? The one with the wild red hair?"

"Medusa? Sure."

"Medusa put spells on people. Did you know that?"

Chris shook her head.

"Not everybody, of course. Just evil men. One afternoon she told me how she goes to the beach during certain times of the moon and casts spells so that evil men will know their actions through the eyes of their victims. She said it will drive them mad because revelation is really a curse."

"She also accused you of stealing souls with your camera, if you recall," Chris added sarcastically.

"And you think I don't sacrifice my own every time I go out on assignment and put off the show one more time?"

"But you don't have to go across the whole country alone to do that show. Your life is here. I'm here. What's here is real." Chris was crying again.

"Don't you see what's happening to me?" Kate demanded. "I'm a photojournalist, dammit. I only survive all the little hells I wade into because I can look at them through little squares of glass. That camera lens insulates me, protects me. It all stops being real, stops hurting. After all, then it's just a picture, then you're safe . . . I'm safe. Or at least it seems that way. But sometimes I have to look, to see. That's when the veil is stripped away. Chrissy, I'm tired of being out there taking pictures, always just watching. Never the doer. I want to be a doer. Can you understand that? I've got to find out who I am. And I can't do that long distance."

"Will you at least let me go with you to Boston to see about the van?" Chris asked, reaching across Kate for the light switch. Her breasts trailed soft and naked across Kate's, sending goose bumps down her spine.

"Next week," Kate promised, pulling Chris on top of her. "Wally owes me some time." Her lips silenced Chris's answer, and the next week, they took the train to Boston where the van was waiting out its retirement.

The van was a weatherbeaten green and yellow Volkswagen microbus that had begun its adventures in San Francisco during the Summer of Love. A group of musical renegades who alternately called themselves Society's Great Pretenders and the Great Society's Pretenders had realized enough profit from a surprisingly successful hashish deal to buy the bus and finance their first cross-country tour, which ended two years later outside Woodstock, New York. The bus was unceremoniously abandoned along the side of the road that thousands of youthful pilgrims were following to Max Yasgur's soon-to-be-immortal pasture. Not long afterward, the bus and a kilo of Acapulco Gold went in trade for a converted school bus with orange headlights and a sun deck. That was the last anyone saw of the Pretenders.

The bus ended up on a commune, where it became the canvas of sorts for the artists in residence, who never quite got

around to finishing their rendition of Eve and the snake smoking a joint in the Garden of Eden. Sometime after starting the
project, there was a long, nearly violent dispute over why the
snake looked so much like Jimi Hendrix while Eve looked nothing at all like Janis Joplin. Everyone had agreed that Janis Joplin should be Eve, but nobody had mentioned Jimi for the snake.

Outraged, the artists railed about censorship, laid down
their brushes, and left to go swimming in the pond by the
pasture. They were waiting for an apology. None came, and the
mural was abandoned when the artists moved on to a commune
across the county where there was a nineteenth-century round
barn in need of a diorama.

Eventually, the bus settled into a middle age that was qui-
eter, if less dramatic, than its beginnings.

Kate's brother John found the bus and the commune thanks
to his girlfriend Sunshine Karma, who had been Mary Jo when
he'd left for Vietnam the year before. At the commune, John
learned to drive a tractor, bake bread, weave baskets, and make
a mean vat of LSD in the summer kitchen—he'd been a chemistry whiz at MIT before Lyndon Johnson and the draft board
had found him. In 1970, after Sunshine Karma ran off to
Toronto with a draft-dodger named Billy, John mourned by
tinkering with the bus's crotchety engine and moving back to
Boston. He wasn't up to another winter at the commune.

Sunshine Karma, who was Mary Jo again by 1973, slipped
back across the border by night. It was only symbolic, though,
because she wasn't the one who'd dodged the draft. She found
John and moved into his drafty flat that came with a free,
almost-legal parking space in the alley under their bedroom
window. The bus made a great guest room for their collection
of friends who were always passing through Boston on their
way to somewhere.

The bus stopped running sometime after 1980. By then,
John and Mary Jo had a rambling Victorian excuse for a house,
two sons, a sheep dog named Magoo, at least three cats, and a
menagerie of guinea pigs, canaries, and white rats. John taught
high school chemistry and Mary Jo studied yoga and Eastern
religions. The bus was stored in the back of the barn where the
boys sacrilegiously used it as a fort. John sometimes talked
about finding the time to rebuild its engine, but he never did.

Then Kate offered to write off the five hundred dollars John
owed her if he'd get the bus running again for one last cross-

country trip. "Cool," said John, scratching his beard and rummaging through boxes of abandoned books to find the VW mechanic's guide for 1967. If John thought it was crazy, he never let on. Then again, John wasn't a good judge of crazy.

It took more than a month to put the bus in running order, but by the time Kate pulled out of John's barn for the trip back to New York, the rebuilt engine was purring as loudly as Berenice Abbott, who had taken an immediate fancy to the bus. The cat spent her days napping on the brand-new road atlas—Mary Jo's contribution to the trip—while Kate fitted out the interior. Chris eyed the bus skeptically but decided to say nothing. She was still hoping Kate would change her mind, although with each day that passed, it seemed less likely.

Kate's only definite plan was to forge a path between the summer music festivals. In between, she'd follow the silent drumbeat that echoed through the lesbian underground, the unmarked but unmistakable highway that links women. The first night found her in the apartment of Leda, a senator's aide whose ex-lover was living on an island just off the Georgia coast.

"They raise goats. Lots and lots of goats. Long-haired goats, spotted goats, old goats, mama goats." Leda's eyes glazed with longing as she took another hit off a joint and passed it to Kate. "That's what we should do, Flash, chuck it all and go raise goats!" Leda was the indispensable right hand to a man who wanted one day to be president. Kate chuckled. It was no secret Leda expected a cabinet post if her senator ever realized his dream. "Black, beautiful, and brilliant, that's me. With a combination like that, look out! This country'll never be the same. And that would only be an improvement." Their sides ached from laughter before she sobered and turned her eyes to Kate.

"So tell me, Flash, how'd you do it—or more important— why?" She and Kate had met years ago when the senator was just another power-hungry congressman. "So, what did you do? Just handed in your resignation one day and walked out?"

Kate nodded, "Something like that." Wally had come through with the leave of absence and promise of a job as a photo editor, "If it ever comes to that," he'd said. "It will, Wally," Kate had replied solemnly.

Leda watched Kate rummage in the camera case. Finding what she was looking for, Kate rocked back on her heels and asked, "How about a picture for the family album?"

"What family is that?" Leda asked as Kate moved around her, the camera whirring and clicking.

"Our family," Kate answered. "The family of women. The lesbian family."

Leda laughed. "Good thing it's a long way to the White House." She threw back her head and posed dramatically. "We'll just say it's progress, Flash."

"And pride," Kate added.

"That too, Flash, that too."

Working her way into Georgia, Kate started to get more familiar with life on the road. She learned to judge time against the road atlas and traveled the two-lane highways whenever she could. "Mrs. Johnson, where are you when I need you?" she would wail when the coffee scorched or the potatoes came out half-raw, but eventually she got the hang of the camp stove. Early one Sunday morning, Kate was perched on a picnic table in a campground that clung to the Georgia shore. She was waiting for water to boil for coffee. Berenice Abbott was stalking a cricket under the bus. Kate was studying the crisp road atlas carefully, trying to connect Leda's directions to the goat women's island with the spidery blue veins on the map in her lap.

In the background the local AM radio station was broadcasting dead air disguised as the winners in an essay contest for young historians sponsored by the Daughters of the Confederacy. A girl with a squeaky voice was reading her entry, "Eleanor Roosevelt: The Journalist's Friend." No doubt Lorena Hickcock thought so, Kate thought absently, raising her eyes from the map. A smile warmed her face. Vigorously shaking what was left in her bottle of seltzer water, she aimed for the bus, spraying its headlights and grill. "I christen you Eleanor Roosevelt. If you were good enough for Hick, you're good enough for me." Kate was so exuberant Berenice Abbott scampered out to investigate. And so, with Kate behind the wheel, the three of them took off in search of an island of goat-raising lesbians.

If Kate had bothered to mark her journey in orange pen the way the A.A.A. travel planners do, the atlas would have looked like the sales record of an erratic company: north for awhile, then a hard dive south. Always, though, her progress inched west. And with every stop, Kate Solomon took pictures and made friends. Anywhere there were lesbians, she wanted to go, to see, to experience, to be. Sometimes she found a darkroom where she developed the film and made proofs of the pictures that were becoming the heart of her family album. It would be an album for all the women in the world . . . the ones in the offices or driving trucks or tending bar or making music or just trying to hang on. It would be her gift, her legacy, her history. In a way, even her future.

One afternoon, sitting on the porch of a mountain cabin outside Steamboat Springs, Colorado, Kate's hands ached. The pain was becoming more persistent, the headaches harder to numb. The mountain cabin belonged to Willa, a silver-haired veterinarian, who was sharing the porch swing with Kate. She'd designed the cabin one winter when she still lived down in the town. The next summer, Willa and a group of women from Denver and Boulder—all good friends—had spent two months on the mountain fashioning a home out of logs and love. When the work had ended, Shar decided to stay and help Willa with her mobile veterinary van, three dogs, a raccoon, and two horses.

Eleanor Roosevelt was parked by the cabin, her ailing engine exposed to the probing fingers of Mia, a mechanic from town. A shy young woman, her dark hair was slicked back in a style not unlike that worn by James Dean who was fading into the blue of the taut T-shirt that hugged small, firm, almost girlish breasts. Mia's arms were dark and well-muscled; her long bare legs were a stark contrast to her short body. She reminded Kate of a young colt. After supper that night, Kate would seduce her. They would talk about New York and mountaintops. Mia would tell Kate about the small town on the Baja coast where her grandmother still lived after eighty-seven years. It was a magical place, Mia said, where whales wintered and poinsettia blooms were the size of dinner plates. Kate would talk of life on the road and promise to come back to ski when the snow piled deep and unforgiving outside the cabin's door. She wouldn't mention Chris or the numbness in her hands or the fear in her belly. She would photograph the mechanic sitting on the ground by Eleanor Roosevelt's exposed heart, a grease streak across her forehead.

"There it is," Kate would say a week later, showing off the mechanic's portrait to a trio of sisters—the fourth generation to run the Wyoming ranch they'd been born on—and their lovers. Even behind the veiled shyness, Mia's eyes flashed out at them. Kate had found the sisters—Dove, Sue, and Myra—in a bar that once had been a grange hall. Their jeans were as soft as their chamois shirts, and their boots were hard-used with worn-down heels, so unlike the ones worn by the city women. Their hands were large-knuckled and calloused. Their eyes squinted as if they'd all looked too long into the sun.

The women had gazed curiously at the photographs, wondering why Kate was showing them an album filled with pictures of strangers. "Who's that?" Dove finally asked, pointing to a large smiling woman standing behind a bar.

"Alta," Kate answered. "She's part owner of a bar in St. Louis."

The sisters and their lovers considered this, looking from one to another and then back at the picture. Myra finally asked, "Were you lovers with this woman?"

Kate laughed and shook her head. How could she make them understand what it had meant to find Alta and her smile? If it hadn't been for Alta, Kate probably wouldn't be here in this converted grange hall. They had met one lonely afternoon when the only options Kate could see didn't really seem like options at all. For two days, Kate had been sick—alone and afraid—huddled on the tiny bed inside the bus. She and Berenice Abbott had camped in the Trail of Tears state park, a wide, smooth, green spot along the Mississippi River. Her body had burned as if muscles and ligaments, blood and bone were warring. She'd dreamed of death and awakened, sure she would die there alone, under ancient trees, the river whispering to the wind. And she had cried—cried for the loneliness, for the pain, for the death of dreams and the loss of power. On the morning of the third day, Kate had reached a decision: The St. Louis Airport was about three hours away. All she had to do was get there and in a few hours she could be home. Chris would take care of everything. It would have happened that way, too, if Kate hadn't taken a wrong turn, then another, then looked up and found Eleanor Roosevelt was stopped at a light in front of one of the city's few gay bars.

What the hell, she'd thought, parking Eleanor, retrieving her camera, and lowering herself into a steamy summer day. If she had to give up, she might as well do some shots in St. Louis. A pair of shirtless young men in tight jeans had been just inside the bar's door, soaking up the air conditioning, like dogs standing in front of an open refrigerator. They'd smiled as she passed between them, then turned their gaze back to each other.

Alta was there at the bar, looking as if she'd been waiting for Kate all along. Her smile was as wide as the river Kate had been following all that morning. Had she said anything or just smiled? Kate couldn't really remember, but that smile had blazed as if it could light the whole bar. Kate had balanced gingerly on the edge of a bar stool, listening to the bar sounds, content to bask in Alta's smile. And then, Kate saw the crutches, the braces. "How do you do it?" Kate had asked later. "How do you get beyond the pain?"

"None of that is me," Alta had confided. "This stuff is nothing but metal and leather and plastic. I'm a whole lot more than that. Just like the pain's not me."

"Sometimes I think it's me, that it's all there is. All that will be left." Tears began to well in Kate's eyes. At first, she'd tried to imagine the pain belonged to someone else, that she could lay it down and go on with her life. But lately, as it had become persistent, she had accepted it, claimed it. Either way, though, she hated it.

Alta nodded. "I hear what you're saying, but it's not you. Unless you let it be."

Kate had stayed at the bar until long after closing. Pawnee, Alta's lover, had stopped by after work and ended up taking them all out for pancakes at the Howard Johnson's. Kate had photographed the two of them holding hands under the table. For the first time on the trip, Kate had checked into a motel. The next afternoon had found her on the road again. And now she was here talking to ranchers who wanted to know about Alta and all the other women in the family album.

"Why do you take pictures of women you don't know nothing about?" Dove asked, closing the book on Alta's smile.

"I just liked how she winked every time she served up a beer," Kate lied, smiling at the women. "Taking pictures is all I know how to do and a long time ago I started to see something in dykes that you don't see in other women." The sisters and their lovers beamed and nodded, understanding. "And it's in these pictures. At least I think it is."

Later, under a streetlight outside the bar that used to be a grange hall, Kate added six Wyoming ranchers to her album. Thinking they were very beautiful together, Kate posed them shoulder to shoulder by the red neon sign that flashed SALOON. They joined the dozens of others who lined Eleanor Roosevelt's walls. Looking into the back of the bus was, by the time Kate arrived in California, a startling experience. Lesbians of every size, color, age, and profession stared out from the walls and down from the ceiling. Kate fell asleep every night under the watchful eyes of the lesbian nation. Like all the women who ducked into the back of the bus and saw the women gathered there, she smiled at the pictures.

Twice a week Kate called Chris collect. The longer she was gone, the more distant and formal their conversations became. Finally they were reduced to sharing anecdotes and lies. Kate didn't tell Chris about the women who had taken her into their hearts and beds, women whose pictures had places of honor on the ceiling over her bed in the back of the bus. She liked waking up with them looking at her. Chris didn't tell her about the actress she'd been dating for the last month. At first, they'd talked about meeting in Denver or Santa Fe or even San Francisco. Now Kate no longer asked and Chris no longer offered. Instead, they marked off the minutes of conversation like polite strangers, and neither of them wanted to know why.

The last phone call had been made from the living room of an aspiring but mostly unemployed screenwriter who had taken Kate home to her Venice beach house that hung on the edges of the southern California coast. The screenwriter shared the house with the members of Vampire Dread, a band of wild women who played music by night and worked for a messenger service by day. Kate and Chris had argued—hateful snipes followed by interminable silences.

"All right, so you made it to California. That's what you wanted. Now just give it up and come home." Chris's voice had turned from sweetly cajoling to hotly autocratic. "I'll take care of you. You're not well, Katydid."

Kate had bristled. "I need you to be my lover, not my nurse. Why can't you just do that?" she hissed, listening to the long sigh and silence at the other end of the line. Closing her eyes, she could almost visualize the wires that connected them running through mountains, across rivers, under city streets. Long threads that tied them to each other. Threads that could be so easily stretched but never quite broken. Finally, they muttered reluctant, angry good-byes. Kate raised her eyes to the band's drummer, whose bed she'd been sharing ever since her arrival three days earlier. The drummer, who called herself Poison, was a squat mean-spirited young woman with striped hair and tattooed hands.

"You're not like most women I've known," Kate whispered later that night, catching one of the drummer's nipples between her lips. It reminded her of a grape, round and smooth under her tongue.

"I'm not like *any* woman you've ever known," Poison corrected, her voice as husky and rough as sandpaper. With her lower lip caught between her teeth, Poison had exhaled sharply, her skin prickling with goose bumps. "So what's your usual type?"

"That," Kate said, her eyes on the TV screen where Chris was standing in front of the United Nations building. The sound was turned off, so Kate could only watch her mouth moving. "That's my lover."

Poison's eyes widened, then narrowed as she assessed the tiny figure on the screen. "No shit," she said, reaching for the remote control, then handing it to Kate with a wicked smile. "Does she want to watch?" Kate considered turning up the sound for a moment, then, thinking better of it, switched the set off as Poison moved under her.

September was beating hot and heavy across the beach when Kate decided it was time to head north, the last leg of her journey. "Come with me," she asked, only to have Poison shake her head. "Maybe I could stay for a while," Kate offered. Poison shrugged. "What's with you?" Kate finally demanded.

"You turned the TV woman off. That news lady. Your woman. You could've left her on to watch, but you turned her off. It shows you still care."

"Poison, look, Chris and I have been together a long time. We have an apartment in New York. We . . ." Poison waved Kate to silence, kissed her lightly on the cheek, and left for work. As if to hurry Kate's departure, Poison stayed away from the house that night, then the next. Early morning of the third day, Kate gathered up Berenice Abbott and pointed Eleanor Roosevelt north.

The trip was fast and angry as Kate tried to push Poison out of her life. By the time she reached San Francisco, late-afternoon sun was washing the streets in gold. "Look familiar, Eleanor? Or has everything changed for you, too?" Kate asked, almost glad the trip was ending. It seemed appropriate, too, that it was ending in California, a place where the landscape sheds its landmarks as readily as New England trees shed their leaves in fall. Kate had expected nothing familiar; she wasn't disappointed. Five years had passed since Kate had been in the Bay Area. Long enough to forget the scraggly palms that wear dying fonds like graying fright wigs, and tangled rosebushes and overgrown fuscia that conspire to hide shacks and shooting galleries. Kate checked the map again as Eleanor wormed her way into the city's interior.

Tattered buildings and rumpled streets, some without street signs, were no help in neighborhoods that were remarkable only for their monotony. A row of secondhand stores. A strip of cheap hamburger stands and gas stations. A used-car lot. An aging school with a ball diamond with asphalt where most of the grass was supposed to be. Counting streets, she was hugging the curb, trying to match the signs with an address scribbled on a napkin, when she spotted the softball team.

Five women, all wearing purple windbreakers with the words BABE'S DYKEBALL HUSTLERS scrawled across the back, lounged at the bus stop. "Dykeball!" Kate laughed, slowing Eleanor to a sullen crawl. Kate eased on Eleanor's brakes and a wide grin warmed her face.

"If you're looking for a ride to Babe's, I'm looking for someone to show me the way!" she called out the passenger window. The women raised their eyes to her, then began a slow survey of Eleanor's fading and rusted exterior and paused by the bumper sticker announcing ANOTHER WOMAN FOR PEACE that rode next to the New York license plates where their eyes settled.

Pushing a crown of unruly gold curls under a straw cowpoke's hat, a freckle-faced young woman with a pitcher's glove under her arm grinned at Kate and demanded, "What part of New York?"

"Manhattan. For me, not for Eleanor here. She's most recently from Boston, before that, San Francisco," Kate answered, looking into the blunt stare from a pair of the bluest eyes she'd ever seen.

"Well I'd say that's one hell of a long way to come for a drink! You're on!" The blue-eyed cowgirl bounded into the van and opened the side door for a brown goddess, a pair of identical twins, a German shepherd—and a trio of gloves, four bats, and two balls all miraculously balanced by a woman who looked just like one of the Campbell Soup Kids.

"I'm Tara," the cowgirl announced, climbing into the passenger seat and pushing her hand toward Kate, who shook it heartily, pushing down the pain that had set in over the last dozen hours behind the wheel.

"I'm Kate. Kate Solomon."

"Of New York and California?" the goddess asked, extending a dainty hand with long gold fingernails. "I'm Luna of California and the world. You don't play softball, do you? We almost won today."

"This season we never win—not even almost," Tara confided, blowing a quick kiss in the general direction of the goddess, who smiled back. "Hey, you got more girls in here than Babe's on a Saturday night!" Tara's eyes scanned the pictures that lined Eleanor Roosevelt's interior. "You a photographer or something?"

"That's what they tell me," Kate answered. "No sports stuff, though."

"Except for this volleyball game" came a voice from the rear of the bus. "Those women are naked!"

Kate turned toward the voice and laughed richly. "It's from Michigan."

"Did they have cheerleaders?" asked Luna, who was straining to see the picture of the nude volleyball game from the Womyn's Music Festival the month before. "I wanted to be the cheerleader for the Dykeball Hustlers, but they put me on second base instead."

"That's where Tara's always wanting to be—on second base!" hooted one of the twins. Tara laughed, but not as hard as the twins, who turned out to be Ronnie and Moe.

"Don't believe a word of it," Tara replied. "Luna's truly great on second base."

"But what about third," interjected one of the twins.

"Or home?" teased the other.

Kate looked at them quickly over her shoulder. Their matching freckled faces were framed by identical masses of red curls. They looked back and grinned identical grins. It must be like living stereo, Kate thought, smiling back.

"Oh, I'm just everyone's dream girl," Luna replied. Her voice was light and teasing. She tied the laces of a pair of spikes together and tucked her feet into a pair of gold pumps. "I'm just better in the night games. Under the lights." She smiled sweetly, pushing the spikes into a large canvas bag. "Don't you love it?" she asked.

"What?" Kate asked.

Luna shrugged and smiled, delighted at her private joke. "Everything. Summer. Manhattan. California. Life."

"I sure do," Kate answered, pulling away from the curb.

Stealing a quick look at Tara, Kate fumbled for conversation. She settled on softball even though she hated the game.

"So, how long have you been playing on Babe's team?" she asked Tara, who was stealing glances at Luna.

"Forever," Tara answered almost automatically, but there was a definite edge to her voice.

"Now, tell the truth, Winston" came a voice from the back of the bus where the woman with the equipment had finally untangled herself and was trying to convince the shepherd to give back one of the balls. Berenice Abbott was curled under the bed, keeping a careful eye on the dog.

Tara chuckled. "Babe's had rotten luck with the team this year. I guess we're the best she could come up with. She keeps threatening to change the name to the Dykeball Losers. You see, we used to always win the city women's championships, but then Pinkie started dating a woman sportswriter last winter. Now all the coaches play on her team and we're all that Babe's got left."

"And Kelly," said Moe.

"She's the coach," echoed her sister, who was staring at the pictures over her head. Ronnie whispered to Moe, who nodded and pointed at the wall.

"They're still mad about the coaches changing teams," Tara explained loudly over the noise of the engine. "But you can't really blame them, I guess. They're loyal in their own way. More to each other than a bar, is all. Campy's just taking it kind of hard."

"Campy?" Kate asked, more interested in the strange name than in the team's history. "Is that short for something?"

Tara giggled, rolled her eyes, and said, "She'll kill me if she finds out I told you, but she got it when we were twelve at Girl Scout camp together. Some of us thought she, well, sort of looked like a Campbell Soup Kid. Her real name's Carla, but only her grandmother calls her that."

"Nice to meet you, Campy," Kate called, her voice light with laughter.

"You ain't tellin' that, are you?" Campy's voice shot from the back of the bus. "Damn you, Tara Winston!"

The laughter started with Kate and Tara and rolled through the bus all the way back to the shepherd, who had spotted Kate's forgotten, half-eaten candy bar on the bed where Campy sat surrounded by the equipment.

Luna's eyes took in the colors and textures of the bus: the

yellow ceiling, the cheap purple and peach cover thrown over the bed, the misshapen rag rug on the floor, the faces that burned out at them from every wall. "So many beautiful women. Are they all your lovers?" Luna drew out the word *lovers* until it seemed to hang rich and full in the still air.

"A few of them," Kate admitted, feeling a blush warming her cheeks. She glanced in the rearview mirror at Luna, who was reclining on the floor next to the twins. She was a goddess on a sun-drenched island surrounded by royal priestesses. Or on a barge moving down the Nile. Or making her way across a hot endless sea of sand, bearing gifts to a sacred temple. Kate smiled.

"I'm putting together a photo exhibit," Kate explained. "Since May I've been on the road taking pictures. Usually I live in an apartment, like everyone else."

"Oh," said Luna, half-closing her eyes. "I lived in a trailer once, a long, long time ago. With Mother. Near the desert, I think. Mother was a showgirl, you know." She wrapped her memories around her, shutting out the snarled traffic that surrounded them, taking refuge on the floor of a long-abandoned sea. "You could take my photograph," she offered, as if her image were a gift. "I'm a dancer, you know. I could use it in my work."

"I'd like to," Kate answered quietly, deciding against her usual discussion about royalties for using her photographs for publicity. Luna smiled.

"She's really a stripper," Moe announced. Ronnie nodded. They both glanced at Luna, who was so still Kate wondered if she was asleep.

"Leave her alone," Tara shot to the back of the bus. "You know she's working tonight."

"They're in love," Ronnie mouthed to Moe, who pursed her lips and nodded.

Kate felt the tension and squirmed slightly in her seat, wishing she were better at small talk. Mother should have sent me to charm school instead of art school, she thought as the silent blocks passed. Finally Tara broke the moment by freeing a plastic bag of photographs from beneath a pile of magazines on the floor.

"These yours, too?" she asked, waiting for a quick nod of permission from Kate before she opened the bag.

"Oh, yes." Kate was relieved at the distraction. "See what you think. Those are just proofs, but I think when they're finished they will be my best work." Tara examined each picture, then passed it back, smiling.

"It's us!" shouted Campy suddenly from the back of the bus.

The twins and even Luna turned to look at Campy, who was giggling with delight at a photograph of a group of dancers, clad in colorful scarves, making music with recorders and small drums. Kate had taken the picture at the music festival. "See, there's Char and Kris, and those two Australian women—I forget their names—and me. See, there's me! Well, most of me. It's a great shot of my leg." Kate smiled, pleased.

Kate turned her attention back to Tara and her complicated instructions on what streets to take to avoid a nest of fire trucks in the next block.

"So, I hear Babe Daniels is quite a character," Kate ventured, turning down a narrow side street.

Tara chuckled. "Well, she is that. I guess I love her anyway, though. Too bad I had to leave her for Luna. Of course, Luna *is* better looking, aren't you, darling?" Laughter echoed through the bus. "But Babe's a real heartbreaker, at least that's what I hear." Tara's tone had turned dry.

"That's enough, Tara," Luna said coolly. "Don't say things you'll regret. Don't even think them. It's bad karma." The twins shuffled. Campy coughed loudly. Kate felt as if she was eavesdropping on a private conversation she didn't quite understand.

Kate shot Tara a questioning glance. The stories of Babe Daniels and her bar had reached across the country. Almost as old as the oldest of the women's bars, the bar and Babe were an institution. Most of the top women performers had played on Babe's stage. More than a few position papers had been drafted at afternoon meetings in her back room. She wondered what Tara's relationship really was to Babe Daniels. Certainly Tara was beautiful, but young, probably half Babe Daniels's age. Of course, there's nothing wrong with liking younger women, Kate reminded herself, remembering Poison. Tara smiled back, her blue eyes snapping.

"Whoa! We're here," Tara suddenly announced, directing Kate into a back parking lot. She bounded out of the bus, followed by the Dykeball Hustlers. As the twins divided up the equipment, Campy edged toward Kate, gathering her courage. Luna led the shepherd to the far corner of the building, where she tied her leash to a post by a large bush. Campy edged closer to Kate and finally pushed the picture of the dancers toward her. "Can I have this? That's me. Really. I could pay you for it—if it doesn't cost too much." Her eyes were hopeful.

Kate laughed, flattered. "It's okay, Campy. It's just a proof. Sure, you can have it. Anything for a fan." Campy smiled and hurried to catch up with the others to show them her treasure. Kate locked the bus door behind her. "Campy, wait up!" Kate called. She was hoping to learn more about Tara and Babe Daniels. Campy turned, beaming; it made her look even more like her namesake. But before Kate could ask, Tara was calling to them.

"Let's hustle. Kate, this is Babe's." Tara was holding the screened back door of the bar ajar. Stepping toward the darkness, Kate smelled the bar long before her eyes adjusted to its dimness.

Piling through the bar doors with her new friends, Kate waited instinctively for her eyes to widen against the permanent dusk. Flashes of light from a music video greeted her, followed by seemingly endless streams of twinkling lights that lighted the bar itself. She fought back the disappointment that threatened. She'd expected so much . . . more . . . or at least different. But more or different from what? That she couldn't answer. Shifting her heavy aluminum camera case from one hand to another, she followed Tara to the bar while the others headed toward the pool table.

"Hey, Ma, we almost won!" Tara approached a middle-aged woman settled at the far end of the bar. Gathering a handful of peanuts from a small bowl, Tara arched her back against the bar, pushed back her straw hat, and grinned.

"Don't call me Ma and what's 'almost'?" the woman admonished, barely raising her eyes from the tarot spread before her.

"Six points. Ronnie made a run after Kelly took off. So she thinks we lost by seven. Maybe she's bad luck, what do you think?" Tara was teasing, but her voice was tense, too.

"Kelly wasn't bad luck when you were winning," the woman sniffed. "Besides, six points ain't almost." The woman folded the tarot cards into a tattered leather bag and looked at Kate for the first time.

"Ma, I've got somebody here who wants to meet you. Kate Solomon, this is Babe Daniels. Mom, that's Kate. She's a photographer from New York. She's got great pictures of naked women playing volleyball at Michigan. You'll love it. And I need to talk to you later, important stuff, okay?" Tara winked, grabbed another handful of peanuts, and headed for the pool tables. Babe looked puzzled as she watched her daughter's re-treating form. It was unusual for Tara not to climb up on the bar stool next to Babe's and fill her in on the game. Babe turned to Kate.

"Tara didn't tell me she has such a famous mother," Kate offered, smiling, extending her right hand. Babe looked toward the back of the room where Tara was holding hands with Luna.

"I wouldn't know about famous," Babe answered, accepting Kate's hand. Seeing the wince in Kate's finely featured face, Babe shook her hand gently. Defying the mortality of her fingers, Kate pressed her hand into Babe's—a hearty show of bravado saved for bars and the women in them. Pulling her hand free, Kate too quickly tucked it in her jacket pocket.

"It's good to meet you at last," Kate said. "And you're wrong, you are famous. There's probably not a dyke in America who hasn't heard of Babe's."

"Well, set yourself down," Babe said, nodding toward the stool next to her, an invitation to join the queen at her throne. Kate balanced uneasily on the bar stool. Her back ached from too many miles behind the wheel. Her knees were stiff. She needed to walk around the block, slowly, painfully, just to be sure that her body was still functioning for one more night. But she'd come so far and the opportunities, like the time, were passing too fast.

Babe listened intently while Kate talked about her work, painting rich pictures with her words. "For months I've been on the road photographing women. And everywhere I stopped, every bar, every place where there was more than two lesbians, somebody would say, 'You've got to meet Babe. When you get to California, you've got to see Babe's.' " Babe nodded slowly, considering this. There were some advantages to being in one place for so long, she decided.

"You're a regular legend," Kate was saying. "Leave it to me and I'll make you more famous than you already are."

"How about better looking?"

"Sure thing, if you want to spring for the airbrush." Kate said and Babe laughed richly.

"Next thing you're going to tell me is I'm centerfold material. Although that's more up Luna's alley. I imagine you met Luna?"

Kate nodded. "She wants me to take her picture. She's very beautiful."

"Oh, she is that," Babe agreed. "So what is it you want to

take pictures of, Kate Solomon? Of me? The bar? My girls? Put your cards on the table and we'll talk about it."

"I came here for you," Kate answered simply. "I came here to find out if you can help me find what I'm looking for."

"And what's that?" Babe asked, studying Kate closely.

"The lesbian nation."

Babe roared. "Well, you've come to the right place, because if they aren't here, they're either on their way or they just left. They never seem to stay in one place very long, but you probably know that. But that's just fine. Shows adventure, wouldn't you say?"

"Or . . . something," Kate answered, smiling.

Babe picked up the little bag with her tarot cards, balanced it on her hand for a moment, then turned to Kate. "Once in a while I read the cards for women. You know the cards." It was more a statement than a question.

Kate smiled as she watched Babe lay out the spread. "My card's the Fool," she offered. Babe only nodded. "Do I get to ask a question?"

Babe shook her head, then winked. "How about if I just tell you what I see?" Kate watched as Babe examined the spread. Then she looked at Kate for a long moment. "Looks to me like the Fool's journey is ending . . . too many obstacles to go on . . . better to go back or go home. Is that true, Kate Solomon, is it time to be somewhere that you aren't?"

"Maybe," Kate said, suddenly realizing she was tired, as tired as she'd ever imagined she could be. "But I've got work to do here, first. I need your permission to photograph you and some of the others in the bar. It would complete my album."

Babe grinned. "Well, honey, I ain't so much to look at no more, but I'd be proud to have you take my picture anyway. Do what you have to do. I'll tell Matty to get you whatever you need. She's my manager, and a real looker—you'll want to save some of that film for her. Just one thing: Don't bother none of my paying customers. Now, I gotta get to work." Babe stepped off her bar stool and made her way toward the back of the bar.

Kate Solomon checked her watch. Soon Chris would be home. They could talk, maybe really talk this time, or at least try to. Together maybe they could figure out what to do next. But for now, Babe's was unfolding around her and Kate still had one last section to fill in her family album.

Saturday Evening

Mother Grew Roses in the Dark

Babe's Dykeball Hustlers were down by seven in the bottom of the fifth when Kelly checked her watch and started toward the parking lot. She didn't look back. Folding herself behind the wheel of the red jeep, she started back to the Berkeley house she shared with two other high school teachers, four cats, and Bronco, a Labrador retriever. A white envelope glared from the dashboard, angry in the afternoon sun. Kelly tucked it into her shirt pocket and turned down the tree-lined street that led home.

The letter was from her mother, the woman who had first rejected her, then banished her, disowned her, and finally denied her fifteen years ago. The first few years, Kelly had prayed for a letter, a sign, anything at all that meant she was still her mother's daughter. Later, she railed and raged. Drowned her pain in a river of whiskey. Wore her anger the way some women wear perfume. Eventually, she settled into bland acceptance, expecting nothing, asking nothing, but still hoping in the quiet still of her soul for a sign. None had come . . . until the letter.

Each tiny word, as tense and unexpressive as her own mother, had marched like a resolute messenger sure of her mission, into Kelly's orderly world: "At the insistence of your grandmother, I am writing to tell you that she is gravely ill . . . doctors say the cancer is inoperable . . . hospital but she is home now. . . . she hopes to see you before . . . ." Kelly had read the letter quickly, then again more slowly, looking for a hint, a word that her mother wanted her, too. There was none.

She'd started a dozen letters in response. "School starts in two weeks . . . difficult to take time off . . . still afraid to fly . . ." But then her grandmother's face, softened with wrinkles, as translucent and white as paper, would rise up before her. Like it or not, Kelly had no choice but to go home.

After loading Bronco and the backpack in the jeep, she pulled onto the freeway, then changed her mind and took the next exit to Babe's. The late-summer sun hung low in the west, sending long shadows across the street as Kelly dodged traffic and headed toward the bar. As she pulled the door wide, dank coolness surrounded her, the trademark of every bar she'd ever known. Air thick with the smell of stale cigarettes and whiskey with beer chasers greeted her: familiar, forbidden smells, like those that spilled out across the sidewalks of her childhood when she hurried to the grocery store for Aunt Nelda or to her best friend Sarah's house. Dark, cool smells of secrets.

"Kelly Marie! Get away from that barroom door!" Her mother's voice charged out of her memories. Even now, a life-time later, she could still hear her mother's shrill whine punctuating the afternoon. And Kelly was nine years old again. "You're asking for trouble, Missy, and that's exactly what you'll get if I ever catch you inside that den of iniquity. Do you hear me? Now, hurry along. Stop dragging your feet, I just spent twelve dollars on those shoes. Do you want them to be scuffed even before school starts? Kelly Marie, I said come on! I swear, you act just like your father's people. Kelly Marie!"

That bar had burned the summer of her sophomore year in high school, but sometimes she could still hear the peals of laughter, the funny tinny music and sounds that seeped onto the sidewalk. Sometimes, breaths of frosty air spilled out through the half-opened doors onto the steaming sidewalks of the little Arkansas town where she was born. Through the gloom, she could see shadows moving, and sometimes a pair of eyes looking out into the white heat of the day.

"But Mama, that's Maybelle Cain there by the window. You see her, don't you Mama? You know Maybelle, she's in my class at school. She's real nice, Mama. Can't I stop and have a Coke with her? Well, why not, I got the dime Aunt Nelda give me. Mama, she's all by herself, just settin' there a-waiting for her mama to get done workin'. Ow! That hurts! Mama, you're a-squeezin my wrist!"

"How many times do I have to tell you she's nothing but

trash? Her mother is nothing but a common barmaid and I will not have you taking up with the likes of them . . ." Her mother's voice faded into the past as the door to Babe's bar closed behind Kelly. A grin washed her face warm. *"Welcome to Babe's, Mama,"* her imagination called back across the miles and years, *"I'm sure you'd be the first to recognize a den of iniquity full of lezzies, queers, and all manner of undesirables. And I like being with them a whole lot better than I ever liked being with you."*

Crossing the floor to her favorite bar stool, Kelly's eyes swept the room, looking for familiar faces. At the far end of the room, a half-dozen of the Dykeball Hustlers were locked in an improvised snake dance. "Yo! Coach!" called Campy, one of the most singularly untalented catchers Kelly had ever had the misfortune to have on a team. The line turned and churned toward Kelly, clapping and bouncing in time to the music.

"You win?" Kelly shouted back.

The dancers shook their heads, turning thumbs down and chugging onto the dance floor. "They just figure they're getting warm," Babe answered from her post behind the bar. "Pinkie's team only won by six."

"That's some improvement. They were down by seven when I left." The two women laughed. No place like a bar to celebrate the little triumphs of life or to try and drown the black clouds that swirl up unexpectedly, hot and hard, like tornadoes across Texas flatlands.

But for Kelly, there'd been hard times in the bars, too. Times when all the whiskey a bottle held couldn't or wouldn't drown out the pain, make you forget you're going home alone— even when the pretty girl, whose name you'll never be able to remember in the morning, is hanging on your arm at last call and will follow you up the stairs when most of the world is lost in the black night of dreams.

Rising off the bar stool, balancing on its feeble rungs, Kelly stretched her long arm across the bar, probing its darkened depths before pulling free a still-dripping beer mug from the little rack by the sink. Shaking the few remaining drops loose, she angled the spigot over it and filled it with soda water before settling back on the stool, which let loose an almost musical groan.

"You're gonna' break your neck one of these days, doin'

that, then you'll probably try to sue me." Babe narrowed her eyes at her longtime friend.

"I ain't gonna sue you, 'cause you got nothing I'd want—except maybe Sharon." Kelly stole a sly sidewinder glance at Babe and winked.

"And you probably wouldn't want her, neither. I saw that girl you had in here last weekend. Dating your students now?"

Kelly shook her head and took a drink. "You mean Linda? She's a student teacher, not a student. She'll be helping out in my classes for a few months. She's just a nice little straight girl with a fiancé in the Navy. He's out there floating around in the Pacific, making the world safe for democracy." Kelly grinned wickedly. "I just thought she'd like to get out of the house for an evening."

"Or out of the closet forever. Next thing Popeye knows it'll be 'Shove off, swabby!' I know how you gym teachers are, Kelly." Babe was laughing, her eyes twinkling.

Peering into the glass, Kelly plotted her revenge, then started to laugh. The sound danced warm and wide around the end of the bar, embracing Babe, who holds court there every evening. And for most of the Saturday nights for the past six years, Kelly had been holding down the stool next to Babe's.

Babe had first met Kelly when she was Tara's high school track coach. Against her better judgment, Kelly had let Babe recruit her to coach the Dykeball Hustlers, who were just ending their first season. "Build me a winning team and I'll keep you in champagne and beer," Babe had offered.

"Going to have to do better than that," Kelly had replied. "I've been sober for almost two years now." Babe considered this for a long moment.

"How about two hundred bucks and all the orange juice you can put away?"

"How about a league party at the end of the season for all the girls and all the orange juice I can drink? You keep the two hundred bucks. You'll need it for the party."

Kelly had built a team of gym teachers and college players who were home for the summer. Babe even had a special glass case installed to hold the Dykeball Hustlers' trophies. And every season for the next three years, the team took the city championship. Then Pinkie Atkins started dating a sportswriter. Pinkie had been Babe's competitor for years, but now she was building a bar that catered to the sporting life. The

Dykeball Hustlers tried to hold on for the next season, but their best players had already defected to Pinkie's team. By the start of this season, Kelly was left with Tara and a collection of former benchwarmers.

"You see the article Pinkie's girlfriend wrote about Martina?" Babe asked, extending the early edition of the Sunday paper across the bar. Kelly shook her head.

"I'll catch it later. Babe . . ." she started, but fell silent.

" 'Course I never did see the woman play. We had tickets to the last Virginia Slims tournament, but Tara talked me out of them, begged me out of them. Wanted to impress *Lu-na*. It must've worked, now I've got strippers. Do I look like a woman who needs the aggravation of putting on strip shows along with everything else? If I wanted to be a producer, I'd move down to Hollywood. It's tough enough to run a bar without havin' to go into show biz, too."

"Luna's okay. Least she works out; some of those girls back there think playing pool here three nights a week is exercise. I could use a few more like her on the team. Maybe that's what the Hustlers need—a bigger Saturday-night show. Go to Reno, recruit a few showgirls." Kelly was laughing. "Loosen up the old purse strings a little."

"You sayin' I'm cheap? You think it's easy to run a bar? I got payroll. I got expenses. I bought this place on nothin' and—" Babe stopped mid-sentence, realizing Kelly was mouthing her words, mugging her expression, her gestures, talking to the mirror behind the bar. Babe shook her head a little and both women started to laugh, a rolling harmonic sound that comes from too many years of living the jokes and the pain.

"Get to work, Babe! You've got a bar to run! Expenses to meet! Tips to collect!" Kelly's words cracked out quick as a drill sergeant's.

"Make yourself useful." Babe snapped a bar rag toward Kelly, who reached up automatically and retrieved it midair.

"I didn't come down here tonight to wipe up spilled beer. I needed to talk to you." Kelly folded the towel neatly, her fingers smoothing the creases.

"So, talk." Babe filled a glass with orange juice and soda until bubbles shot up the side. "I'm going nowhere, least not for three hours. You got more'n three hours' worth to say, I'll hang out a sign says 'psychiatrist' and charge seventy-five bucks an hour. For that kind of money, I'd listen till you're in your grave." Amused by her own wit, Babe laughed, pushing the glass across the bar to Kelly, then leaned tired and heavy against the back of the bar.

"Long day?" Kelly asked, testing the drink. Babe shrugged. "You should take a vacation. Why don't you and Sharon go to Hawaii or Tahiti? You could just sit down and relax. Or at least give up working back there every night."

Babe shook her head. "And what'd I do all night? Sit over there and listen to you complain? Or maybe watch videos of that miserable excuse for a softball team you coach and I sponsor? No thanks."

" 'Course not." Kelly countered with a sly wink. "You could always bore me with how you were in the Roller Derby—you know, about the time they first invented the wheel." She shot an impish grin at Babe, who snapped the bar rag at Kelly's left hand, chuckling when the damp cloth plopped untouched on the bar, leaving Kelly's hand closing on air. "Should've caught it," Kelly muttered.

"Well, you just ain't as quick as you used to be." Babe winked, turning her attention to the cash register.

"So I've been told," Kelly answered, her eyes surveying the scene reflected in the mirror before her. Reflections of women—young, old, in pairs and clusters—bounced the length of the bar, their faces all shining, distorted, by the tiny lights.

"Cheers." She raised her glass, toasting an all-too familiar reflection. A pair of dark-green eyes rimmed with tiny wrinkles watched Kelly intently. As she raised her glass, the reflection raised its glass, too. The eyes looked deep into her face, moving from one feature to the next: the sandy-turning-gray hair that never seemed to go in any one direction; the round face and flushed cheeks that always made her look younger than she could ever even remember being; the soft mouth that seemed, as the years marched past, to draw tighter, just like her mother's. She was used to the reflection; it had watched her year in, year out. When she was drinking, though, it had been easier to ignore. Now it was always there, waiting, unchanged but changing.

"I'm thinking I should probably go home," Kelly announced with finality when Babe returned to her end of the bar. Her fingers were tapping out reveille on the bar, waiting for Babe's reaction.

"Kind of early. Don't you want to stay for Luna's show?" Babe asked absently, her mind on the night ahead.

"Babe, I mean back home." Kelly started, then paused, rummaging in her pocket for the letter.

"You mean Texas?" Babe asked, looking at Kelly closely.

"Arkansas," Kelly corrected.

"What the hell difference is there?" Babe countered. "I thought you said there wasn't enough money in Fort Knox to ever get you back there. Now you're talking about going 'back home' like it's someplace you've been pining over for the past, what is it, fifteen years?"

Kelly nodded, fingering the letter, then pushing it toward Babe. She turned her eyes to the glass before her as if she were trying to memorize each line of sweat that slid down to the paper napkin. Babe was silent as she read, raising her eyes to Kelly every few lines.

Watching Babe with the letter resurrected the last words her mother had ever spoken to her. *"You want to go! Then go! You think I don't know what you are, what you're doing with that girl? You're going to hell, both of you. Do you hear me? To hell, where you'll burn forever for your sins! Don't you dare call yourself my daughter ever again! You're no daughter of mine! Thank God, your father's not alive to see this day! Get out of my house! Get out and don't come sneaking back trying to beg my forgiveness! You're dead! Do you hear me? Dead!"* The venom echoed and rebounded through Kelly's memories, swirled in front of her, pounded at her temples.

At first, Kelly had tried. Every Mother's Day, Christmas, birthday, even Valentine's Day for years, she'd sent cards to her mother. And two weeks after each holiday had passed, those same cards were back in her mailbox—each unopened. "Return to sender" written in her mother's tight, uncompromising script was the only contact Kelly had with the woman who bore her. "Mother doesn't want to talk about it," her brother had muttered over the phone when Kelly had called one Christmas morning. "And frankly, neither do I." He'd lowered his voice to a whisper and added, almost furtively, "Don't call here again, okay? It only upsets her." Then the line went dead. Kelly had spent the rest of that Christmas in the arms of Jack Daniels.

After that, Kelly had kept her end of the bargain: no more phone calls, no letters, no Mother's Day cards. And finally the memories of Arkansas began to blend into the dust of her life, mostly forgotten. Except for Grandma, dear kind Grandma, who never, at least as far as Kelly knew, questioned the circumstances that surrounded the departure of her eldest grand-daughter one summer afternoon so long ago. Kelly sometimes wondered what her mother had told Grandma—if she'd told the truth or nothing at all. Kelly couldn't imagine her mother lying; the wages of defying the ninth commandment were too great.

In those early years, Kelly fantasized that one day her mother would overcome the fire-and-brimstone fear that kept her riveted in the church pew every Wednesday night and almost all day Sunday for as long as Kelly could remember and would reach out to her only daughter, denying the guilt and shame. But that didn't happen. For just as long, Kelly had wondered if her grandmother could ever understand why the road or anyplace else at all was better than the two-story frame farmhouse just outside Crossett, Arkansas. Then in a birthday card one year, her grandmother's shaky script asked Kelly if she and Carolyn were happy. God, Carolyn. So many years since Carolyn. It had been Carolyn who had held her arms wide to Kelly when her mother sent her screaming into the wilder-ness. Carolyn, who had faded out of Kelly's life, to be replaced by Ginny, then Lou, finally by Becky. And Becky had been gone almost three years now. Grandma had understood, though Kelly doubted her mother had ever told the old woman. Grandma. No matter what else changed in the succession of lovers and addresses, she always remembered her grand-mother.

And now Grandma was dying, reaching out across the miles and years to Kelly, asking her to do the one thing she'd sworn she would never do again—go back, go home. Funny no matter where she'd lived, home was still the farmhouse with its porch swing where Grandma had rocked her to sleep under August sunsets. So painful to remember, so impossible to forget, so difficult even to try.

Back home, they'd think she'd come to see her grandmother one last time, accepting the female legacy of watching old women die, and about that, at least, they would be right. Gath-ering around the bed, holding midnight vigils of the heart, waiting for death to steal in, soft and silent, tossing out its comforter of hope, they would wait. Her mother would be there, watching the old woman, as thin and pale as the bleached sheets they'd have her on. Then, after a time, Grandma would be in the family plot down the road near the creek, where the wildflowers bloom in spring.

Only that's settled, Kelly thought. I can't remember half of where I've been and don't know where I'm going, but I sure as shit know where I'll end up—there with Daddy, and soon enough Grandma, and all the dead aunts and uncles, and the babies that never lived long enough to even cry. The thought sent a strange shiver down her spine. Goose bumps.

"A goose walked over your grave," Grandma would say when Kelly was little and determined rain beat at the windows, making delicate patterns on glass where the wind seemed as if it could almost rattle through, so loose in its frame it was.

"Out there in the cemetery by the road?" Kelly would always ask the white-haired woman with the strong, wrinkled, blue-veined hands. And Grandma would nod every time, smiling a little. In those days, Kelly imagined the smile came because her grandmother coveted the concrete angel that stood over Great-Aunt Luwanda's grave. The angel had big feathered wings and was blowing a trumpet with chipped flowers flowing out of it. Her grandmother would always laugh and say it wasn't the angel. "There's a comfort, child, in knowing sure where you belong, where you'll be spending eternity." And she'd smile that strangely quiet smile.

Funny—Kelly hadn't thought about that in years, and now she was going back to it all. Back to where songs of the wild geese echo across flat fields, heralding their travels along an invisible unchanging path to the far north country. No matter how far they traveled, the geese always found their way back. Back to big country kitchens with windows that opened onto cornfields and kittens in the chicken coop. Back to country dirt roads with barefoot children dancing in creeks that gurgle through woodlots. Back to her childhood, and she didn't even know if she wanted to find it again. Home.

Sometimes when Kelly was pulling back, caught up against the years like a mouse backed into a corner by a hungry barn cat, the cities and bars and women all tumbled together. Jumbled memories. The good and the bad could no longer be sorted out, becoming nothing more or less than a kid's ball of twine, multicolored, endless. Just there, cluttering up the afternoon of better days. At other times, it seemed her life was like that old road map that didn't have but half the new interstates on it or even all its pages left anymore—crumpled and leading from one place to the next, yet going nowhere at all.

Still, the memories kept nagging, sending her mind racing across the years. She could still smell the perfume of her third-grade teacher, the one who always wore violets in her long black hair every April. Could see her second-grade best friend Donna, brown pigtails with red ribbons, dimpled knees bent, pink ruffled panties around her ankles as she squatted in the woods, pissing on a clump of dandelions to see if they'd turn white like Bobby Jay said.

One of the last good times Kelly had spent with her mother was at the kitchen table, just shelling peas and drinking coffee, and talking. Nothing more, nothing remarkable, just the warmth of being home and knowing there's no place you need to go, at least not in a hurry. In the background the radio on top of the refrigerator was batting out an endless diet of Lord-she-done-me-wrong-so-I-blowed-her-brains-out music. And just like all the summer days she could remember, every time a pickup truck jogged past, road dust rolled up into the yard, leaving a fine clay film on the day lilies by the porch. As children, Kelly and her brother and all the cousins would wave at the truck that passed, hooting with glee when the driver honked. They almost always honked. Then they'd chuck the rocks the truck had spit off the road into the ditch where the grass stood tall and untended, lush from summer rains. When the rains came, they gushed as if the black sky had been ripped open by the thunder, by the lightning that cracked into eternity.

Those things she remembered well. The rest of it? Well, some things are better left forgotten. No memories, no regrets. Only rarely did she wonder what might have been if she'd stayed in that land where cornstalks sway gently in summer breezes. She could have married a farmer, taught physical education and girls' hygiene at the local high school, produced grandchildren for her mother to coddle. She could have raised chickens and gone to church on Sunday, wearing pink polyester dresses and white patent-leather high heels with a plastic purse to match. The good ladies of the church would elect her president of the Thursday Night Ladies' Aid Society because she had the living room with the most chairs.

Kelly laughed aloud. I surely could give some of those fine ladies some aid they wouldn't soon forget! she thought, then eyed Babe, who was folding the letter back into its envelope. "You ever think about going home, Babe?" Kelly asked when Babe handed the letter back.

"You mean back to Joliet?" Babe shook her head. "No reason to. I did when my old man died, but haven't since. There's nothing there for me anymore, and I'm smart enough to know where I don't belong."

"Well, I guess you could say I never did fit in back home," Kelly agreed. "Good thing, too, or I'd have ended up like my brother's wife Betty—two husbands down and a boyfriend on the side!" Babe snorted at the idea. No, that wasn't for Kelly— no station wagon, or honeymoon in Little Rock, or Christmas dinner at Mom's house for the next thirty-five years or death— whichever came blessedly first.

"But Babe, sometimes in that mirror of yours there, I see my mother looking back at me, her face all screwed up with worry and hate, and it scares me. You see, when I was run out of there, nobody ever let me look back. Now I can find out if that place, those people are like I remember them, if I'm still a part of them, because they're sure as shit a part of me. Maybe going back there will put it to rest, for one of us, at least."

Babe nodded, rubbing at an imaginary spot on the bar, trying to find the right words. "It's a long trip," she finally managed.

"They all are, aren't they?" Kelly was already pulling on her jacket. Oh, she wasn't who they'd wanted her to be, that was for damned sure. But then, she wasn't who she wanted to be, either. "I think it's time for me to go home now." The words were proud, determined. She would see her grandmother one last time, the wrinkled old woman who had pulled her close so many years ago, hugged her tight, kept her warm and safe in the big old four-poster bed in the farmhouse with the rattly windows. Maybe she would even try to make peace with her mother.

The bad days had driven Kelly out onto the road. The fear that if she ever dared go back, she'd die, or worse, end up nothing more than a dusty reminder of who she was, who she might have been; this was her private demon. It was the fear, more than her mother, that had kept her bouncing across the country from one city to another. For a long time, she'd been little better than a restless leaf looking for a gutter. But no longer. This time was her time, not theirs.

She'd become hard and lean from her years gone. She wasn't like them back home anymore. They had never been able to chain her, to hold her to their kind of life. And even if they all thought like her mother, shaking their heads and saying, "Poor Kelly, threw her life away," she was going back triumphant, not all beaten-down, worn-out, and used up like the women she'd seen reflected in the eyes of girlhood. No, she hadn't married a farmer and spent her life driving a tractor and raising too many kids. And she hadn't ended up cooking eggs in the local café for early-morning coal miners and hunters who greeted the dawn with cigar nubs and yellowed teeth. They'd never been able to rope her into PTA meetings on Wednesday afternoons and square dancing on Saturday night.

"Do you even really know what you're looking for back there?" Babe probed, then uncharacteristically reached out to smooth a tuft of runaway hair from her friend's eyes.

Kelly nodded. "Nothing. I'm looking for nothing. Really. I used to imagine that I could go back and make it be like it was when I was a kid—you know, good again? But I don't believe that anymore. Like the man says, you can't go home again. You know that line?" Babe nodded. "In a way he understood, but I'm not going back there because I need them. I'm going back there because I have to find out if any of them, maybe even Mother, just might need me. Do you understand?"

"And what if you're wrong, Kelly? What if you get back there and all these ideas you're building up don't amount to nothin' but so much dirt under your fingernails? You're going back. So what? So who cares? You think your mother cares— the same woman who sent back her own Mother's Day cards? Who writes to you only when your dying grandmother asks her to? Tell me, does she care?"

Kelly studied her fingernails a long time, noticing each little jutting hangnail, each ragged cuticle, each tiny scratch. Babe was right, her mother didn't need her, maybe none of them did. But if that was true, then why the letter, why the come-back call after all these years? Did her mother really write only because her grandmother was dying, only because the old woman asked? "Like I said, I've got to settle it . . . one way or the other," Kelly finally said, softly, raising her eyes to Babe's. Babe nodded, caught for a moment in her own memories.

"So, when do you leave?" Babe lighted a waiting Lucky, then studied the smoke rings that erupted from her mouth, as if there was more to say, but no words to say it.

"Soon as the door closes behind me," Kelly answered.

"So you've already made up your mind? Can't just let it rest?"

"Babe, even if I don't go back there, it still won't rest. And maybe if I go, it won't, either. But it's worth a shot."

Kelly looked across the bar for a long moment, her eyes straining through the blue-pitch smoke and tiny twinkling lights—sucking it all in, like a drowning swimmer choking for a final breath.

"You ain't gonna find nothin' there," Babe interrupted Kelly's thoughts. "It ain't never the same. It's never the same even when you stay in a place all along, ridin' it out."

"I know, Babe." Kelly nodded. "Believe me, I know." Taking a deep breath, she started toward the door, raising her hand in a determined half-salute.

"Keep my stool warm for me," she called, opening the door. "When I get back we'll go fishing down at the pier, maybe catch a mermaid." Babe's rich laugh, accompanied by snatches of music and bar smells, followed Kelly onto the sidewalk. Then the air was silent, cool and crisp, the moon hanging low and clear. Kelly wondered what it would be like to wander aimlessly in space, circling the moon for eternity.

Climbing into the jeep, she leaned against the seat, quiet for a moment, surveying the street, the pink and lavender shadows chasing across the concrete. Bronco bounded into the front seat, her nose twitching in anticipation. "So, now it's you an' me, buddy," Kelly said, gunning the jeep a little. The dog thumped her tail against the seat as Kelly pulled into traffic.

"Had to bring you along, Bronco, 'cause you're just like too many women I've known. Three days gone and you'd be off in somebody else's bed without even a backward glance." Kelly laughed loudly as the dog dropped down on the seat.

Pulling onto the freeway, Kelly toyed with the idea of turning around, heading back to the bar. She could catch a few games of pool, maybe line up some interest in a late-night poker game in Babe's back room. Maybe Babe's right, she thought. Maybe it had been too long. Too many miles, too many years, too many bars and better places to be. Life here had been comfortable for a long time. She wasn't the same woman who'd crisscrossed the country in a weather-beaten pickup truck, like a flea searching for a friendly dog. In those days a trip like this would have been nothing more than a little diversion. But if that was true, the thought nagged, why didn't you make that trip? Kelly shook the thought away.

"You sure we're ready for this?" she asked Bronco, who was lying on the yellowed dog-eared road atlas that had ridden shotgun for Kelly for nearly as long as she'd been driving. "One more exit and that's it. No looking back after we reach Sacramento. You know the rules." The dog grinned, drooling on the map that marked Kelly's path.

The exit signs slid past until finally the highway stretched out like a black satin ribbon. "We'll make Nevada by morning," she said aloud, scratching the dog behind her floppy ears. "You know, Bronco, that's what I like about you. You're a damned good listener." Kelly's fingers massaged the dog flesh. "All told, it should take three days, four tops, if we don't blow up somewhere between nowhere and Timbuktu." Settling back against the seat, feeling the vibrations slipping up her legs, liking the feel of the wheel trembling under her hands, Kelly hummed a little ditty, a wordless song accompanied by the spin of the tires against the pavement. The song turned to a lullaby her grandmother used to sing so many years ago.

"Sunday afternoons when Mama was in church—and believe me, Bronco, Mama was *always* in church—I'd bake bread with Grandma. I don't believe I've ever told you about my grandmother, but you'll like her. Her daddy was a union organizer for the mine workers way before the turn of the century, and she would tell about what it was like in those early days. She was fifteen years old when she married my granddad and only thirty-two when she buried him. By then she had seven children, one of 'em was my dad. And she'd always say to me, 'Kelly, girl, your mama's not to blame, because she's a Yankee. She just don't know no better.' " Kelly's voice rolled warm and strong into the night. The memories would carry her home, heralding her homecoming, and when she wheeled into the drive by the farmhouse, she would raise a cloud of pebble-spitting dust.

Kelly was the one who'd won out, after all. She'd made it on her own in spite of her mother, in spite of her broken legacy and tattered dreams. Maybe Grandma had known that part all along, too. Maybe that was why the old woman was calling her back, not so Kelly could watch her death, but so she could witness Kelly's life. "Your grandmother is a proud woman, stronger than you'd think . . . " the letter said.

"And so am I, Mother," Kelly answered her mother's silent pen, "despite all of it, despite even you, so am I."

And finally it seemed very right that after all these years Kelly was going home.

Somebody Called It the Blues

With an all but imperceptible groan, Fearless Faye Fletcher settled hard and heavy on the last stool next to the wall at the far end of the bar. Shafts of early-evening light filtered pale and dusty through the tiny windows, cooling the checkerboard tile floor, making the empty tabletops glow. The light can't reach Faye, who is settled into the bar, all her weight balanced on her forearms in the way of women who spend much of their time sitting at bars. Even when the bar is alive with light that twinkles and flashes, pulsing blue and red and yellow, Faye's corner is filled only with shadows.

Her basset eyes narrowed, beginning a slow march along the bar, past the mirror and cash register, hesitating at the spot where the whiskey is lined up like an army of armless dwarfed soldiers standing at the ready to battle another assault of the Saturday-night blues. The eyes smiled a little, then stumbled on to where Matty leaned across the bar, talking to a shapeless figure lost to the glare. Faye shook her head, squinting, trying in vain to focus. She could put on the glasses kept in her shirt pocket—there just in case she needs to read something—but that would be a lot of trouble to go to for a drink.

"Matty, honey, bring me a rye and soda?" she croaked loudly, drumming her fingers against the bar. "An' where's that good-for-nothin' boss of yours? Late again! Probably off seein' her bookie!" Faye laughed, thumping the bar. "Did she tell you how I took her for a fin on Thursday? Or was it a week ago Thursday?" Faye's face sagged as she fell silent, trying to remember. Setting the drink in front of Faye, Matty smiled tolerantly and moved back to her conversation. Always, she was uncomfortable with Faye, who had become as much a fixture in the bar as Matty or even Babe herself.

"Oh, she's not so bad as all that," Gail would protest when Matty complained about Faye and how Babe not only put up with her but wouldn't even listen to reason. "She's harmless and kind of sad. Faye's a little loud, sometimes, but some of the customers get a charge out of her. If you get her going, she has some really weird stories."

Matty didn't see it that way, but Gail had a kind heart, everyone said so, even Faye, who rarely had a good word to say about anybody, even Babe. Gail and Faye had each arrived at the bar a couple of years ago: Gail as a bartender, and Faye? Matty scowled. What, indeed, was Faye? A fixture, perhaps. A piece of Babe's past, certainly. An anachronism lost to time. That bothered Matty more than anything about her.

If Faye could only have been a victim, Matty might have forgiven her. Instead, she was a woman, once strong but no longer, who had tripped over her own ambition and then lay wallowing in self-pity, too lazy to even try and pick herself up. A pitiful affront to the women Matty studied and admired. Those women had managed to keep turning with the world, churning through its storms and torrents until time itself forced them down. Only then, kicking and screaming, had they given themselves up to the earth that gripped them tight, holding them still in damp black eternity. Once in a while they'd even managed to cheat death and chip out another moment or two, they'd fought that hard. Matty imagined she understood those women, was even a little like them. So like them that she could feel only contempt tinged with a very little sympathy for the ones like Faye. The discards. The ones that life has sapped of the fight, leaving them crippled capitulators, stumbling along clutching a couple of tattered dreams, a handful of tarnished golden-moment memories all wrapped up in shadows. She didn't yet understand that, in their own way, they were survivors, too.

It takes a practiced eye to tell them apart, the fighters and the capitulators. The differences are so small and so few: a stooped shoulder here, a nervous twitch there, a hand that fists in rebellion before trembling, almost intangibly, as the fight melts away. The fighters rage against the coming of night; the others sigh and turn toward it and their memories, finding a kind of solace there.

"Sometimes I see her little face and it's like she's, you know, lookin' at me," Faye muttered, turning only her face toward the young woman who was perched like an elegant parrot on a nearby stool. The young woman looked at Faye, her eyebrows arched, her head tilted, wearing a small smile, as if to ask: I'm sorry, what was it you were saying? Faye's puffy, worn face edged toward her, like an ancient turtle sniffing the air for danger or death or even love. The young woman looked help-lessly at Faye, who was recounting the dream that had shouted her awake that morning. It was a familiar dream born of hang-overs and hungry memories.

"I keep sayin' to her, 'Here I am, Charlene baby. It's me, Mama Faye.' Only I know she can't really see me, 'cause of how her eyes are all rotted away, burned-out, like. But I keep feelin' them eyes on me." A large tear rolled down Faye's cheek and hung on her chin. "She keeps cryin', 'Mama Faye! Help me, Mama Faye!' and holding her little hands out to me. Such tiny hands. I try to grab onto one of them little hands, but they're so tiny that I can't keep hold of them—of her. And she starts to fade away, with that look on her face like she's blamin' me, only I can't never remember what it was I done. Then I wake up. And that's what I remember . . . mostly." Faye's eyes dropped to her hands; they trembled slightly, clutching her half-empty glass. The young woman continued to smile, stiff and polite, as she picked up her drink and slid off the bar stool, making her escape. Faye ignored her.

Wiping her mouth with the back of her hand, Faye sighed deeply, wishing Babe would come. She wanted to tell her about the social worker she'd been to see the day before. Not that this social worker understood any better than the rest of them what it really was like. Too much liquor, too many memories. It didn't really matter which; it had all gotten mixed up and turned around such a long time ago that there weren't a half-dozen people left in the world who could remember how it was or might have been before. So long ago that all even Faye can really remember about the little girl she gave birth to in the middle of her mother's living room floor in a dingy fifth-floor Philadelphia walk-up are burned-out eyes that keep burning out at her from shadowy corners and hung-over nightmares.

Faye peered toward the clock behind the bar, but the numbers all ran together. "I gotta get me a watch. Next month when my check comes, I'll do that," she announced, though no one was listening. Finally, her face crinkled into a wide smile at the sight of Babe. "Thought you was takin' the night off, late as it is," she jeered when Babe stepped behind the bar.

"Dammit, Faye, I own the place. Who's gonna fire me? You?" Babe chided, tying a towel around her waist.

"Well, you been at the track? How'd you do? You said you'd let me know the next time you went." Faye's lower lip began to extend in a pout.

"I wasn't at the track." Babe took a quick drink from glass that was more water than bourbon and winked. "And where I was is none of your business." Babe smiled. Her hands moved automatically while she talked. Faye relaxed, pleased that Babe was in a good mood. For Faye, most nights went the way of Babe's moods. When her mood was high, she liked being with Faye, introduced her as Fearless Faye Fletcher, the Roller Derby queen. But when Babe's mood was black, she ignored Faye and spent all her time in the office. Lately, Babe had been especially happy.

"You got a new girl, Babe?" Faye suddenly asked. For as long as she'd known her, Babe's humor was always related to a woman. Babe shrugged and winked, setting a fresh drink in front of Faye.

"That social worker lady called me to come in again, Babe. Said she'd get me some new eyeglasses. Seems to think I'm missing out on somethin' I need to see. Hell, she's just doin' everything she can to get me back on my feet. Says to me, 'Faye, listen up now! You got to do what I say . . .' Somethin' like that. Shit, I ain't been doin' what nobody said since I was seventeen years old. Seven-teen years old," she drew out the word, testing the sound. "That's how old I was when Charlene was born. I went out on the circuit the next year." The raspy voice faded into the curling blue smoke from a nubby cigarette. Faye studied the sweat on the outside of the glass as if she were looking for a sign or maybe just an answer to one of the questions she was no longer really interested in asking.

The days before her stretched as empty, as listless as those of a dying alley cat. The girl she had been had long since abandoned this shell of a woman she'd become, this woman the years had made her. But once, she had been Fearless Faye Fletcher, the Roller Derby queen who burned up the tracks all across the country. Nobody could catch her. Nobody could tame her. Nobody could stop her. Even death couldn't destroy her. No, she had done that herself. Faye closed her eyes, drumming her fingers against the bar in time to a fading skating song that kept spinning in her mind.

On the wall above the cash register hangs a large picture of Faye's old Roller Derby team, taken in 1965, a month before Babe broke her leg. In the center of the team, Faye Fletcher smiles, beautiful, blond, desired and desiring, posing for the camera like a Vargas pinup girl. At the end of the second row, a twenty-one-year-old Babe Daniels glowers at the camera. Faye opened her eyes and studied the photograph as if she'd never seen it before. Turning her eyes on the mirror, she sought some resemblance there with the beautiful skater in the center of the picture. And for that single stolen moment, she was the golden girl once again, frozen in a spotlight that would never fade.

"Faye, why don't you go down to Park's and let Wan Lo fix you something to eat? You eaten all day?" Faye shook her head like a guilty child. "Tell her I'll settle up with her on Monday." Babe stepped from behind the bar, anchoring one arm around Faye's shoulders. Guiding Faye off the bar stool, Babe began to pilot her toward the door. "Hey, remember when we were both Roller Derby queens?" Babe teased, stumbling a little under Faye's weight, her faltering steps. The pair of them listed across the barroom floor like a johnboat fighting the river's currents. "Those were some times we had! Broke hearts all the way across America, you and me. Left a trail of broken hearts and broken bones in every city in this country." Babe chuckled. Faye looked at her hollowly; then a light began to glow in her eyes.

"Oh, I was somethin', wasn't I?" Faye joined in the memory, her voice almost reverent. "I was the best. Now, you had some good moves, too, don't get me wrong, Babe. But you remember that steamroller I had? Drove the crowd crazy." Faye stopped short at one of the little tables where a pair of young women were holding hands and sharing secrets. Alarmed, they looked to each other, then to Babe for rescue, unable to see any golden moments in the haggard faded woman before them. "See, I had this move . . . I'd, you know, fake 'em out and bam! I was gone!" But the moves are gone, and Faye stumbled into the table when she tried to demonstrate. Babe tightened her grip and more insistently began guiding Faye away from the table, saying a silent prayer that she didn't see the knowing grins that passed between the young strangers at the table. That prayer, at least, was answered.

"You never met my Charlene did you?" Faye peered intently into Babe's eyes, trying to conjure up some tiny spark of recognition, pity, sympathy, maybe even love that might be left just for her. None came. Faye's voice stumbled into the past where a blond cherub runs down the steps of a yellow frame house, her tiny arms extended, crying "Mama Faye! Mama Faye! You're home." Faye moved her head from side to side, an ancient feline trying to clear its vision, and stared into the shadows, memories teasing the night. "Oh, she was a pretty baby. My pretty baby."

"I'm sure she was real pretty, honey," Babe answered softly. "If you don't want to eat, why don't you go on upstairs, get some rest? Maybe come back down later when you feel better?"

"Too early, Babe. The party's just startin' to cook." She shot Babe a sly look. "You want me upstairs, you're gonna have to carry me." She laughed loudly. Babe sighed and settled Faye into a chair at a table in a remote corner of the room. "Remember when you used to carry me to bed?" Faye laughed wickedly.

"That was a long time ago, Faye," Babe said. "There was less of you and more of me." She sounded irritated. Faye narrowed her eyes and looked at Babe closely.

"You sayin' I'm too big or you're too weak or maybe you're just not interested no more?" Faye's tone was wicked, searing.

"Just busy, Faye," Babe lied. They hadn't slept together in more than twenty years. "Why, you always were a real looker. There wasn't another woman around that could hold a candle to you. 'Course there was better skaters, like me, you understand." Babe's voice was a teasing lullaby of memories of better days, designed to chase away visions of burning children, to let them skate off into eternity, finally at peace.

"I was gonna teach Charlene to skate, I really was." Faye recited a mother's litany of promises and regrets. "Right after I got off the road for a while. Oh, she would've been a natural. Remember when we was in St. Louis and I got her them little pink leather skates with the real rabbit's fur pom-pom that had a little bell in it? You remember them skates, don't you, Babe? I got 'em for her for her birthday. I was gonna surprise her. We was gonna be in Philly for her birthday and I was gonna go out to Mama's, maybe take the whole team out there with me. Have us a regular party. We was gonna have a big time and I was gonna teach her to skate. I really was."

"I know honey." Babe started back across the floor, leaving Faye alone at the table.

"Babe . . ." Faye's husky voice pleaded, "could you send over a little somethin'? You can put it on my tab. I'll settle up with you come payday."

"Sure, honey, whatever you need," Babe answered automatically over her shoulder, repeating the scene she'd played night after night, ever since Faye stumbled back into her life two years before. There was no tab; payday never came.

Faye looked around the room. A worn smile tugged at her face. It was still too early to go upstairs, where the night stretched out sad and lonely. Endless. She needed to be with people—couldn't Babe understand that? Faye smiled at Matty, who gingerly set the drink in front of her. "Here, honey, this is for you." She handed Matty a pair of quarters. "I didn't get to the bank this week, so just run a tab tonight. I'll settle with Babe." Matty nodded and when she got back to the bar, pitched the quarters into the jar by the cash register. Faye's face fell.

Matty had once asked Babe why Faye always tipped when she couldn't even pay for a drink. "Faye was a big spender," Babe answered, "and she liked to tip. Big. She wanted to hand it over personally, too. None of this leaving it on the table stuff for her. She wanted to see a little gratitude. It was one of her more disgusting habits." Babe had smiled and Matty understood: Babe had once loved Faye, and in a secret way, the part of her that would always be twenty years old, still did.

That was why Babe did for Faye what she would never do for anyone else. Whenever anyone challenged her reasons for taking Faye in, for trying to take care of her, Babe answered quick and hard: "You didn't know her before. I did." The finality of her tone stopped more questions. Eventually, Matty and some of the others had pieced together the patchwork story of when Faye was a real Roller Derby queen who stormed the circuit with guts, talent, and determination.

Fearless Faye Fletcher was the Roller Derby's darling, until her career was short-circuited in October 1964, when a bus filled with schoolchildren on their way back from a museum field trip was struck head-on by an out-of-control tanker truck filled with gasoline. It had taken three hours to extinguish the fire, which left a blackened place on the pavement that couldn't be washed away. The story made the network news, and the mayor called for an investigation. Sympathy cards from well-meaning strangers poured into the school's office. A group of schoolchildren in Florida who had been saving up for a trip to Cape Kennedy sent the money instead to buy a small granite marker. It still stands next to the highway where the flames inhaled seventeen third-graders, the bus driver, two nuns, and the mother of one of the children who survived. Eleven children suffered second- and third-degree burns; three of the children and the driver of the semi escaped unscathed. The survivors had nightmares of burning children for years after the accident was forgotten. The truck driver blew his brains out with a .32 Colt revolver eight months later. Every year on the anniversary of the accident someone leaves a bouquet of white daisies by the little marker.

The newscasters called it a "senseless tragedy" and a "nightmare that touched the nation." And over the years all the mothers of the other victims lighted candles on special days and talked fondly of the dead child who would always remain a child, while their other children went on with their lives. For Faye, though, the accident was the near-fatal blow that makes the fighter lay down his gloves. Even when she came to understand that there was no why to be found, she carefully tended the pain and hatred of loss, letting it erode her life like a bit of porcelain under a dripping faucet that no one will ever bother to repair.

Destiny turns strangely, sucking the innocent as well as the guilty into its web. Days passed, spilling out newer history, but for Faye and even Babe, that lone October day was to hang frozen, strangely suspended, burned into the blackness of time. Every moment, every movement of that afternoon, of the next day, and the day after that remained etched into her brain. For Babe, it could have been yesterday. For Faye, it was.

Babe had been in the shower of the hotel room she shared with Faye when the phone rang that afternoon. She could still hear the water running, could still see the crack in the tile by the faucet. Two hours earlier she and Faye had been out combing St. Louis for a pair of tiny roller skates, the best money could buy. Faye, who was used to autograph sessions, was busy signing them: "Happy Eighth Birthday, Charlene! Love Always, Mama Faye." She planned to have those skates covered with autographs of the top skaters by the time the team hit Philadelphia. Charlene smiled from behind the glass of a chrome picture frame Faye kept propped on the dresser. Every year Faye's mother sent a new picture to take the place of the one from the year before.

"She ain't gonna turn out like her mama—married too young to a no-good son of a bitch that lit out before Charlene was even born." It had taken a long time to find the skates and Faye's mood had turned ugly even before they entered the children's department of a sporting-goods store that had a picture of Fearless Faye Fletcher in the window. The salesman with a painted-on smile had waited patiently as Faye examined each pair of skates he produced. She had inspected the skates so carefully they might have been for Faye herself rather than for an eight-year-old to use at the local skating rink. Sticking her hand in one of the skates, she'd continued ranting about her ex-husband, a topic equally hated and familiar to all who knew her. "Wasn't my idea to marry the bastard and I didn't have no choice but to divorce him. Still, do you think the church could see it my way? No ma'am. Couple of years ago, he even turned up after a show. Brought me a bouquet of flowers. Talkin' some shit about gettin' back together, and all the time just wantin' to climb on Fearless Faye's gravy train." For the first time, she raised her eyes to the salesman. "You got these in pink?"

The salesman nodded and disappeared into the back room while Faye continued her tirade. Babe slouched in a chair next to a moon-faced man and his son, who was trying on hockey skates. "You're going to show those other boys what for, just like your old man," the father kept repeating. Babe looked at him skeptically; the man didn't look like he could show anybody what for about anything. The salesman reappeared with the pink skates. "You have an excellent eye for skates. These are the top of the line." He was obviously pleased with his good fortune. Few people bought such expensive skates for children.

"Well, I guess if anybody knows roller skates, it'd be me." Faye was looking for some glimmer of recognition in the salesman's face. None came. "What's the matter, you don't follow the derby?" She spit the words at the thin-lipped man, pushing him the hundred-dollar bill she'd been waving for emphasis a moment before.

"No, no. Can't say that I do," he muttered. "I don't suppose you have anything smaller?" He was still smiling. Faye's clear blue eyes glinted, suddenly hard and angry. The thin lips, the silent smirk belonged to her ex-husband, who'd run off to join the Merchant Marines. It belonged to the priest who'd so unceremoniously refused Faye communion but who so quickly sent her a bill every month for Charlene's school tuition. It belonged to the sportswriter who refused to take her seriously but always asked for a couple of free tickets, ringside, if she didn't mind. The salesman was none of these things, of course. He was only the blistered toe, the unhealed hangnail, the unexpected downpour that spawned silent curses.

Faye inhaled, raised herself to her full five feet eight inches of glory, looked at the man, and answered loudly, "Smaller? No, honey, but I'll just bet you do." She deliberately dropped her eyes to his beltline. The words sunk deep into their target; the man flushed a deep red. That the man first held the bill up to the light, then scurried off in search of change, taking a full fifteen minutes to return, only fueled Faye's smouldering ire.

Ignoring Faye, Babe remained slouched in the chair, avoiding the gaze of the young matrons with their children, there to buy high-topped basketball shoes, figure skates, and colored gym shoes. Faye stayed by the cash register, hurling insults at anyone who looked her way. Finally, the man returned with the big white box with its pink ruffled bow. Faye accepted the box, which she pitched wordlessly at Babe, tossed her golden hair back, and with roller skates and Babe in tow, waltzed past the pyramid of basketballs and into the afternoon chill. Babe raised her chin and walked a little faster. Just being with Faye made Babe feel like a queen, too, and that day the whole of St. Louis was their kingdom.

Three rye whiskeys later, Faye offered to race Babe back to the hotel. Four luxurious untapped hours lay ahead of them. "Winner take all!" Faye called, shooting past Babe and down the street, her blond hair flying, the box of skates tucked under her arm. Babe took off after her, wondering why she even bothered to race; Faye always won. Bursting into the hotel room, Babe found Faye lying face down, gulping air like a winded racehorse.

"I won! Say it! I'm the best! Go on, say it!" Faye leapt from the bed, grabbed Babe, and pinned her against the wall, tickling her ribs until she threatened to double over in breathless laughter.

"Okay. I give up, you're best!" Babe's words were muffled by Faye's kisses.

That she was only one in a succession of girls Faye had taken under her wing and into her bed didn't matter to Babe. She knew Faye's eye would stray sooner or later, but for the moment she was content to bask in the glory of Faye's star. Faye proved her devotion by spending hours coaching Babe, teaching her the moves, the bravado that made the fans crazy with excitement. That Babe didn't have the street-fighter's guts, the unharnessed fury that had pushed Faye into the spotlight and kept her there since she'd stormed onto the circuit when she was barely eighteen, didn't stop either of them.

"We're gonna make history, you and me," Faye would confide in rare, tender moments. "Just give it time, honey, that's all it takes." Babe wanted desperately to believe Faye, to take her place in fame's fleeting spotlight, to feel like she really could take flight and soar to the moon.

Then the telephone rang and it was over. Faye's scream pierced the early afternoon and shot Babe, naked and dripping, out of the shower. Looking into Faye's eyes, Babe knew she was seeing death. They drove all night to get to Faye's mother's house, where only the day before, little Charlene had been practicing long division at the big oak dining room table. The table, the house, all of it was paid for by Faye's fame. And it was all for Charlene.

Streetlights hung dim and low, twinkling off one by one against the late gray dawn, by the time Faye and Babe pulled into the driveway. The house was dark. No matter how the years tried to erase the picture, Babe would always remember how abandoned that house looked, as if the neat shutters were really hanging loose, untended from the windows, as if the prim screen was really rattling on one hinge in the breeze. When they stepped through the door, Faye's mother was sitting in a rocking chair, an open Bible beside her. Faye crept to her mother's side, slipped to the floor, and lay her head in the old woman's lap. Faye cried until Babe was sure she would spill out her very guts. The forgotten outsider, Babe finally slipped upstairs and fell asleep across a twin bed that smelled vaguely of pine and mothballs. In the distance, a train howled in misery.

That afternoon, Babe stumbled through the tiny house, feeling lost and helpless, while Faye's mother made phone calls. A parade of cakes and casseroles borne by neighbor women moved through the front door. Finally, Babe escaped to the mortuary with Faye, who hung over a tiny blackened form, sobbing until her stomach churned and she vomited spit and air and whiskey into a wastebasket in the mortician's office.

Hundreds of people came to the funeral in the cathedral. The tragedy was of such magnitude that a bishop celebrated Mass. Babe thought it was remarkable that there were that many little matching white caskets available on such short notice. She wondered vaguely if the morticians kept that many around, or if they had to send out for them. Visions of a factory that made only little white caskets welled in her mind, making her head ache. She decided some things are better left unasked, and escaped to the sidewalk where reporters and photographers crowded up the church steps. No one recognized her as a mourner, and she was content to mingle with the crowd of curiosity seekers who spilled onto the sidewalk. Later, when the families had separated into small groups for the silent trip to the cemetery, Babe had shivered in confused silence, trying to smile at the plump nun who kept patting her arm. The nun had mistaken Babe for Faye.

The days muddied together, and finally there was no longer any reason to stay.

"The priest said God wanted her," Faye had whispered hoarsely on the drive back to the team, which was by then in Indianapolis. They were the first words Faye had spoken since they'd left the cemetery. "What in the hell is God going to do with my baby?" Faye suddenly roared into the night. Babe was so startled by the outburst that she jerked the steering wheel. The car swerved; Faye didn't notice. "I guess I wasn't good enough for the old bastard. Just my money was good enough for him. Well, God got enough of that. Mama said she'd be safe with the nuns, that they'd take good care of her. Well, they took care of her all right. And what have I got left? A goddamned string of beads."

With that, Faye cranked down the window and flung Charlene's tiny rosary into a ditch by the side of the road. When Babe started to pull over, Faye hissed, "Keep driving. What the hell do I need that piece of shit for?" And Babe kept driving in silence, counting every mile, every moment that passed under the tires. It was as if the venomous blasphemy had drained Faye, who slumped in the corner, her hand cradling a pint of whiskey, her eyes closed, her tears flowing.

Some, like Faye's mother, find faith in the face of tragedy, turn their voices and songs to a never-ending piety. But for Faye, there was no comfort, no solace—not that night, not ever again. In the weeks ahead, Babe came to understand that Faye had puked up her heart, her drive in that mortician's office. But that night Babe didn't yet know that all she was hauling back to the team was the empty shell of what had been Fearless Faye Fletcher.

When they got to Indianapolis, Babe saw the white box with the forgotten pair of pink roller skates still nested in their pink tissue paper, carefully stowed on top of Faye's uniform. She quietly slipped the box out of Faye's locker and into the trash bin, hoping Faye wouldn't notice. But Faye found the box, and no matter what happened in the years ahead, no one was ever able to separate her from those size-four pink roller skates.

Babe had been determined to salvage what she could of Faye after Charlene's death. She'd stood by her in Philadelphia and now Faye needed her more than ever. In her innocence, Babe had believed the star could still shine, given enough love, enough time. When Faye was too drunk to skate, Babe would half-push, half-drag her up and down the halls outside the dressing rooms, douse her in cold showers until she screamed, pour coffee down her, even dress her. When anyone complained, Babe would lie, "It's just the flu. She'll be fine. Just give her a couple of days." And so long as nobody put the pressure on, so long as Babe and few of the others were there to protect Faye, it worked. But as the hollow weeks turned into nightmare months, those willing to coddle Fearless Faye Fletcher fell away until only Babe was left. Soon there was a new darling cradled in the crowd's adulation, and as the spotlight began to fade, Faye drank even more.

It had been in trying to protect Faye, who was too drunk to skate but actress enough so it didn't show, that landed Babe in the hospital with a broken leg and shattered career. After that, news of Faye Fletcher came sporadically, if at all. The sports pages said Faye had moved on with the team until they fired her one snowy night in New York City. Then Babe heard Faye picked up another team but that hadn't worked out either. By then Babe was in California and Faye Fletcher didn't make the newspapers anymore. Finally, Babe heard nothing more. Faye never wrote, never called, and Babe settled into the quiet of life without Faye, without spotlights, without rolling from town to town.

Faye had kept on drinking. She'd skated when she could, when anyone would have her, which wasn't too often as the years passed. Finally, she'd ended up making personal appearances and giving demonstrations at grand openings of skating rinks on the back roads of America. By 1986, nobody really remembered Fearless Faye Fletcher. Nobody except Babe, who spotted an ad for a local skating rink offering lessons by Fearless Faye Fletcher: Roller Queen Extraordinaire.

Only Faye was no longer anybody's idea of roller royalty. A fall a dozen years before on a bad floor at a demonstration had left her barely able to skate. And the mothers who took their children to be coached by the Roller Queen Extraordinaire complained when her majesty's breath smelled of whiskey and beer. By the time Babe found her in a roadside motel near the roller rink, the queen had received a not-so-royal pink slip. It didn't matter to Faye; she'd just added it to the pile. Babe had unceremoniously picked up what pieces she could find and took Faye home with her.

Sharon didn't want Faye in the house, so Babe moved Faye into the apartment over the bar. Like Faye, it had been mostly empty for a very long time. Welfare paid Babe the rent and Faye helped out around the bar. When the social worker suggested living above a bar contributed to her alcoholism, Faye answered, "I've seen the world drunk and I've seen it sober. I like how it looks drunk a whole lot better." She spit on the floor for emphasis, then grinned at the social worker, who pursed her lips and told Faye to come back next week for job-training assessment. Faye curled her lip in contempt. "I'm Fearless Faye Fletcher. Perhaps you've heard of me? Even now I'm considering several offers to come out of retirement."

The social worker looked bored. "Your appointment is at 10:00 A.M. Wednesday. Don't be late this time." The woman handed Faye a card with an address on it. "It's on the number 83 bus line."

Faye didn't keep that appointment or any of the others the social worker made for her. The truth was, Faye couldn't think of any job for which she could be trained. So she spent her days recovering from her nights, and her nights were spent battling demons that spit fire at children. If Babe expected anything more, she never let on.

And now it was once again Saturday night at the bar. Faye stirred in her chair. How long had she been sitting there? An hour? Two? A cluster of empty glasses were on the table in front of her. She didn't remember ordering more drinks, but then she didn't remember not ordering them, either. One more thing to try to remember, and it wasn't really worth the bother. The bar was filling rapidly, but not one of the women approached her table to buy her a drink or ask her to dance. Not like the old days, she thought. Not like when they all wanted to get next to Fearless Faye Fletcher. Next to the queen.

Faye stood, a little unsteady, and started toward the bar. Her eyes were shining. The idea she'd had that afternoon had come back to her, and Babe would want to know. Babe was perched on her regular stool, talking to Kelly about the softball game. Kelly made Faye nervous, partly because she was still an athlete of sorts, mostly because she was a recovering alcoholic. Faye grinned broadly at Babe and nodded at Kelly, who smiled slightly and turned away. Faye, after all, was Babe's problem.

"Babe, honey, I been thinkin' about goin' out on the road again, maybe doin' some demonstrations," Faye said, pulling close to Babe. Her breath was hot and sour. "I been watchin' them skaters on the TV. They even got roller skaters in the Olympics now. Ain't that somethin'? The Olympics. Whooee, if we'd had the Olympics back when we was skating, them sportswriters wouldn't have dared make fun of us. Could've had us a couple of gold medals!" In her glee, Faye slapped the bar so hard her hand stung. She glanced around to make sure no one was listening to their conversation. Her voice dropped to a hoarse confidential tone. "I figure I'll need a partner, though. And I been thinkin' we could really do it up right this time. Maybe even join up with the Roller Derby again. Hell, we could be breakin' hearts and bones, just like in the old days. What do you say, Babe?"

"Faye, what would I do on roller skates?" Babe leaned against the bar and chuckled. She smiled at Faye. "I ain't been in a pair of skates in—honey, I don't even know how many years. Neither have you. We're too old, Faye, too old. That kind of thing's for young girls and I got about all the young girls I can handle in this joint." Babe laughed, not unkindly, and winked.

Nodding slightly, Faye raised her eyes to the old team picture, ignoring the tears that threatened. The reality of Babe's words stung like an undeserved slap. She was quiet for a moment, then smiled hopefully. "But I was the best, wasn't I, Babe?" Stealing out, the words fell soft against the night.

"Yeah, Faye," Babe answered absently, "you sure were. We both were."

Even Fat Girls Don't Sing Beatles Songs No More

Stars spilled like rhinestones from a broken bag of midnight across the sky and down the cliffs into the sea as the '67 Mustang pushed away the miles of Highway 1, which winds up the peninsula to the heart of San Francisco. The car is a classic, a tribute to Motor City's gluttonous fantasy of unchained horsepower and endless rivers of twenty-five-cents-a-gallon gasoline. An American dream that had burned out like a meteorite. Like its driver, the car wears the passing years both badly and well.

Sixty-five. Seventy. The engine spewed pure raw energy, blanking out the world until only wild blackness remained. Sheer cliffs rose hard and rocky on one side, dropped into black ocean surf the other. Seventy-five. Eighty. The road twisted sharp and treacherous. Level it off. The ocean crashed against the shore five hundred feet below.

Sharon Winston rummaged absently through a box of tapes, one hand on the wheel, her eyes flickering from the road. Her fingers closed around one. Smiling, she pushed the plastic film of memories into the car's stereo. "Let It Be" swirled around her, through her, engulfing her, teasing her back as if her very life were being rewound. Whirling, twirling, screeching as fast as the roller coaster she'd loved throughout her childhood. She leaned, grinning until her jaws ached, into the feeling.

She was seven years old and the roller coaster screeched

under its load of screaming children. Heavy and cold, the metal safety bar dug into her lap, leaving dark angry streaks on tender thighs bared by her favorite polka-dot shorts. By the next morning the red streaks would have darkened, angry purple storm clouds on a horizon of pink flesh. They were her war medals: some aged and yellow, others bright pink, shaded green. They made her remember the moment when the world trembled and collapsed against the rush of speed, when she could let go, step away, or maybe even fly. Up there, alone with the speed and wind and light, she was beautiful, numb, free, invisible, magic. She could do anything. So different from her life on the ground, where she was just another little fat girl.

Every day of every summer until she was old enough to drive, Sharon Winston rode the roller coaster. On her sixteenth birthday her father had presented her with her own key to his blue Lincoln Continental. The car wasn't hers, but with the windows down and the radio blasting Kansas City's top-ten hits, it didn't matter. Only the speed mattered. The boys in their heavy Chevys wouldn't race her because she was just a fat girl in her rich daddy's Lincoln; the girls wouldn't because racing wasn't ladylike. So Sharon raced alone, roaring down the two-lane highways that still skirted Kansas City like a nervous suitor.

In winter, when the amusement park was closed and the highways were glazed with ice, Sharon sulked in her room, a ruffled confection of blue dotted swiss and white french provincial furniture from Sears. The room had been her mother's idea, right down to the four-poster canopy bed complete with bed curtains that actually closed. Behind those curtains, the bed was a stage where dreams could come true. Sharon could be anything—beautiful, popular, glamorous. She didn't have to wish to be smart, she already was, just like she already was the secretary of the Kansas City Chapter of the Future Teachers of America, and the band's second-chair flute who grudgingly dated Rodney Mittsfield, the first-chair french horn. But Sharon Winston didn't want any of those things—she wanted adventure, excitement, whatever was out there waiting for her beyond the flat fields of Missouri. But to find it, she first would have to be glamorous—that much she'd learned from Lottie.

Lottie was Sharon's aunt, her father's baby sister, who had lived everywhere, even New York City. The year before when she collided with thirty-five and looming obscurity, she'd come home. There wasn't much modeling work in Kansas City except for the spring fashion shows at the country club and a few newspaper ads for the big department stores downtown, so she started waiting tables in the Holiday Inn's Safari Lounge. Lottie danced the bossa nova, wore miniskirts before anyone in Kansas City, and had once met Bobby Darin at a cocktail party. She'd had two legal husbands, a third of questionable legality, an assortment of live-in boyfriends, and countless one-night stands. Lottie was five foot three, a natural blonde with the fresh-scrubbed looks of her country-girl background. She was too short for the runway and too bland for high-fashion magazine work, so she modeled junior petites until she was thirty-one. Once her picture was even in *Glamour* magazine. Lottie was a runner-up in the 1947 Miss Missouri Pageant, a cheerleader every year of high school, a homecoming princess twice, and in her senior year of high school was queen of both the sweetheart dance and the prom. Lottie was beautiful. Lottie was fast. And Sharon loved her.

Lottie had escaped the spirit-crushing boredom that was Kansas City the week after she'd graduated from high school. She hadn't been much of a student, but the American Modeling Institute in New York City didn't care. All that mattered was her good looks. "With a face like that you can go anywhere," she would tell the mirror every morning of her life, even when it was no longer true.

But to Sharon, her aunt had boarded a train as a Kansas City high school girl and come home years later a glamorous, worldly woman. Lottie's life was one of tuxedoed lovers who rode in the back of white limousines and provided very expensive gifts in small satin boxes from only the best jewelry stores. That was the life Sharon wanted and it seemed so much more than what Kansas City could ever offer. It would take a little style, a little glamour, a lot of ambition, and guts. Sharon knew that what she lacked in style, she could make up for with ambition. First, though, she would need a makeover, like the ones in *Seventeen.*

Margaret Winston had early on denounced the magazine as frivolous and refused to allow it in the house, so Sharon had to settle for the back issues her best friend Sally Meyers smuggled to her. Sharon inhaled the magazine articles that commanded her to agonize over her hopelessly round face, her dimpled thighs, her freckles. Then she saw Twiggy posing by the Eiffel

Tower, then in front of Buckingham Palace, and then at the base of the Statue of Liberty. Suddenly Sharon wanted very much to be that girl—not so much for the fame but because that was a girl who could see the world on her own terms. Sharon's eyes shone with possibilities. And because she didn't yet know how to be someone without looking like them, she secretly practiced outlining her eyes and putting on false lashes as thick and fuzzy as caterpillars. All she needed now was the hair—and the legs. Margaret Winston said if Sharon wanted a hair cut, she would make the appointment with Bonnie of Bonnie's House of Beauty. Sharon had hoped for one of the new high-fashion salons downtown instead of where her mother went every Tuesday morning for a shampoo and set. Only, her mother refused to budge on the issue, and Sally said even Bonnie couldn't blow the Twiggy style. So, Bonnie could take care of the hair. The three-month supply of Fat-Away that Sharon had sent for would take care of the rest.

The Fat-Away ad had been in the back of Sally's *True Confessions* magazine. For only $17.95, the Fat-Away people would send their "wonder cure for ugly flab" all the way to Kansas City, where it would "magically melt away pounds of fat without dieting" while Sharon slept. It certainly sounded better than her last diet of grapefruit and hard-boiled eggs. Sharon hadn't told anyone about the Fat-Away, especially her mother, who'd heard from Bonnie about a woman who'd once taken some mail-order diet capsules that had tapeworms in them.

Sharon had begged Bonnie for the whole story. "A bag of bones, that's all she was," Bonnie had confided that afternoon when she had Sharon under her plastic cape. Bonnie had never heard of Twiggy, but Sharon had provided a magazine picture. "Just look at all that hair hanging in that girl's eyes. And flat as an ironing board. Wouldn't you think she'd use a little something?" Bonnie had cluck-clucked, waving her shears for emphasis. "She looks just like poor Myrtle Rae after the tapeworm got her. I swear, no matter what she ate, it didn't make a bit of difference. Not a bit." Sharon was secretly hoping for such good fortune with Fat-Away. "And finally her hair fell out—all of it." Bonnie's voice dropped to a whisper, she arched her eyebrows and nodded emphatically. That was the only part of the story Sharon didn't like.

She also didn't like Bonnie's version of the Twiggy look. Not even an inch long, the cut had only encouraged the bounce in

Sharon's already naturally curly hair. The result was unusual: Sharon looked as if she was wearing a fuzzy yellow knit cap. "I'm supposed to look elfin!" Sharon wailed. Her hair curled around her face like a stiff halo.

"It's a bubble cut, honey," Bonnie had cooed, pleased with herself. "It's what your mother ordered."

"My MOTHER!" Sharon shrieked. "You listened to my mother? My mother hasn't changed her hairstyle since nineteen forty-three!" It was true. Margaret Winston bothered little with her appearance. The weekly trips to Bonnie's were like a washing machine, just a little convenience that came with being the wife of the vice-president of the First Farmers National Bank of Kansas City. Sharon's mother was a plain, bony, ungiving woman who spent every afternoon, except Thursday when she played bridge, in her darkened bedroom taking Valium, reading *National Geographic,* and planning trips to the Galapagos Islands, treks through Nepal, expeditions to the Tequendama Falls. She was a high school geography teacher when Harvey Winston, a serious young bank teller, married her just after V.J. Day. She'd dutifully produced a daughter two years later and settled back to wait for the child to grow up, counting the years to her freedom. One day she'd leave Kansas City, just as she'd been planning all this time, with or without her husband; it didn't much matter one way or the other.

"Mother, I'm bald and it's your fault!" Sharon raged, bursting into the kitchen where her mother was washing a chicken for dinner. "How could you *do* this to me? I look like Bozo the Clown, not Twiggy." Margaret Winston turned, looked at her only child, and frowned.

"You look fine," she answered, picking up a meat cleaver and neatly splitting the chicken in a single motion. "Go tell your father and Baby Clark dinner's in an hour and if they're late it goes to the dogs."

Baby Clark was Lottie's son, the result of her first doomed marriage. He was conceived in a borrowed Manhattan penthouse where Lottie was living with Billy White, a washed-up minor-league catcher who left her seven months later with his name and not much else. She'd come home to have the baby, named for Clark Gable, her favorite movie star. Lottie tried motherhood for six months, then moved to Chicago to pick up her modeling career. There was no question that she couldn't take a baby to Chicago, so Sharon's mother had grudgingly agreed to take the boy in. Harvey Winston already thought of the child as his son, the son his precious Lottie had presented to him, the son that his arid wife would never provide.

Sharon thought her mother disliked Lottie because of Baby Clark—she'd once overheard Margaret Winston call her sister-in-law a cowbird—but it was deeper than that. Margaret Winston suspected there was no one her husband loved more—not his daughter, his nephew, certainly not his wife. Only Lottie. Lottie who loved and was loved by everybody. Even the men who kept connecting their fists to her perfect face with its laughing eyes and smile as big as the Montana sky. That was how her modeling résumé described her. That was how Baby Clark and Sharon and Harvey saw her, no matter how many loosened teeth and bruises she had when they rescued her. Somehow she still managed to look beautiful, like a wounded gazelle.

Harvey Winston had been rescuing Lottie all her life. When she'd fallen on the school playground, he had been there to pick her up. When she was fifteen and tried to elope with the Hodges boy, he'd found them even before they reached the justice of the peace and brought her back. He'd waited up for her when she was out on dates; sent her money when she was between jobs; hired the lawyers for her divorces; bought her train ticket when their mother died. As the years passed and Lottie's taste in men worsened and the beatings increased, so did the late-night phone calls. And always, Harvey Winston would be there to pick up the pieces, nurse her back to health, then watch her fly away again, waiting until the next time. Always, there was a next time.

When Lottie called, Margaret would set her lips in a hard line and make Harvey promise that this time would be the last. "Tell her that you have a family," Sharon would hear her mother say. "She calls and you come running. What about us? What about me?" The words disintegrated into tears of pleading. Years later, Sharon would sometimes hear the same pleading tone in the voices of women caught between lovers and mistresses.

Sharon never questioned Lottie's late-night calls or the way her father answered them. All she knew was that sometimes long after midnight the phone would ring once, twice, a dozen times until Harvey answered, his voice low and comforting, the way it only sounded for Lottie. Sharon would strain to hear the muffled words. Then silence. Sharon imagined her father sitting in the darkened living room, smoking, watching the shapeless night. The stairs would creak under her father's step, heavy and deliberate, for Harvey Winston was a big slow oxlike man. Then the rhythm of secret voices would throb against the common wall that separated Sharon's bed from her parents'. Her mother's voice would rise angry, then be silenced by her father's pleading sobs. Her mother would go then, first to Sharon's room, later to Baby Clark's, rousing the children, guiding them to the station wagon where she would tuck them into makeshift beds made of sleeping bags and frayed quilts. With her father behind the wheel, the station wagon would fly across blackened highways lined with soybeans and corn in summer, snow fences and the frozen carcasses of road-killed rabbits in winter. Two hundred, three hundred, four hundred miles or more. It didn't matter. Lottie was in trouble, hurting, waiting. For him. And he was coming.

Sharon would lie awake during these night flights, listening to Baby Clark whimper like a puppy until his soft sobs filled the back of the station wagon. The boy always cried himself to sleep, sure that his mother was dead this time. Sharon spun elaborate fantasies. She was a mortally wounded spy, like Mata Hari only more famous, more beautiful; the ambulance driver had orders to get her back across enemy lines to where her lover, the general, waited to hear her last words, the ones that would win the war. She was an astronaut hurtling a thousand miles an hour through space on her way to Mars, where she would establish the first outer-space colony and meet a tragic end when her spaceship was lost on the return voyage.

Sometimes the ride reminded her of the roller coaster, only better. She tried not to smile from the feeling that wrapped around her, tried to squeeze a tear out of the corner of her eyes for Lottie. She recited the rosary. She was an angel floating, dipping, soaring through silver clouds into a tangerine sunset. Sometimes, she fell asleep still smiling.

Always by the time they arrived, the night was long ended and Lottie—who was never dead, only broken—would be sitting at her kitchen table smoking cigarettes and plotting her revenge. She'd wait until Harvey burst through the door shouting, "Sis! Where are you?" before she'd run to him, burying her head in his barrel chest, sobbing. "You came, I knew you'd come. Don't leave me, don't ever leave me." Sharon's mother would look away embarrassed, humiliated at being reduced to a voyeur. But no matter how her father cajoled or pleaded, Lottie would never leave with him.

Finally, for Baby Clark's eighth Christmas, Lottie had come home alone and for good. Maybe she'd figured out that Sharon's father wanted to adopt the boy. More likely, she was simply tired of waking up in a strange land with strangers and wrinkles that weren't there the day before. Sharon didn't know or care why Lottie was back, only thankful that she was. Lottie was one of the few adults in the whole of Kansas City who could remember what it was like to be young.

Lottie would know the difference between Twiggy and Bozo the Clown, Sharon fumed to Sally, who had been her best friend since fourth grade. They both played flute in the high school band, were junior editors of the yearbook, and planned to be roommates at the University of Missouri, where Sharon would major in English or maybe journalism and Sally in music or maybe chemistry. They were sharing Oreo cookies and the bottle of apricot brandy that Sharon had pilfered from the downstairs liquor cabinet. Sally was sitting cross-legged on Sharon's bed, painting her toenails with pearlized white polish. She was wearing white cotton underpants and a real French décolleté bra from Miss Marie's Hollywood Lingerie. Miss Marie's, in a tiny shop downtown, was where Lottie bought all her lingerie.

Sally had blossomed from being distressingly flat-chested through ninth grade into a C-cup the summer of her junior year. So Sharon, whose own breasts were unremarkable, had convinced Sally to buy the bra—a fortress of wires, elastic, bones, and foam rubber covered in stiff black lace. Sally was too shy to wear it in public, even though it made her feel a little like Elizabeth Taylor in *Cat on a Hot Tin Roof*. Sharon agreed the effect was stunning.

Sally's were the only naked breasts Sharon had ever seen besides her own. Certainly the only ones she'd ever touched. And they were beautiful. Rounded and full, the nipples pouted, firm and pink. Pale-blue veins showed through the translucent flesh, beginning near each perfect swollen rosebud nipple and moving like highways on a road map into her chest. Sally worried that boys would want to touch them, although her Saturday nights were as dateless as Sharon's own. None did, but Sharon did.

For most of that year, Sally and Sharon had been practicing kissing. It had been Sharon's idea. Sally pretended she was kissing Dennis, the drum major she had a crush on. Sharon occasionally moaned, "Oh, Rodney," even though she hated kissing Rodney Mittsfield, who was always trying to stick his tongue in her mouth. After reading *Lady Chatterley's Lover,* Sharon suggested practicing kissing with their pajama tops off. Sally blushed and shook her head. Sharon was insistent.

"What if you met a really dashing Frenchman this summer and you took him for your lover and he found out you were just an inexperienced little high school virgin?" Sharon cajoled. They were still trying to walk the fine line of protecting their virginity while seeming to be experienced. Sally continued to shake her head. "Girls in Swiss boarding schools do it. It's practically a required class, like home ec. Only instead of Miss Bidwell teaching how to make cheeseballs, they have real French courtesans teaching them how to *make love.*" Sharon whispered the last and rolled her eyes. Neither girl knew exactly what a courtesan did or was, but the idea sounded exciting, daring, exotic. Eventually, Sally agreed.

Sharon loved to feel Sally's flesh tickling against her when they stepped into each other's arms. Each time their bare nipples brushed, sharp shock waves rocked through Sharon. It was 1965. They'd never seen a penis. Virgins didn't wear Tampax. It was Kansas City, Missouri. They'd never known a real lesbian, except maybe Miss Markham, the Spanish teacher, and her friend Teddy Bates, the women's tennis pro at the country club. And they couldn't get a straight answer from anyone about that, especially their mothers, who blushed and told them to hush every time they raised the subject. But Sally never liked to kiss for more than a few minutes. She'd quickly pull on her pajama top and dive under the sheets, clutching a stuffed tiger against her chest, leaving Sharon to turn on her side, watching the moon compete with the streetlight outside her window, dreaming of places with exotic names, places far from Kansas City.

"Too bad you don't have one of Lottie's wigs," Sally finally mused, handing Sharon the bottle of brandy. "She'd have you looking like Sandra Dee, Doris Day, anybody at all."

Sharon considered this. Lottie's wigs were legend—at least

in her family. So the next morning she was at her aunt's front door where Lottie greeted her with: "Honey, what is that? A poodle cut?" Sharon nodded solemnly as a pair of giant tears chased each other down her cheeks.

"Mother *made* Bonnie do it. She even likes it." Sharon was wailing again, as much for effect as from outrage.

Lottie's eyes widened until her false eyelashes brushed her eyebrows. Lottie was the only woman Sharon would ever know who wore false eyelashes to breakfast. "No doubt about it, you need Aunt Lottie." She motioned her niece into the master bedroom, past the living room where "Uncle" Nicky, the night bartender at the Holiday Inn, was watching a Bugs Bunny rerun. He laughed loudly.

"Like a lazy dog," Sharon muttered to herself, curling her lip in what she imagined was worldly disdain. Nicky didn't even glance her way. None of the "uncles" ever paid any attention to her—even the ones she'd unsuccessfully tried to seduce.

Sharon had been in Lottie's bedroom often. The dressing table had a three-foot-square lighted mirror, with dozens of lipsticks and matching nail polishes, foundation, powder, rouge, a can of brushes, eyeshadow, liner, eyelash curlers, and rows of false eyelashes carefully arranged by length. A large open box of bath powder that had left a fine dust on the floor, marked by small footprints, was the only sign of disorder. The room smelled of Tabu and sex.

A dozen plastic heads, each with an identical smile and Cleopatra eyes, lined a bookshelf next to the dresser. Each head was wearing a wig. Red, blond, brunette, curly, straight, long, short, some in curlers, some with flowers interlaced in the intricate curls. Sharon beamed as her aunt selected a free-flowing strawberry-blond confection that curled delicately around her face and fell long past her shoulders. Lottie had worn that wig to the 1963 Fourth of July country club dance.

That had been Lottie's first summer home. She had selected a lace dress with a full skirt and a low neckline, and a matching picture hat with blue ribbons that, like the wig, tickled her waist. It was a costume more suited to a garden party than a dance, although for years after, all the women would wear picture hats and lace dresses to the Fourth of July dance. That's just how it was with Lottie.

Sharon's father had arranged a date with Lottie for his new assistant, an ambitious young banker fresh from the state university. Margaret had been shocked. "She's a good ten years older than that young man. What can you be thinking?"

"Lottie's still the prettiest girl in Kansas City." Sharon's father had fairly beamed. "Besides, she doesn't look a day over twenty-five."

"He's just a boy . . ." Her mother had stopped abruptly when Sharon entered the room.

When Lottie had arrived that afternoon, Sharon dropped broad hints about the conversation she'd overheard, and was shocked when her mother and Lottie had actually laughed.

"Maybe we're not so different after all," Margaret confided later when the afternoon sun and sherry had loosened her tongue. She and Lottie were playing gin on the far end of the porch where the honeysuckle hung sweet dark shadows. Sharon was draped across the porch swing, her eyes closed, an open copy of *War and Peace* on her stomach. The women thought she was asleep. Sharon opened one eye a slit and peeked into the shadows. She couldn't imagine any two women less alike than her dowdy mother and her glamorous aunt. "Only one of us ran away because freedom was more important than pity or honor, and the other stayed because they were more so." Her mother's voice sounded bitter.

"Cowbirds under the skin," Lottie had replied, and they had laughed, a secret laugh that rose up and wrapped them in the conspiracy of women. And for the moment Sharon was still on the outside.

Lottie had never looked more beautiful than she did that Fourth of July, even though her affair with the young banker ended badly a few weeks later. But that night, with all that hair falling soft and golden across her shoulders, she really was the prettiest girl in Kansas City. And now the wig was Sharon's. The girl turned her back to the mirror and looked over her shoulder, admiring the long hair. She was Hollywood's newest and greatest discovery and Troy Donahue was waiting for her on the set.

"You sure do look like Harv," Lottie observed, breaking the spell. Lottie was the only one who ever called Sharon's father Harv and it sounded secret, special the way she said it. Sharon blushed deeply. She didn't want to look like either of her parents. She wanted to look like Lottie, be like her. She wanted strangers to call her "sweetie" and have bartenders ask for identification until she was nearly thirty. Instead, she looked like her hulking father—even Lottie thought so.

Later, at Lottie's kitchen table, over a lunch of Kools and Budweisers, Sharon spun dreams while Lottie applied a second coat of pink polish to her niece's stubby fingernails. Her mind was on the real estate license exam next week. For two years, she'd been taking the test but had never passed. It was as if the questions all stopped making sense when she read them. No matter how much she tried to study before the test, it always happened. Once, she'd even slept with the proctor afterward. She didn't pass that time, either. It wasn't until later that she found out a computer graded the test.

"Tell me about the time you got to go backstage and meet Elvis," Sharon probed, hoping her aunt would bring out her scrapbook full of photos and clippings. "God, that must have been something." Sharon's voice was quiet with awe.

Lottie looked at her niece closely. "That was a long time ago, Sharon. And look what it got me—Mister Wonderful in there sacked out on my couch. When he wakes up, he'll come in here and get one of my beers out of my refrigerator. My beer. He doesn't even buy his own beer." Her voice was as bitter as the beer in Sharon's mouth.

"But you could've been Miss America," the girl pleaded, trying to break her aunt's mood. "You almost were, everybody knows that." Lottie moved to the window, where frost made the world look like it was wrapped in cellophane.

"Sharon, I wasn't even close to being Miss America. Although if it hadn't been for the talent competition . . ." her voice trailed. Lottie turned to Sharon, chuckled, and winked. "You think it would take Miss America five tries at the real estate exam?"

Sharon studied her hands. If only life were as easy as taking tests, she thought; then offered, "I could take the test for you. School's about the only thing I can do right all the time."

Lottie laughed kindly. "Kiddo, you do a lot of things right. There's just some things in life you've got to do yourself, no matter what. But, hey, I appreciate the offer." They sat quietly, listening to the radio, feeling the afternoon fade.

"Aunt Lottie," Sharon finally spoke, "do you think I'll ever get out of Kansas City? Sometimes I have this dream where I go to Mother's room to look for something on her globe and all I can find is Kansas City. All the countries, the oceans, the mountains are gone. I never wonder what happened; I just feel so sad that now I'm stuck here forever. I'll never get out, never be anybody different. Never be really happy. Or free. Never be like you." Sharon blushed deeply at her confession and blew on her fingernails, even though the polish was already dry.

Lottie looked at her niece for a long moment and started to laugh, filling the room, filling Sharon's whole world with the music of the sound. And then Sharon was laughing, too, even though she didn't know why.

1965

Tara Winston was still a speck of dust, a breath, a motion, a whiff of honeysuckle in the night air, a sliver of silver, a wish, a whisper, a snatch of a song sung on a clear morning. She would have remained so, too, if not for a collection of seemingly unrelated events that occurred on March 20, 1965. If the girl who was to be her young mother hadn't been reading the seduction scene in *Forever Amber* and suddenly lost interest in her virginity. Or if her equally young father hadn't lost his nerve in Martin's Main Street Drugs and bought four Three Musketeers bars instead of a box of Trojans. Or even if Timmy Thompson hadn't broken his leg, which meant Baby Clark had to go to his house to sleep over. Or especially if the Missouri Bankers Association hadn't asked Harvey Winston to speak on escrows and estates at their annual meeting in St. Louis that very weekend. But all those things did happen and so, Tara Winston was dreamed out of the cosmos.

Three months later, in an obstetrician's office on the seventh floor of what passed as a skyscraper in Kansas City, Sharon Winston's stomach knotted and she upchucked her future.

"I'm sorry," the doctor said. He looked sad. Pale. His eyes were blue and cloudy. He reminded Sharon of a very old dog.

"No, you're lying," Sharon said, her eyes widened, defying the edge in her voice. "You have to do something. I'm the

Lillian Parkhurst Scholarship winner. I'm going to Vassar next year." For once nobody had cared if she was fat, only that she was smart, smarter than any other seventeen-year-old girl in the entire state of Missouri. Little fat girls from the Midwest could only dream of going to a school like Vassar, no matter how much money their daddy's made, and Sharon had made that dream real. For four glorious years, a trust established by the late Miss Lillian Parkhurst would pay Sharon's tuition, room, board, even a small stipend. And then in her junior year, Sharon would study in Paris. It was all arranged. Just one more year in Kansas City, then Vassar, even France. For the first time, Sharon Winston could be anybody, and there would be no one around to remind her of who she'd been, who she really was.

"I can't have a baby," she whispered finally. "I'm supposed to go to Vassar." The old doctor patted her hand. His nails were short, cut almost to the quick. He bites his nails, Sharon thought, and started to cry.

Lottie was in the outer office, turning the pages of a dog-eared *Vogue,* trying to concentrate, although her mind kept wandering to her niece. How a girl as smart as Sharon could end up in such a mess puzzled her. Didn't Margaret ever explain anything to the girl? No, of course she wouldn't. Damn, I should've done it myself, she thought, raising her eyes to a woman about her own age but in the far stages of pregnancy who was lowering herself onto the couch next to Lottie. The woman smiled almost apologetically. Lottie smiled, then her face crumbled into a scowl. Harv's gonna have a fit when he hears about this, she thought, the vision of her older brother towering in her mind. Shit, he'll probably blame me. Say I'm a bad influence, again. Well, I know one thing, if she was my kid, she wouldn't be knocked up. I'd make sure she was smarter than that.

Sharon had gone to Lottie for the name of an abortionist. But if her aunt knew of any, she wouldn't tell. Maybe it was fear for Sharon's immortal soul or her mortal uterus. More likely, she didn't have the money and knew Sharon couldn't get it. Whatever the reason, Lottie had offered to make the appointment with the doctor, even go with Sharon for a pregnancy test, but nothing more.

"I only did it once," Sharon muttered on their way back to

the car. She was dragging her feet, feeling the pink leather of her princess pumps scrape across the concrete sidewalk. The sun beat hot on her shoulders; it was already eighty-five degrees and only ten o'clock in the morning. Lottie was putting the top down on her yellow Pontiac convertible.

"Once?" Lottie turned to her niece, her eyes wide. "You only did it once and you got knocked up? That doesn't seem fair. You should at least get two or three shots. Well, did you at least like it?"

Sharon shook her head. "It's better in the books."

Lottie started to laugh. Sharon eyed her quizzically, then suddenly it all seemed very funny. It kept on being very funny all the rest of that summer, as if Sharon Winston had just heard the funniest joke in the world. Or maybe it was the world playing a joke on her, only she'd beaten them all to the punch line.

She laughed when her mother announced Sharon would be spending what Margaret Winston delicately called "your confinement" in a nearby convent where she could finish her senior year early and then go on to the University of Missouri as they'd originally planned. And no one, especially Sally, was to know. "Isn't it a little late to confine me with professional virgins and amateur lesbians, Mother?" Sharon had sneered, for the morning sickness had brought up a decidedly sarcastic streak that no one had really noticed before. "And Sally already knows, but I swore her to secrecy. You think I'd want anybody else to know it was Rod-ney," Sharon dragged out the name. She'd already made her parents promise never to tell Rodney or his parents about "the situation," as her mother called it.

She'd laughed when the summer band director, Mr. Brestleman, who was so unpopular the boys called him 'Mr. Breast Man', asked Sharon to stay after band practice one July afternoon. "I've been meaning to talk with you for quite a while," he began, his voice timid, halting. She'd shot him a cold look that instead of silencing him, fueled his voice with confidence. "You have such a pretty face. You could be one of the prettiest girls in this school—hell, in the whole state—if you'd just lose some of that weight. Why with the right program, you could be in shape for the Homecoming Court." He'd smiled, pleased with himself, until her peals of laughter washed his face sober again.

She'd laughed when Rodney Mittsfield brought her a pink leather diary with a tiny brass lock. "You lucky duck," the bon voyage card read. It had a picture of a duck wearing a life preserver boarding the *Titanic*. He and Sharon didn't see each other much anymore. He'd stopped calling, could no longer even meet her eyes. It was as if that one March night had been wiped from the calendar. He'd even asked Janey Parsons to the Independence Day dance. His mother had made him come to tell Sharon good-bye. Like everyone else, he thought she was going to a private school in New Hampshire to prepare for her glorious career at Vassar. Sharon could think of no reason why he should know more.

She'd even laughed when Sister Mary Agnes welcomed her to Saint Mary's Home for Young Women. It was a huge brick and clapboard mansion built not long after the Civil War that sat back from a tree-lined street. It originally had been built as a boarding school for young women but had been a convent since World War I. In the mid 1950s, the nuns began doing officially what they'd been doing unofficially for years: taking in pregnant girls. Margaret Winston had chosen the home because the nuns said Sharon could get her high school diploma by the time her baby was born. The child would be adopted by a good but childless Catholic couple. Sharon's life would be back on course by the time the snow cleared.

"We have heard some very good things about you from your former school," the sister had said, showing Sharon to her room. "We understand you are a very gifted girl, very intelligent." Sharon had laughed until she nearly doubled over. "And lucky, too," she'd gasped through peals of laughter, "don't forget lucky!"

Those were the last words she spoke for a week. She went to class. Did her homework. Listened to the radio in her room. Finished her chores. Went to dinner. Fell asleep in a twin bed with springs that creaked under her weight. Kept her doctor's appointments. Celebrated her eighteenth birthday alone. And started to cry. All the tears that she'd pushed down for so many months spilled out of her. The girls who had made Sharon Winston the butt of their cruelty took credit for the tears, but they were wrong. They were the tears of hopelessness, of stupidity, of ruination. Sharon cried them all and then one day, she realized Babe could dry her tears, make her laugh, even think she was beautiful, as beautiful as Sharon had always wanted to be. Maybe that was how it started. Later she could never be sure of the exact beginnings of their life together. Only the place and the circumstances, but never the exact moment in time.

Running away to California had been Sharon's idea, she was sure of that, just as the idea to keep Tara had been Babe's. And despite the odds, Babe had made it all happen. She'd convinced Sister Timothy to help smuggle Sharon and the baby out of Saint Mary's lying-in hospital and into a run-down motel near the stockyards. "This place stinks," Sharon had announced, her face screwed up in distaste. The strangely sweet odor of disinfectant was no match for the stench of cow dung from the boots of the farmers who stayed there after driving their stock to the Kansas City market. Tears had welled in her eyes as deep sobs wracked her body. "I hurt all over," she'd whispered hoarsely as Babe put her to bed and tucked Tara in beside her. "What am I going to do? Who will take care of us?" she'd asked over and over while Babe spun tales of the California sun that shone all year round, and oranges the size of a softball, and grapes heavy and sweet and black with juice. Babe had talked and soothed Sharon until she was strong enough to travel and then, without looking back, they'd boarded a Greyhound bus bound for San Francisco.

The rhythm of the bus rocked Sharon all the way across the country. She watched the plains rise into foothills, then disappear into the deep forest of the mountain ranges as the bus trailed along behind the sun. It was surely a dream. Girls like her didn't run away on Greyhound buses bound for California with lesbians and babies. None of it was real, it couldn't be. Sometimes she'd look at the baby and wonder where its mother was. Certainly it couldn't be her. She was an honors student, winner of the Lillian Parkhurst Scholarship. In September she'd leave Kansas City and the old Sharon behind. She'd become Shari—witty, pert, popular. She'd join a sorority, a good one. She'd lose weight and style her hair and buy new clothes—lots of miniskirts and boots. She'd laugh a lot. She'd have a foreign sports car and go for drives in the country. She'd spend her junior year in Paris. She'd be happy for the first time in her life.

Sometimes as the countryside fell away to dusk, Sharon would see herself speed past in a red convertible. She was the

star of the new hit TV series "Runaway" about a brilliant
woman undercover agent who was combing the country trying
to find an amnesic princess who had been separated from her
baby in the Kansas City bus depot when an evil spy drugged her
Coke. Every week viewers would watch Sharon and her
gumshoe sidekick, Babe, and the baby in a new adventure as
they tried to find the missing princess. In this week's episode,
they were all on a bus, traveling undercover. There were rumors that the princess was hiding out in California. They had
to find her before the spies did. The camera panned down the
aisle of the bus, taking in the faces, some sleeping, others just
closed to the night, then out to the highway, a close-up on the
girl in the convertible. Her hair was flying on the wind, streaming behind her like Isadora Duncan's scarves.

But then Tara would cry or Babe would want the window
seat or the bus would sway, rocking Sharon back to her reality.
The transistor radio Babe had tied to the window set the trip
to music. Crossing the California state line, the Beatles were
serenading them with "Kansas City" followed by "Run for
Your Life."

"It's an omen," declared Babe, who believed in magic. She
handed Sharon the baby and began to dig through the makeshift diaper bag for her tarot cards to tell their fortune for the
fifth time that day.

Sharon had run away with Babe Daniels more for adventure than love. If Babe loved her—and she'd never really said
that she did—Sharon thought it would be either very wonderful or very terrible. She'd been reading paperback novels Babe
had given her about lesbians. The women in the stories were
always deliriously happy in their passionate, sometimes even
perverse love nests—for a while. But in the end they either died
or got married. "Is it really like this, always?" Sharon had
asked after the third novel.

"Don't know," Babe had shrugged. The only woman she'd
ever been with for more than one night was Faye Fletcher, and
Faye had run out on her.

"Well, why don't they write books with happy endings?"

"Maybe there aren't any," Babe had answered, rocking
Tara on her lap. In the way of frightened, lonely girls, Sharon
sometimes imagined that Babe might love the baby more. Still,
she'd fallen in love with the idea of loving Babe one night when
the moon hung low and blue, washing the sea in pale light.

1966

The ocean had roared like a relentless lion outside the door of the aging summer cabins that held a motley assortment of beats, weekend junkies, would-be poets and sometime artists who clung to the California coastline like barnacles. At first, Sharon had imagined them all to be romantic characters in one of Jack Kerouac's novels. She liked to think her life belonged on a library shelf, and she was still waiting to see how the story would end, to close the covers and feel the little letdown that always came with the end of a novel.

Sharon Winston was eighteen years old. In less than a year she'd had a baby she didn't really want, run away to California with a lesbian she didn't really know, and was living a life she didn't understand. No matter how she tried to sort it out, she was one hell of a long way from Kansas City.

Sharon was letting the little white pill dissolve under her tongue. It was Thursday. Every Thursday afternoon, she dropped acid with Rasha and wrote haiku on the handmade paper Babe had brought her from Chinatown. Rasha was a doe-eyed former Stanford graduate student from Cleveland who had moved to the cottages with her husband, Tomas, the week after the Marin acid test. Tomas had been a doctoral candidate in economics until he took a three-month sabbatical at Harvard, where he joined a group of devotees of Dr. Timothy Leary. Following the advice of his guru, he had taken the rest of his fellowship money and never bothered to go back to Stanford.

Rasha and Tomas had followed the acid tests with their vats of electric Kool-Aid and flashing lights and fantasies up the peninsula into San Francisco and finally to the one abortive attempt in Marin County. That one had been the undoing of Tomas, who said the trees in Marin County talked. "Far out," said Rasha. It was the only response she was capable of at the time. She'd been stoned for three days. They had gathered up their toddler, Free, and moved to the beach, where Tomas eavesdropped on what the trees were saying to the waves.

Shortly after their arrival, Rasha began painting portraits of pain. Rasha was convinced she knew the color of pain; she'd seen it when she'd dropped acid for Free's delivery. She was finishing her eleventh oil, entitled "Pain," as were the previous ten. The walls of their cabin were lined with her paintings, quotes from *A Midsummer Night's Dream* in Tomas's tense script, and a banner over their bed that had the words TURN ON, TUNE IN, DROP OUT—T. LEARY embroidered in rainbow colors. Sharon thought Rasha and Tomas were the most exciting people she'd ever met.

While Babe cut bait on the fishing boats, Rasha taught Sharon to bake bread, to gather wild mushrooms, to write haiku, to drop acid, to paint, to sew, to play the recorder. Every afternoon they took the babies for walks along the beach, passing the spot where Tomas sat quiet as a stone listening to the trees talk and occasionally making notes in an oversized leather notebook. Sharon had peeked inside the notebook once but only saw page after page of undecipherable glyphs.

Even when she wasn't tripping, Sharon was content. When she was turning on with Rasha, though, she was awash in a sea of wildflowers. The countryside, the cabin, the ocean, the baby, all were so beautiful that Sharon couldn't believe she'd never seen it before. The world was special. She was special. Kansas City was nothing more than a memory of a bad trip.

"I'll never marry," she confided to Rasha one rainy afternoon. They were baking bread in Sharon's kitchen. Through the wavy glass they could see Tomas and Free making mud pies in the driveway. Rasha smiled and folded her hands across her second child who lay beneath her ribs. "My baby and I will be nomads, wandering the back roads, getting to know the people," Sharon pressed on, her face was young and intent. Since arriving in California she'd been reading a strange but steady diet of John Steinbeck, Allen Ginsberg, and Lawrence Ferlinghetti in a desperate quest to find the heart of what's real, as she'd taken to saying.

Rasha was considering leaving Tomas, maybe moving down to San Francisco or back to Palo Alto, and putting her life in order. In the sixth month of pregnancy, she was worried about this baby. It felt different. Somehow wrong. All morning she'd been feeling sharp tugs, as if a temperamental giant had her full uterus suspended by a taut rubber band. The baby had been quiet for more than a day. Too quiet. "Probably tripped out," Tomas had offered that morning. They had done magic mushrooms the day before. "Man, can you imagine what a fetus sees? Dinosaurs. The beginning of the world. All kinds of shit. Far out." Rasha frowned, biting her lower lip. She'd wanted to stop the drugs when she first found out she was pregnant, but Tomas had called her uptight and laughed. "This is going to be the *most beautiful* baby, Mama," he'd said, his face glowing. He'd taken the trees an offering and after a day came back to announce the baby would be named Enlightened Tree.

The giant tugged on the rubber band again. A sharp pain shot across Rasha's back. If only Sharon would shut up, she thought, gasping for breath, suddenly angry at this girl and her endless prattle. "Who the hell are you, if not *the people*?" Rasha flared. The giant let go. She could breathe again. Lowering herself onto a kitchen chair, she looked a little more kindly on Sharon, who was standing next to the stove, her eyes wide in terror. She'd never heard Rasha speak sharply to anyone, even Tomas, who deserved it if anyone did.

"I officially christen you one of *the people*. Take a look around your kingdom. As we *people* say, 'This is it, there ain't no more.'" Rasha's voice oozed sarcasm, cruelty, as she swept her arm wide, a matador's veronica exposing the shabby cabin for what it really was: a thin-mattressed double bed under a threadbare pink chenille spread; two wooden chairs, the green one that supported Rasha, the other painted yellow, tucked primly under the rusting chrome table; a brown loveseat with a large red scarf gaily draped across the back to hide a rip in the upholstery; Tara's secondhand playpen, a makeshift affair pieced together by Babe and Tomas.

Sharon trembled, unaware of the tears that threatened. The fantasy was crumbling and she desperately needed to bring it back. Turning away from Rasha, she leaned across her sleeping baby, watching hot tears splash one by one against Tara's soft pink back. Reality came crashing through the fantasy. *Failure* taunted the cheerleaders in their short red skirts that skimmed tight thighs. *Fool* hooted the Pi Phi girls in their matching winter-white cashmere sweaters. *Fatty* jeered the majorettes in their tall white boots, which ended just below dimpled knees. Shards of doubt and pain cut deep across her brain. Soon Babe would find out the truth, if she didn't already know—that Sharon was a nothing, a worthless failure, a despicable fat blob. There was nothing to do but try to save face. Sharon inhaled sharply, swallowing her tears, when a deep sob echoed by a groan coursed through the cabin.

When Babe came back that night, she found Sharon on the

porch, staring morosely at the moon. "What'cha see?" Babe asked, balancing herself on the porch railing.

"A liar's moon," Sharon answered, not meeting Babe's gaze.

"Looks more like a lover's moon to me," Babe teased, looking from Sharon to the moon and back again.

Sharon shook her head sadly and studied her hands. "Everybody's leaving here. They say the place has bad vibes."

Babe looked around the horseshoe of eight identical cabins casting eight identical shadows. She hadn't been comfortable here since the night she heard spirits howling on the ocean wind. Even without LSD, Babe knew what Tomas was talking to in the woods, and she wanted no part of it. "Wood spirits," Babe mused, pulling out her pocketknife and beginning to pare at her nails.

"Vibes. Wood spirits, what does it matter now?" Sharon started to cry. "An ambulance came and took Rasha away this afternoon. The baby was dead inside her. For two days, she'd been carrying a dead baby. She told me she couldn't remember it moving since Tuesday morning. All this time it was dead, and she didn't even know!" Sharon sobbed, hugging herself so hard that her fingers dug deeply into her sides. "Tomas says they're moving down to the city as soon as she's out of the hospital. Rasha begged him for weeks to move back to the city, only he wouldn't go. Said the trees told him to stay."

"So now that the baby's dead, he's willing to tell the trees to go to hell?" Babe shook her head, wondering what Rasha saw in him.

"He wanted to bring the baby back here . . . to bury her . . . under one of his trees, but they won't let him 'cause he's not an undertaker and this isn't a cemetery. I guess you can't even bury an unborn baby where you want to. I always thought those laws were just for real people." Sharon suddenly fell silent. There was nothing left to say.

Babe leaned against the porch railing, dabbing at her eyes with the back of her right hand. She blinked hard. The stars blurred. "I've been thinking about some things, Winston. Maybe clearing out's not such a bad idea . . . this place. These people," she started.

"You don't have to stay," Sharon interrupted. "I know we're a burden. You should go." The words seemed to explode all at once. She'd been practicing what she'd say when Babe wanted to leave. Sharon had braced herself for the inevitable. Eventually Babe would leave. Little fat girls shouldn't expect anything more; it was a lesson she'd learned too well. She was a burden, a mistake, a nothing, just like all those girls had told her so many times. And she had swallowed their poison, their hate and made it her own. Why prolong the agony? Babe should go now, leave the bad little fat girl to march into her nondescript future alone.

Only Babe didn't smile, relieved, the way Sharon had expected. "*I* should go?" Babe raged. "Just like that?" Babe's voice was loud, angry. Sharon's head snapped up, surprised. "What right do you have to tell me to leave you and our daughter! You just decide and that's it? No discussion? Just thanks a lot and get the hell out?" Sharon kept shaking her head, confused. She wanted to speak, to cry out even, but a knot in her throat threatened to choke her every time she tried. The angry words stood between them like a cobblestone wall. Minutes froze against the night. The two women looked at each other for a long moment, then one turned to the house and the other strode off the porch, climbed on her motorcycle, and roared into the blackness. From the window, Sharon watched the red taillight retreat until it was nothing more than a red speck on the blacktop highway.

Dawn was teasing the darkness away when Sharon heard the motorcycle rev then shudder into silence, heard the cabin's front door creak, heard Babe's footsteps move through the familiar darkness. Sharon slipped from the bed, wrapped a blanket around her pink cotton nightgown, and padded silently across the room. Even when the kitchen chair scraped against the worn linoleum, Babe didn't turn away from the sink where she was running water for coffee.

"How's Tara?" Babe finally asked, her voice terse.

"I think she missed you."

"And you?" Babe waited a long minute. "What about you?"

A deep sob answered for Sharon, who huddled deeper into the blanket trying to become invisible. And then Babe was there, holding her, rocking the tears away. "I love you," Sharon whispered. "Even if you don't love me, even if you love the baby better, I still love you."

"Hush," Babe cooed, kissing her lightly, petting her hair.

Later that morning while Sharon slept, Babe lay beside her, watching sunbeams chase through the windows. "I love you, Winston," she whispered into Sharon's naked back. "I know you don't believe me now, but it's true. I really do love you."

1987

On the occasion of Sharon Winston's fortieth birthday, Babe Daniels rented a trio of searchlights, a tuxedo, a 1936 Rolls-Royce limousine that had originally belonged to a movie star she'd never heard of, and a sound system. She got a special permit from City Hall to park the searchlights in the street in front of the bar and had the PA system's speakers mounted over the bar door. At ten o'clock, the limo was to pull up in front of the searchlights where Babe, dressed in the tuxedo, would be waiting with a dozen roses. "Yesterday" would spill onto the sidewalk through the rented speakers. Sharon, in the satin evening gown Babe had selected from the designer's queen-size collection at Macy's, would step out of the limousine looking like a golden goddess. Babe would hand her the roses, kiss her lightly, and lead her through the parted crowd into the club decorated with a thousand lights and pieces of mirror that would transform the ceiling into a summer night sky. After the party, Babe would give Sharon a diamond and sapphire ring shaped like a flower as the limo whisked them through the Berkeley hills to their suite at the Claremont Resort for what was left of the weekend. Babe had been planning the party for months. Every detail was smoothed into place.

Seeing the limo round the corner, Babe waved the crowd to silence and took her place next to the curb. "Go get 'er, Tiger," a voice called from the back of the crowd. The music started. Babe grinned. The door to the limo opened and Sharon, in a tuxedo identical to Babe's but with a fedora pulled low over her forehead and a lighted cigarillo clenched between her teeth, scrambled out of the car. "Gotcha!" she hooted, planting a damp kiss on Babe's cheek. She slung the roses across her shoulder like a baseball bat, took Babe's elbow, and ploughed into the cheering crowd. "You're the one always saying there's no such thing as a femme after forty," Sharon whispered to Babe, who could only grumble in reply before the crowd of well-wishers closed in around them.

Sharon didn't spend much time at the bar anymore. In the days when they'd lived upstairs, she and Babe had worked side by side. But those days were a long time gone, and now Arlan and their business needed her more. More and a little more with each week passing.

"I have dreams of driving," Sharon had told her therapist the week before the party. "It's dark. Foggy. I see the headlights shoot into the distance like a tunnel. I'm driving very fast. I'm chasing something just beyond the headlights. Sometimes I can almost see it, like a shadow. But no matter how fast I go, I can never catch up."

"And how do you feel about that?" the therapist had asked, making a brief note on her yellow legal pad.

Sharon's eyes had roamed the room, skimming the collection of diplomas and licenses on one wall, the bookcase, the trio of Imogene Cunningham prints on another. She'd selected this therapist because of those prints, a little thread of commonality in a world of anonymous feelings, she'd thought at the time. Like the little fat girl running up the sidewalk calling, "Wait! Please wait for me!" Like a reject, a failure, because the others won't slow down, no matter how much I beg, she'd started to say, then a troubling thought surfaced in her mind like the form of a drowning swimmer being sucked under the surf. No matter how much Arlan wants to slow down, he can't. He . . . can't. It doesn't have anything to do with me. The thought surprised her, but before she could begin, the therapist had signaled the session over, leaving Sharon alone with her angels and demons for another week. Leaving her alone with Arlan, with Arlan's dying.

She'd promised to go to his house the evening of her birthday party. He had a special gift for her. Watching her cross the yard at the house that clung to the side of a cliff overlooking the sea, his once-handsome face crinkled into a smile, perhaps a little too bright, and only slightly out of character for Arlan Mendenhall—author, raconteur, celebrity gardener, personality on two continents. To eyes that didn't know him well, did he seem himself? She wondered. Thinner, perhaps, or forgetful or pained or tense? "Is it so obvious?" he'd ask Sharon two, sometimes three or four, times a day when they were alone in the office. And she honestly wasn't able to answer, so subtle were the changes, like a rose day by day going to seed.

Soon . . . Arlan . . . will . . . die. Sharon turned the words over slowly, letting them glut with memories and madness, bits of happiness, more than a few tears, all shredded like remnants from the years they'd built together. They were partners; more than that, they were friends. But no longer equals. With every day passing, the work was becoming more hers than theirs. And she wasn't ready.

When Arlan Mendenhall thought of dying, as he did so often these days, he imagined it as a way of brushing against immortality. The world would remember him for the beauty he'd given it. A generation would possibly remember him for his books, but the roses he'd created would outlast them all. And Sharon? How would she remember him? As partner? Mentor? Friend? Or as the one who helped her to free the beauty locked deep in her soul?

Certainly, she'd been the one who first had the idea of turning his little books on aristocrats' rose gardens into the flashy volumes that made Arlan Mendenhall a beloved household personality. He'd rescued Sharon from life as a legal secretary at Hobbes, Crenshaw and Markes, but she had saved him from something worse: obscurity.

With her poetry, his essays, and Charles's photographs, *Sweetheart Roses* had surprised even the most skeptical with its success seven years earlier. Every year after, there had been a new book, each more popular than the one before. Sharon feared fame as much as Charles had scorned it, so Arlan had basked in the spotlight alone. After Charles's death, Arlan had pursued fame almost frantically, as if he could become the image he'd so carefully crafted. A man in the mirror that nothing could touch or tarnish. Not death. Or disease. Or despair. A man made immortal by the sheer strength of beauty.

He wouldn't allow himself to become like Charles, who'd so quietly withdrawn, resigning himself to the inevitable. Charles hadn't known how to fight, even in the beginning. Sometimes as Charles leaned over the lightbox, studying a dozen transparencies of red roses, his face glowing, rouged by the reflected light, Arlan could see shadows of the boy he'd first loved half a lifetime ago.

They'd met in New York when it was still reeling from the end of World War II. Anything was possible in those early years, especially for two handsome young men. Arlan had been at Oxford when the war had erupted, freeing him from living out his mother's dream. She had raised him to be a true scholar. After spending the war years as a secretary in Her Majesty's Navy, Arlan booked passage as a purser on a cruise liner that was ported in New York. When the ship sailed for the U.K. two weeks later, a new purser was aboard and Arlan was settled into room 537 of the Sloane House YMCA.

Charles was in room 536—home since his arrival two months earlier from Salt Lake City, where the local chief of police had encouraged his abrupt departure in exchange for tearing up an obscenity charge filed by Horace Dobbs, a local wedding photographer. To Dobbs, who lived with his wife of thirty-three years and their three spinster daughters, Charles Anders was more than just another apprentice, he was the son the middle-aged photographer would never have. Horace Dobbs might even have offered Charles a small part of the business if he hadn't dropped by the studio late one Wednesday night when his apprentice was in the middle of a session. By night, Charles had been photographing willing cowboys, football players, swimmers, construction workers, and students under the same lights where, by day, Dobbs recorded the anniversaries, graduations, reunions of his God-fearing clientele. Charles considered his photographs of nude men art. Horace Dobbs and most of Salt Lake City's upstanding citizenry called them trash, plain and simple.

So, with his future as a Salt Lake City wedding photographer behind him, Charles arrived in New York with a camera, two suitcases, a high school diploma, and a box of photographs that at first paid the rent and eventually made him famous. When middle age began to yap at his heels, Charles turned his studio over to his own younger, more flamboyant apprentices and began to spend ever-increasing blocks of time photographing Arlan's gardens. It was as if he was trying to capture, or perhaps to understand, beauty.

"The roses burn with beauty, but we are too weak, too cowardly to hold their fire," he'd told Sharon on one of his final visits to the office. Eventually, he no longer left his mirrorless rooms, which bloomed even in winter with roses of every color from Arlan's greenhouse. Through the final months, Sharon and Arlan had mourned together, had shared shifts so Charles was never alone. "If only this weren't such an ugly way to die," Charles would sometimes muse, during his rare lucid moments. And his friend and his lover would tell him that he was imagining things, that of course he was still beautiful. They meant, of course, his soul.

Two years later when it started with Arlan, Sharon was

there, already devising a battle plan, like Troy's last soldier. As Arlan made the rounds of San Francisco's medical offices, Sharon found healers willing to promise what none of the doctors could or would: a way to shore up Arlan's debilitated immune system. As the time constricted, Sharon became more desperate, Arlan more resigned. Ronaldo, the houseboy, had strict orders from Sharon to cook only the special diets from the nutritional healer in San Mateo, no matter what Arlan ordered for dinner. Twice, Sharon took Arlan to special meditation retreats at Big Sur, where they sat in a wide circle, chanting with a dozen others until the room vibrated. When he was too weak to finish the last part of the pilgrimage up Mount Shasta to the shaman who lived deep in the timber, Sharon had climbed on alone and somehow convinced the grizzly bear of a woman who never left her cabin to go down to her friend. They fought the battle well—Sharon, the guerilla warrior, and Arlan, the increasingly impotent general.

Through it all, Arlan tended to the rituals that accompanied the deaths of old friends. And death moved against him like a whisper. Some nights she'd find him on the patio, work abandoned, watching the sun set across the bay. "Farthing for your thoughts," she'd offer, her bright voice always defying her fear.

And he'd chuckle softly, answering automatically. "You've not got a farthing, Miss Winston, m'dear." Only he was lost already to the night.

And now her worst fear and his worst anguish were confirmed, not by the healers or even by the doctors, but by Arlan himself. She could see it in his pale blue eyes: The battle was lost. Maybe he was just too tired, or too alone. If only all his money could buy time, Sharon thought, watching the sunset drip flames into the sea. But they'd gone through all that with Charles, hadn't they? And like so many of the others, Charles was gone, too.

"Tuxedoes become you, m'dear," Arlan was saying, extending his hand. Dark shadows crossed the patio, cast by lights from the house and garden. Arlan had been watching the fog roll across the ocean. Lights from distant houses up the shore began to twinkle like fireflies dancing at dusk. They sat in silence. They no longer had the capacity for talking of small things.

"I should like to die here at home, with my work," he said

finally. He walked into the garden, his back to her, his gaze lingering on the terraces, heavy with the last blooms of summer. "Not in the meager grip of strangers in some sterile hospital. Just here, with my things. Will you help me to do that, m'dear?" He turned to her and smiled.

"Arlan . . ." Her voice trembled against his words and she despised its weakness. He waved her silent.

"Finish *Roses for My Love,* at least promise me that. Oh, I expect to be here long enough to oversee, if you'd like. Although I doubt you'll really need me, you'll soon know that."

"I'll always need you," she whispered, her voice cracking from the tears she'd hidden from him for the past year.

"I despise crying females," he answered dryly, starting down the path to his greenhouse. "Come along, I've a birthday gift for you. But only if you stop blubbering."

The greenhouse was a glass dome, warm, humid. Tears streamed down every glass pane. It was private, secret, like a beginning. In the day, it had a view of the ocean, the mountains that stretched south. At night, though, the glass walls reflected only what the greenhouse held. A tape of jungle birdcalls played continuously. It was one of Arlan's many unproved theories about horticulture. A fountain gurgled against the far wall. Whenever she was in the greenhouse, Sharon felt like a fly in a terrarium. In the center of the dome were Arlan's famous roses, some of which even caught the fancy of at least one queen and a few royal ladies.

His long, slender fingers stroked the petals of his newest rose, a spectacular blossom tinged with lavender and white that exploded from a thorny stem. "This is my last rose," he said, as much to himself as to Sharon. The words made her shudder. During his career, Arlan had developed many new roses: strong yellow-orange blossoms, ruffled pinks, frivolous tangerines, sophisticated reds. Each new rose represented years of work. He had marked the seasons of his life with roses.

"I've chosen a name. I considered calling it Arlan's Last Stand." He chuckled dryly. Sharon winced. "But I've reconsidered. I'd like to name it Arlan's Sharon, with your permission, of course. Think of it as my birthday gift to you. What do you say?" His voice was excited, almost childlike. "It would make a splendid cover for the next book. *Rose of Sharon* you might call it. A wonderful title, although the purists would scoff and the real aficionados would call it egocentric at best. Either way, it would be a cheap play on words." He looked at Sharon and smiled kindly. "Call it whatever you like, m'dear. It will be, after all, your first truly independent venture." Arlan already was laying plans for her future. Sharon sighed. The sound rattled against the dusk.

"Only a fool defies the inevitable," he said finally, misinterpreting the sigh.

Sharon's mind whirled, trying to settle on an answer, the right answer, any answer at all. "Do you know how old I am today?" she finally asked.

"Far beyond the age of consent, I should imagine," he answered, his mind on the new rose.

"Forty. I'm forty years old today. And for every one of those years I've been somebody's child or mother or lover." Her voice trailed.

"Or partner," he added almost absently.

"Or partner," she echoed.

"And is it so terrible to be all those things?"

"Arlan, my father's been dead for six years now. He dropped dead at work one afternoon. A twenty-six-year-old man replaced him. They didn't even wait until after the funeral. I get picture postcards from my mother. She's in China this month . . . or maybe that was last month. I can't keep track anymore. And it doesn't matter. My daughter's in law school. She lives with a stripper on the side of a hill in Mill Valley. They have a view of the bay and a hot tub. And my lover? My lover has a bar for a mistress. Sometimes she even sleeps there, or at least that's where she says she's sleeping, and I don't have the courage or maybe the interest to try and find out otherwise." She inhaled deeply, tasting the air that was thick with humidity and the perfume of roses. "All that's left is the partnership. Our partnership."

"And that, too, soon will be ending." Arlan finished the sentence for her. They regarded each other silently for a long moment. "Which brings us then to the ultimate question: Who is the real Sharon Winston?"

"Every week for the past two years I've been paying $125 to a woman with a wall full of diplomas to tell me that. The jury's still out, I'm afraid."

"And you believe that the . . . jury, as you say, is still out . . . for you, too?"

"Does it matter?"

"A little." Arlan smiled and studied his hands. Fingers that might have belonged to a concert pianist locked and unlocked. "The closer I come to death, the more I find it to be an interesting taskmaster," he mused, examining his new rose closely, looking for any hint of imperfection that might be lurking in its petals. "I have found myself to be not such a bad fellow, after all—a most remarkable discovery." He raised his eyes to meet hers. "But what is more remarkable, looking back across my life, is I find so few regrets. I had always imagined they would be legion. Oh, boyhood disappointments, certainly. A few doomed dreams unfulfilled, to be sure. But real regrets?" He shook his head.

"Regrets, you say? Have I got a deal for you!" Sharon's voice rose, edged in bitter laughter. "I could run a blue-light special on regrets. Two for a dollar. Have your checks, cash, credit cards, money orders, even promises ready. No waiting on aisle two!"

"Good. You still laugh with a dying old man, but one day you'll understand."

"I hope so, Arlan. For my sake, I certainly hope so."

Chuckling, he clipped one perfect half-opened bud from the bush and handed it to her with a small stiff bow. "For my dear friend."

At the spot where the path turned to the garden, he left her, walking in the direction of the house.

"I love you," she whispered, watching his back sag a little more when he thought he was out of her view.

Following a different path, Sharon started toward the Mustang that was waiting to take her home to Babe and then to her birthday party. A pale breeze rustled through the empty garden. The heady scent of the rose touched her. The first star of the night twinkled to life on the horizon. How many stars had she wished on in her forty years? Thousands surely. And had any of those wishes come true? Or had they all, and she'd just been too blind to know it at the time?

"Starlight, star bright . . ." she began, then fell silent. She could no longer think of anything to wish for. Raising her eyes, she saw that the star was no longer alone in the night sky. And she could hear a radio playing "The Long and Winding Road" somewhere very far away.

Park's Cafe

Two doors down from Babe's, Park's Café huddles against life. A fading Korean diner where hapless spiders spin anxious webs in fading plastic poinsettias and watch the widow Wan Lo fill bellies with eggs and surprises for $2.95 fourteen hours a day, six days a week. That Wan Lo or any of her ancestors never saw Korea doesn't matter to the customers, who never saw Korea either except from a television-eye view on "M*A*S*H" reruns. Some of their fathers or brothers or sons saw Korea from behind a rifle beam or a jeep windshield or peeking out of a foxhole. But Wan Lo doesn't know, doesn't ask, doesn't care.

And the customers don't ask, either, in this neighborhood where a regular is somebody who comes around more than once in a lifetime, where every place is just one more stopover on the way to a dream. Like the neighborhood, they're zoned for transiency, mementos and promises of other days. In another time, Park's Café would have been a bright spot on a child's walk home from school, where a smiling middle-aged lady doled out bits of candy with dime ice cream cones. But now it waits for better times that come disguised as fern bars and art galleries.

Only, Wan Lo has stopped waiting, for waiting is a passion reserved for those who still hope, still dare to dream. Women like Wan Lo, the ones who have seen beyond the gaunt masks of monsters and survived in death's belly, don't allow themselves the luxury of hope. For them, dreams only steal in unannounced on cats' paws.

Her black eyes follow the shadows of the men and women who haunt the tiny restaurant. That Wan Lo isn't much of a cook doesn't matter to the gaunt mechanics and fading old men whose weathered mouths gobble down the gruel she places before them without a smile, without a glance. Theirs is a silent pact. The cash register rings, the customers edge out the door, cooked cabbage riding hard on their bellies.

Once, a young girl came in selling pictures of Buddhist shrines and red sunsets burning quietly on silver silk. Wan Lo fingered the pictures, one by aching one, pushing back the silk and watercolors until she found her memory. With a green thumbtack, she pushed a scrap of her past onto chipped paint and cracked plaster. Looking into the still waterfall, she could see a young teacher that only shadowed the woman she had become, hurrying across a schoolyard while small voices sang familiar nonsense children's rhymes. The snatches of songs turned over in her mind, making her tired withered mouth smile, wiping out the dark acid memories that etched her soul the way the revolution etched the heart of her Southeast Asian home.

Blue and silver, the waterfall washed away the memories, taking her back to the time before the war shook her loose, left her sick, dying, alone. Finally, after almost a lifetime had come and gone in the dank pools of decay and desolation, she'd found her way first to a refugee camp then finally to Iowa, where the snow beat her into submission. She'd escaped then to the warmth. Joe Park, the aging Korean, had found her in a parlor with red and gold flocked wallpaper, beyond a flashing red sign that winked ORIENTAL GIRLS! MASSAGE: NOON TO 3 A.M. He dragged her back from the shores of death and poverty, hired her, married her, and died.

Wan Lo never questioned that her husband was dying just as her new life was beginning. She'd learned the ways of death far too well to ever wonder at how its gray fog crept across life, dampening, shrouding all it touched. Watching him sit by the window that looked out on the overgrown patch of weeds that only the summer before had been his tidy garden, she saw the light leave his eyes. The doctors had promised him two years of agony, two years of watching all he'd spent a lifetime creating being eaten away by bills from hospitals and specialists. If he had been a rich man or a young man or a white man, they might have promised him a new liver. Instead, they shook their heads, one by one, and turned away. In the twilight of the rooms Wan Lo shared with Joe Park, the pact was formed. Joe Park didn't ask, for the words were unspeakable, but Wan Lo knew what his eyes, now so yellowed from his dying liver, were willing her to do.

The fragile shell that held what little was left of her husband shattered quietly, without pain, without notice. In his last days, as the final traces of life drained from his sapped body, the light returned to his eyes. It was just as he had wanted it. Joe Park was satisfied. As always, Wan Lo had provided the requested service, distasteful but necessary all the same. This time her payment was freedom.

"Is this why you married a whore?" she whispered into the clean white hospital sheets that contained what was left of what had been her husband. Graying jowls hung loosely, stagnant against the hard pillow. Dead eyes gaped at the ceiling. Wan Lo understood the look. It was the one she had lived when Joe Park and all the faceless men before him heaved their sweating nakedness on top of her fragile body. Her stomach churned at the memory. In death, Joe Park looked to Wan Lo much as he had in life: a molting cabbage.

Wan Lo watched the motionless chest for a long moment until she was sure it was ended. She didn't call a nurse. Joe Park was dead; there was nothing a nurse could do to change that. She flushed down the hospital toilet the last traces of the strange tea she'd used to eat Joe Park's heart out and then walked the twenty-seven blocks back to the restaurant. Wan Lo would never be any man's slave or any man's whore again.

On the walk back to the café, Wan Lo shed no tears, felt no remorse, no guilt, no shame. Chopping cabbage for the dinner gruel, the cleaver slid easily through the tight leaves, which suddenly reminded Wan Lo of her husband's head. She threw the cleaver down, pushed the cabbage away, and let the tears finally flow. The deed was done. She had given him what he wanted. So little but so much. A small frown crossed her delicate features. No one would ever question that a sickly sixty-year-old man who had lived alone in a pair of tiny rooms over his restaurant for twenty-five years should die a few months earlier than his doctors had predicted. No one would suspect or even care.

"His time had come. You made his last days happy," his sister from San Diego said to Wan Lo before the funeral. "I thank you." Two days later, the sister went home to her Lincoln Continental and import-king husband. Wan Lo was alone—with her secret, with her treasure. She would never be hungry or homeless again, for Joe Park had kept his part of the bargain, too, naming only Wan Lo in his will.

It mattered little that Joe Park's café, under his young widow's strange tutelage, had few customers. She had his insurance policy, his delivery truck, his restaurant, his savings. War had fed her the bitter apple of destitution. She spent little and earned enough to get by. If customers came back, it was for their own reasons.

And so it was when Rose found Wan Lo and the café that was to become her solace, her private window on a world she coveted. By the time Rose arrived every Saturday night just before nine, the place was as silent as dust. Wan Lo would push the tattered menu toward this woman who was her only real regular and ten minutes later shove a steaming, heaping plate across the table. Some nights, they would exchange glances, half-smiles, broken attempts at conversations that hung heavy and pregnant, as if waiting for a sign. Other nights they would sit at separate tables, silent, locked in thoughts that tumbled and sputtered like the fading neon that glossed the tabletops.

Rose never pondered the restaurant, the food, the dust that gathered on the plastic flowers by the window—Wan Lo's only attempt at what the finer restaurants called "ambience"—although she memorized it all as the Saturday nights tumbled into months. She'd stumbled on Park's Café by accident one night when her feet had frozen to the sidewalk on her way to Babe's, the promise that she knew was her destiny.

Rose had discovered Babe's one winter afternoon as she hovered by the bulletin board at the women's bookstore, stealing glances at the customers who all seemed to laugh so easily, to touch so freely. More than anything, Rose wanted to be like that, to reach out across the desert of her life and whirl into the oasis she'd read about in the paperback books she smuggled into her room. The books told her how it was supposed to be, how soft fingers would reach out and touch her throat, stroke her aching virginal breasts, hold her safe and close when the long night had faded into morning.

Every Friday afternoon on her way home from work she stopped at the bookstore where she knew every title and missed no new additions to the shelf marked "Lesbian Literature." Lingering, she greeted favorite titles like old friends and welcomed new ones. Clutching each new selection, she carried the book with its title turned outward—brazenly, she imagined—for any passing customer to see, although none ever indicated any interest. Rose then made her way to the bulletin board, where she jotted down the times and dates and places of the meetings she would never have the courage to actually attend. And it was there that the lavender poster asked her to dance.

The next ten days crawled as Rose waited for the night of the dance as anxiously as she'd waited for the prom invitation that had never come. She'd memorized the poster, the bar's address, the time, the band, even the sliding cover charge. Still, the afternoon of the dance, she nervously checked and re-checked the bar's address in the fat telephone directory in case she had made a mistake. Rose planned for the dance as care-fully as a girl preparing for her first date, although, Rose re-minded herself, she was well beyond the age for first dates. Still, she didn't know what women wore to dances—surely not the casual jeans and bright shirts and sandals that they wore in the bookstore. Her novels didn't tell her. Neither did the magazines and newspapers; they were far more concerned with child-custody suits and comparable worth than dances. Finally, she settled on a new baby-blue blouse and matching linen slacks, black leather flats polished to a high gleam, even a new purse to match. A cultured pearl barrette held her dark curls carefully. The bathroom mirror smiled back as she strapped on her watch, dabbed her wrists with Chantilly.

Rose's mother, who had given her only child the most beau-tiful name she could think of, sat on the daybed in the living room, eyes glued to the television. "I'm going to the movies, Mom," Rose called to this woman who had shared her life for nearly thirty years. Her mother nodded, eyes never leaving the tiny black and white screen.

That first night, the eight blocks to the bar had loomed like a promise. But the bright neon of Babe's struck too soon. Sud-denly she remembered her sophomore dance, the one her mother had made her attend, the one where nobody talked to her, the one where Rose had finally slipped into the girls' rest room, where she sat on a cold toilet until it was time to go. Music and laughter had seeped through the bathroom walls, taunting Rose with promises she had known, even then, would never be kept. And now, fifteen years later, she was still locked in a nameless fear that came as intimately as her own breath.

Rose walked slowly those last few yards to the bar, but as she reached the door, a group of laughing women suddenly burst through the doors, pushing past her, letting the laughter and music spill onto the street. Once again Rose was the fifteen-year-old wallflower with acne and no breasts, the girl who heard the muffled laughter as she passed in the hall, the girl whose mother wouldn't let her shave her legs or wear lipstick or heels, the girl who didn't belong. Her heart froze and Rose quickly crossed the street, pretending to wait for the bus that she knew well enough wouldn't come for another thirty-five minutes.

From her vantage point, she watched the early-evening stragglers drift into the bar. When the bus came, she waved it on and crossed the street to Wan Lo—who offered weak coffee and a momentary haven—promising herself that in fifteen minutes she'd get up and go into the bar. Rose settled into a corner table by the window, hoping the coffee would give her courage. Only, the coffee, like her courage, was stale. Fifteen minutes passed, then a half hour, and still Rose couldn't muster enough nerve to carry her the last dozen yards into Babe's.

Hours later, when Wan Lo turned the red and black CLOSED sign to the door, Rose made her way home, each step a promise that the next Saturday night would be different.

"How was the movie?" her mother would call from the day-bed in the front room when Rose's key turned in the door every Saturday midnight. "Fine, Mother," Rose would answer, slipping into her sensible blue terry robe and into the darkened room illuminated only by the "Late Show" in miniature. The next morning, just like all the other Sundays, Rose would help her mother off the couch, help her down the stairs, into the waiting taxi for the twelve-block ride to church. On the way, they would pass the window where the world peeked in on Wan Lo, past Babe's, where the Saturday-night fantasies unfolded and where, Rose knew, her own destiny lurked if only she could find the courage to step through that door.

Each Saturday night, filled with promises and dreams, Rose slipped into her window seat at the restaurant. From her perch, she watched the silent parade of women march and stumble along the sidewalk, arm in arm, faces turned up in laughter or sometimes painted grim with pain. Rose made up a name, a history for each woman until they were friends that she might have known well. But none of the regulars recognized her or even noticed the plain round-faced woman huddled in the restaurant window. Sometimes, one or two of the women would stride through the door at Park's, flop into a booth, and send shock waves of hope coursing down Rose's spine. But before

Rose could gather the courage to look into the eyes of these women she'd named Karen or Rhonda or Helen, they were gone, leaving her alone with Wan Lo's silent company.

Once, a striking blonde had even smiled at Rose, who carried the memory close to her heart until the February rains washed it into the gutter one night when she saw the blonde she'd named Jamie huddle close to a winsome brunette. Rose had paid Wan Lo quickly and scurried deep into the night. "Movie let out early?" her mother had asked. Rose had only grunted. Jamie Lee Curtis screamed on the screen. Rose smiled. Justice was done; passionate transgressions avenged. Rose slipped silently into her narrow bed with its clean white sheets and hospital corners where she devoured the books that painted a world of women in love. She pulled the pillow to her, curling her soft belly next to it as if it were her lover. The world passed away to morning.

Five mornings a week, Rose rode the Broadway bus eighteen blocks to the hospital where she spent the next eight hours wiping babies' bottoms and watching new mothers hold tiny pink mouths to swollen nipples. The babies were her only real joy. Their tiny innocence piqued her curiosity, stirred her wonderment. Once she had hoped to be a real nurse, the kind who wore starched white hats and stiff uniforms that buttoned down the back, and who scuttled through the halls on missions of mercy. But there had never been enough money or time for that, so she had settled for the short course for nurses' aides and the blue polyester uniform the hospital offered. Rose had been secretly outraged when the nurses abandoned the starched hats and uniforms for sensible slacks and lab coats. She knew if she'd ever been allowed to wear one of the hats, she would never have taken it off, no matter what.

One night while she was curled into her window, a familiar face strode by. Rose recognized the young doctor who turned, smiled, waved cheerfully, and continued on her way to the bar. Embarrassed, Rose ducked quickly into her thoughts, pretending great interest in the last few floating tea leaves that sulked in the bottom of her cup. Lena Burns, Rose knew, was one of the few interns who ever had a kind word for the scared young mothers, some of them barely more than girls themselves, who passed through the maternity unit. Rose smiled into the glass and waved slightly at the empty sidewalk, as if the doctor was still there, and imagined all the things she would say the next time their paths crossed. She imagined striding into Babe's and talking to the young doctor. They would become friends. Rose wondered if she would call her new friend Dr. Burns or Lena? Definitely Lena. She and Lena would have lunch in the hospital cafeteria, laugh, share secrets, go to the bar together after work sometimes. The fantasy kept Rose warm on the silent walk home. But the next week she found out that the doctor had transferred to another hospital. Rose had lost another friend.

And then as quickly, as quietly as she had come that first night, Rose stopped taking the window seat. The first Saturday night, Wan Lo's head jerked like a startled sparrow with each customer's arrival as she waited patiently for the patent-leather shoes to move across her tile floor. The sweetcakes she'd started baking each Saturday in honor of Rose's arrival stood sodden on the counter, attracting flies. The second week, Wan Lo hovered anxiously, dusting, scrubbing as she waited, wondered, watched the street turn to darkness. The final traces of life seeped out of the pink snapdragons Wan Lo had so carefully arranged on what she had come to think of as Rose's table. By the time a month had passed, Wan Lo stopped making special sweetcakes, stopped looking to the door, turned the CLOSED sign against the glass even as the last customer was lingering at his table. Then she slowly climbed the two flights to her upstairs rooms. Music from the bar seeped through her windows, lulling her into a dream where she danced on the wind, a bird flying against time.

Wan Lo was in the back room almost two months later when Rose finally slipped into her familiar corner one Saturday night. The last traces of summer hung cold and heavy from the fog that chilled the sunset. The patent-leather flats were gone, replaced with blue running shoes with clean soles. The neat slacks had given way to jeans so new their creases stood strong and firm. Rose had taken her hair down and it fell in brown ringlets across her narrow shoulders. Wan Lo smiled. She unthawed a pair of sweetcakes in the microwave oven, secretly hoping Rose would notice their warmth, their honey.

Over tea and cakes, Wan Lo edged into the chair across from Rose, who pulled her eyes back from the window and smiled, genuinely pleased at the company.

"You have new clothes. Now you look like all the other women." Wan Lo nodded out the window where Rose had kept her eyes riveted for so many Saturday nights. "I think you were more beautiful before." The words stirred inside Rose, who looked intently at her companion. Wan Lo smiled again, an almost hopeful smile. Rose was trying to decide what to say, but the words came too hard. She shrugged slightly, a self-conscious act that made her more uncomfortable, and looked hard at the last crumbs on the plate.

"You didn't come. I worried." Wan Lo pushed on, her voice quiet, hesitant. A single tear escaped, then careened down Rose's cheek, trembling against her chin.

"I'm sorry . . . my mother . . ." Rose started, then looked away, pushing her fist hard into her cheek as if she could shove the threatening torrent back inside. "My . . . mother . . . passed away." The last words spilled out in a rush. Wan Lo watched in silence as Rose squeezed her eyes tight, gasped for breath, looked into the street and then down into her empty cup as if some sort of answer or solace was waiting there. Finding none, she raised her eyes to Wan Lo's waiting face.

In all the months of shared Saturday nights, they'd never spoken, really. Two strangers caught on the edge, where memories somehow blend into fantasy and destiny, they had hovered together as silent as changing seasons.

"My mother is dead, too," Wan Lo offered, her voice still quiet, tugging at the nightmare she had tried so desperately to forget for so long. "A long time ago." And then, almost in a whisper, "At least, you were with her when she died?" The words shuddered through Rose, who nodded. Wan Lo smiled, slipped her hand across the table, and offered, "And I with my mother, too. This is important." The two women smiled.

Through the night, long after Wan Lo had turned the CLOSED sign against the door, Rose spilled out her story and her tears. And Wan Lo listened. Some of the memories made her smile, remembering the light, the beauty she had known. Rose's eyes fell on the paper placemat with a nameless artist's rendition of a Parisian sidewalk café in the shadow of the Eiffel Tower.

"Mother always wanted to go to Paris," Rose said, smiling for the first time in the long night. "She wanted to be on a game show and win a trip to Paris."

Wan Lo's eyes glowed, fueled by memories. "She would have liked it there, I think, very much."

Surprised, Rose looked into her companion's face and saw Wan Lo the way she once might have been, filled with sunshine. "You went to Paris once?" Rose asked, hoping the question wasn't silly.

Wan Lo shook her head. "No, many times. I lived there. It was a long, very long time ago."

"But I thought . . . I mean the war and all . . . aren't you . . ." Rose's voice trailed away and her eyes fell on Wan Lo's hands where there was a tiny stub where her left little finger was supposed to be. Self-conscious, Wan Lo slid her hands beneath the table. Memories floated back as she talked of how her mother, then still young and beautiful, was so desperate to save herself and her daughter from the war that seemed to never end. How it had taken all the money and influence her family could find to send both of them to the safety of Paris. And there they lived, Wan Lo growing, surrounded by beauty, while their homeland became more desolate. Wan Lo was to have been a great dancer but the war had claimed first her grandfather's wealth and finally her mother's heart. "We had to leave. Our country . . . it was dying, you understand. How could we stay apart?"

And Rose nodded, although she didn't understand, could never really understand. "And so you went back to a war? Just like that?"

Wan Lo looked at her curiously and shook her head. The words *just like that* confused her. They were too light, too simple to express what had really happened. Nothing was ever "just like that." Not life, not death, certainly not escape. Rather it was a maze, one path leading into another and yet another on the journey to freedom. There were no accidents, only people doing what had to be done. And each deed led into another and yet another after that.

"What was it like?" Rose looked deeply into Wan Lo's face, asking the unanswerable question.

"War is the whoremonger and we pander to its whims," Wan Lo said finally, the words formed so carefully, so slowly that Rose was sure Wan Lo was somehow not understanding the meaning. Rose shook her head, confused. "Like the belly of the beast, the hunger it carries is huge. It takes all. Yet it searches always for more. And it feeds until nothing is left. The soldiers come. Some say, 'We are the revolutionaries.' Some say, 'We are your protectors.' Others . . . say nothing. They are alike, very much, I think. They all pay, some with honor, some with blood. But still they do not pay the way the women pay. The way of my mother . . . and of me. We pay with our hearts . . . and when we die, even then the beast, the whoremonger, hungers."

Rose was silent. She had read of the Vietnam War, but it

seemed so long ago, so far away. Now it was here, reflected in the eyes of her friend. She sighed. "I'm so sorry," she said. "For you. For your mother."

Wan Lo looked at Rose closely. "We do what we must, whether we believe it right or not, so that we can survive. All my life, since I was a child, I did things, many things, some unimportant, others not, so that I could survive. I did what was asked of me, always. I was paid badly." She laid her hands on the table, turning them over slowly. "Very badly." The war had claimed one of her fingers and two of her toes for its own. She danced now only in her dreams.

Rose fell silent, then reached across the table, taking each of Wan Lo's hands gently. "Only now is it different," Wan Lo said carefully. "I have survived the whoremonger. I no longer am his consort." And she smiled.

When dawn tickled the pavement, Wan Lo made coffee and eggs. Before Rose stepped through the door into the light of a new day, Wan Lo pulled the thumbtack loose and handed the silk picture to her new friend. "For my dear friend Rose." The words came slow and an embarrassed silence fell between them while Rose, as unaccustomed to presents as she was to friends, let her fingers curl around the cool silver waterfall. The pair shared a secret smile.

As the weeks gave birth to months, the women's lives wove a tapestry of memories and shared secrets, with the loneliness that had been so much a part of them spun into a golden thread. As carefully as she had ever dressed for an imagined night at the bar, Rose dressed for her Saturday nights with Wan Lo. She sat primly in her window seat waiting until the CLOSED sign bounced against the door before she scurried to the back booth to be with her friend. Through the open kitchen window, scraps of bar music floated around them.

"Do you like music?" Rose asked one night. In her mind, she had asked Wan Lo the question a thousand times during the week. "I mean to dance?" Wan Lo's face shone and she nodded anxiously. Had Rose forgotten Wan Lo's dream of being a famous dancer? How she'd abandoned that dream for the classroom, where she'd gladly accepted the adulation of little girls instead of an audience? Rose smiled, a secret kind of grin, and reached into her back pocket, producing a purple piece of paper announcing a dance the next Saturday night at Babe's. "Should we go . . . I mean, you and me?" She stumbled over the words, forgetting her well-planned speech. "If you want to . . ."

Wan Lo's fingers traced the outline of the words, the drawing of the dancing figures, but she still did not raise her eyes
to Rose's waiting face. "We don't have to, I mean . . ." And Rose
felt hope seeping away. She so much wanted Wan Lo to look at
her, to give her some sign, some hope. And finally, when the
silence was too much to bear, she offered, "I'm sorry . . ." The
words trailed as Rose reached for the paper, starting to slip out
of the booth, out of Wan Lo's life.

Wan Lo's fingers clamped hard against the paper, then fell
into her lap as Rose pulled it free. The moment hung hard and
long. Rose was back in high school gym class, caught looking
too long at the rich full breasts of the cheerleaders who care-
lessly dropped their towels and stepped into white lace bras and
panties. "What are you, queer or something?" echoed in Rose's
memory. Hot tears of humiliation burned in the back of her
throat. The books hadn't prepared her for this moment; they
didn't have to, the cheerleaders had done their job well. And
Rose cursed her stupidity for wanting to dance with Wan Lo,
for wanting to feel her softness deep into the night.

As Rose started to move away, fat tears splashed against the
table where Wan Lo had her head bowed. But Rose could see
only her own pain in the reflection of the glass where the word
CLOSED was illuminated by the streetlamp. Stepping away from
the table toward the front of the darkened restaurant, Rose felt
Wan Lo's hand, as soft as a butterfly, brush her thigh. Then the
hand reached up, taking Rose's fingers in her own.

"You don't understand . . ." Wan Lo's whispered words were
more a question than an answer. Rose shook her head and
looked toward the window where a pair of women, hand in
hand, waited for the bus. Wan Lo's eyes followed, remembering
another flower woman from another life. A young ballerina
who whirled and turned like petals on a waterfall. The woman
she had been. The woman she had left Paris for so very long
ago, the woman she would never see again no matter how far
she traveled. The woman she no longer allowed herself to remember for the pain was too deep, even now.

"I would like to dance with you . . . very much." The words
came strong, determined, borne on the winds of memories and
magic.

When she raised her eyes to Rose, Wan Lo saw not shadows
but light for the first time in as long as she could remember.
And the two good friends smiled and walked hand in hand up
the two flights to Wan Lo's quiet rooms.

Saturday
Night

The Ground
Shaking

The ginger cat nestled more deeply into the soft crevasse between Shelly's naked legs. Propping her head on the dark forest there, she began to purr. Morning sun sent shafts of pure gold light across the sleeping pair, nudging Shelly back to consciousness. Slowly, like a child being led from a candy store window, she stumbled through the strange silent netherworld that separates dream from reality. With each step, she became more aware of the heavy warmth that pressed into her belly, tickled her bare thighs, hummed against her. Fighting to keep the dream close, alive, Shelly closed her eyes tightly against the intruding day.

Warmth born of desire pulled her mind back into the dream. The ginger cat became Julia's face nesting between Shelly's legs, Julia's hair tickling her thighs, Julia's breath warm and even against her want. Lying still, even after the dream had given way to the harsh light of day, Shelly was unwilling to let the sweetness fade or to disturb the ginger cat, who would only scamper away demanding breakfast. That would all come soon enough. For now, the stolen moment was hers alone.

Closing her eyes, Shelly smiled. It was Saturday. Tonight she would see Julia. Julia, who would, if she was here, rip open the blinds and hit the bed like a divebomber, tickling Shelly until she curled into a ball held tight by spasms of laughter. Who would nibble at Shelly's throat, her breasts, the inside of her thighs, threatening to gobble her up for breakfast or lunch or dinner, whichever was closer. Who would then forget about breakfast and lunch and dinner, content to spend the rest of their stolen hours tucked away in Shelly's bed, with the ginger cat serving as guard to their private kingdom.

The very thought of Julia sent a hard throb of desire into Shelly's belly, then beyond, deep into the warmth where the cat pressed tightly against her. Shelly imagined Julia, awake since the first rays of sun approached the mountain, pulling on the well-worn jeans, wool socks, cowpoke boots, then the no-nonsense T-shirt that hid her soft full breasts, and finally the red or the blue or the gold flannel shirt that her scratched nubby fingers always snapped closed with such finality. Shelly had watched Julia's dressing ritual each Monday morning for nearly six months, bracing herself against the moment when the door would finally close, leaving her alone once again with only the ginger cat.

"Don't go," Shelly had whispered once, early on, when she had imagined she could somehow cajole or manipulate Julia into staying. She'd held her breath, waiting for Julia's reply, watching while she shoved the heavy black leather belt through the loops in her jeans. Julia had looked out the window by which she always dressed for what seemed a very long time, examining all the options carefully, one by one, and coming up empty.

"Oh, I don't think so," she'd finally answered, slow and easy, as if Shelly had offered ice with orange juice.

"But why not?" Shelly had tried to sound coy, teasing, light-hearted, anything to cover the desperation that blanketed her each time Julia's strong back strode down the street and out of her life for another week. The voice might have belonged to a little girl crying after the moon, not to a woman who prided herself on always maintaining a cool, even icy exterior every-where but with Julia. For Julia's presence, her very essence transformed Shelly into a willful, wild child, stripping away with only a whisper or a glance the armor built so carefully over so many years, leaving her naked and vulnerable, open and explosive, and most of all unashamed.

"You could get a job in the city or teach at the university." Shelly had pressed on, trying to ignore the muscles she could see tightening in Julia's arms. Julia was a geologist who had turned down more than one teaching offer. To her, school was a pastime; her real work was on the mountain. "You could keep the ginger cat company . . . and me." Shelly's voice had sounded soft, faraway, hopeful and hopeless all at once. It was the sound of it more than the words of it that caught and tugged at Julia, who finally turned, raised her eyebrows, smiled, and winked at the ginger cat. The cat had flicked her tail and winked back. The ginger cat merely tolerated Julia, just as she tolerated every other human. Still, the cat and Julia shared the deep understanding of shackles and freedom far better than Shelly ever could.

Julia had turned back to the window then, the morning sun silhouetting her against the open blind. "And do what?" The question came edged with the hard glint of anger. Shelly had quaked silently, not daring to let Julia see the tremors that shuddered deep in her core. "I'm a mining engineer, a geologist, a seismologist. That's what I do. And I do it on my mountain, not chained to some office and a bunch of machines like those atrophied, parasitic old desk hogs downtown, or teaching earth science to a bunch of snot-nosed freshmen who'd rather be out drinking beer. I belong on my mountain. Not here. You couldn't live there, I know that, so I don't ask you to. Well, I can't live here. So don't ask that of me."

Silence had descended around them, shrouding the room, sending a hard chill across Shelly's naked shoulders. Julia's eyes had burned intently on the fuschia that grew beyond the window. Shelly had stared at her hands folded on the sheet draped across her lap. Then the radio had begun to play "You Made Me Love You" and Shelly had giggled, breaking the moment. Julia had turned and with a running leap had landed on top of Shelly, pinning her against the bed. "You know I can't stay," she'd whispered between kisses and Shelly's fingers that had burrowed and teased beneath buttons and zippers.

"Except on weekends . . ." Shelly had offered the words like a question, a promise, a hopeful gift.

"Except on weekends," Julia had agreed, smiling, relenting, the unspent fury quieting.

And now it was the weekend again. "My weekend lover," Shelly whispered, hugging her pillow tighter, pretending it was Julia, extending her legs, daring to disturb the ginger cat who stretched and indignantly slipped away. "And tonight we get to see Julia," Shelly told the cat, who blinked twice, as if to say "big deal," but smiled a secret smile.

By the time Shelly arrived at the office, it was already late
morning and the message from Julia had been waiting for two
hours. "Be home early, I've made plans." The note was printed
in the secretary's terse hand, but it was Julia's name that filled
the all-important line that read A MESSAGE FROM. Shelly tapped
the note against the edge of her desk. Debating. Deciding. Dialing Julia's number. Letting it ring too long. No answer. Wait
five minutes. Redial. No answer still. So like Julia to rocket her
missives into an otherwise quiet day, as if Shelly could just drop
everything and run.

Of course, Shelly had always done just that. She smiled,
remembering, trying to concentrate on the pile of neat papers
on her desk that silently commanded her attention. But Julia
was lurking in every corner, every hidden doorway of her mind.
Those brown eyes that could look at the coldest mountain and
see the bubbling molten treasures hidden deep inside, that
knew how to bring it all churning to the surface. Julia peered
into Shelly's every thought, leaving her skin to prickle with
memories and want.

Those eyes that first sent Shelly's heart pounding down to
her belly, then on to a throbbing tribal dance in her cunt. Julia
needed an attorney, and a friend had provided Shelly's number.
That Shelly knew little about the mining industry hadn't
swayed Julia. "So, you'll learn," she'd announced bluntly.
Julia, as much as the words, had taken Shelly by surprise. She
was, after all, a woman used to being in command. It had taken
Shelly a long moment to compose her comeback.

"It's not that simple, Julia," Shelly had explained quietly,
trying to recapture control of the situation. "There are people
better prepared in your area. I could recommend . . . someone . . ." Reaching for her Rolodex, Shelly had trailed her
words, then stumbled under Julia's stark gaze. She'd suddenly
felt very naked, very open, and at the same time, very wicked.

"I don't want somebody better . . . prepared," Julia had
answered, measuring out the words as if they were heavy
cream destined for an elegant dessert. "I want you. And I've got
a feeling you're very good . . . exactly what I want." Shelly's
eyes had darted to her own hands, then ricocheted into Julia's
eyes. And those eyes had smiled back, knowing, like a cat who
suddenly discovered the untended parakeet's cage door ever so
slightly ajar. "We can discuss it over dinner tonight. I'll pick
you up here at seven. Don't keep me waiting."

Julia was leaning against a brown Porsche parked by the curb when Shelly emerged from her office just before seven that evening. "Don't get excited," Julia had said, seeing Shelly's eyes move past her to the car. "One of these'd last about five minutes on the mountain. I'm over there." Taking Shelly's hand, she had dodged through six lanes of traffic.

"Don't you ever wait for the light?" Shelly had demanded when her heartbeat finally returned to normal. "We could've been killed."

"I never wait for anything," Julia had replied, gunning the four-by-four and roaring into the night.

Everything was like that with Julia. She ran and Shelly tried to keep up. Never had Shelly met a woman so determined, so consumed with the very act of living. Julia was as tireless as she was relentless, as spontaneous as she was ruthless. She was a woman used to getting what she wanted, and she always knew exactly what that was. Now she wanted Shelly, had since that first afternoon, that first dinner, that first afterdinner drink at the bar. Shelly had wanted her, too.

Only over Shelly's weakening protests had they bounced the nearly hundred miles out to the mountain, Julia careening up the narrow dirt roads, Shelly hanging on in the passenger seat. "I want you to see my operation," Julia had insisted. The afternoon sun was beating warm through the windshield. Julia had shrugged out of her flannel shirt and let the wind beat against her sleeveless T-shirt, which left the flesh of her breasts slightly exposed. "The air feels good; you should take off that jacket," she'd said, her eyes never leaving the road. "Your shirt, too, if you want. I'll let you know if anybody's coming." Shelly had blushed but slipped out of her tweed jacket, letting the wind from the open window whip through her short hair, rustle the silk of her blouse. Julia had laughed loudly. "You city women sure do mind your manners," she'd hooted, turning up the radio, singing along to Bruce Springsteen a little too loudly. Shelly had gazed out the window, trying to imagine what it would feel like to ride bare-breasted across dusty back roads with this wild woman.

Many miles later, while Julia was explaining the intricacies of mountain reclamation, Shelly had felt a hand slide under her skirt. She'd stolen a quick look at Julia, whose eyes had met hers only for a moment. They'd both smiled, and Shelly slipped back in the seat, letting the truck and Julia's fingers rock her toward orgasm. Julia's words had been sucked away by the wind, and no matter how Shelly had tried to concentrate, her mind was paralyzed, powerless, had given way to the demands of her flesh.

But it wasn't until they reached the deserted outpost that Julia had let Shelly's fingers wander over her own long, finely muscled body, and only then after the last traces of afternoon sun had pushed into the tiny engineering shack with all the clutter of a project not yet underway. They had made love there on a dusty sleeping bag Julia had pulled out of the back of the four-by-four.

Even now, on the rare times when she made the long trip out to the site, Shelly's heart pounded at the thought of Julia's touch that first afternoon, how she'd somehow felt this woman could sweep her off her feet and carry her through the door. It hadn't happened that way at all, of course, but Shelly always found the strange image exciting. So easy to imagine Julia in a tuxedo—strong and beautiful, her short black hair shining like the satin lapels. Would she wear a white gardenia? No, a black orchid. Shelly wove the fantasy in her mind. But try as she might, Shelly could never picture herself in anything other than what she'd worn that first time: the sensible tweed suit and, of course, that red silk shirt—her only concession to the rebellion that raged in her soul—that picked up the highlights in her short brown curls.

Shelly's heart had pounded as Julia led her through the door into the tiny office, with dusty light making patches of gold on the plank floors. Julia had peeled away the silk shirt as if Shelly were a fine orange waiting to be savored. And she had savored Shelly, tasting all her deep dark secrets, until they both had trembled, stark dampness threatening to consume them. Trembled until those strong blunt fingers had plunged deep into Shelly, until she had convulsed hard and long, her body bucking into Julia's power, her demands. And when Shelly had turned to touch Julia's small breasts, her narrow hips, she was astounded by how soft the skin was that encased muscles that seemed always taut beneath.

When they'd dressed for the ride back to the city, Julia had watched, amused, at Shelly's frantic search for the silk blouse. "Guess you'll just have to go without it," she'd said, striding toward the four-by-four where Julia had left her jacket on the front seat. And Shelly, afraid of being abandoned, had hurried out the door, her arms trying desperately to cover her tiny naked breasts that prickled indignantly against the cool damp evening air.

Julia had been leaning against the side of the truck, laughing at the sight of Shelly stumbling across the gravel lot, looking about frantically to see if anyone was around to view her exposed secrets. "Didn't your mother always tell you to wear a bra?" Julia had demanded, still laughing. "We might have an accident and what would the people at the hospital think?" Then she'd laughed so hard, so long that Shelly's face had begun to burn. "This what you're looking for?" Julia had asked then, waving the red silk shirt like a matador.

Shelly's eyes had flashed. At that very moment she'd hated Julia, who dared to torment her, to laugh at her. But when Julia had opened the door, the dome light sent shadows of softness across her cheek, sent tiny stars to shine in her eyes. Shelly's thoughts had turned back to the shack, to the hour before, to her mouth lost against Julia's strong beautiful neck. As quickly as it had come, the anger faded.

"Get in the truck," Julia had said, stuffing the shirt in her back pocket, then smacking Shelly's rump as she hauled herself into the unfamiliar territory. "If you're really good on the ride back, I'll let you have it before we get to the city."

Eagerly, Shelly had settled into the passenger seat, letting herself be pulled toward Julia, whose hungry tongue burrowed and licked and teased the naked trembling nipples. For the next hour, Shelly had savored the wickedness of riding half-naked next to Julia, whose right hand had alternated between shifting gears and stroking Shelly like a large luxurious cat.

By the time the city lights had beckoned them, it was too late for Julia to drive back to her little house on the mountain, so she'd stayed with Shelly. One day had turned into two and then three and then she was gone. Once a week, though, she still came down from her mountain to be Shelly's secret, perfect, private lover. The rest of the days fell away, pale next to the promise of Julia, of her arms, her lips.

Shelly's own trips to Julia's mountain home, up a long winding road, far removed from the mining shack where they'd first made love, were rare and uncomfortable. The two huge rooms that Julia shared with her books and strange machines and a half-tame ferret named Farlo seemed strange and alien. On her first visit, Shelly had walked slowly around the huge room, taking it in, trying to imagine Julia sleeping in the hard narrow bed, stoking the Franklin stove. The walls were lined with Julia's photographs of mountains, some ice-capped, others in bloom. "Pictures of my lovers," Julia called them, and in a way it was true. For each woman who had touched Julia's life, there was a picture of a mountain. Julia said they were portraits of woman-souls, for she believed mountains were all female, all fertile, all beautiful.

"So which one am I?" Shelly asked, after looking over each of the pictures. "This one." Julia was pointing to a mountain so beautiful, so snow-capped, so pristine in its sheer majesty that Shelly's breath had come hard, quick.

"Which one is it?" Shelly asked, her eyes riveted on the glass where the reflection of her face seemed etched in the side of the mountain.

"Mount Saint Helens." Julia was wearing a half-smile, her eyes shining.

"But it blew up."

"I know," Julia whispered, "and in a way, she was even more beautiful after she came."

The words sent an eerie shudder through Shelly, who listened to Julia talk about the mountain and the volcano that lurked deep beneath its surface as if they were alive, bound by orgasm rather than destruction. And with each word, Julia's eyes glowed and flashed, excited. Later that night, Shelly had awakened suddenly to find the room glowing with candlelight. From every corner and crevice of the room, candles glowed, and Julia crouched almost expectantly by the window.

"What's going on . . ." Shelly asked, her voice sleepy, confused.

Without turning, Julia shushed her. "Soon, just wait . . ." She was whispering although they were alone in the room.

"What—wait for what?" Shelly started to ask when the earthquake hit, rolling the room for a moment, rocking and shaking the cabin. Shelly sat petrified in the bed listening to the machines whirring and chattering in the next room, the pictures rattling against the wall, watching Julia with her arm raised, howling. The ground shaking lasted only moments, and when it had ended, Julia turned to Shelly, her eyes flashing, her face flushed. She slowly walked to the bed, her naked body glowing in shadow and yellow light.

"She came," Julia whispered, "make me come." The hunger, the need in her voice propelled Shelly's hands across Julia's body, deep into her open core until they both howled, Julia coming like aftershocks.

It was that kind of excitement that had kept them inseparable, insatiable, with Shelly savoring each moment, knowing it couldn't last, hoping it would, wanting the magic to keep on. Even now, only a little of that first fire was gone. More often it still was that first day on the mountain.

If Julia had made plans for the evening, the least Shelly could do was keep them. Shelly smiled, picked up her briefcase, and started toward the outer office, waving good-bye to the secretary and offering no excuse for her unusually early departure. If the secretary was surprised, he didn't let it show. "Have a nice weekend," he said. Shelly blushed. Was there a hint of knowing in his voice, or was it just her imagination?

Waiting for the elevator, then all but running toward the parking lot, she hoped her anxiousness was less obvious to casual observers than it felt to her. Her mind was tumbling with the plans Julia might have made. It better be good, she thought, easing her car out of the too-tight space and into the pounding traffic.

Julia knew there was nothing Shelly hated more than being called home from work early. She knew better than anyone how devoted Shelly was to the office, to the plans she'd made a lifetime ago when she was just a kid from nowhere determined to make a name for herself. It had been no accident that Shelly had ended up with a law degree, no accident that she'd landed a plum post in one of the city's top firms.

"What you see is real," she'd told Julia one Saturday night over dinner. "I love my work and I work sixty hours a week. I have no social life, few friends, and I see my family four days a year at Christmas. I plan to be a partner in five years, seven at the outside. I have it all planned. So if you can stand all that, then I'll tell you I love you and mean it. If you can't, then I'll try to understand." She had rehearsed the speech for most of a week. Julia had listened, her mouth turned in a slightly patronizing smirk that Shelly hated. And when Shelly had let the last words out, Julia had sat in silence, studying the traces in her wineglass, then had reached across the table, kissing Shelly so hard even their waiter, Raoul, had blushed. That night they'd left the restaurant before the main course arrived.

Caught in traffic filled with sports fans and Saturday shoppers, Shelly replayed the message in her mind: "I've made plans." What plans? Julia never made plans; she was far too busy with her damned mountain. It wasn't their anniversary, nobody's birthday, no holiday anyone had ever heard of. What plans? By the time she eased the car into her parking space, Shelly was frantic with anticipation, sure Julia would be waiting for her. But the apartment was empty.

"So like her," Shelly muttered, turning on the answering machine, which had a message from her dentist, who wanted to change her appointment, and her sister, who wanted to borrow fifty dollars, and her mother, who wanted to know why Shelly didn't call more often. "Because my sister always wants to borrow fifty dollars," Shelly hissed at the machine. "The least you could do is call!" she screeched at Julia's picture, but Julia only smiled back as if the sun was in her eyes.

It wasn't until Shelly stepped into the bedroom that she saw the box on her unmade bed. Beneath the tufts of tissue paper was a note in Julia's broad script: "I'll pick you up at nine; don't be late. Julia." Pulling up the rest of the tissue, Shelly found a dress, and not just any dress. White beaded satin gleamed in the afternoon light. Shelly had never in her life owned such a dress and couldn't imagine where Julia planned to take her in such a creation. The top of the dress dipped open and low, and the narrow skirt was slit high, so high that Shelly wondered how anyone who wore the dress could ever sit without it falling dangerously open. Tucked in one corner of the box was a pair of satin high heels. Shelly sat down on the bed and started to laugh as the ginger cat invaded the box, shredding the tissue paper.

"Do I look like Tina Turner? Only Tina Turner can walk in shoes like these." The ginger cat ignored her, nesting in the tissue paper. She tried on the shoes and practiced walking across the room. Inspired, she let her work clothes fall to the floor and slipped into the beaded dress. She studied her reflection in the mirror, turning this way and that. She was a little girl playing dress-up in her mother's bedroom on a Sunday afternoon. The dress clung seductively to her chest, discreetly covering her small breasts. She was standing on the dress-maker's platform in her sister's wedding dress, a dress like Shelly herself would never wear or want . . . until now. How had Julia known?

By eight-thirty Shelly was already pacing her apartment building's lobby, waiting for Julia, watching her reflection in the glass. She was no longer Shelly Helms; she was a wild, slightly wicked woman looking for adventure. Her eyes scanned the street, looking for Julia's truck. When a taxi pulled up next to the curb, the driver, a woman who looked vaguely familiar, hopped out with a half-dozen long-stemmed white roses and beckoned to Shelly. "Where's Julia?" Shelly asked, settling into the back of the cab.

"She said to tell you she'd meet you at the restaurant." The driver shot a conspiratorial grin into the rearview mirror. Shelly had never been to the Top of the Mark before, but the place made her feel like a child. Imposing, elegant, it was a place out of touch with reality. While she stood waiting for the elevator, an elegantly dressed late-middle-aged couple came up behind her. There they stood, all three, the mommy and daddy and their little darling out on the town. Shelly stepped on the elevator and shivered just a little, though there was no breeze.

The elevator stopped, they stepped off, and there was Julia, waiting, smiling, beautiful and easy in a white tuxedo that glowed like moonlight. "I have the whole night planned," Julia whispered, leading the way to their table by the window. Beneath them San Francisco spilled out like lust, quiet and shining.

Shelly was laughing, shaking her head, burying her face in the palm of her hand. "I had the *strangest* feeling on the eleva-tor . . . all afternoon, really . . . ever since I put this dress on. Julie, why did you buy me a dress like this? No, forget that; why did you buy me *this* dress?" Shelly giggled; it was all starting again; any minute the elevator doors would open and there would be her mother.

"Because when you saw it in the store window, you said, 'I always wanted a dress like that.' And I wanted to see how the mountain looks snow-capped and icy."

"Julie." Shelly was laughing again. "I meant a long time ago, when I was a kid. My mother had a dress like this; she only wore it once or twice, but it was always there in her closet. I *loved* that dress, trying it on. I'd prance around in that beaded dress and pretend—oh, I don't know what I'd pretend, maybe that I was the most beautiful woman in the world or something. You know, I'd forgotten about that dress—the one in the store window, I mean."

"I played dress-up, too," Julia said, her eyes smiling. "I'd take my dad's pickax and put on a pair of boots and a beat-up old hat I found out in the garage, and I'd go prospecting. I had most of the neighbor's stone wall picked out before the summer was over. My dad was so mad. He made me help him fix it, then he took me out to an old quarry—he figured it was safer than Mr. Shaffer's wall." She laughed, warm and easy. "You sure do look pretty."

Shelly beamed and whispered, "I love you" just as the waiter arrived. After he left, they collapsed in giggles.

"We're worse than fourteen-year-olds," hissed Julia.

"That's what I was trying to tell you before. Julie, I feel like I'm in my mother's dress. Surprise! It's Mom! Believe me, neither one of us is ready for that."

"So'd your mother ever do it in the ladies room at the Top of the Mark? Or was she more the elevator type?" Julia suggested wickedly, arching her eyebrows as Shelly blushed. "Or was she a good girl and rented a room? By the way, don't suggest that one; my credit card's at the limit."

"Let's get out of here," Shelly hissed.

"Aha! I should've guessed, the back of a taxi? I've got my sleeping bag. We could do it in the parking lot. I will do it anywhere, but I will not go home! These clothes demand that we do it in the road!" Julia's voice was becoming progressively louder as they made their way toward the elevator. A few heads turned to look at them, and to each one, Julia turned and nodded a polite little greeting.

"Are you drunk?" Shelly asked once the elevator doors had closed, leaving them alone.

"Less drunk than hungry. How about stopping for a taco, then going to the bar and catch the show there?" Julia was smiling, hugging Shelly, nibbling at her neck.

Babe's was humming by the time Shelly and Julia arrived. Still, Shelly was met by the curious gazes of a group of women huddled around a table near the door. It was true, nobody else there had on white satin. "They probably think you're one of the dancers," Julia whispered evilly as they found an empty loveseat in the corner. Kissing her lightly, Julia stroked Shelly's throat. With a quick wink, Julia stepped toward the bar, where she was swallowed up by the crowd.

Minutes ticked away and Shelly was still waiting. The bar was full of friendly strangers; no one they knew was there. From behind her, a husky whisper asked her to dance. Turning, Shelly smiled, expecting Julia, but found herself face-to-face with an intense stranger. "I'm waiting for someone," Shelly said, smiling.

"Yeah, you're waiting for me. I know I've been waiting all my life for someone like you." The words slurred and Shelly recoiled.

"No, really. She's at the bar."

"Well, you can dance with me while you wait." Then, more softly, "Please?" Shelly nodded and found herself half-lifted off the couch and led to the dance floor. With the stranger's arm locked around Shelly, they plowed the dance floor to a slow beat. As they moved with a half-dozen other couples, Shelly caught sight of a familiar form leaning against the wall by the pool table. Watching. And Julia was laughing. Finally, the music changed tempo and Shelly's partner abandoned her with a stiff bow and a sloppy whiskey-soaked kiss.

Shelly joined the few women lined up outside the rest rooms by the back door. Leaning against the wall, it felt cool and rough against her bare arms. When the back door opened, as it sometimes did, the women who passed her wore whiffs of smoke and night air, almost cold but not quite. She heard the door creak open, felt the coolness raise anxious goose bumps across her chest; she turned toward it. "I can't right now. I'm waiting for someone," she said and giggled, trying to ignore the warmth of the wine, the outstretched hand daring her. She took it and stepped into the night.

Following the night shadow around the corner under the fire escape, Shelly stepped carefully through the darkness. Under the full moon, white satin glowed soft as new snow. The bricks, the earth that fringed the sidewalk smelled damp and musty. Letting her eyes adjust to the darkness that was inter-rupted only by a streetlight, Shelly could make out the barred windows on the next building, the wooden gate at the end of the walkway. Strong hands pulled her close; a soft mouth that tasted of whiskey muffled her voice. She leaned into the cold rough wall. Hands roamed her body, pulling the dress back to expose her breasts, moving quickly under the open skirt. Her skin prickled from the rough wall, the wicked dampness of the night. Bar sounds filtered out the window, traces of music, laughter, women sounds. Her body was responding to the beat, pulling her along. She was trembling not from damp or cold but from something yet unknown. She was opening, rocking, wanting. Fingers. Tongue. She could hear her own breath coming hard, shrill. Hands moving, mouth sucking, nibbling beneath the dress. With a deep moan, Shelly leaned heavily into the wall and let it fall away. When she opened her eyes, the walkway looked smaller than it had only moments before, the gate dangerously close. Looking back only for a moment, she let herself be led back inside.

Slipping onto a bar stool, Shelly took a sip from the glass of white wine the bartender set in front of her. Cool. Sweet. Like night air. Turning to watch the dancers, she saw her old dancing buddy piloting another woman back and forth across the floor. Shelly closed her eyes for a moment, listening to the music, feeling the tingling in her cunt subside, wishing for a moment that the sensation, like the fingers, could have lingered a little longer. Opening her eyes, she smiled at Julia. "Miss me?" Julia asked.

Shelly giggled. "Just a little."

"Still love me?" Julia asked, teasing. Shelly nodded.

"I saw you dancing earlier. I was watching you. Would you dance with me or do you do it only with strangers?" Julia took a drink and raised her eyes over the glass, arching her eyebrows, smiling wickedly.

Shelly shook her head and closed her eyes, remembering kisses in the walkway, wondering how she ever could have imagined this dress was anything at all like her mother's. Her mother would never have worn such a dress into a walkway under a fire escape outside a bar. Or would she? Shelly opened her eyes and looked into Julia's. "Ready to go home, baby?" The question was whispered into Shelly's neck. Shelly nodded, then turned to kiss Julia, who tasted like whiskey, whose white tuxedo glowed like moonlight, and whose fingers smelled of Shelly.

Sunday's Child

Tara groaned and turned on her back, careful not to disturb Luna. Locking her hands behind her head, she watched the last traces of sunset-pink shadows streak through the windows. Times like this, she was glad the bedroom windows faced west. It was always easier to think when you could see the sky.

The blue plastic clock on the dresser read 8:17 and 33 seconds. Why the hell does anybody need to know that? she wondered. It wasn't as if anyone ever said, 'I'll meet you at 8:17 and 33 seconds.' Except spies and Army bombardiers. And one wrong step with either one of them, there's a good chance nobody'll see 8:19 anyway. Maybe it's all that olive drab. They should have a selection of decorator colors just like everybody else. Powder blue. Daisy yellow. Mint green. Camouflaged like a French garden. World War III averted by pastels this spring. Cheery thoughts there, Winston. Well, no matter, it's an hour before Sleeping Beauty has to haul it out of the sack.

"I'll set the alarm for 9:30," she told Luna, who peered at Tara through sleep-clouded eyes. "You don't go on until 11:30. That should give even you enough time." Luna mumbled into the pillow and pulled it over her head.

Naked except for a pair of leather thongs made from a water buffalo's backside, Tara Winston padded through the house, stopping at the refrigerator for a Coke, then out onto the deck where the hot tub breathed puffs of steam into the chill night air. Tara lowered herself into the water, draped her arms over the edges of the tub, and exhaled as her body floated to the surface. The hot tub was definitely a plus. Not that she wouldn't have moved in with Luna without a hot tub. Hell, she thought, I would have moved in with Luna if the woman lived in a pup tent. She smiled at the thought of Luna in a pup tent. A pup tent pitched by a hot tub in a glade of eucalyptus. She breathed deeply, letting the water warm her. The hot tub was nice. And Luna was nice. Tara smiled.

Summer vacation was fading. In two weeks she'd be back at law school, living out her mother's dream. She wondered what it would be like to be a lawyer. Sharon should know; it's what she'd drummed into Tara since first grade: "Get your law degree and you can do anything, go anywhere." So Tara had taken a scholarship to Boalt Hall at the university in Berkeley. Sharon was proud. Babe was proud. Even Luna was proud. And Tara didn't really give a damn; she wanted to be a pilot, to fly. Next to the sun. Circling the stars. Soaring just a breath beneath the sound barrier. Too bad the Joint Chiefs of Staff didn't have a sense of humor or she'd be up there right now fucking Luna at thirty thousand feet, the plane piloted by radar.

Tara turned onto her belly. Her breasts dipped into the hot water, her ass steaming against the night air. The hot tub was her favorite part of the house. From her spot on the deck, Tara watched the city lights twinkle. Leaning into the heat, beads of crystal sweat ripened her skin like apples. From the heart of her steamy cumulus, the world looked almost soft, harmlessly pleasant.

White bubbles churned around her hands, reminding Tara of cake frosting. "I am a cupcake," she repeated slowly, her fingers moving to massage her shoulders. The words reminded her of a nursery rhyme Sharon used to sing to her: "I'm a little cupcake, short and stout," she sang. Frowned slightly. It's teapot, stupid. She chuckled slightly, relishing the silence of the night. Over her head, a perfect orchid draped across a trellis, turning her corner of the deck into a tropical jungle. She was Esther Williams in a bottomless pool at the base of the Angel Falls. Her best scenes were always played underwater.

Tara smiled and sank down into the tub. The hot water would last as long as she needed it to, maybe forever or longer. Closing her eyes, she savored the heat. It felt like love.

The hot tub, the house, and almost everything in it was Luna's—paid for by breakfast cereal and cough syrup. Luna had spent her childhood making television commercials. Now, she was a stripper, although she preferred to be called an erotic dancer. The work was steadier without so much rejection, Luna said. Luna didn't believe in competition or rejection; she was too used to getting her own way. Tara also suspected she liked the rush of taking her clothes off in a roomful of strangers.

"What's it feel like?" Tara had asked when they'd first started dating. In those days, Luna was still headlining one of the big downtown shows frequented by visiting conventioneers.

"You're up there on that stage, with the lights going . . . the music just right. Everything's perfect and you're looking good. So fine. So beautiful. And you can feel them out there, wanting you, aching for you. Not even for you, really, but for what they think you are. What they think you can make them be. And no matter what they do—they can't have it because it doesn't exist. But they don't know that and you won't tell them. So you just go on letting them want you like they've never wanted *no-body* before. And all the while you just go on being perfect. And fine. So very, very fine."

Luna's mother had been a dancer, too, before she realized there was more money in putting her only daughter in commercials. When Luna reached the awkward teen years and the commercial work dried up, her mother started teaching belly dancing in the basement of the neighborhood center. Housewives and secretaries, Sunday school teachers and shop clerks paid Luna's mother ten dollars every week to teach them to dance for their husbands—the foremen and church deacons and janitors. Luna had started there but quickly graduated to the studios downtown.

The money from the TV commercials was in a trust, so she danced nights at a Greek restaurant to pay for dance lessons. While Tara was memorizing equations for college-entrance exams, Luna was rehearsing for an audition as a Reno showgirl. Life in the casino show lounges didn't agree with her, though, so she came back to California and the clubs. While Tara was studying ancient history, Luna was designing costumes that would come off easily onstage. By the time Tara was in her third year of college, Luna was headlining in her own show in the top club in the city. She and Tara had met the last semester before Tara's graduation. Tara had been filling in behind the bar when Luna came in with some of the other dancers from her show.

At five feet nine with black hair that curled to her waist, an olive complexion that tanned golden, and wide-set black eyes that seemed to slant slightly in a perpetual question, Luna was a stark contrast to Tara's athletic blondness. Tara was more at home on a softball pitcher's mound than at the theater, happier buried in the stacks at the library than out dancing. It was their differences that kept their life together interesting.

Tara had started courting Luna in earnest just two days after their first meeting. Soon she was spending every weekend with Luna, waiting for her after the shows, surprising her with theater tickets and small gifts. Finally, she announced she was moving to Luna's house in Mill Valley.

"Your daughter is going to live with a stripper," Sharon had announced at dinner one night.

"Erotic dancer," Tara had corrected. Sharon had shot her a black look and Babe had laughed as if to say Don't push it, kid. Sharon had ignored her daughter and glared at Babe. "I suppose you think it's a good idea?"

Babe had considered this for a long moment. "I don't think it's a *bad* idea. Seems to me like it's her business, not ours. It's not like *I'm* going to go live with the stripper." Babe had chuckled at this, then waved her hand. " 'Scuse me, I mean *erotic dancer.*" Sharon had glared. Tara had smiled, choking back a laugh. "Maybe she'll get us free tickets for her show." Babe had winked, slapping Sharon on the rump. "From what the kid tells me, it's *hot, Mama!*" Babe had grabbed Sharon, buried her face in her neck, and whispered something that made Sharon blush.

With that, Tara moved out of the house she'd shared with Babe and Sharon and moved in with Luna and her roommate Arlene, a third-grade teacher who spent her summers with a small group of amateur archaeologists digging for Amazon burial sites on tiny islands off Greece. Every few weeks a postcard would arrive with sketchy details about their progress. Tara had found one in the mail Friday morning. Luna was rehearsing for her show.

"Says here, they're at the same site they were last year," Tara shouted over the music. "If they don't dig any faster than that, they're going to be artifacts themselves before they find any Amazons." Luna smiled, never missing a step, and mouthed, "I love you."

Luna probably would never have considered a show at Babe's if the club she'd worked at for three years hadn't been closed by the IRS. One morning she'd joined the small crowd on the sidewalk to read the official notice that was glued just above a very large ominous padlock. "Toddy'll get it straightened out," Shala, one of the younger dancers, announced. "It'll just be a day or two," offered Val, the afternoon bartender. "End of the week at most," volunteered Jason, another dancer. The club didn't reopen by the end of that week or even the end of the month. Toddy's lawyers were never able to straighten out the income-tax-evasion charges that landed the show club owner in a federal penitentiary, with not a few former government officials. Luna, like the rest of the crew, was out of work. Unlike most of them, though, she didn't want to go on to the next club and the one after that.

Dancing at Babe's had been Tara's idea. A bad one, Babe would have said if anyone had bothered to ask. "Do I look like a woman who needs the aggravation of strippers?" Babe had huffed at Tara's suggestion. "Maybe you're mistaking me for a Hollywood producer? Or you think I got nothing to do on Saturday nights?" But Tara was as used to getting what she wanted from Babe as Babe was to giving in to her daughter. "Tell you what I'll do," Babe had finally offered. "You set it up—publicity, stage set, whatever it takes—so I don't have to do nothin' but watch and you got a deal. But I don't want no part of it—except the profits." Babe had chuckled under Tara's thank-you kiss. "Hey, kid," Babe had called after Tara. "Twenty bucks says it don't work."

"Thanks for the vote of confidence, Ma," Tara had answered, making an obscene gesture as the door closed on Babe's laughter.

And so the stage was set. Under Tara's supervision, the planks were covered with a deep dark plush. The plain blue backdrop was exchanged for black velvet shot with electrified streaks of silver and mists of net. New lights and sound were installed. Luna hired a deejay and two other dancers; she was both costume designer and choreographer. Her mother came out of retirement in Ventura and moved into Arlene's vacant room to make costumes. Tara argued with printers over posters; charmed the electricians who didn't want to work on Sunday; and wiped Luna's tears when everything went wrong.

"It looks like a harem," Babe snorted, fingering the fluff, ruffling the plush with her boot toe. It was no secret that Babe thought strippers were a waste of time, space, and money. Not that Luna was the first stripper to perform in the bar. How many years had she watched . . . what was that boy's name— Tony? Well, no matter—leap on top of the bar itself, pumping and prancing, churning the length of it? Stripped till he was buck naked. And the customers lining up three deep and cheering until you could hardly hear the music. Luna was definitely an improvement, Babe decided.

"It'll be fine, Mom," Tara had said, as if she could read Babe's thoughts. "You'll love it."

"I doubt that," Babe had observed, moving back to the bar, wishing for the old days when all a bar needed was a pool table and a couple of pinball machines. Then it was live bands on Fridays, and after that disco with live deejays on Thursdays, now strip shows. Barkeeping, to Babe's mind, wasn't what it used to be; sometimes, neither was motherhood.

Tara Winston was an unexpected combination of the two women who had raised her. A near mirror image of her natural mother, she was short and blond, with crinkly blue eyes and a pouty mouth that looked as if she'd been too long eating cherries. But Babe Daniels had played an integral part in the child's upbringing, giving her a keen sense of people and a razor wit. Reaching womanhood, Tara was as much Babe as she was Sharon.

Let those who worried about such things think she was disadvantaged being raised in a world of women; Tara had never known any other way of life. Some days it was exhilarating; other days, monotonous. Either way, she didn't miss what she'd never known—father, brothers, uncles, even grandfathers with any great regularity. Few men had passed through her childhood: Tommy Agres, who had been her Santa; Arlan and Charles, who had doted on her; and Grandpa Harvey, who arrived for a week every August of her childhood with Tara's grandmother in tow. Of them all, Tara had loved Charles best; she'd cried for days when he died.

It was only in the crannies and chasms of her earliest memories that Tara could even remember wishing for a father. Tara had kept the idea tucked away under her pillow, a well-kept secret, until one fateful afternoon when she was five.

Babe had been looking for the keys to her motorcycle for almost a half hour. As she charged through the three-room apartment like an unleashed bulldog, Tara tittered from the corner of the couch. "Did'ja look behind the chair?" She giggled. Babe snorted and upended the chair. "Maybe they're under the TV," Tara offered, convulsing in laughter when Babe crawled along the floor, her arm waiving under the bookcase. "How about . . ." Tara began, when Babe snapped.

"Shit, Tara, I'm late! Did you do something with the damned keys?"

"April Fools! April Fools! I flushed 'em! April Fools!" Tara was doubled over in mirth. Babe turned, enraged, her eyes flashing fire. It was the first time Tara had ever seen Babe truly angry and the shock of it startled her so that she only laughed harder. Babe lunged, jerking Tara off the couch, and spanked her all the way to the bedroom. Tara wailed as she heard Babe slam out the door. She sobbed as Sharon called the locksmith. She cried until it felt like the world had curled up and died in her belly. By suppertime, the neighborhood locksmith was forty dollars richer.

Tara had heard the house grow quiet and could smell supper. Her small face was swollen from the tears and her throat ached. She wanted to crawl into Babe's lap and look for sugar cubes in her vest pockets. Tara slipped out of bed and padded into the living room.

"Don't you have something to say?" Babe demanded as Tara approached. Her eyes stayed riveted on the evening news. Tara shuffled her feet, looked at the floor, then pretended to watch the news, all the time stealing quick glances at Babe. "Well, I'm waiting," Babe said. She was trying to live up to her parental duty and to make sure the locksmith didn't eat steaks on her forty dollars again. Babe leveled a stern look at the child, but Tara was as stubborn as Babe herself; the child just stared back. Black silence hung between them. Finally she spoke. The words were meaningless, accidental, an empty threat overheard on the playground, but lethal nonetheless: "When my daddy comes back, he's going to get you."

The words hit their mark, jerking Babe's heart free from her chest. She inhaled sharply and her eyes shot back to the television screen as if she'd been knocked off balance. Tara shuddered, unsure of what would happen next. As soon as she saw the effect of what she'd said, she was sorry, but her child's pride kept her from running to Babe, from burying her head in the lap that had shielded her so many times. She stared at Babe, bracing herself for the explosion. Instead, large tears slid down Babe's cheeks as she pretended to watch the news. Tara trembled. Many times she'd seen Sharon cry, but never Babe. Babe always said her hide was tougher than an armadillo's. That she was stronger than even Ironman, the wrestler. Tara began to back away, afraid, ashamed as tears streaked her freckled cheeks.

Later, after Babe had gone to work, Sharon silently opened the bedroom door and stared through the dusk at her weeping child. "You hurt your mom. Why would you do such a thing?" Sharon wasn't waiting for an answer; her words were cold and harsh. "What you did was wrong and you didn't even apologize. Instead, you hurt Babe."

Tara sobbed in reply, wanting her mother to pull her close, to hug her, to forgive her. Instead, Sharon stood in the door like an alabaster statue. "What you said was evil and mean. You hurt someone who loves you more than her own life. You're a bad child." Sharon's words slashed deeply. Tara looked at her mother, her eyes wide.

"Is that why my daddy left?" Sharon had always known Tara would someday want to know about her father—the boy whose face Sharon could no longer remember, whose fumbling attempts at manhood had created Tara, who never even knew about this child who lived in a Haight Ashbury walk-up with his one-time girlfriend and her lesbian lover, who, the last Sharon knew, was a band director in a small town in Florida. How she'd hoped she could sweep him into the shadows where she would never have to think of him, where no one would ask about him ever again. Tara regarded her mother silently, watching as Sharon plucked a discarded doll from the floor and absently smoothed its dress. The moment hung heavy. "You don't have a father," Sharon finally answered. "You have me and you have Babe. But you don't have a father—and you never will."

"I do too have a daddy! I do! You're lying! Dickie Dinwiddle says everybody has a daddy!" Tara's tantrum escalated to new heights, until Sharon stormed from the room.

"Damn you, Dickie Dinwiddle!" she raged at a faceless little boy. She was so angry, she was shaking. "Goddamn you!"

Huddled in the darkness of her room, Tara listened to her mother curse the dishes she was washing. Tara no longer understood her world. If what Dickie Dinwiddle said was right, then she had to have a father. Dickie Dinwiddle was a big kid, eight years old and almost in third grade. But Dickie was dumb, too. None of boys would play with him—unless they wanted to steal his glasses or his pants. Of course, no one had ever seen Dickie's father, either. Dickie said he was a CIA agent on secret assignment in Africa and when he got back he was going to beat up the boys who were always stealing Dickie's pants and peeing on him. He even swore on a comic book about Moses that his father had a big Cadillac and he was going to let Dickie drive it. He said Tara could ride in the backseat.

Tara considered this. If Dickie knew so much about his father and nobody had ever seen him, either, did that mean she had a father, too? And if she did, why had Sharon lied? If talking about him made Babe so upset, then he must be real, Tara decided. Maybe Babe and Sharon were kidnappers and they were afraid they'd get caught. Maybe her father was out there right now looking for her. If Sharon and Babe were so afraid of him, he must be rich and important, somebody special. Just like the kindly fathers who lived in the TV. He would be so happy to see her. He'd never yell at her. He'd probably even let her drive his car, just like Dickie's father. All she had to do was find him. She wasn't sure where or how, but she'd do it.

She had planned to leave that night, but she was afraid of the dark, so she waited until morning. Just as dawn was breaking, Tara slipped down the steps and out the front door. Clutching her Cinderella suitcase, which she'd emptied of doll clothes and carefully packed with a piece of cheese, a bottle of orange Nehi, two slices of bread, and Gruff Beardog, Tara stepped into the dawn. The street was quiet, deserted, ominous. She sat on the front stoop for a very long time, waiting for Babe or Sharon to come running down the stairs to find her. But no life stirred inside the building.

Making her way down the steps, she looked back over her shoulder, saying good-bye to her life on Bertha Street. A siren howled in the distance. She walked slowly up the street, her head turning quickly at every sound. A spotted tomcat, home from his evening prowl, stopped to be petted by the little girl, who buried her face in his scruffy fur. He yowled in indignation and wiggled free when she squeezed him too tightly, his tail whipping back and forth as he marched up the street. She began to follow the cat. He would be her traveling companion. He was probably a magic cat who would help her find her father. The frightened tom led her up streets and down alleys, with Tara close behind. Finally, the cat escaped through a hole too small for even the smallest child. She crouched by the hole, pleading with the cat to come out. When that failed, Tara made her way out of the alley and into a strange street that was alive with morning.

A corner bakery reminded her it was breakfast time, but the cheese and bread she'd packed was dry and tasteless. Cookies and hot rolls beckoned her through the bakery window. With her nose pressed against the glass, she watched a swarthy man carry trays heaped with glazed cakes to the display window. Tall men in business suits pushed and jostled past Tara as they entered the bakery, their minds on breakfast rolls, not lost little girls. All, that is, but one.

"Here, kid, you want one of these?" Tara looked up, her hungry eyes focusing quickly on the extended muffin and then beyond that, on the man's open fly. With a sharp cry, she pulled back and started to run, fast as she could, faster than she'd ever imagined her legs could carry her, the man's raucous laugh chasing her through the streets.

She desperately wanted to go home, but no matter where she turned, nothing was familiar. Trees glowered. Strangers scowled. Bushes trembled with lives of their own. The whole world loomed ominous, filled with danger. Tara had forgotten about her father and about being mad at Babe. She was sure she had somehow walked to another city, maybe even another country. Buses roared past her, threatening to suck her under their massive wheels. Dogs bared their teeth and growled when she drew too close. Old men with blank eyes sank away from her into doorways when she stared too long. Round women with white aprons and full arms shooed her away from the front of their produce stands. She wandered on through the streets. But no matter where she looked, she couldn't find the way home.

Squatting between a mailbox and a news rack, Tara watched the streetlight change red to green and back again, tears streaming down her face. Traffic roared past, loud and angry, so she didn't notice the motorcycle that pulled up next to the curb or the heavy boots that stopped in front of her until it was too late for escape. A strong hand dropped down on her shoulder.

"Hey, you! Ain't you Babe Daniels's kid?" Tara focused on the motorcycle boots, then looked up, all the way up to Andy's broad grinning face shining mahogany brown in the sunlight. "Looks like you're plannin' a little trip. Where you headed?" Andy asked, lowering herself on her haunches next to the child. Tara shrugged. She hadn't really thought about where she was going, only that she was going. "I been a lot of places," Andy offered, her face softening with a wide grin. "Any place you want to know about in particular, I'm the one to see!" It was the same voice Andy used when she was holding a pair of aces at Babe's Monday-night kitchen poker game. Andy settled on the curb by her motorcycle and pulled Tara onto her broad lap. Tara snuggled close to Andy, letting the woman's big arms enfold her, protect her. Glad, very glad she'd found a friend in this hostile land.

"When I was about your age, I figured to go to California, but since you're already in California, I guess you'll be goin' east?" Tara nodded, though she wasn't sure which way was east. " 'Course, it gets pretty cold back east," Andy continued. "Snows there, too. I reckon you thought of all that. Probably got yourself a good warm coat there in your suitcase. Couple of sweaters. Some boots." Tara shook her head. "No boots? Kid, you're goin' the wrong direction, then. Must be plannin' to head south. Maybe down Mexico way?" Tara nodded again.

She'd heard of Mexico. Jesús and Manuel in the second-floor flat were from Mexico, and on their birthdays their mother always had a big purple piñata shaped like a donkey that spilled candy all over their living room floor. Tara laughed at the memory of scrambling across the carpet like a mouse looking for treats. " 'Course you can talk Spanish, can't you?" Andy asked. Tara shook her head sadly and looked up at Andy, who was scratching her chin, pretending to ponder the situation. "No boots. Don't speak Spanish. Don't sound to me like you got this here trip too well planned out. You know what I'd do if I was you? I'd go on back to my house and wait it out till I got enough stash to buy me a decent pair of boots or at least learned me some Spanish, then I'd take off."

Tara brightened with thoughts of her room and Sharon smelling of talc in the morning and Babe's coffee on the stove. Then the tears started again. What if they wouldn't let her come back—or worse, what if they did but Babe never forgave her? "I can't go back," she confided. "Babe doesn't want to be my mom anymore."

"She told you that, did she?" Andy asked.

Tara shook her head sadly, tears welling up in her eyes. "I flushed her keys for April Fools. Only Babe didn't laugh. She spanked me."

Andy rubbed her chin again. "So you run off 'cause Babe walloped you for flushing her keys? I would-a done worse'n that." Tara's lower lip trembled. She was a little afraid of Andy, who stood over six feet tall, had a voice that rumbled and a laugh that sounded like a lion's roar. She worked the graveyard shift at the loading docks and always had a pocketful of watches that she gave to people she liked, usually tiny women with huge dark eyes and long red fingernails. Tara had been disappointed when she found out that the graveyard shift only meant that Andy worked nights, not in a cemetery. Ever since Babe took her to see *Night of the Living Dead,* Tara had wanted to see a dead body. With a puzzled look, Tara turned to Andy.

"I thought you slept in the daytime. You should get to bed," she scolded.

Andy laughed. "Well, I was just about to hit the sack this morning when the phone rings. I figure it's probably Diana Ross in a red dress with spangles and she's callin' me for a hot date." Andy had a large poster of Diana Ross over her bed. "Only I'm too tired even for Diana, see? So I answer the phone and you know that it ain't Diana at all. It's Babe Daniels. Let me tell you, that ain't no wake-me-up compared to Diana." Tara giggled, watching Andy roll her eyes and grin. "Anyway, Babe says to me, 'Andy, my little girl's gone. We gots to find her.' Well *no-body* tells your mom 'no' when she's hot for something. You know that, don't you?" Tara nodded again.

"Was she mad that I run off?" Tara asked.

"Not mad, exactly, mostly scared. A lot of bad's out here just waitin' for a plump juicy chicken like yourself to happen along." Andy tickled Tara, then swung her up on the bike. "Believe me, kid, this ain't much of a world to be in by yourself."

"Babe was scared?" Tara couldn't imagine Babe being afraid of anything. "Was she scared of my daddy?"

"Your what?" Andy let the words out with a long whistle and chuckle that sounded to Tara like a freight train moving across the night. "Honey, I ain't never seen Babe Daniels afraid of no man, no how. No, she's just scared that you'd get hurt real bad. But now you're with Andy, so you're okay. But there's gonna be hell to pay if I don't get you back home, pronto! C'mon Tonto, let's ride. I'll drive. You and the bear there can ride shotgun." Andy zipped Tara and Gruff Beardog in under her thick leather jacket that smelled like Babe and Monday-night poker. With an angry roar, the Harley's engine sprang to life. Fantasies of television fathers blew away in the wind that whipped across Tara's smooth cheeks.

Riding on Andy's broad shoulders up the stairs to her apartment, Tara giggled in delight at being home. Babe lifted Tara down and hugged her until she squirmed for air. Sharon, who'd spent the previous four hours curled into the darkness of Tara's tiny bed with a pint of gin, crept into the living room and knelt, weeping, by her daughter.

"Mommy! Why aren't you at work?" Tara asked, her eyes so wide with surprise that the three women had laughed and hugged each other and cried—even Andy, who called it road dust.

"Seems some kid name of Denny Dimwit gave our little buddy some high ideas," Andy said after the homecoming excitement had quieted and Tara was settled into her bed with Sharon. Over her mother's regular breathing, Tara listened to snatches of Andy and Babe's conversation.

"Dickie Dinwiddle," Babe corrected. "He's one of those slimy kids that always has to play with the little girls because the boys keep pissin' on him. You know the type." They laughed.

"She told me on the ride back she'd been figuring on heading out to New York to find her dad. So I asks her about it. Seems his name is Rob Petrie, he's a TV show writer. I says, 'Kid, I watch TV, too. So let's cut the crap.'" Tara heard Babe laugh again.

"You know, I had a father, if you want to call him that. Beat the shit out of me and my brothers for as long as I can remember. Was hell on wheels for Mama, too. Then one mornin' we gets up and the bastard's gone. He just lit out. Never seen him again. Left my mama with four kids and thirty-seven cents. I was ten years old. I remember Mama took that thirty-seven cents and laid it out on the table and said to us, 'This here is what your father left us, this is what he thinks of you. You kids ain't even worth a dime apiece to the bastard. Now forget him.'" The room fell silent.

Tara thought of Andy's faceless father, the one who didn't think she was even worth a dime. And of Mr. Rodriguez, who mostly just laid on the couch downstairs, cursing Manuel and Jesús. How he threw beer bottles at them, sometimes empty and sometimes not, if the boys walked in front of the television screen while he was watching. And of Jennie Pierce's father, who always drove her to school in a shiny blue convertible but who never smiled when Jennie kissed him good-bye. Real fathers. None of them were much like the fathers who lived in the television. Tara hugged Gruff Beardog tighter, pretending she was invisible. If Tara pondered fathers again, she never let on.

So it was that the family grew up together. Tara had Babe to do battle for her and Sharon to wipe her tears. They both bandaged her scraped knees and fixed her supper. Sharon was a room mother and went to PTA meetings. Babe was a popular chaperone for the bus trips to the girls' track meets—although her chaperoning career was cut short after the trip back from the state meet when she taught twenty-seven girls how to play poker. Tara always suspected Babe was secretly disappointed, even though she never let on. But she did threaten to frame the terse letter the Board of Education sent regarding chaperoning improprieties.

"Ought to send 'em a bill. The little devils cleaned me out," Babe grumbled, passing the letter around the poker table. "Went on that trip with three bucks worth of change and ran up against a busload of thirteen-year-old hustlers. I wouldn't be surprised if Mrs. Weed wasn't behind this," Babe snarled, and Tara laughed. Mrs. Weed had, over the years, become a family joke that had spread throughout Babe and Sharon's circle of friends. Tara's third-grade teacher, Mrs. Weed, was hauled out everytime Babe wanted to illustrate in graphic detail exactly what was wrong with American public education. And Babe Daniels had been, and was until the day Ermajean Weed died, her bridge-table example of the depths to which American motherhood had sunk.

The chances of Ermajean Weed and Babe Daniels ever meeting face to face should have been, by all rights, slim. But the world revolves on ifs and this chance encounter was no different. If Babe hadn't bought the bar from Tommy Agres, the little family would never have moved out of the old neighborhood into the apartment over the bar, which put Tara in a different school district. If Ronald Weed hadn't lost his job as a quality-control inspector at the packing house when it closed, his wife would never have returned to the classroom, which she loathed. And if none of those ifs had come together, Babe Daniels and Ermajean Weed would have continued, each in her own way, blind to that part of the world that the other inhabited.

It had all started innocuously enough. Tara had written an essay on the class topic "My Family." Mrs. Weed had held the paper up, displaying the big red *F* that blazed above Tara's name. The teacher then made her way up and down each aisle, making every eight-year-old in the room take a long look at what their fate would be if they ever dared to indulge in what Mrs. Weed labeled "dreadful fantasies." She came to a halt by Tara's desk. "Tara Winston, stand up and read to the whole class what you've written."

Tara accepted the paper with trembling hands. Confused, she began to read: "My family is special because I have two mothers." Mrs. Weed cleared her throat. Some students in the back of the room giggled. Tara looked around, then back at the paper and continued reading: "My mothers are Sharon and Babe. We live in a big apartment over the bar that Babe owns. Sharon works for a lawyer. She is a legal secretary. She goes to work early. She wears dresses with flowers on them, because she likes roses even if we don't have a garden. On Saturdays we go to the arboretum and she tells me the names of plants." She raised her eyes to Mrs. Weed, who smiled slightly. Tara sighed. Mrs. Weed nodded toward the paper.

"My other mother is Babe."

"Yeah, like the blue ox," hooted a boy from the next aisle. Tara's face reddened but she pressed on, tears burning at her eyes. "She has a black leather jacket with lots of zippers and snaps on it. She wears cowboy boots with silver spurs. We don't have room for a horse, so Babe has to ride a motorcycle. On Sunday morning we go for a ride on her motorcycle. Sometimes she lets me steer. We go very fast, much faster than a horse. We meet Babe's friends, JoJo, Red, and Andy at the beach. They all have to motorcycles, too." By then, the class was roaring with laughter.

"And tell us, Tara Winston, are these other motorcyclists all women, too? Even the one called Andy?"

"Oh, yes," Tara readily agreed, smiling.

"Lies," hissed Mrs. Weed. "There is one thing I will not tolerate in my classroom," she intoned, her narrowed eyes looking from one frightened face to the next, "and that is lies. And this is what happens to children who think I will be deceived." She grabbed the paper out of Tara's hand and underlined the big *F*. The woman's face was red with rage, her eyes bulging. "Take this paper home and have your *two mothers* sign this and bring it back to me in the morning." She shoved the paper back at Tara as the dismissal bell rang.

Tears of shame and fury streamed down Tara's plump pink cheeks. She hid in the girls' bathroom until she was sure all her friends were gone and then she began her long walk home alone, clutching the tear-stained paper in her fist.

"She wants my autograph?" raged Babe when Tara told her the story. "How about if she meets the real thing?"

Ermajean Weed was just finishing her work when Babe Daniels charged into the classroom.

"What the hell do you mean embarrassing my kid in front of a classroom of other brats?" Babe roared at the frail bespectacled woman who quaked primly behind her desk and who, Babe would think later, seemed to shrink before her very eyes. "What's wrong with you? Don't you know nothin'?" And Mrs. Weed, who had never before been confronted, at least to her knowledge, with a living, breathing lesbian, much less an angry one, stared at Babe in disbelief. "Her mother's home right now trying to explain to Tara that she didn't do nothing wrong and that you're an asshole! At least she'll believe that last part."

"Her mother?" Mrs. Weed asked. She was trying vainly to translate what was happening to her, but the state teacher's college had prepared her for none of it. She gaped at Babe standing before her in all her glory: the leather jacket, the heavy silver belt buckle, the boots, complete with the spurs. "But I thought you said you were her mother."

"I am," Babe answered, as if she was explaining a complex physics theory to toddler. "What the hell do I look like, the damned maid?" Mrs. Weed raised her eyebrows. Babe looked like no other mother Ermajean Weed had ever even imagined, much less actually seen.

"But how can she have two mothers?" Ermajean Weed pondered aloud.

Babe shook her head and snorted. "You are one *stu-pid* woman." Babe drew out her words until they filled the room, hovering like a black cloud. "Now do you want to tell me what's wrong with this story my kid wrote?"

"Lies—I thought . . . she . . . nobody has . . ." the teacher stammered, her face turning white under Babe's rage.

"Lies!" Babe roared. "There ain't a lie in the whole damned thing! You show me the lies, lady!"

"I suppose . . . I must have been . . . mistaken. So unusual . . . the essay."

"Yeah, you were mistaken all right. Now change this grade to what it ought to be." At that, Babe had pushed the crumpled essay across the teacher's desk. Mrs. Weed regarded Babe carefully, trying to decide what her chances of survival or even escape would be if she didn't change the grade. What if this woman, this deviate, wanted something else? What if . . . Ermajean Weed blanched.

"You waitin' for Christmas, lady? I ain't got all day," Babe said, nodding toward the paper.

Ermajean Weed slowly picked up her red grading pen, paused, and looked over the paper for what seemed to Babe to be a very long time. Babe shifted her weight slowly, then encouraged, "Let's not dawdle."

"This is very unorthodox," Mrs. Weed said, handing Babe the paper, which now carried a *B* at the top. It was obvious that the *F* had simply been reshaped.

Babe scowled and pushed the paper back. "Let's be adding a plus mark there. Tara never gets nothing less than a *B* plus." Ermajean Weed knit her brow, pursed her lips, and sniffed. Babe smiled, almost sweetly. "Now, let's not get huffy." Babe was still smiling. Mrs. Weed picked up the pen again, made a cross next to the *B,* and silently handed the paper back to Babe, who seemed even more ominous when she smiled.

Babe silently accepted the paper, carefully folded it, and tucked it away into the recesses of her jacket. Offering no thanks, Babe turned and made her way slowly up the aisle past the long rows of desks, past the American flag that hung limply in the breezeless room, past the colored posters with pictures of unsmiling presidents. She didn't look back to see Mrs. Weed raise her bifocals to follow every step of her visitor's retreat, or how the teacher looked heavenward and silently crossed herself.

"Asshole," Babe muttered with finality as the door whooshed closed behind her.

That night, Tara pretended to be asleep while Sharon and Babe discussed the grading incident. *"How can she have two mothers?"* Babe was mocking Mrs. Weed in a falsetto voice. "Hell, you should've seen her, Winston. I thought she was gonna crap right there. *'Well, I guess I was mistaken,'* she says. Hell, yes she was mistaken. But what good does that do the kid?"

"We've got to expect things like this to happen," Sharon offered, sounding as she always did when things went wrong, apologizing even though she didn't know why. "People don't understand."

"Well, they damned well better learn to or they'll have Babe Daniels to answer to."

"Babe, you can't protect her all the time. You can't be everywhere for her."

"Then she'll learn to protect herself. I'll teach her. And you can make book on that, Winston!"

From her bed in the next room, Tara smiled. Everything was back to normal. It would be all right. She turned over, hugging Gruff Beardog tightly, sure that Babe would take care of things no matter what happened, and that Sharon would be there to take care of them all. "Two mothers are much better than just one," she told the stuffed bear. "No matter what anybody says!" It was to serve as her answer to an unfeeling world's questions, spoken and unspoken, for the rest of her life.

Ermajean Weed was just one in a long line of misunderstandings—some humorous, others not. But with Babe as coach and Sharon as mitigator, Tara managed to grow mostly unscathed, armed with a natural brilliance and brash wit. When Tara entered high school, she joined the track team, where she earned a reputation as being a deadly opponent in the low hurdles. In her senior year, Coach Kelly joined the faculty and Babe made a new friend. That same year Tara won the state track meet, turned down two prom invitations, and accepted a college scholarship from the University of California at Berkeley and the keys to a new motorcycle from Babe and Sharon.

The next morning, Babe was up early, pounding nails over the fireplace to hang Tara's graduation picture. "The flea market was out of Elvis on black velvet," Babe teased. "That was my first choice." She chuckled. And so it was that life went on there at 73 Archer Lane in Sherwood Forest.

Sherwood Forest, a nondescript suburban subdivision, was first conjured in the midst of Robert Sherwood's painful hangover. The developer is a memory to everyone but the Internal Revenue Service and a dozen credit agencies that still faithfully scan computer printouts every month in hopes of turning up the name Robert Sherwood. But Robert Sherwood long ago escaped with his nineteen-year-old secretary bound for a tiny island south of Tahiti. The girl took three bikinis, a pair of jeans, and a teddy bear, all stuffed into one carry-on bag. Robert Sherwood took four suitcases, all stuffed with American currency. The girl and one of the suitcases disappeared at the Honolulu airport. Robert Sherwood bought an island and a sailboat—named both for himself—and made arrangements to have a case of Canadian whiskey shipped in every month. He was content. Three suitcases of currency can buy a lifetime of contentment.

For Babe Daniels and her neighbors, though, Sherwood Forest was the realization of a dream. It was a long way from the cold-water flat over the Smokey Joe's that had been home for most of her childhood. Ten years after Robert Sherwood hauled his first ill-gotten case of whiskey up from his beach, Babe Daniels spotted an ad for a real estate auction. A month later, she turned the key in the lock, stepped into the empty house, and announced, "Hot damn! We're home! Sharon, honey, c'mere, I'm gonna carry you over the threshold!"

Carrying her mop like a lance, Sharon strode onto the concrete-slab porch, shoved a plastic bucket toward Babe, and announced, "That'll be the day. Here, carry this across the threshold instead." Babe peered into the bucket, which held two bottles of undiluted Lysol, three cans of bug spray, and a package of mousetraps.

"Expectin' company, I see," Babe observed, setting the bucket by the door and stepping inside.

"These country places are always full of vermin," Sharon replied, easing past Babe.

"I imagine that's what the neighbors'll think once they get a load of us." Babe laughed. She was pleased with the house. The split-level ranch was at the end of a cul-de-sac, butted up against the unfinished back side of Sherwood Forest. The result was that all the houses on that side of Archer Lane had backyards twice the size of any in the rest of the subdivision. Sharon finally had room for her rose garden.

Tara came to think of the rose garden as a private place where she could talk to Sharon. Mother and daughter would dig and prune happily, sharing memories, bits of gossip, hopes, even fantasies. Babe would watch them from the kitchen window, smiling. It was in the garden that Tara first told Sharon she'd won a scholarship and then, four years later, that she'd been admitted to law school. It was there, too, where she introduced Sharon to Luna. In the garden Sharon found solace, comfort in things beautiful and growing. The garden was hers, just as the bar was Babe's.

And as busy as she was—with Arlan and their business—Sharon still spent every Saturday morning in the rose garden. She found peace in the rich smell of earth and roses. September roses blooming still, Sharon thought, turning the line over and over in her mind. She was working on a new book about the seasons of flowers and life. It would be a tribute to Arlan and to Charles. She leaned back on her heels, looked toward the house and smiled. Through the window she could see Babe moving through the kitchen.

They had grown more distant in the past several months. Sharon charged it to being busy; she hoped that was all it was. Babe never wanted to talk about it. "It ain't like we're newlyweds, Winston," she'd grumble. "What do you expect after twenty-three years?" "Twenty-four years," Sharon always thought, but never said so. And now it was September. One more September in a string of Septembers. Just like Babe's Saturday night would be just one more added to a pile of Saturday nights. Sharon was thinking of all these things when she heard Tara's motorcycle in the driveway.

It wasn't unusual for Tara and Luna to arrive unannounced on Saturdays, even though it was early. They'd been at the beach watching the sun rise when Tara decided to take Babe and Sharon out for pancakes. They'd found Babe standing by the kitchen window watching Sharon in the garden.

"What's up, Ma?" Tara asked, looking out the window at Sharon, who was crouched by a large, yellow rosebush.

"Nothing now, but you should've seen your mother a half hour ago. I put a ceramic snail out there by her new rosebush," Babe chuckled. "Thing's as big as my fist. Even has rhinestone eyes. But your mother don't put her contacts in until after she's had coffee. I pretended to notice it. You should've seen her light out there. She even took a shovel. Funniest thing I ever saw before noon."

"Well, she should have smacked it with that shovel," Luna observed.

"Damn! If she'd done that, I'd be out two bucks and she'd have me out there pickin' glass out of that garden of hers till I'm ninety." Babe rapped on the window, motioning Sharon into the house.

Temporarily forgetting Luna, Tara leaned out the window hollering, "Hey, good lookin', get in here. You've got company." Sharon smiled and waved and picked up the snail with its rhinestone eyes glinting in the sun. She started toward the house, stopping along the way to collect a handful of blooms from the garden. She walked slowly across the yard.

"Is a rhinestone-studded snail anything to do to a woman who's not even had her morning coffee?" Tara scolded, pulling a pair of cups free from the drainboard.

"Have to do it before she has her coffee, it's the only time she'd fall for it," Babe observed, watching Sharon cross the yard. Turning from the window, she looked first at Tara and then at the sloe-eyed Luna, who was leaning against the door. "So, you girls been out all night, it looks like," Babe observed dryly.

Tara pushed a lock of hair out of her eyes and handed a cup of coffee to Luna, who didn't look to Babe as if she'd seen too many sunrises from an upright position. "You're just jealous, Mom," Tara teased. "Anyway, be nice to us; we stopped by to see if my two best moms want to go out for pancakes."

Babe shrugged. "It's up to Sharon."

Tara laughed, then confided in a mock whisper, "Babe hates making decisions away from the bar, but she'll go. She just can't pass up that icky, gooey strawberry syrup." Tara locked her arms around Babe's waist, hugging her tightly. "And Sharon won't let you keep it in the house, will she?" Tara teased.

"I think you forgot this, Babe," Sharon said, trying to sound irritated as she set the snail on the drainboard. Babe grinned impishly.

"These two cuties invited me out for breakfast. You can come, too," Babe teased.

Sharon kissed first Babe, then her daughter lightly, smiled at Luna, and headed down the hall. "Not this morning, honey. I've got a meeting." In recent months her books and Arlan's illness had taken increasing blocks of time, leaving Babe alone more and more often.

"Sharon doesn't like me," Luna ventured later at breakfast. "She never invites us to the house. She avoids us. She's never even been to the show, except that first night."

"She likes you well enough, Luna," Babe said, polishing off the last of the pancakes. "She's just busy and worried about Arlan."

"It's true," Tara agreed. "That and she's still upset because I moved out," she added smugly, slipping her hand under the table to squeeze Luna's knee. "Mother was sure I'd move in with you and forget all about law school, become your manager or something. All her life, Mother has been rehearsing how to introduce me as her daughter the lawyer. Right, Ma?"

"Don't call me, Ma," Babe scolded. Tara grinned; it was their private joke. "You're too hard on her," Babe said, waving for the check. "Sharon should have been the lawyer; it's what she always wanted. That's the rub about life—you don't just get what you want, you get everything else, too. And if you expect too much, then you're that much more disappointed when it falls flat. Your mother just doesn't want you to be disappointed, that's all."

"And what about you, you're never disappointed, you never expect too much?" Luna asked, only half-teasing.

"That's why I'm a happy woman, honey, I just always take what life hands me and say thank you with a smile. See, that's the difference between me and Sharon. I'm happy; she's more . . . content."

"It's a mixed marriage." Tara winked at Luna, who giggled.

"Whatever. It's still good, and it's been working since before you were hatched." Babe ruffled Tara's hair affectionately.

"I was a turkey-baster baby," Tara observed dryly. "Only it was before they invented turkey basters."

Babe chuckled and checked her watch. "Looks like it's about tee-off time, kid," she announced. "You kids got places to be, too. Don't the Hustlers play this afternoon?"

Tara groaned and slid deeper into the booth. "I forgot about the game." She grinned at Babe. "You coming?"

Babe shook her head. "I never went when they was winning. No way am I going out of my way to watch 'em lose. Sorry to disappoint you, kid, but I got some business to take care of." She slid out of the booth, taking the check with her. "Thanks for breakfast," she said, heading for the cash register.

"Do you think it's true?" Luna finally ventured as she and Tara left the restaurant.

"What's true?" Tara asked, mounting the motorcycle.

"That Babe's . . . well . . . seeing Roxie?"

Tara whirled to face Luna, her eyes wide. Roxie was one of the dancers Luna had hired. She was a short redhead with huge tattooed breasts that she decorated with spangles and fringed pasties. Tara shook her head as if to clear it. Her brow furrowed. "Where'd you hear that?" she all but shouted.

Luna drew back, instantly sorry she'd said anything, thinking, So the wife isn't always the last to know—the daughter is. "Look, Tara, it's just something I heard. Something Roxie sort of said."

Tara settled onto the motorcycle with Luna behind her. They sat in silence. Tara didn't know whether to laugh or cry. Scenes from her childhood were flashing across her mind. Sharon and Babe holding hands as they walked along the beach. Sharon in a black evening dress, cut low to show off her cleavage, dressed up for her tenth-anniversary dinner with Babe. Babe wailing like a lost child when Sharon threatened to leave and take Tara with her if the gambling didn't stop. Sharon falling asleep over her textbooks because the only way she could go to college was night school; Babe massaging her neck and feet the next morning. How they'd all held each other, crying, when Charles died. Even how they'd been just that morning, laughing together over one of Babe's terrible practical jokes. Then each of them going her own way—Sharon to work, Tara with Luna, and Babe to . . . where? To Roxie? Tara blinked back a tear and tried to smile.

"Hold me tight," she finally said to Luna, firing up the bike. "Whatever you do, don't let go." And Tara roared full tilt into the day.

Table Topics

The table wasn't set for lovers. No candles flickered. With scratched Formica, it listed slightly from too many glasses, too many elbows and asses propped on its surface. Shoved into the bar's farthest corner behind a pair of overgrown ficus trees, the little table was only the forgotten invitation, the wine no longer shared, the dance too long ended. No view of the dance floor intruded into its shadowy depths, nor glimpse of the spangled strippers or sultry singers who swooped and slithered across the stage. Only the music found the corner easily. It was simply the worst or the best seat in the house—depending on its occupants' intent.

On nights when Babe's exploded with gyrating bodies that spilled across the dance floor and down the back hall into the parking lot, the little table was a repository for empty bottles, a hiding place for bartenders wanting a few moments of peace from the press of women four deep against the bar. Every other night, the table sat empty.

Kit had spotted it only by accident on a crowded Saturday night when she tried to make her way to the main bar. Pink lights from the stage sent eerie clouds across its surface. Soft green branches bent low around the table like a hidden glade in a forest. Ignored, nearly abandoned, the little table seemed to be waiting, a patient lover. For two weekends, Kit watched it jealously, laying her plans carefully. Soon Sissy would be back, the miles and months falling away like an unkept promise, and Kit was saving the special table for her.

*   *   *

"Tell me your secret fantasy," Kit whispered into the blue plastic receiver that sent her voice across miles and mountains, rivers and prairies until it spilled out in Sissy's ear, a warm soothing fog. Stretched full length in the middle of her bed, which soon would be their bed again, Kit ran her left hand gently along the bare curve of breast, belly, until her fingers tickled the dark hair, teasing out the dampness between her legs. Listening to Sissy's whispers, she closed her eyes, willing the miles to melt away, willing her fingers to be Sissy's.

"You know my favorite," Sissy crooned, her voice dripping with sleep and love. ". . . a table in the far back of the bar, one of those tropical bars where they have beautiful women with large knowing eyes and sheets of hair caught with orchids or gardenias . . . under palms and ferns with only one candle to light our corner . . . drinks in coconuts with tall straws and cherries, bits of orange and pineapples, with names like Tropical Temptation . . . making love under the table so nobody knows—except the woman in the red-flowered sarong behind the bar." Kit smiled, seeing Sissy's face, sweet, rosy like the lights that fell across the little table. Sissy's voice lulled Kit deeper into the fantasy. The pink tips of Sissy's soft breasts beckoned Kit like a beacon across a black night sea. As Kit's fingers circled in the silken fluff of hair between her own legs, Sissy loomed in the darkness over her bed. As Kit's fingers dipped deeper into the damp heat of her own cunt, she could see Sissy's mouth open, her long tongue darting quickly over her lips, her eyes closing slightly, her face going soft the way it always did when they made love. Sissy continued her lullaby fantasy, her voice and Kit's own fingers wooing orgasm across the miles and time that separated them. "Soon," Kit whispered, pushing herself over the edge. "Soon."

Waiting at the airport, Kit's jeans were already dampening for want of Sissy. An hour early, she paced, prowled, roamed the terminal like a hungry animal. Making love to every woman who passed, her eyes rummaged beneath the prim white blouses of the teenagers who sold ice cream cones, licking their nipples erect . . . while they squirted mustard on another hot dog. Shameless eyes pulled off the sensible beige nylon slips and panty hose of the young matrons, buried her face in their warm juicy cunts . . . while they herded toddlers past the display of stuffed bears wearing T-shirts that read CALIFORNIA, HERE I

COME! Hungry eyes nibbled their way past the patent-leather high heels up the stockings to the hearts of the businesswomen in their dress-for-success navy-blue suits, who leaned back, their cunts open, extended, offered up to Kit's ravenous tongue . . . while they flipped absently through this week's copy of *Time*.

Occasionally, one of the women would look up to find Kit staring blankly, frankly, hungrily at her. Inevitably, each one would smile hesitantly, trying vainly to place this haunting young woman with the tattooed snake slithering up her fore-arm. Kit's eyes would devour her, the snake diving deeply into each waiting stranger's cunt, while the woman vanished through the open door that would transport her to New York or Chicago or St. Louis.

Finally, the great silver and blue door parted and Sissy stepped through. Slightly drunk, her blue silk blouse rumpled from the four hours that it took for her to cross plains and mountains and gushing rivers, she looked quickly around the waiting room. Spotting Kit, she smiled, shyly at first, afraid that the months and miles had changed them; then came her bright, happy "I love you" grin. Kit, leaning nonchalantly against the post, felt her legs go weak, the floor move under her. She was sure she would collapse for want of this woman. She wanted to consume Sissy, to take her right there in the middle of the airport waiting room. Instead, she leaned harder into the post, waiting for Sissy to come the twenty yards to her. And then she was there, her tongue dipping dangerously in Kit's mouth, mindless of the stares and danger of the strangers who pushed past them. Sissy's breasts pressed hard into Kit's chest. Their fingers intertwined.

"I have to go to the bathroom," she whispered hoarsely, her breath smelling of gin and stale cigarettes. "Come with me." Pushing past the matrons and shop girls that Kit had ravaged only moments before, they squeezed into a tiny orange-doored cubicle. Kit's cowgirl shirt unsnapped with one quick tug from Sissy's hands and her tongue took the throbbing, pulsing rose-buds that waited there for her. Kit groaned, sliding her hands under Sissy's linen skirt, until she gasped in protest and lust, her cries first silenced by warm lips, wet tongue, then urged on by trembling insistent fingers that rolled her clit back and forth, a fine pearl being examined by the most discriminating buyer.

With passion's fire barely fanned, they finally emerged from the cubicle, smiling at the knowing looks of disgust and veiled eyes of the women who huddled close to the mirror, painting on ruby mouths and blue eyelids. Sissy's hips swayed a little more than usual as she swished past the silent clucking tongues of disapproval.

On the way back from the airport, Sissy curled down on the seat, her head warm against Kit's lap. Traffic lights passed in a swirl of color. Palm trees swayed in the moonlight. Sissy raised her ass lightly every time Kit shifted, making sure her cunt was settled on the vibrating head of the gearshift, her breasts dancing loosely against the rough edge of the bucket seat where Kit squirmed in anticipation.

Babe's beckoned them across the dark side streets. Only over Sissy's protests were they even going to the bar. "I want to go *home*," she hissed, while Kit parked the car, rebuttoned her pants, smoothed her rumpled hair. Kit, grinning with the delight of anticipation, ignored Sissy's pleas, held the car door open, and nodded toward the bar. She could barely keep from laughing, so delighted was she at her plan. Sissy exhaled, irritated, and stepped out of the car, her neat heels clicking across the concrete.

"Four fucking hours in a damned airplane, eating crap you can't even tell what it is, sitting next to some old goat who belches all across the damned Rocky Mountains, to go to a damned bar. I can go to a bar in Chicago. I want to go HOME!" The tirade had started out distinctly enough, but the faster she walked, the faster she talked, and it delighted Kit, who loved jokes and surprises almost as much as she loved Sissy. Running slightly to keep up with Sissy, Kit suddenly caught her arm, pulled her close, and whispered, "Remember your secret fantasy?" Sissy looked puzzled, then giggled.

Holding the bar door open and bowing slightly as if she were a doorman at the St. Francis, Kit kissed Sissy lightly. A pair of women in matching satin bowling shirts with pink mohawks and oversized safety pins as noserings pushed by. The sight delighted Sissy. "I just love how they dress out here! Okay, just one drink." Her voice fell to a whisper when she added, "But then I want to go home." Kit winked as they stepped through the door, and mouthed, "Trust me."

Threading through the cluster of women around the bar's edge, Kit elbowed into the waitress station, ignoring the sign that read NO CUSTOMERS. Sissy settled on the edge of the crowd, her cunt pounding out a rhythm of want. Watching Kit's sharply defined ass shift slightly left, then right as she waited for the drinks, Sissy felt her skin go hot, then prickle with anticipation. Kit's jeans rode low and tight across her hips where a set of keys played against the light, covering her strong legs that protected dark secrets. Sissy felt her nipples harden, her breath rise. Kit was more exciting than any woman she had ever known, teasing and tempting her even across the two thousand miles that separated them more time than she liked to think about. Sissy moved her hand casually across her chest up to her neck, pretending to check her hair, just to feel the silk tease the tiny hard peaks that ached for Kit's mouth, her fingers, her cunt to move across them.

By the time Kit returned with the drinks, Sissy was nearly frantic with desire. "I've changed my mind. I *want* to go *home,*" she hissed. But she let Kit lead her through the crowd, past the stage and the cluster of pool players to the tiny table that waited for them. On the way, Kit casually lifted a candle from a table littered with half-filled glasses and the elbows of a drunk. "What the . . . ?" the woman managed to slur. Kit silenced her with a quick wink. The woman went back to watching her friends on the dance floor. Sissy smiled and licked her lips in anticipation.

Parting the ficus leaves, Kit gallantly pulled a chair out for Sissy, who sat primly as if she were a queen, wondering all the time if the wet had seeped through leaving a dark telltale splotch on the borrowed skirt. The skirt had been Kit's idea; tucking her white lace panties into her purse somewhere over Nevada had been Sissy's own.

They sat quietly, suddenly shy. Sissy's green eyes slid down the rounded cheeks she knew so well, stopped to nibble Kit's neck, licked and sucked just inside the place where the shirt opened casually. Kit moved her chair a little closer to the table and studied Sissy, her short curling hair, the full ripe lips that were flushed pink. Music throbbed and pulsed across the tiny table, drawing them closer.

"How was your flight?" Kit finally asked. Sissy laughed.

"Terrible," she answered, then suddenly inhaled, her eyes widening as Kit's naked left foot moved under the skirt. The sharp edge of her jeans scratched Sissy's soft inner thighs; the strong toes moved slowly up and down savoring the warmth, sliding in the wet that anxiously greeted them. "There was turbulence over the mountains." Sissy slipped farther down on the chair, leaning into the table where Kit's ready hands cupped and squeezed her breasts. Looking quickly around, Sissy slipped her right hand into Kit's shirt, letting her fingers lightly brush the hard nipples she found there.

"What did you eat?" Kit asked, her toes massaging Sissy's wet clit.

"Chicken," Sissy answered, her breath coming short as she raised her own foot to Kit's jeans. "Or veal. It's hard to tell on airplanes." Kit's eyes never left Sissy's. Burying her foot deep in Sissy's cunt, which opened to welcome it, Kit's breasts trembled under Sissy's warm fingers.

"How long were you at the airport?" Sissy asked, pushing harder against Kit's throbbing pussy until the jean's inseam connected with a flash of fire and wet.

"An hour," Kit answered, her breath coming harder, trying to concentrate, trying to make her mouth form words as the music surged down on them. Sissy was riding Kit's foot in earnest now, her face flushed, her head thrown slightly back, her breasts now out of Kit's reach, the foot rubbing and demanding her bounty. "You always were early," Sissy finally managed to gasp, her chest rising and falling in time to the music.

"I couldn't wait for you to come," Kit said, her eyes closing on the image of Sissy's mouth slightly open, her eyes slightly closed, the ficus leaves framing her hair and shoulders. The bar swirled and tilted slightly, fell away until they were in a forest clearing, a fern glade. Sissy was pulling Kit down on top of her, guiding her hand through the marsh of her cunt, open, gushing up to meet her. They were flying across the beach mounted on the bare back of a great white steed, sand flying to meet surf and sky, bare cunts burning in vibrating horseflesh. And then the moment passed; the bar shifted level again. Sissy leaned heavily into the wall, leaves touching her cheek. Kit slipped her foot back into its boot, gently moved Sissy's fingers back to her side of the table. They smiled, a strange whisper-secret smile.

"How are you folks doing?" asked a voice just beyond the leaves. Surprised, Sissy jumped, looked up at the waitress, then blushed, suddenly embarrassed. "Sorry to keep you waiting. I didn't know anybody was back here. Can I bring you anything?"

"No." Kit laughed. "I've got everything I need."

Sissy smiled, bit her lip lightly, then motioned the waitress closer. "Unless you've got any of those drinks they serve in coconut shells with cherries and little paper umbrellas." She shot a quick look at Kit. "You know the kind I mean, the ones with names like Tahitian Tornado or Secret Fantasy." And she laughed, the sound rising like bubbles on the night air.

The Bottle Count of Sadie Belle Curtis

Sometimes there's nothing left to do but the bottle count. The checklist of life's little successes and big failures—that's mostly how it looks coming up. See, there's no real reason to do a bottle count when a woman's feeling fine about herself. When she's looking good and everybody knows it. When there's money in her pocket and not a thing to spend it on but good times, because that's all there is.

No, the bottle count's something you do when it's finally time to add up your troubles. When it's only the tenth of the month and already the landlord's hollering about how he's going to evict you and move in a respectable tenant—just 'cause he's allergic to cats, or dykes. When your lover just left you—or you wish she would. When your mother's coming for a visit . . . with your brother's second wife . . . and her Great-Aunt Millie . . . for 3 weeks . . . 21 days . . . 504 long hours. And they want to stay with you. But not the cats. Or the lover, who's either leaving or not. Because hotels are too expensive. How expensive? You begin to wonder.

"If you get a job as a hotel maid at a place like the St. Francis, say, do you get to live there?" you ask Gail, from across the hall. She's a bartender down at Babe's and while she's never been a hotel maid herself, she maybe knows somebody who knows. Bars are like that. Bartenders know a lot of things you wouldn't ordinarily think they'd know. "Or the Claremont? I mean they have all those tennis courts. Hell, I could learn to play tennis." Gail says she'll ask around.

Gail's all right. Just lonely. Sometimes Maggie stays over at her place—they were lovers for a while—but even then it's still like she's all alone. Lonely. You know the kind of look that says end-of-the-world empty? That's how she looks, even when Maggie's around. Gail's a woman who does the bottle count a fair amount, although she's not one to talk about it much. That's why everyone was so surprised Saturday night down at the bar when she was sort of glowing.

Seems she met this woman, Sadie. Sadie Belle Curtis, formerly of New Orleans, Louisiana, who only recently found herself in sunny California. She'd moved out here because of a woman named Jessie. So, it's been foggy ever since she got here—of course, that's not unusual for San Francisco in the late summer—and her lover had another woman all along, which is to say Sadie Belle Curtis was a woman doing her own bottle count. At least that's how it started . . . .

It's always crazy in Babe's on Saturday night. Early enough and there's all the aftersoftball leftovers and afterwork hangers-on, and not much else. Everybody hates the early shifts—except for Babe, who's been through so many shifts they must all look the same to her. But everybody else hates them. The only thing worse than the boredom is the tips—which are pretty much nonexistent. Early morning's pretty bad, too. That's when the serious drinkers come out, and the ones who don't have any place better to go. There's a lot of loneliness in a bar after midnight and the closer it gets to morning, the worse it gets.

Now the 10 P.M. to 2 A.M. crowd's another story. That's when the hard-core partiers show up and there's nothing they like better than a good time. They know how to make it happen, too. Not that they're always happy, but it's as if they have that potential: They could be if they really wanted to, or like actresses, they're just between shows or parties. Sadie Belle Curtis was like that. She had the look of a woman who knew how to have a good time. Of course, who can say if she'd look that way in the light of day. Dim lights have a way of making things look a little better than they really are.

Gail had been doing the bottle count for a while when Sadie climbed up on a bar stool and just sat there, waiting for somebody to notice her. Not that she was an easy woman to miss, with this wild curly black hair and blueberry eyes that are about as big as the ocean. She's one of those women who was probably a pretty funny-looking little kid with eyes that were too big for her head. She probably wore glasses, too, the big thick kind. But as a woman, the rest of her caught up with those eyes that could look through granite.

If Gail hadn't been busy at the cash register, no doubt she would've seen Sadie the moment she sat down. But as it was, it took her a few minutes to notice Sadie, or, rather, those eyes that were kind of crinkled up and smiling like the eyes on the Miss Coca-Cola 1945 sign that Babe keeps over the cash register.

"Would you mind wrappin' your hand 'round that bottle of tequila there and bringing a sunrise to a lonely lady?" Sadie said in this kind of husky voice that sounded like magnolia trees and mint juleps on the lawn, only clipped, too, like they talk down in New Orleans. So Gail pulled the bottle free, and Sadie was watching her and smiling, easy, happy. "And cherries," she prodded. "Don't forget the cherries." Gail gave her a few extra. If anyone had asked, she would've said it was because it was still early, but that wasn't the only reason. Gail knew it and Sadie knew it, too.

They danced a little verbal shuffle for a while, trying to find a common ground as strangers sometimes do when they really want to get to know each other. Finally Gail settled on the cigarettes that Sadie had sitting next to this little pile of neatly stacked bills. Black cigarettes from Turkey, and next to them was a package of lemon drops.

"You like those?" Gail asked, nodding to the cigarettes.

Sadie laughed, just a little airless chuckle, and pushed the pack across the bar. Only it was more like she was daring Gail to try one instead of making an offer. And she was still smiling that easy, open smile.

Gail reached for the pack, even though she had quit smoking a couple of years ago. It was just something to do. Besides, she'd never met anybody who smoked Turkish cigarettes. Sadie handed over a black monogrammed lighter and nodded as Gail flicked it to life. A foul aroma rose from the cigarette and Gail coughed deeply into the blue smoke. "What the hell is wrong with this?" she gasped when she could finally talk again.

"Not a damned thing, darlin'," Sadie answered and started to laugh. "That's just how they taste. You don't like it?" Sadie was teasing; she had to know Gail would hate those cigarettes. Even Sadie didn't like them much—except for the color. She only smoked them for the effect . . . and that was *something* . . . especially when she put one in this mother-of-pearl cigarette holder she had, although she usually didn't bring that out until later, much later.

"Let me tell you something," she said, leaning across the bar like a conspirator. "You can always trust a lady who drinks tequila."

"Why's that?" Gail whispered back, trying to match Sadie's mood.

"Because we never lie." Only *never* came out like *nev-ah,* all soft and strange and a little dangerous. Sadie smiled again and winked.

A pretty woman, with a sense of humor, Gail decided. Not movie-star beautiful or cheerleader cute, just pretty. Sadie ran her fingernail around the top of the glass, poking a little at the worn-out twist of lemon that sort of huddled against the ice cubes, then ran the finger over her bottom lip, all the time looking at Gail and smiling with those crinkly blue eyes. She was teasing the way Gail wanted her to.

Sadie was unwinding a long story about her cross-country trip to California when she got sidetracked by the tequila and started telling Gail about a winter she'd spent in Mexico a few years ago. Sadie's stories were like that, one feeding into another and another after that. "Let's make that sun rise again, woman!" she demanded, giggling madly. "In fact, you can bring me as many sunrises as you'd like . . . anywhere . . . anytime . . . my place, if you have roommates." She smiled slyly, seductively enough to make Gail blush. It had been a long time since anyone had flirted with her. "So tell me, darlin', is it true what they say about bartenders?"

Gail shrugged. "What's that?"

"That you hear the troubles of the world and dole out advice that'd put Dear Abby to shame?"

"Right," Gail laughed. "Babe's putting a confessional in the back room next week. Matty's going to be in charge 'cause she looks great in black."

"And all the broken hearts can go there and be absolved of their hurt, their pain. All for the price of penance—or a beer." Sadie sounded a little too hard, a little too hurt, and Gail found herself trying a little too hard to break the spell, to get her to laugh again.

"I can hear it now: 'Say three Bloody Marys, take two aspirin, and call me in the morning.'" Gail laughed. Sadie laughed, too, but it sounded shallow and a little strained. Sadie was silent for a long moment, then she raised her eyes to meet Gail's. She looked a little sad, but maybe it was just the tequila.

"You know what the place needs more than a confessional?" she finally asked. Gail shook her head. "A checkroom for everybody's troubles. See, everybody could just unload them there—put 'em in a little purple bag, or if they were really big ones, hang 'em up on a peg. It would be a true service to womankind," she said, raising her glass in a kind of toast.

"But what if everybody just forgot about them? Left them there forever?" Gail teased. "Or what if the little bags got all mixed up and you ended up with somebody else's troubles?"

Sadie chuckled, only it sounded a little dry. "That, my dear bartender, would never happen. Everybody knows their own troubles. My grandma used to say we could all hang out our troubles like sheets on the washline and all the neighbors could come by and take a look, sort of to pick and choose among them, but you know what would happen?" Gail shook her head, again. "Everybody would just take down her own and head on home with the same old troubles. Rich people, poor people—it wouldn't matter. Not because they were so much better or worse, as troubles go, just because they were familiar. Is that what you would do?"

"I don't know . . . I don't think so." Gail was suddenly embarrassed.

Sadie looked at Gail closely, studying her round face, her eager eyes. She smiled; Gail smiled back. "Well, it's what I would do . . . . Say, I don't even know your name? I'm Sadie. Sadie Belle Curtis. Named for my daddy's prize racehorse. She was supposed to win him a million dollars—but she never won a race. Of course, he named me before he knew that. My daddy, you see, was a gambler."

"Is that true?"

"That my daddy was a gambler? Of course."

Gail shook her head, giggling, but just a little. "No, that you were named for a horse?"

"Maybe," Sadie answered, smiling impishly. "And tell me about you. No, let me guess. Your name is . . ." She thought for a moment. "Ellyn. Spelled with a *y* instead of an *e* at the end. You're twenty-six years old. You're a double Scorpio. You've lived in San Francisco all your life. Your mama wanted you to be an English teacher, but you became a bartender instead. And you hate Turkish cigarettes. Am I right?"

Gail was laughing in earnest. "None of it. Not one word. Except about the cigarettes. My name is Gail—no special spelling—just Gail. I'm twenty-eight. I'm a Capricorn with Pisces rising. My mother . . . hell, my mother just wanted me to get married and have a bunch of kids, I think. And I moved out here five years ago from Tulsa, Oklahoma."

"Really? Oklahoma?" Sadie's eyes were half-closed in thought. "I knew a girl from Oklahoma in college. Janice Marie Watson." She raised her eyes to Gail's in the unspoken universal question: Maybe you know her? Gail shrugged and shook her head. "No, I guess Oklahoma's a big place. Not that it matters." Sadie rescued a drowning cherry, and holding it by the stem she sucked the juice from it. She smiled at the sweetness.

"Janice used to drink Tequila Sunrises, too. She's the one who introduced me to them, you might say," Sadie confided. "If I were her, I would've taken on a bottle of tequila, too, until the only thing left was the damned worm. Until the worm and I were on a first-name basis. Or maybe not." She half-smiled. "Of course, you don't know Janice, but she was the first woman I lost my heart to. Janice Marie Watson studied French in the morning and drank tequila in the afternoon. And I loved her. Only we were just kids, and I wasn't smart enough to know I loved her. I didn't figure it out for a long, long time. So we hurt each other because I loved her but she never loved me back. So you know what she did?" Gail shook her head because she, of course, had no idea but really did want to know.

"She ran off with a soldier boy she met one summer. That boy beat her in the yard one night until I swore to get my daddy's shotgun and blow his brains out just to watch the blood splatter. I remember those words as clear as if it was yesterday. He must have believed me, too, because he took off that night. I guess he just didn't believe me long enough 'cause he did come back for her." Sadie studied the dregs in the bottom of her glass and rattled the ice, her signal for another drink.

"Did you ever . . . make love . . . or anything?" Gail asked, watching Sadie closely as she set the drink before her.

"Oh, not so you'd notice. One night when it was so hot that it felt like hell itself had sprung a leak, we were sitting on the daybed on the side porch of this house where we boarded with Miss Lela Johnston. Miss Lela always had eight girls boarding with her from the college—two from each class, freshmen right up to seniors. Most of the girls moved in with her when they were freshmen and just stayed there every year until they graduated. Janice and I were the freshmen. Our mamas thought it would be a fine experience for us. Miss Lela, you see, was genteel, which is a polite way of sayin' that she could trace her family back to the Louisiana Purchase but didn't have a pot to piss in. The only thing Miss Lela did have was her house, and she wouldn't have had that if she hadn't taken in boarders. But everybody was too polite to say anything; they just let on like she wanted the company. She probably did, come to think of it." Sadie smiled, a sad, faraway kind of smile.

"Anyway, Janice and I had this stolen bottle of tequila. We'd been matching shots that night until we were both so drunk neither of us could walk, so drunk we just fell across that bed laughing and swaying and swooning. Maybe each of us was less drunk than the other imagined, but either way, she let me, as my grandma would say, have my way with her. Right there on the daybed on Miss Lela's side porch. I remember smelling the honeysuckle all night. Funny, I can't clearly recall another thing about that porch—except the honeysuckle and Janice. Of course, the next morning, we both pretended nothing had happened—and even if it had, how could we possibly remember, being so drunk and all. Next thing I knew, she was gone, leaving me with nothing but a dead worm in an empty tequila bottle. I never even saw her again. Oh, I tried writing once or twice, only she never wrote back. Sometimes I still wonder why it was she couldn't love me enough to make it stop hurting, even now."

Large tears welled up in Sadie's eyes. She pushed them back, trying to forget Janice and her full soft breasts, the soft dark hair that framed classic features so startling that strangers used to stop and stare; but mostly trying to forget her eyes, painted with a pain and knowing that hung on no matter how many years passed. Gail has eyes like that, Sadie decided. Too sad, too quiet. She took another sip of the tequila, trying to drown out memories of Janice and her brutal soldier boy, but the feeling wouldn't budge.

A knot of customers were all wanting Gail's attention, so she left Sadie alone for a while. Maybe Sadie got bored or had a better offer; either way, by the time Gail got back to that end of the bar, Sadie was gone. After most of an hour passed, Gail gave up looking for Sadie, figuring it was just her streak of bad luck holding up. That had been happening a lot lately. Then Sadie was back, with a smile bright as the morning.

"I tried to stay away, but you are my sunrise."

"I missed you." Gail tried to sound nonchalant, but the words were too loaded.

Sadie shot her a warning look and started to sing "I'm Popeye the Sailor Man . . . ." Gail giggled. "You remember that little guy in the sailor suit? Popeye. And how he was all the time singing 'I am what I am, and that's all that I am?' " She hummed a few bars, then stopped and pretended to flex a muscle, wiggling her eyebrows. "Only he sang *am* like *yam*." She started singing again, "I yam what I yam." Pretty soon that whole end of the bar was singing the Popeye song and laughing. And Gail was falling in love.

Sadie hummed a few more bars, then reflected. "Sort of like Grandma's at Thanksgiving. You know, yam pies?" Sadie laughed.

She is one of those rare women with a Christmas-tree kind of smile that lights up her whole face, Gail thought, but she only asked, "It's a joke, right?"

"Isn't everything?" Sadie answered.

Gail nodded dumbly, trying to think of something clever to say and coming up empty as Babe's after last call. Sadie chuckled, then started to hum again, her head bobbing from side to side, all the time drumming her fingers against the bar, impatient, as if she were waiting for somebody who was very, very late.

"Did you ever watch Mickey Mouse on television when you were a kid?" she suddenly asked. Gail laughed, caught unaware. She kept expecting roses and poetry, and instead she was getting cartoon characters. "Did you ever wonder what would happen if Minnie Mouse and Daisy Duck lit out to see the world? I think they'd end up here—only onstage. Who wouldn't pay to see Minnie Mouse take it off?"

Gail laughed, caught up in the zany fantasy. "Luna would have to do a whole new show. And Disneyland would never be the same."

"Neither would Minnie and Daisy, but c'est la vie!"

Gail looked into Sadie's eyes and smiled, and could have sworn she saw Minnie Mouse dancing there. One thing was certain, nobody could tell a story like Sadie Belle Curtis, not even Babe herself. Laughing at her own jokes, Sadie stitched up crazy-quilt portraits of people and places that were fantastic but believable, too. And it was catching. First she was laughing, beating her palm against the bar, then it tickled the woman next to her and on down, until finally half the bar was hooting and gasping for breath and laughing until they were crying.

Even Babe laughed at Sadie's story about smuggling her cat Hildegarde into the MGM Grand Hotel in Las Vegas—"That cat loved the mirrored walls"—feeding it out of ashtrays, and then turning half the place upside down and crazy when Hildie vanished. "One of the showgirls had found her. You should have seen that cat! Dressed up with a rhinestone bracelet on for a collar, she was all set to strip and strut. She's like that. I like to never convinced that animal to come along to California with me." Through it all, Gail was feeling like she'd just come home after being gone a long, a very long time. She wanted Sadie to stay on that bar stool forever.

"Is Sadie Belle really your name?" Gail finally asked, after things had calmed down a little. She'd never met another woman named Sadie Belle.

"Why not?" Sadie replied, rising off the stool, leaning across the bar, studying Gail's face closely. "Is Gail yours or is that an alias for Moonbeam?"

"I'm Gail."

"Then I'm Sadie," she answered, smiling, then raising her eyes to study Gail's face slow, long, and hard, almost as if she was looking for some secret that might be hiding there. Finally she lowered her eyes to the drink in front of her.

Gail checked the clock. Most nights all she could think of was getting out from behind this bar for a little break. With Sadie, though, she found herself wishing them both out of there. Wishing the night gone and them walking home, holding hands along the beach, watching the sunrise.

"Look, Sadie, I got a break now. You want to come out back with me?"

At Babe's *out back* means the parking lot where the dope smokers congregate. Every month or so, Babe rolls out there on a tear, hollering, "Haul it back inside, ladies, or haul it on outta here for good!" Mostly, though, Babe stays inside unless things get rowdy, and everybody guards against that. Nobody wants to cross Babe on a Saturday night. It also helps that Babe Daniels is as regular as Big Ben: in the bar at four, out at nine for supper, back at eleven, home at two. The only time it varies is when she takes off early after the show, and it's a rare night that she bothers to come back. Even if she did, almost nobody goes out back that late—they just go on home.

Crisp night air shot down Gail's arms when she pushed open the back door. A dozen women were protected by the shadows, huddling in little groups, leaning on Babe's car, perched like friendly night birds along the little cement wall that rims the bar's dirty brick walls. Any other night, Gail would have joined them, but she wanted to be alone with Sadie. Settling into a corner by the dumpster, Gail lit a joint, inhaled deeply, passed it to Sadie, and studied the sky. Full moon, brighter than any streetlight ever made, smiled down on them. Sadie was watching the moon, too, and when she handed the reefer back to Gail, her fingers lingered a little too long. The touch caught Gail unaware, sending shivers down her back.

A chill breeze took off across the parking lot, rattling the leaves on little trees that tickled the moon. "It's hanging so low and heavy it could be a big yellow balloon," Gail observed, meaning the moon. "When I was a kid I used to beg my dad to follow the moon when we went driving on nights like this. I was sure if we drove long enough, fast enough, we'd be able to catch up to it and see what was pulling it along. But he never did; he'd just laugh at me when I asked. A few years ago, I tried to follow it, but I never did catch up with it." She shuffled her feet, a little embarrassed. "That probably sounds pretty stupid to you."

"No it doesn't," Sadie said, reaching up to kiss Gail lightly, then more deeply. "I'd go with you to chase that moon until we caught up to it, made it show all its secrets," she whispered as the night opened to take them in.

Leaning back, feeling the cold bricks through her flannel shirt, Gail smoked, her eyes half-closed so that the moon and the streetlights all became little stars. Ice stars, she decided, circling the moon. Sadie was lost in her own thoughts, chasing the moon in her own way. She leaned warm and gentle against Gail and shivered, maybe from the night, maybe from the way Gail wrapped her arms around her. Gail smelled of the bar and smoke and Ivory soap that clung to her throat. Warm smells against a cold night.

There with Sadie in her arms, Gail was spinning a fantasy of wispy dreams and promises. A fantasy of Sadie tucked warm and soft under pink sheets, looking out an open window, waiting for Gail, watching the moon. Gail would let herself into Sadie's room using the key Sadie had given her one special day after they'd left a thousand footprints in the sand, made love in a hidden cove. She would close the door like a whisper and step into the room she knew so well that the moonlight was enough to guide her. "I've been waiting for you," Sadie would whisper, her eyes still on the moon for one last longing moment before opening her arms. She would turn back the sheet, inviting Gail to join her there, naked in the moonlight. They would smile as the sheet fell away, exposing her soft eager flesh.

"You ever live on the outside, Gail?" Sadie asked, finally breaking the silence. Her voice was sad and serious. Gail shook her head, puzzled. "No, you don't look like you would."

"What do you mean, *outside*," Gail pressed. "Outside like camping or outside like prison is inside?"

Sadie was silent for a long moment, her eyes still on the moon. "No, just outside. Like everybody else belongs but you. Everybody else knows what's going on, knows how to play the game, except you. Everybody else says the right thing and does the right thing, but not you. Never you." Her voice choked as if it were caught deep in her throat. Gail hugged her more tightly, trying to hold back the tears that she could feel Sadie trying to push down.

"Sure, everybody feels that way once in a while."

"Not once in a while," Sadie said, turning to look at Gail. "All the time, always, until you don't know any other way. More than breathing, you want things to be different, but it never happens—at least not for you. They never love you best or quite enough. They say they want to take care of you, so they turn you into their very own private Barbie doll that they dress up and play with. Then when somebody they'd rather play with comes along, whoosh, back you go into your little dollhouse, like you don't matter anymore. It's like you're not real." Gail nodded. Sadie felt very small and sad in her arms.

Then Sadie stopped talking and she sobbed so softly it sounded like the wind. Gail hugged her more tightly, vowing silently to never let go. This is how it would be if they could wrap themselves in each other's arms, pushing the world away. Gail felt Sadie's hard nipples move a little under the blue silk shirt that draped her chest in folds as soft as her skin. She could almost feel Sadie's fingers, long and strong, clinging to her back, pulling her close, insistent, determined. Gail was suddenly thankful for the shadows that hid the passion, the want, the hunger in her eyes. And Gail was suddenly ashamed. She looked away, smiling a little.

"Oh, enough of that," Sadie said a little too brightly, producing a tiny vial from the depths of her pocket. "I get this way when the sun rises a little too often on a Saturday night. Speaking of which—this'll put a whole new shine on the moon. Bolivia's finest marching powder, straight from an animator I know down in La-La Land. He paid up an old debt on my way through."

Gail shook her head. "What'd you mean about living on the outside?"

Sadie shrugged and returned the bottle to her pocket, her mood, like her voice, suddenly escalating. "Oh, you know, living on the edge. They have a lot of names for it, for me, names like *other woman*. I always wonder, Other than what woman? But we all know the answer to that, don't we? Or *mistress*. That's my personal favorite. Sounds like you own something, even though you don't have a pot to piss in. Or *nonmonogamy*. That one's a hoot—I mean it's not even in the dictionary! I know, I tried to look it up once—no, twice." Her laughter was brittle, like ice cracking.

"Jessie said to me . . . Well, it doesn't really matter what she said to me, anymore, does it? Just that she loves me. Oh, yes, she was quite clear about that, but she loves Gloria, too. If this were the comics, we'd all go off and raise chickens and live happily ever after. Of course, this way, we run the risk of killing each other first. Either way, deliver me from nonmonogamy," she said brightly. "And from understanding girlfriends, and electric blankets three nights a week, and dinner for one, and from things that go bump in the night."

" '. . . ghoulies and ghosties and things that go bump in the night . . .' " Gail finished for her dryly.

"Yes, indeed, all my little buddies. They're not so bad as they sound, so long as they leave me some hot water in the morning and don't use all my towels. Besides, they keep me company at night." She smiled a silent dare; Gail smiled back, confused.

"It's not funny," Gail said finally.

"Sure it is." Sadie's eyes were studying her the way beggars size up the mark. The look was cold, heartless, deliberate. "I'm the one who bought a handful of promises and pocketful of wishes. She said, 'Come to California. It can be like it used to be.' And I didn't have sense enough not to believe her. Well, now she can't or won't keep the promises and all that leaves me is the wishes, which is to say a pocketful of nothing."

"So why do you do it? Why not just leave and be happy?" Gail asked. It suddenly seemed very important to know, to try to understand. To save her or to protect her. To just make her laugh, really laugh again. Only Sadie wasn't looking at Gail anymore; her eyes were locked on the moon, staring, wide-eyed. The eyes of a fawn frozen in the road under the headlights' glare.

"Gail, I ran out of options and offers," she said after a long pause. "How do I know what I'd end up with would be any better than what I'm already living? Do you have a guarantee for me, little ghosty? My lovely little ghosty that I very much want to spend the night with." She reached her lips to Gail's, her fingers all the while exploring. Burying her face between Gail's breasts, she sighed deeply. "All my life people thought I was taking them for a ride, and it never was that way at all. It always was the other way 'round. See what I mean? Funny." She smiled a little and began to sing, "I yam what I yam," then closed her eyes, inhaling the scent of the night on Gail.

Closing her arms around Sadie, Gail rocked her gently. I'll take her home, Gail decided in that moment, take care of her, let her take care of me. I'll love her and not let anybody ever hurt her again. Gail moaned slightly and bent to kiss Sadie's throat. Sadie turned to kiss her back, this time in earnest, her arms locked around Gail's neck. They stayed that way for what seemed to be a long time, and then as if she could read Gail's thoughts, Sadie pulled back and smiled at her.

"Cold," she lied. "Let's go back inside." Sadie took Gail's

hand and led her through the door. She was buoyant, humming, bouncing as she made her way to the bar. Then she stopped short, staring across the room. "What's over there that's got you so interested?" Gail teased, turning on her very best smile, her hand on Sadie's waist. Sadie barely heard her, though, just nodded, her eyes narrowing. Nothing unusual, just a couple of women pulling up chairs at a table by the bar. One of the women raised her eyes and looked hard at Sadie, then tilted her head a little, smiled, and possessively dropped her hand on the arm of the woman next to her.

"She shouldn't wear black," Sadie said absently, "doesn't do a thing for her." Confused, Gail looked at the woman who was whispering into her companion's ear. Sadie's voice sounded strained, bitter, but quick and unconcerned, too, as if she were talking about the weather. "Red, she should wear red, better color for her, don't you think?" Gail nodded, not caring what color the woman wore, just wishing Sadie would stop staring at her.

"Is that Jessie?" Gail finally whispered.

Sadie smiled brightly, her hand gently stroking Gail's cheek. She shook her head. "No, my darling. *That* is Gloria. The one in the leather jacket is Jessie. The leather jacket I gave her for our anniversary. Our very happy anniversary." She smiled evilly and climbed onto a bar stool, one strategically placed so she could watch Gloria and Jessie in the mirror.

Embarrassed or guilty, it was hard to tell which, Jessie kept studying her own hands, then the tabletop for what seemed like an eternity. Finally, she looked up and caught Sadie's eyes in the mirror wearing this dark, sad, almost pleading look. Sadie trembled as if a night wind had suddenly swept across the bar. A single tear fell untended on the bar.

"She said that if I loved her I'd understand. Well, I love her and I don't understand." Her voice trailed to a whisper; her eyes dropped to the little ring of tears her glass left on the bar. Picking up one of the napkins, she dabbed at the moisture left behind.

"And that is the reality of my life," Sadie finally said, taking a long breath. Only, her voice was flat, as if something deep inside her was frozen, and she was trying very hard not to cry. "Usually this doesn't happen, us in the same place and all." She nodded toward Jessie and Gloria. "Even so, you'd think I'd get used to the hurt after a while, wouldn't you? Used to always coming in second, being left out?" Gail nodded even though Sadie was talking more to the mirror.

"Well, Sadie, I guess we better get this show on the road," she said quietly, as if she'd forgotten about Gail.

"Hey, Sadie," Gail said, desperately trying to recapture what they'd had in the parking lot, hoping to bring Sadie back. "How about another sunrise? On the house."

"Maybe some other time, my pretty little ghosty," Sadie answered, still smiling, but her voice was heavy and tired. Sadie pulled a pair of kid driving gloves from the same pocket where she kept the little vial and smoothed them, studying the leather. Jessie was watching closely, but Sadie wasn't looking in the mirror anymore. Maybe she needed to stop seeing Gloria all snuggled up against the leather jacket, smiling up, cute and coy, and all the while stealing glances in the mirror—just in case Sadie might be watching. Or maybe Sadie just couldn't bear to see what was waiting there beyond the looking glass.

Sadie produced a few folded bills and pushed them across the bar, smiling. She started to pull on the gloves, but then, as if thinking better of it, tucked them loosely in her pocket. One fell to the floor, unnoticed. "Thanks for the memories, Gail," Sadie said, moving toward the door.

"Sadie, wait!" Gail called after her. She wanted to scream, Wait for me! Give me your phone number or call me. Or just come back to the bar. Instead, she made a little half-salute. Sadie smiled back.

"Maybe some other night," Sadie whispered, pressing a pair of fingers to her lips, then toward Gail.

"Sadie, you got a million-dollar smile," Gail said.

"Sure." She laughed a little. "And that and a buck'll get me a beer. Right?"

"Right," Gail said, then, "You going to be okay?"

"Sure," Sadie answered, her voice trembling and a little too light. "I'm always okay—just like Popeye." She tried to smile, to hum "I yam what I yam," but her lower lip was shaking so that all she could do was bite it hard and take a deep breath. She looked at Gail for a long moment, then walked quickly to the door. But her back was a little too straight, her step a little too quick.

"Take care of yourself," Gail called after her, but Sadie probably didn't hear.

And across the room, the woman in leather looked as if she was watching a kitten freeze in the snow.

Shadows in the Looking Glass

Shadow slipped into her favorite darkened corner and vanished. She did it so easily and so well that she no longer pondered how she became invisible or even why. It was as natural for her as breathing, as unpremeditated as a heartbeat.

Mostly, she considered her invisible state to be accidental providence, stumbled on so long ago she could no longer remember when it first began nor point to a date on a yellowed calendar and announce, "That's it! That's the first time I vanished." Not that anyone would ever ask; when you're invisible, nobody ever asks anything of you or expects anything in return. That was the best part of what she eventually came to consider an ideal, although sometimes admittedly bothersome, condition.

The worst of times, which she came to believe were far better than even the best of times that she'd ever known before, were in restaurants. Waitresses kept looking through her when it was time to order, but magically rose up, surrounding her like a herd of dragons, whenever she tried to fade out the door without paying the check. Bars were different, though: Dark secrets that were so very easy to slip into fermented there like wine waiting for its season. Babe's was like that—full of private corners where Shadow could sit and listen to the music and watch Matty, Babe's manager, who could be found most evenings behind the bar.

At first, Shadow had been content to sit in the deserted twilight of the bar's corners, huddled there like a squirrel cautiously watching the hound's approach. Silently, breathlessly she'd waited for those few times Matty moved past her, coming so close Shadow could smell her perfume: Chanel No. 5. She'd spent most of one afternoon at a perfume counter sniffing all the different bottles until she found the one that had Matty in it. That tiny bottle cost Shadow's lunch money for a month, but it was worth it to be able to carry a little part of Matty's beauty with her. Just before she went to bed in her rented room in the women's residential hotel—which advertised itself as being near theater and shopping, although Shadow was interested in neither—she opened the bottle and set free a drop of the golden essence on her pillow, hoping she would dream of Matty. Sometimes she did.

Eventually, familiarity turned the bar less foreboding and Shadow was even brave enough to claim a small table—still away from the stream of bar traffic and sounds, but within view of the dance floor and the pool tables and, most important, the main bar, where Matty moved with the grace of a dancer. There, Shadow penned verses about the sea and magic butterflies, and the starbursts that exploded across the crescent of Matty's breasts. And then before stealing back into the night, she carefully wrote Matty's name on the folded piece of paper before tucking it under the ashtray on the little table. Even though she didn't smoke, Shadow always took a single cigarette out of the package she'd brought with her, lit it, then carefully extinguished it in the ashtray, just so the note would be found. She knew Matty found the poems—at least she hoped so.

After a while, Shadow started finding excuses to go to the bar more often. Her favorite night was Wednesday, when Babe and the softball players didn't come by until late. Shadow was content to sit at what she thought of as *her* table, just out of the mirror's vicious reach but close enough to watch the little tattooed stars rise and fall on the horizon of Matty's cleavage while she laughed and poured drinks and flirted with all the other women perched along the bar's rim. Shadow liked to imagine she was one of those lucky few basking in Matty's glow. But if that ever happened, would it mean she was no longer invisible? Shadow didn't know and decided better no Matty than to go through it all again. It hadn't been easy learning how to vanish, and now that she was finally good at it, didn't seem the time to stop.

Then one Wednesday night, the bar was empty except for Matty and three beer-drinking pool players in the back room. The little twinkling lights danced the length of the mahogany bar, uninterrupted by human hands or elbows. The mirror was a clear cascade of icy color. So beautiful, Shadow thought, just like 2:00 A.M. Christmas morning in Union Square—all the lights shining and not a soul around. Smiling at the memory, she stepped back to get a better look when a sweet voice pulled her back. For the first time in almost as long as she could remember, Shadow forgot about being invisible.

"Why don't you pull up a chair and join me?" The voice came from Shadow's favorite darkened table. Matty's voice. She'd heard it so many times saying those words in her mind that Shadow was sure she was hallucinating. She laughed, shaking her head slightly, when the voice came again. "Come on, sit down. I don't bite, you know." Shadow's heart began to pound and she froze, almost trembling, trying desperately to remember how to disappear, all the time knowing it was too late. Chanel No. 5 drifted up to meet her as she turned, then stumbled into the chair Matty had pushed out with one high-heeled boot. "By the way, what'll you have?"

Already, Matty was starting to rise from the table, to move across the floor toward the icy twinkles. Shadow exhaled slowly. She was invisible after all. Matty didn't really see her. Then she realized with a sudden start that green eyes were burning into her, waiting for some sort of reply. Shadow opened and closed her mouth half a dozen times, trying to decide what to say. No one in Babe's had ever asked her anything before.

"Is that your fish impression?" Matty was laughing, waiting for Shadow to either take life or take flight, anything but opening and closing her mouth. "What do you want to drink?" Matty's words came out slowly, carefully, as if she were talking to someone from another planet. "You do want a drink, don't you?" Matty was as confused by this haunting woman as Shadow was at being asked a question.

Shadow's mind raced. She didn't drink. It never really occurred to her to actually buy a drink in the bar. All these months she'd been content to listen to the music and watch Matty and the other women. Certainly, it had never come up before. Every other night, she'd simply found a half-empty glass and put it in front of her. But now Matty expected her to actually order something. Visions of all the drinks she'd ever heard of tumbled across Shadow's mind. The only drink she could ever remember having was a sloe gin fizz one time after

the high school prom. She remembered it tasted like strawberry soda pop.

"A sloe gin fizz," she said finally, very carefully, hoping she
had the name right, that it wasn't just something she imagined
remembering.

"Well, we don't get many orders for those, but I'll see what
I can do," and with that Matty was gone, moving behind the
bar, taking down bottles and glasses, humming in time to the
music while she worked. Shadow, overcome with her good fortune, watched Matty closely. She was, Shadow decided, the
most beautiful woman she'd ever seen. A storm of passionately
red hair curled and flowed down across Matty's shoulders. Rich
heavy breasts moved free under a shirt the color of the forest
floor. The cascade of stars shone beyond a half-dozen brazenly
open buttons. A velvet vest with scenes of stars and mountains
shimmered in the flickering light. Tight black jeans tucked into
tall boots defined long legs, slightly spreading hips. Shadow was
sure she was gazing on a goddess at work.

For the first time in a very long time, Shadow turned and
looked at her own reflection in the mirror. A wan young woman
with giant brown eyes peered at her intently. Shadow studied
the woman in the mirror, trying to see her through Matty's
eyes. Brown hair hung straight to her chin, no remnants of a
stylist's magic wand left there. Pale skin, even paler in the dim
bar light, seemed to stretch too tightly over high cheekbones
and long fragile fingers. Corduroy jeans two sizes too big only
accentuated her thinness. The reflection pulled herself deeper
into a baggy brown jacket as if she was trying to hide. She
reminded Shadow of a sparrow after a summer rain, all speck-
led and pitiful, and she felt like a trespasser in someone's soul.
Quickly averting her eyes, she turned her attention back to the
bar, to Matty's confident stride as she moved across the room.

"So, I'm Matty. Who are you?" The voice sounded like the
women on Sunday-night public television, all from someplace
very far away that Shadow thought she should remember but
would never know.

"Where are you from?" Shadow heard a voice that sounded
very like her own ask this woman who set the drink in front
of her. She couldn't let Matty know that she was stalling for
time, rummaging through her pockets, trying desperately to
come up with more than a bus pass and a library card.

"You don't waste any time do you?" Matty settled back in

the chair, poured some white wine out of the carafe in front of her into a half-empty glass. "Do you use that line on all the girls or just us lucky ones?" Shadow heard the teasing lilt in Matty's voice, saw her warm smile, and smiled back.

"I just wondered. Your voice, I mean."

"Would you believe me if I said L.A.?" Matty, who was still smiling, winked at Shadow, who shook her head. "It's true, or at least since I was six years old. Before that, me folks and me brothers and sisters come from what you Yanks call the 'Emerald Isle.' " The voice descended into a deep Irish brogue, so thick it made Shadow giggle. "It gets 'em every time." Matty's own voice was back again. "I only bring the other me out for St. Paddy's day, you know. Goes good with the green beer."

Shadow very much wanted to learn how this woman could change her voice back and forth. "You should be a movie star," Shadow blurted, surprised at her own daring. "I mean the way you do that . . . with your voice." Matty was laughing, this time in earnest, as if Shadow was telling the funniest joke she'd ever heard.

Shadow looked into her drink, trying to choke back the tears, then raised the glass and took a gulp. The sweet fizz caught in her throat, though, and she started to cough and wheeze, gasping for breath, until Matty was beating her on the back, fighting back another frenzied attack of laughter.

"I'm sorry, honey, it's been a rough day," Matty apologized when Shadow was finally breathing again. "Now, let's start over. I'm Matty and you are . . ."

"Shadow." The voice sounded very far away, so far away Shadow wondered if she were disappearing again, right before Matty's eyes. For the first time, she didn't want that to happen.

"Shadow? Okay, Shadow, it's nice to meet you. I've never met a shadow before. Did your mom name you that or did you pick it out yourself?" Matty seemed genuinely interested and Shadow began to bask in the attention. She couldn't remember the last time anyone had ever even looked at her closely, or if she had ever wanted anyone to look at her at all. Yet here she was, smiling and talking to Matty, even drinking, just like she'd always seen the other women do. It was a wonderful feeling, one she'd pushed so far back in her mind it was only a vague recollection of another life, another time, another woman named not Shadow but Marla.

Marla would have known what to do, how to act, Shadow

thought. Marla wouldn't be sitting here in baggy clothes that didn't match, drooping hair, scruffy shoes, not being able to figure out what to say next. Shadow hadn't thought about Marla in a long time, so long it might have been forever. The last time she had seen Marla, in fact, was right before she'd walked out of the apartment with a backpack and not much else. But she could still hear Marla's mocking laugh following her down the stairs as Shadow stepped into the world to start her new life all alone. And while she couldn't remember much about what happened before or after Marla, those few weeks with her hung like icicles in Shadow's mind.

"Marla gave it to me," Shadow finally confided. She'd never actually told anyone that before. At first, she'd tried, but nobody seemed to understand. Finally, she'd stopped trying. She wondered if Matty would understand, if anyone really could ever understand how Shadow stopped being Marla and just disappeared one day, faded into the shadows. That was where the name came from. Picking it had been easy enough: She didn't have to find an exotic animal or ancient goddess or some strange land her ancestors might have trod a thousand generations ago. She simply called herself what she had become: Shadow.

It had all started while she was in the shower one morning. Before that, everything had seemed normal enough. But when she stepped out of the shower and was getting ready to brush her teeth, she noticed a naked stranger standing there in her bathroom. Of all the things she'd ever expected to find in her bathroom at 7:30 A.M., a naked stranger was not one of them. Shadow distinctly remembered it was a Wednesday because that was the day she always wore—or had before she disappeared—her navy-blue suit to the staff meetings with Mr. Hastings.

On Wednesdays all the women in the firm—although she could no longer remember what it was everyone was firm about—wore navy-blue suits to meet with the junior partners, who wore navy-blue suits, too. Shadow liked to imagine that somewhere in the blue and white binder she'd found on her desk the first day she'd started work at the firm, there was a rule that read: "On Wednesdays, everybody will wear navy-blue suits." She never found the rule but bought the suit anyway. It seemed like the thing to do at the time.

It was that suit that affixed Marla's arrival in Shadow's

mind. It had been hanging just beyond the bathroom door, where the naked woman was standing, staring at Shadow and, she would realize later, laughing. Shadow had blinked once, then closed her eyes for a very long second, and promised herself she'd be alone when she saw light again. She wasn't.

"Who are you and what do you want?" she asked, mustering up all her courage, although years later when it all seemed beautifully normal, she would no longer be able to remember why she was frightened that first time. "Who are *you* and what do *you* want?" the stranger replied. The voice sounded a little hysterical.

"I live here," Shadow answered the question quickly, irritated that the woman was already pulling her toothbrush from its little chrome holder. "And you're using my toothbrush!" Later, Shadow regretted that last comment. Her mother had always taught her to be gracious and, above all else, to share. She wondered if uninvited naked strangers counted, even in her mother's perverse view of transplanted Southern hospitality.

But the stranger, never blinking, looked straight at Shadow and replied, "*I* live here and you're using *my* toothbrush." Shadow looked down. To be sure, she was holding a toothbrush in her right hand. Shadow assumed it was her toothbrush, but this woman seemed so sure of herself, her rights, her belongings, maybe it was her toothbrush after all. Shadow quickly tucked it back in the holder and hurried into the bedroom, hoping the stranger wouldn't follow.

It was unnerving. Each time she asked the woman a question, the answer came so quickly Shadow was sure that somehow this strange woman really did belong here and she, Shadow, was the intruder. When Shadow opened the closet door, there was the woman again, still naked, but this time fingering the white silk blouse that went with the navy-blue suit, taking the silk slip with the heavy lace insets, stockings, even underwear out of the bureau drawers as if she not only knew exactly where everything was but had every right to those things. Finally Shadow settled into the chair to watch the woman dress. She had to admit the stranger looked very nice in the clothes. The slim skirt and high heels accentuated her long legs. High cheekbones and big dark eyes were framed by the shiny brown hair so carefully turned and curled it was obviously well-tended by stylists.

"That's my blue suit. I wear it always on Wednesdays to meet with Mr. Hastings," Shadow confided from her perch.

"That's *my* blue suit. *I* wear it always on Wednesdays to meet with Mr. Hastings," the stranger replied, squirting perfume on her wrists, then stepping away from the mirror where she had so carefully been dressing. Shadow was puzzled. How did this woman know Mr. Hastings? Had she seen her at work? Perhaps that was why the woman looked so familiar? But before Shadow could ask, the woman was gone.

At first, Shadow had been distressed by the incident—the way this stranger seemed to come and go with such familiarity, such abandon through her life. The woman was absolutely shameless: entertaining her friends in Shadow's bed, mindless of whether her unwilling hostess had an early meeting with Mr. Hastings; buying clothes, pieces of jewelry, even exotic plants, then leaving the things lying about the apartment. At first, Shadow had mistaken them for gifts, tokens of appreciation for her hospitality. She didn't realize until the bills came that this stranger had somehow obtained a key to her life, her finances, her very being.

"I don't know who you are anymore, if I ever did," Shadow finally announced one morning while the stranger was, as usual, naked as a jaybird and brushing her teeth with Shadow's toothbrush. "And I wish you'd get your own damned toothbrush," she started to add, but then thought better of it.

"I don't know who *you* are anymore, if *I* ever did," the woman answered, her words strangely muffled by the toothbrush but her eyes flashing in anger.

Shadow settled into her chair and watched while the woman took out her very best forty-dollars-on-sale slip. The stranger had invaded Shadow's closets that first day and her appetite was by now insatiable.

"Do you like it here?" Shadow finally asked, for she was, despite all the aggravation, beginning to grow almost fond, certainly tolerant, of this familiar intruder.

"Do *you* like it here?" the woman asked, looking hard at Shadow, who was beginning to think this stranger made a lot of sense. There was, after all, something to be said for those rare beings who are of like minds.

"I can't stand the reality of my life," Shadow said, never realizing the words took voice only in her own mind. She waited for the woman's reply, but none came. "I don't even know how it happened." The words splashed and spilled across her mind, but the room remained silent as a stone. "One day I was in school, happy, in love. You know, just regular life, only mine was this big silver balloon, the kind you see at fairs, the kind mothers always tie to the wrists of their children so the balloon won't get away, so the kid won't cry as it sails off into the universe. Then it all started to go sour.

"At first, it was like bad cream: just a few little curdles, but still okay to use. Then a little more time passes and it goes a little more sour. Every day it gets worse and worse and there's nothing you can do to stop it." The words kept spilling across Shadow's thoughts, given voice only in great, gut-wrenching sobs that sent torrents spilling out of her eyes, across her cheeks. She cried as she hadn't cried since she was the girl nobody bothered to ask to the sophomore dance, cried as if her very heart would burst from her chest, squirting blood across the room's white walls.

Shadow raised her eyes to see the woman's reaction and noted, with a start, that she, too, was sitting on the bed, still in her slip, crying. She's not so bad after all, Shadow suddenly decided, except for being greedy and wanting to wear all my best clothes and never bothering to apologize when she spills wine on a scarf or dribbles clam juice on a lapel.

And then, Shadow was laughing because it was all so funny. A strange woman who just appeared in her bathroom one morning had taken her place and nobody had noticed. Not Richard, the doorman of the apartment building. Not Woody, the newspaper vendor on the corner. Not even Mr. Hastings at the Wednesday-morning meetings. The idea of Mr. Hastings sitting behind his big ugly antique oak desk, droning on and on—about what, Shadow could no longer remember—to a total stranger was very funny. And when Shadow looked up, the woman was laughing, too. The vision was as sobering as a cold shower. What right did this strange woman have to laugh at her? What right did Mr. Hastings have not to even notice?

"I want out," the words were barely a whisper, so soft they drifted into the room, lost, falling from all but silent lips. "How do I get out?" she asked the woman who was by now trying to repair the not-so-waterproof mascara.

"How do *I* get out?" the strange woman asked Shadow, dabbing at her left eye.

"The same way you got in here," Shadow wanted to scream,

but decided there was no point in being rude after all the two of them had been through. The woman went back to repairing the sodden makeup, preparing, Shadow imagined, for the Wednesday-morning meeting.

"If you want out, just go. What's stopping you?" Shadow finally said. After all, she thought, what had she expected? Surely this woman wouldn't want to go on like this forever? Still, what right did she have to be looking for a quick escape? And after all Shadow had done for her, too.

"If *you* want out, just go. What's stopping *you*?" the woman asked.

Easy enough for her to say, Shadow thought. After all, she's the one who's run up the bills, ruined ties and blazers, turned the place upside down with her girlfriends and dinner parties— always leaving the mess for somebody else to clean up. Still, it was true. She could go. Just walk out. Good-bye, Mr. Hastings, whoever you are. Good-bye, firm, whatever you are. Even good-bye, Marla. That was what the strange woman called herself. *She even took my name,* Shadow had written in her diary a few days after the stranger had confided that her name, too, was Marla. Since they couldn't possibly both be Marla, and the stranger was so sure of herself, Shadow had begun to doubt her own existence.

Lost in thought, Shadow barely noticed that the woman in the mirror had stopped putting on makeup, unplugged the curling iron, and sat down on the chair, square on Shadow's lap. Any other Wednesday morning, Shadow would have let Marla sink into her, but this time, she suddenly stood up, dumping her brazen guest on the floor. Without looking back, Shadow marched into the living room, pulled off the slip, jerked on a pair of jeans, and began rummaging through closets for the backpack she hadn't touched since college.

Careful to stay away from the mirrors, which always attracted Marla, Shadow stuffed the pack with socks and jeans, sweaters and underwear. It was then the revelation hit her: If she wants to be me, Shadow thought, then I can be anybody else at all, or even nobody. And she knew it was true.

One last time, she hurried into the bedroom, peeked around the corner of the closet door, and, sure enough, saw Marla's smiling face waiting there for her. Shadow smiled then, too. "You'll probably do okay without me," Shadow said, trying to contain a giggle.

"You'll probably do okay without *me,"* the woman replied, peering deep into the shadows as if she were looking for something as fleeting as a moonbeam.

"Well, so long," Shadow called over her shoulder, never waiting for the reply, letting the door slam behind her, rattling the mirrors on the wall until she was sure she could hear Marla's laugh following her down the hall to the elevator.

For a long time after that, Shadow was sure Marla had followed her. In the first days, then weeks, finally even months, Shadow would see Marla standing just behind her in the reflections of store windows, sometimes even in the mirror at Babe's. As time passed, Shadow noticed she was alone more often, until finally, when she sought out her reflection, Marla was gone.

That was when Shadow had first understood she could be visible sometimes, too. Still, she kept her new invisible job—in a typing pool in a huge company where all the executive women wore navy-blue suits on Thursday; Shadow wore a red kimono and jeans. She got raises because she could spell and nobody minded if she sat on the fire escape and wrote poems instead of eating lunch with the other typists in the company cafeteria. Once, they'd even tried to send her to night school to learn word processing. Shadow had replied you were supposed to process food not words. Nobody asked again.

Even now, when she sometimes was perched in a corner of the couch in the ladies room—the one the typing pool shared with the women in blue suits who sat in little glassed-in offices—Shadow would watch a woman in a navy-blue suit tying and retying a silk scarf, looking hard into the mirror, trying to smile at a reflection Shadow knew the woman couldn't quite see.

How could Matty understand any of it? How could anyone, really? No one else had ever understood. Not the white-jacketed men with all their pills and machines. Not the women with their clipboards and pencils. Shadow had talked and they had nodded until finally, one day, Shadow had just drifted away, out across the yard, down through the gate, out to the highway, into a passing truck, and she was gone. No one had missed her, she was sure of that, for how do you miss a shadow? And now she was here with Matty, listening to bartender stories.

"You want another one of those?" Matty was saying, nodding toward Shadow's empty glass. Shadow didn't even remember drinking the sweet fizz, but it was gone. Her fingers closed around the bus pass, the library card, the lint in her pocket, and nothing else. She shook her head miserably. What would happen when Matty found out she'd ordered something she couldn't pay for? Flashes of Matty scowling, dialing the phone, calling the police, having Shadow taken away surged across her brain. A few tears escaped as Shadow huddled deeper into her jacket.

"Honey, what's the matter?" Matty was reaching across the table, brushing Shadow's hair back. Her hand was cool, soft, just like Shadow had always known it would be.

"I don't," Shadow began, but great sobs broke her words, "have any money. *Please* don't call the police."

"The police!" Matty's eyes widened, astonished. If Babe's was struck by lightning and then invaded by street gangs, nobody would call the police, didn't this girl know that? "Shadow, honey, it's okay. Really. Nobody's going to call the police. Besides, I didn't ask you for money; I asked you if you wanted another drink. I never figured you for a Rockefeller." Matty was smiling. "Anyway, I guess I owe you a couple of drinks, after all those poems you wrote for me."

"You knew?" Shadow was trying hard to focus through tear-dimmed eyes. "You got them?"

Matty nodded, then smiled. "Every Wednesday night for six months, I'd get a poem that smelled like Chanel. It's my brand, you know."

"I know," Shadow answered, then smiled back. "But how did you know it was me?"

"Oh, me and Mickey Spillane got our ways of keepin' our eyes on the dolls."

"Who?"

"Never mind." Matty's eyes were laughing again and Shadow felt warmed by the glow. "Now, let's get on over to the bar before somebody else shows up and thinks there's nobody home. I'm a working girl, you know." Matty led Shadow across the room and sat her down at the bar, square in front of the big mirror. Shadow looked into it and smiled. Her own reflection smiled back.

Every Saturday evening after that at precisely seven o'clock, Shadow slipped onto her favorite stool in the corner of the bar, ordered a sloe gin fizz, and settled back to watch the women, listen to the music, feel her spirits dance with the little twinkling lights. And exactly three hours later when Matty took her turn at the door, Shadow slipped back off the stool and into the night. But only after she solemnly folded a little square of pink stationery scented with Chanel No. 5 and placed it under an ashtray that magnified the word *Matty* encased in its hand-drawn heart. Nobody ever asked for anything more.

The Changer and the Changed

Matty O'Donnell was a beautiful woman, and that was the crux of the problem. Things might have turned out differently if she hadn't been a lesbian or a feminist, or if it hadn't been 1978, a time of innocence and anger, an unkind world for the vaunted and the vain. Certainly it would have been different if she could only have beaten down her beauty, battered it, denied it, or even ignored it. But she couldn't or wouldn't do any of those things and so Matty O'Donnell was destined to be seen as little more than a heretic. The real tragedy was that years would pass before she really understood why.

Looking back from the luxury of time, it's easy enough to see that she was simply a woman who stepped too close to the line. In another place in time, it all might have seemed unimportant, even silly to care so much about hair or a splash of perfume. But Matty O'Donnell was a beauty in the days when real lesbians were beyond it all—or thought they were.

Real lesbians shaved their heads or said they wanted to. And made love a political statement. And didn't let their eyes linger too hungry or too long on an uplifted bare breast exposed to the sun, or never admitted it if they did. Real lesbians knew hatred because so much of it had cauterized their hearts. And fear because so much evil had slashed through their lives. Real lesbians thought they were following a road no one had traveled before. They dreamed and loved and wanted more than they could believe was ever possible before. Real lesbians were building the new order of sisterhood. And real lesbians knew one another so little and so well.

1978

Matty O'Donnell knew she was a real lesbian when she first walked into Babe's one August afternoon in 1978. Folded in her back pocket was the yellow index card she'd found that morning on the Women's Center bulletin board: Bartender wanted for women's bar. Part-time. No experience necessary. Will train. References. Ask for Babe.

Matty climbed onto a bar stool, ordered a beer, and rechecked her options: She was twenty-two years old with a degree in women's studies that equipped her to do practically nothing, according to the job counselors. The only place she really wanted to work was the Radical Womyn's Center, where she volunteered four mornings a week, but that ran on volunteer labor. Her rent was due in two weeks and all she had left in the bank was $27.32. She took a deep breath and smiled as if she had nothing to lose; she didn't. "Is Babe here?" she asked the bartender, a great black woman with huge hands and wide eyes that seemed deep as the ocean itself. "I'm Matty O'Donnell. I'm here about the job."

The woman nodded and reached for the phone by the cash register. Turning her back to Matty, she mumbled into the receiver, then looked over at Matty and growled, "She wants to know can you wait?" It was a demand more than a question. Matty smiled and nodded. The bartender turned back to the phone. The mumbled conversation resumed, with the bartender glancing at Matty occasionally and chuckling as she mumbled into the receiver. Finally she replaced the phone and set a second beer in front of Matty. "Babe said for you to hang loose, have another beer, make yourself comfortable. I'm Andy." A beefy hand shot across the bar, enveloping Matty's in strength and softness.

"So, Matty O'Donnell, how come you want to be a bartender at Babe's?" Andy boomed, not unkindly. Two months earlier, an accident at the docks had left her temporarily deaf in one ear, so she shouted most of the time.

Matty smiled and shrugged. "You're a bartender."

"Nah, I'm just here to help out Babe. I'll be back at work in a couple months." Andy was more than six feet tall, with iron muscles and an easy smile. All but a few select longshoremen she worked with thought Andy was a regular guy; those who knew otherwise had as much to lose as Andy if the truth leaked out. "Working behind the bar keeps me out of trouble." She winked at Matty. "Besides Babe's okay. Knows what she wants and what she don't. Gotta admire a woman like that, even if you don't always agree with her. Know what I mean?"

Matty nodded automatically. She had no idea what Andy was talking about.

" 'Course bartending ain't nothin' compared to my regular job, still it takes a certain skill. Relating to the customers and all. But you would know that from where you worked before. By the way, where were you before?"

"College," Matty answered simply. "I never worked in a bar . . . or hardly anywhere else."

A laugh as big as Andy herself erupted from the recesses of her chest and rolled across the bar toward Matty. "So what brings you here?" she finally managed. She was still laughing, but her eyes were warm and friendly.

"Because nobody's advertising for revolutionaries in the want ads."

Andy chuckled. "So that's what you are—a revolutionary? I always wondered what one looked like."

"Well, revolutions are obviously attracting a better clientele this year, Andy." Matty turned toward the voice and came face-to-face with Babe Daniels, who looked almost soft and a little dreamy. It was, Matty would learn, how she always looked after lovemaking. Babe winked. Matty smiled. Andy laughed.

In the beginning, Babe and Matty were an unlikely pair. "Women's studies," Babe mumbled, looking over Matty's job application. "You have to go to school to learn that now, do you?" Babe lit a cigarette and sniffed. "Well, I've been studying women most of my life. You need a teacher at that college of yours?" She laughed richly, her eyes twinkling.

Matty tried to smile, to carry the joke. "What is your specialty?" she asked, raising her eyebrows, trying to look studious.

Babe looked at her carefully. Matty was young. Her emerald eyes had seen little enough of the world: enough to know what she wanted but not yet how to get it. She was serious but with a crackle of wit, vitality. Babe winked again. "Pussy."

"*What*?" Matty gasped, her eyes widening, her veneer cracking.

"You heard me," Babe said, smiling, pleased with herself. "Two bucks says you never even took one class in it. Am I right?"

Matty was quick, though. "And I suppose you're going to tutor me?"

"Why? You think you need it?" Babe asked, lowering her eyes to Matty's chest. She was wearing a T-shirt with Virginia Woolf on the chest; her nipples made Virginia's eyeballs bulge. Babe laughed wickedly. Matty blushed and looked at her hands, unable to think of a reply.

Without a word, Babe reached over and took Matty's right hand in her own, looked at its palm closely, then laid it gently back on the bar. After a long moment she asked, "When can you start?"

"Why did you do that?" Matty asked, looking at her hand.

"Just curious," Babe answered. "How about tomorrow night?"

"Can you read palms? What did you see?"

"Nothing much. I'll tell you someday. When we've got more time." Babe winked. The interview had ended. "So, I'll see you tomorrow. About five." She extended her hand to Matty, who shook it. Babe winked. The deal was made.

There was no real reason why Babe should have hired Matty. Except she liked her, and she very much wanted to kiss her. Besides, Matty was different. She had the kind of wild untamed beauty that leaves men and some women humbled, but it wasn't so much the beauty, for Babe had known many beautiful women. No, it was more the hunger that burned, unacknowledged and untended, beneath her surface, an ember gathering power around its core. Babe wanted to touch it, to hold it, to feel that fire before it was lost to time and the wisdom of age.

So, the first week, Babe taught Matty to mix drinks. And the second week, she took her to bed. By the third week, Matty was in love.

Even though Babe and Sharon had moved to a house in the suburbs the year before, Babe still kept the apartment over the bar open—furnished with Goodwill specials—for poker games, she said, although the bedroom was furnished, too. Matty wasn't the first woman Babe had taken to the apartment, but she was by far the most unpredictable. About the time Babe Daniels decided to seduce Matty O'Donnell, Matty decided to convert Babe Daniels to radical lesbian-feminism. She imagined it would be her greatest achievement. Certainly it was her greatest challenge.

Matty had never met a woman like Babe—a woman who brought her flowers and gave her bottles of Chanel No. 5 and pouted when Matty tried to explain why real lesbians didn't wear perfume. A woman who kept a dildo under the pillow and back issues of *Penthouse* under the bed and laughed when Matty patiently explained that real lesbians didn't see other women as sex objects.

Babe, though, had known lots of women like Matty—women who left copies of *Off Our Backs* in the bathroom and organized marches to take back the night; women who wrote articles about how to castrate rapists and how to ensure that the turkey-baster baby was a girl; women who were angry and scared and outraged and determined all at once. Babe had known lots of women like that; she'd just never made love to one before.

In retrospect, getting Matty into bed had been easy. Keeping her politics out was another thing altogether, for Matty was a zealot. Any encouragement—or none at all—was inspiration enough to launch Matty into a nonstop discussion about the contents of the pile of magazines and manifestos, pamphlets and periodicals that she kept on the night table by the bed for easy reference just in case Babe ever had any questions. She almost never did. Still, the pile grew like unspent passion.

One evening, as Matty's skin glowed pink and golden in the candlelight, Babe lay watching her breathe softly on the edge of sleep. The regular rise and fall of her breasts. Freckled, with shockingly pink nipples. Babe had buried her face in those breasts and cried from happiness not an hour before. Her hand moved slowly, barely touching the soft down of Matty's belly, to the wild red curls that glistened damp, like moss. She stroked the fine skin of her thighs, freckled there, too. Matty moaned slightly, opened her eyes, and smiled, shaking her head no. Babe kissed her lightly and pulled herself up in bed, reaching for a Lucky. Matty flicked on the overhead light and began rummaging through a sheaf of papers on the night table. Babe sighed and blew a smoke ring, wishing Matty would forget about the movement just once.

"I brought you that article I told you about," Matty said, her eyes bright with excitement. "Notes on the Etymology and Usage of 'Dyke'." She smiled; Babe rolled her eyes toward the ceiling. "It was in *Sinister Wisdom*," Matty added with an air of finality.

"I know how to use dykes." Babe chuckled. She blew another smoke ring. "In fact most of my—what'd you call it? etymology?—has been in using dykes. By the way, what the fuck is etymology?"

"It's like the history of language," Matty explained absently, her eyes buried in the page. "This is all about what *dyke* means and why."

Babe roared. "I know what it means and why!" She roundly smacked Matty's rump. She liked Matty. She even liked some of her crackpot ideas. And she wasn't as aggravating as most of those political women who showed up in the bar. They weren't any fun; one of them had even told Babe she oppressed women. Never mind that Babe paid her help twice what they could make anywhere else, or that a man hadn't set foot inside the place in years. No, Matty was different, fun—at work and in bed. Babe grinned wickedly and pulled Matty down on top of her. "Let's practice using dykes," she mumbled, feeling Matty warm and naked against her, letting Matty's long hair fall around them, blocking out the light like a curtain.

Later Babe lay on her back watching the room fill with streetlight shadows. Matty was quiet, absorbed in her own thoughts or no thoughts at all as she traced the outline of Babe's skin against the night. She moved her hand gently, stroking up Babe's arm, disturbing the fine down of hair that she could not see. Across her shoulder, the fingers traced, dipping into the hollow of Babe's collarbone, stroking her throat. The fingers might have belonged to a questioning child, so tentatively, so gently did they move. Following a path as familiar as time, they moved down Babe's chest to the chasm between her breasts, which hung like small ripe pears. Pink and gold. Matty flattened her hand then as she stroked Babe's belly, soft but rounded only a little.

Babe had never let Matty make love to her, and Matty very much wanted to feel Babe move under her, to touch her, to have her passion spill out across her hands. Laying her head on Babe's ribs, she could hear her heart beating, loud and regular. Matty lay her hand on the overgrowth of dark hair, soft, curling, feeling the damp warmth against her fingers. She could feel Babe watching her, burning her, or trying to.

"I want you," Matty whispered. "I want to make love to you." She turned her head to look at Babe, who smiled only a little and said nothing. Matty raised her mouth to Babe's, her fingers beginning to probe, to explore.

Babe stiffened, caught her hand, and whispered, "Don't." Only it meant never, not later. "Private property."

"Whose?" Matty said, trying to sound light and teasing. "Yours?"

Babe shook her head and looked at Matty for a long moment, judging her words carefully. "Sharon's. That's just how it is," she finally said, pulling Matty's head down on her chest, petting her, kissing her hair.

Matty felt hot tears burn against her eyes; her throat constricted. She was trying very hard not to cry. "But I thought you wanted me," Matty finally said, her voice trembling with tears. "I could make you happy . . . I could try," she added miserably.

"Shhhhh," Babe whispered, rocking Matty slightly. "I do want you, honey. You do make me happy. Someday you'll understand. Someday things will be different." And Matty took it to mean that one day she and Babe and Sharon would all live together, bound by love. Or even, maybe Babe would leave Sharon. She couldn't have been more wrong.

The truth was that Babe saw no reason why the women who clung to her life like bits of straw should touch her world with Sharon and Tara at all. If Sharon knew about Babe's affairs, she never let on. Matty was special, but she would never be Sharon. Family.

Matty had always known about Sharon but rarely thought of her. Like Babe's old Roller Derby picture that hung behind the bar, Sharon seemed shadowy and distant, a part of Babe's life that wasn't real. It might have remained that way, too, if Babe and the women's movement hadn't formed an uneasy alliance. At Matty's urging, the bar had become the town meeting hall for Saturday-afternoon lectures. In the afternoon, movement leaders and poets found a place on Babe's stage that was taken over by singers and dance bands at night. Mostly, Babe stayed in the background, listening, wondering about the future that was being mapped there in her bar—a future that didn't seem to include her or Sharon or Andy or JoJo or any of the old crowd. And she kept quiet—until the afternoon of Alice Wood.

Speaking in a bar wasn't Alice Wood's first choice, but Matty convinced her it was the only option since the Radical Womyn's Center was crowded into a one-room office and didn't have enough money to rent a hall. Alice was an arid angry woman who had been dismissed from her teaching position at a midwestern state university the year before for openly harassing male students who attempted to register for her classes. A small woman, she pinned her shoulder-length hair at the very top of her head in a tight silver knot that bobbed while she talked—she imagined it made her seem taller. Alice was frequently moved to tears by her own words and so by the end of every lecture, sweat beads and tears soaked her face as her fists pounded out a cadence. Alice Wood was a memorable orator.

But after the adoring had departed, each carrying an autographed copy of at least one of her manifestos, she would dissolve in tears in the arms of her lover—a solid jovial butch who had been her student the year before. The lover was the same age as Alice's daughter, and fond of motorcycles and cigarillos.

If Alice Wood had reservations about speaking in the bar, they paled next to Babe's own reservations at having her there. For weeks, Matty had been stocking the bar with pamphlets announcing Alice's appearance, and had piled the night table with mimeographed copies of the manifestos. Babe hadn't much liked what she'd seen, but Matty had been relentless. Eventually, Babe had given in.

The afternoon of Alice's appearance found as many women crowded into the bar as on a Saturday night. Alice was enough of a draw that Babe considered opening the bar early to catch the overflow crowd. Babe always kept the bar closed during the lecture, but she and a few of the regulars usually sat on the bar stools, sometimes listening, sometimes playing cards. Babe was in her usual place at the end of the bar and Matty was hum-

ming through the room trying to make sure everything was
perfect for Alice when a large beautiful blonde in a velvet
jacket and leather pants that ended in a pair of high-heeled
boots stepped into room. Her hair was deliberately styled, her
fingernails long and, like her face, painted. She smelled of forbidden flower gardens. "There are seats at the back," Matty
whispered, anxious for the woman to sit down before anyone
noticed her. "We're about to start." The woman just smiled.

"I'll just sit at the bar," she answered softly, although there
was no real reason to whisper, and headed toward the bar,
where she slipped onto the stool next to Babe, kissed her
lightly, and leaned back against the bar, smiling. When Babe
leaned close to her to whisper, her arm draped easily across the
blonde's shoulder. When they smiled at each other, it was a
familiar smile, a lovers' smile. Babe kept her arm around the
woman's shoulders.

Sharon hissed a knowing whisper inside Matty's head. In
all the months Matty had been working at the bar, Sharon had
never come in. But Matty had always known how it would be
when they finally met. Babe would take Matty by the hand and
introduce her to Sharon. *"This is Matty,"* she would say. Her
eyes would be smiling. *"I've asked her to come and live with us
and she's agreed!"* And Sharon would leap up, her face beaming, take Matty's other hand, and kiss her lightly on both
cheeks. *"Babe has told me so much about you,"* she'd say. *"I'm
so glad you're joining us. Tara will be so thrilled to have another mother."* And the three of them would hug, holding nothing back. *"We're so lucky,"* they would agree.

Only, Babe seemed to have forgotten Matty was even there.
Instead, she and Sharon were talking together, laughing, waiting for Alice Wood to take the stage. Deadly curiosity drove
Matty from her front-row seat to the back of the bar where she
could watch Babe and Sharon. During the lecture, Babe raised
her eyes to meet Matty's only once and even then she couldn't
read them. It was as if Babe had locked herself far away. On
the stage, Alice Wood was delivering highlights from her newest manifesto: *Butches and Femmes: The Real Enemies of Lesbian-Feminism.* As the talk neared its conclusion, Alice was
openly weeping. Her hands shook as she tried to turn the pages.
In frustration, she grabbed up the pages in her clenched fist and
waved them over her head. Her voice trembled. Her hair came
unleashed and fell wildly around her shoulders.

From her seat at the bar, Babe leaned forward, listening intently, her fist clenching and unclenching. Sharon had turned her back on the speaker and was studying her hands intently. She was trying, Matty thought, not to cry. Finally, Alice's voice rose, her words spun to a crescendo, and she looked as if she might collapse on the lectern. The room held its breath, then Alice pulled herself up, smoothed her hair, wiped her brow, and took a deep breath. The room sighed and waited.

Babe dropped off the bar stool, walked to the center of the room, and demanded, "Sounds to me like all your fancy labels are good for is to try and make us respectable. You ashamed of what you are, lady?" The room was silent for a long moment, then a titter started from the back and moved across the crowd. Alice Wood clenched a half-filled glass of water. Her eyes swept the audience. A long moment passed. Finally, she smiled.

"Does anyone have any questions?" she asked. An audible gasp shuddered through the audience, followed by silence.

"Why won't you answer her?" Sharon's voice came from the back of the room, clear and crisp, without emotion. Then she was standing next to Babe, her manicured hand resting lightly on her lover's shoulder.

The room rustled slightly as Alice leveled her gaze on the women in the front of the room. "You have a question?" she asked a young woman in the middle of the second row. The young woman cast her eyes helplessly around her, then to Alice, who was still smiling. The young woman could think of nothing to say; she shook her head miserably.

"I have a question, Alice," Matty said, stepping from the shadows. Alice smiled, visibly relieved, and nodded. "Why won't you answer Babe?" The audience was beginning to stir; Matty O'Donnell was on the wrong side of the fray.

Alice dabbed her upper lip with the back of her hand. Then, meeting Matty's eyes, she formed her words carefully. "We must fight the patriarchy's pawns wherever we find them . . . and in whatever form."

"Answer my goddamned question!" Babe shouted. "Or did you forget it already?"

"Sexism is insidious. On page twenty-three of my manifesto, as I have discussed . . ."

"Answer the question!" Sharon demanded, cutting off Alice.

"Answer the question!" Andy had taken up the cry. Then

Matty. But it was an isolated chant. The room was beginning to quake with unrest. Some of the women turned to openly gape at Babe and Sharon, who continued to stand arm in arm in the center of the room. Others looked at each other with questioning eyes. Still others shuffled their feet and looked uncomfortably at the floor.

"That concludes the question period," Alice abruptly announced, stepping from the stage and disappearing into the crowd that quickly swallowed her, leaving Sharon and Babe and, for the first time, even Matty, standing on the outside. Babe's face was purple with rage; Sharon was trembling. Matty moved back into the shadows.

After closing that night, Babe and Matty were finally alone for the first time that day. Matty sat at the far end of the bar trying to sort out all that had happened. Babe had refused to talk about the incident all night. Finally, Matty gathered her courage and ventured, "Alice didn't mean anything personal. She doesn't know you—what you're really like. She didn't mean you."

"Who the fuck do you think she meant?" Babe asked, her back to Matty, her words acrid.

"She meant women like . . . like . . ." Matty stumbled over her words, trying to think of an example that wouldn't offend Babe and coming up empty. Ending miserably, she added, "She didn't mean you."

"Maybe she meant Andy? Or Sharon?" Babe asked viciously, turning to face Matty for the first time. "Or . . . you." Her face was dark and angry.

Matty blanched. Surely Babe knew Matty wasn't anything at all like Sharon, or those other women Alice was talking about. She had to make Babe understand; if she never understood anything else, she had to understand this. Matty formed her words slowly, carefully. "Alice isn't like you think, really. Her theories are so . . . she's so . . . she wants us to be so . . . politically . . . pure," Matty finally offered, hopefully.

"Alice's theories are pure all right. Pure shit! She don't like how I look, so I'm a sexist oppressor of women. I believe that's what Alice said wasn't it, or did I miss something? And Sharon. She's the pawn of the patriarchy. Let me tell you a little something about us. When I bought this place, it took every dime Sharon and I could put together. She was working days and going to night school. But every goddamned morning before the sun was up, Sharon came downstairs—we were still living up-stairs then—to scrub the johns. How many bar johns has Alice Wood scrubbed before she went to work for some asshole who could spend more on one lunch than he paid his help for a week's work?"

Matty looked at Babe, her eyes welling with tears. Why wouldn't Babe listen? Why couldn't she ever make Babe listen? Alice Wood had a vision for the family of women. Alice loved women; she'd sacrificed so much already. Why couldn't Babe see that? Why wouldn't she join in the struggle? Why couldn't she see this was the dawning of a new age? Instead, Babe only wanted to talk about the bar. The damned bar, as if there was no other life, nothing before it, nothing after it, nothing outside it. As if life began and ended inside the bar.

"I know," Matty agreed, reaching out to touch Babe's arm. "It must have been so hard for you."

"You don't get it, do you? It was hard for all of us. There was nights you could've fired a cannon in here and hit nobody. Not because I was a sexist oppressor of women, but because my customers were scared. Scared of the vice squad. Scared of losing their jobs. Scared of what would happen if the neighbors found out that those nice girls living next door really weren't sisters. Just scared they'd break us . . . or worse."

"But you don't have to be scared anymore. Things are dif-ferent now. Now you can be proud of what . . . of who you are." Matty's eyes were shining. "We're everywhere and the whole world knows we're here to be reckoned with!" At that, Babe shot Matty a hard look and for the first time, Matty felt as if she didn't know Babe at all.

"You girls really think you discovered something, don't you?" Babe was tired. Her leg ached. She was tired of arguing and tired of remembering. Most of all, she was tired of trying to explain what Matty seemed incapable of understanding. Maybe the distance between Babe's reality and Matty's dreams was just too great. Babe sighed. "There's not one damned thing new about us . . . or you either, for that matter. Just a fancier label, so that now everybody's a radical lesbian-feminist, as if that makes us nice and respectable. Only, what you ain't figured out yet is it don't matter. We've always been respect-able and low-down ass-kickers that don't need Alice Wood or anybody else to tell us what to do or how to do it. We're respect-able because we survived. And we survived because we knew how to kick ass. And we'll be here long after Alice and the rest of 'em has gone home." Babe closed her eyes for a long moment, remembering.

"It wasn't easy for Alice, either," Matty mumbled. It was common knowledge that Alice Wood had been a professor's wife with three children until four years before when she'd embraced radical feminism. Not long after that she ran away with the assistant women's dean. That made her a lesbian. The rest was history.

"I never said it was," Babe said, softening. "But don't ever think it was easy for me and Sharon or Andy or JoJo or Red or any of us, either. You girls talk about being outcasts? You don't even know what it means. You talk about building a revolution? Well, just remember whose backs this revolution of yours is built on." She turned to the cash register, which opened with a loud *ching*.

"We're all dykes," Matty whispered, her mouth puckering with tears.

"Are we?" Babe asked suspiciously as she scooped out the change. *Dyke* was a word she used only judiciously. She'd never believed one word could ever describe all the different kinds of women who strolled through her bar, her life. Babe Daniels had little use for a word—or an ideal—that reduced all those women to a single common denominator.

"If you'd just try to see Alice's point about . . . about . . ." Matty faltered as if the words would burn her tongue, then all but whispered, "butches and femmes."

Slamming the cash register shut, Babe whirled to face Matty. "What do you think I am?" she hissed. "But more important, what the hell do you think you are?" Babe pulled on her jacket and stomped toward the door.

"Babe, please," Matty whispered. "I didn't mean you." A tear escaped and ran down her cheek. "I didn't mean you."

Matty stayed away from the bar for three days, waiting for Babe to call. She didn't. Finally on the fourth day, Matty swallowed her pride and went back to work. Babe was sitting in her usual spot at the end of the bar, a tarot spread in front of her. "So you're back" was all she said. "I figured you would be."

"The cards told you that?" Matty asked.

Babe shook her head. "Just intuition."

"Do I still have a job?" Babe nodded, waiting. Matty flushed, wishing apologies came more easily. "I'm sorry," she finally began, "I shouldn't have said . . . those things . . . to you."

Babe waved her to silence. "Don't apologize. Apologies don't mean nothing unless you know what it is you're apologizing for."

"We could talk about it," Matty said, wishing Babe would touch her, would take her hand and lead her upstairs. Instead, she reached behind the bar and brought out Matty's collection of papers from the night table, tied together with string. Babe set them on the bar.

"There's nothing to say, Matty. You just don't know who you are. Maybe someday you will, but right now you don't, no more than Alice Wood or the rest of them." Babe folded the cards away, a signal that it was time to get to work. But unspoken words hung heavy in the air between them and nothing was ever quite the same with Matty and Babe after. And they never made love again.

A few months after the Alice Wood incident was buried if not forgotten, Matty and a few pool players were left alone in the bar one hot afternoon in late August. Babe and most of the regulars had chartered a fishing boat. "Going for mermaids," they'd said. The air conditioner had been out for a day, waiting for a part that couldn't be had until Monday. Inside the bar the air hung, thick and stuffy, even with the doors open.

"Hot n' nasty," sang Matty under her breath as she cha-cha-cha'ed behind the bar. She couldn't remember the beat, only the words, which she sang over and over. She unbuttoned the Hawaiian shirt she'd bought that morning at the Goodwill and knotted it under her breasts, which were damp with sweat. She unbraided her hair and piled it on top of her head, securing it with a lavender bandana. A few rebel curls escaped and hung dark and damp against her throat. Still humming, she danced across the room to the jukebox. Linda Tillery could love her in a "special kind of womanly way" or she could be Meg Christian's "sweet darlin' woman." Tough choice, she thought, punching up Holly Near and cha-cha-ing back to the bar and the beer she'd left.

"Well, hello," Matty greeted the woman who was sitting there. "Hot enough for you? You know, I always promise myself every year to get away to the coast or maybe the mountains when this heat starts, but I never make it. What'll it be?" Her smile was wide and warm.

"Apple juice," the woman said. "Unfiltered. On the rocks."

There was something familiar about the new arrival. The

thin shoulders where a bright green hummingbird fluttered, ready to dart under the woman's baggy green T-shirt that had the words KILLER DYKE emblazoned across the front. The tattoo was familiar, Matty thought, trying to place it from among the hundreds of women she saw march through Babe's in a month's time. But where? When? A pewter labyris the size of Matty's fist, hung from a purple ribbon, glowed softly against the woman's chest. And then Matty remembered. She'd seen the woman at Alice Wood's lecture. She was the woman who'd pushed past Matty on her way out the door, muttering angrily.

"Well, it's been a long time . . ." Matty started, extending her hand as she set the juice on the bar. She'd forgotten the woman's name.

"Sarama," the woman answered, ignoring Matty's extended hand and counting out eighty cents. Sarama scowled. Maybe she was angrier than usual because the Equal Rights Amendment still wasn't doing well in Illinois. Or maybe it was because the article she'd submitted on parthenogenesis had been turned down by both *Plexus* and *Big Mama Rag*. Or because her lover had left her the month before for a divorced mother of two boys who lived on a marijuana farm in Humboldt County. Whatever the reason, Sarama fixed her gaze on Matty, taking in the shirt that was dangerously unbuttoned and tied, exposing a flash of midriff, the tight white jeans, and all that hair. Wild red tousled ringlets curled in an untamed ponytail down her back.

"Nice name," Matty offered, leaning against the bar. "One of the goddesses?"

"The mother of the hounds of hell," Samara answered proudly. "Alice Wood helped me find it. You've met Alice, haven't you? I know you have; I saw you here when she spoke."

"Alice is . . . interesting," Matty said. "Very."

"She conducted four workshops at the music festival. I was at them all," Sarama announced, her face glowing. "She's been focusing on how passing oppresses our sisters in struggle. So she shaved her head right there at the workshop. It was wonderful. I have her latest manifesto here." The woman was digging through a canvas daypack. "You should read it."

The words hit their mark, but Matty smiled and accepted the sheaf of papers the woman pushed toward her. "Thanks. It looks . . . interesting." Matty had been organizing a Take Back the Night March, which left little time for reading.

"It's a dollar," said Sarama.

"Of course," replied Matty, digging a dollar out of her jeans. "Well, hey, looks like you're keeping cooler than the rest of us," she said, meaning Sarama's crew cut. "Looks great—cooler than this." Matty gathered up a handful of hair and retied the bandana. Sarama eyed her coldly.

"You should try it," Sarama suggested, only it was more an ultimatum, and her voice was hard. Matty blanched. She knew that after the Alice Wood incident, her loyalties had become suspect, and that when no one could find fault with what she said or did, they focused on her hair. At first it had been a joke, but she was beginning to wonder. After all, real lesbians did not, as Matty's friends pointed out, have hair like Rapunzel. If she would only cut it or do *something* with it. Her enemies were less kind.

"Guess I never thought about it," Matty lied. The truth was she loved her hair, the way it hung soft and curling, how it tickled her back, or sometimes clung damply to her chest after lovemaking, how it glinted like fire in the afternoon sun. But Sarama would understand none of that, so Matty smiled weakly.

"What kind of a lesbian are you, anyway?" Sarama suddenly demanded. She'd come to the bar looking for Babe, hoping to finally avenge the wrong done to Alice. Just because Babe was nowhere in sight didn't mean Matty should escape unchallenged.

"Just your regular card-carrying kind," Matty answered, attempting a halfhearted chuckle.

"Women who pass are supporting the patriarchal oppressor," Sarama announced, with no glint of humor in her eyes. "You should think about that, Matty."

Matty looked at her for a long moment. "Come on, we're all dykes."

Sarama glanced around the bar, her eyes narrowing. "Well, I can vouch for the rest of us." The venom of the words slapped Matty and the color drained from her face. A long moment passed. She smiled slowly, patiently. It was her cordial bar smile, nothing more. She didn't want to fight with this woman, certainly not over the length of her hair. Matty ignored the remark and moved to the far end of the bar.

Sarama, though, was relentless. Leaning across the bar, she shouted, "Bad enough it's that long, why is it that color?"

Matty sighed and looked at Sarama for a long moment. "It grows out of my head this color." Her voice dripped with sarcasm. "You want me to dye it green, maybe? Or shave my head so it wouldn't worry you so?"

"Why don't you?" Sarama asked, leveling her eyes at Matty. And then the inevitable happened: Matty blushed and Sarama saw. A secret smile slid onto Sarama's face. Matty felt naked and a little scared, like a guilty child. Her vanity was exposed.

"She's passing," Sarama declared later, and a trio of heads nodded.

"Maybe she's bisexual," one hissed. The others widened their eyes and looked one to the other.

"Well, I heard she was having an affair with Babe Daniels." The heads cluck-clucked. "You can't be more politically incorrect than that." The heads nodded again.

"I heard Babe Daniels has a . . . uses a . . ." began one of the whispers before fading into silence.

"A what?" asked another.

"A dildo," finished Sarama confidently, although she was only guessing. Again the eyes widened, the heads nodded.

"Well, I heard they broke up."

"Who Babe and the—you know?" They tittered.

"No, silly, Matty and Babe."

"Because of the . . ."

"Will you forget about that!" hissed Sarama. "It just proves that Matty O'Donnell is P.I." The heads nodded again.

"And probably not even a real lesbian," added a whisper.

In the weeks that followed Sarama's visit to the bar, Matty pretended not to hear the whispers, tuned out the obvious slurs, and threw herself more deeply into work and the cause. Of course, the Radical Womyn's Center collective scheduled meetings only when she was working, or so it seemed, so she had to be replaced as the coordinator of Take Back the Night. She still volunteered four mornings a week, but she was more often alone in the office than not, and even when she wasn't alone the silence was oppressive. None of this was lost on Babe, who made it her business to keep track of every whisper, every five-dollar poker pot, every stolen kiss that happened under her roof. She knew Matty would eventually hear the whispers; what she didn't know was whether Matty would listen.

It all came to a head one Tuesday afternoon when Sarama slammed into the bar looking for Matty: seventeen dollars and ninety-three cents was missing from the Radical Womyn's Center war chest. Someone said Matty had been seen leaving the office the night before. And Matty, of course, could no longer be trusted. None of it was true. Babe knew it, Matty knew it, even Sarama knew it. But Matty was willing to be crucified for the sin of vanity and at Alice's bidding, Sarama was anxious to serve as judge and executioner; she had no trouble finding a jury. When it was over, all the whispers, the speculations, even the lies had found voice. By the time Matty tried to defend herself, the silence that had descended around her was too great for mere words to pierce. Alice Wood had won. The movement was purged once again from evil.

Babe saw what was happening, how the fire and heart were beaten out of Matty all in the name of sisterhood. Matty moped around the bar for nearly a week. None of her friends returned her calls. The locks on the Radical Womyn's Center were changed, even though she returned her keys when Sarama demanded them. And when the money turned up in a desk drawer, the apologies that came were faint and halfhearted. Through it all, Babe kept quiet, thinking Matty needed time to sort things out. Finally, though, she broke the silence.

"I've been around this life for a lot of years, honey," she offered one night when they were finally alone, "and one thing I know is a real lesbian. Who the hell would pretend to be a dyke? It ain't like they're giving out fifty-dollar bills down at the bank for every one of us that comes in. Shit, I can remember when it used to be the other way around. Lot of pain in that, too, I can tell you. But hell, you're as real a lesbian as me and I've been a dyke long as I can remember. 'Course they probably don't have nothing better to say about me, am I right?" Matty giggled. Babe was, indeed, right.

"They say you're P.I."

"What's that?"

"Politically incorrect. Don't scowl, Babe; it's better than being a sexist oppressor of your sisters." Matty was teasing for the first time in more than a week.

Babe snorted. She had little use for Alice and Sarama, and even less for their rules. To Babe's mind, Alice Wood's brand of sisterhood made for a movement with precious little variety, and Babe was a woman who thrived on variety. "Well, I always did say you were a looker. Maybe now you'll do something about it. Find yourself a good woman, one who appreciates a *real lesbian* femme." Babe chuckled at her own joke.

Matty averted her eyes. Her friends, who didn't speak to her anymore, said she wasn't a real lesbian and Babe, who didn't sleep with her anymore, thought she was femme, which was worse. Femmes were nothing more than anachronisms to be scorned, pitied at best. They were weak, everyone said so—everyone except Babe, and she didn't understand. She even though it was funny. No real lesbian could ever be a femme. They were soft and stupid, warts on the skin of radical lesbian-feminism. Matty couldn't be that. She could be anything, but never a femme. "No," she whispered, "I'm not like that." She was starting to cry.

Babe picked up a bottle of wine and a pair of glasses, took Matty's hand, and led her to one of the little tables. "It's time you and me had a little talk, Matty. I always said you didn't invent nothing, but you never really believed that and maybe women like Alice Wood never will. But you're going to hear me out because no woman should ever be ashamed of who she is and she should never think she's alone. But you didn't invent that, either, and neither did Alice Wood or anyone else that's still alive to tell it." And that night, Matty O'Donnell heard stories that she'd never even imagined of women who'd risked everything to be who they were, who built lives not so very different from the dream Alice Wood thought she'd drafted. Women who didn't march to take back the night because it was already their domain. Women who dreamed and danced and fought and lived as best they could in a hostile world. Finally Matty was starting to hear what Babe had been saying all along, and for the first time, she began to understand.

1988

Ten o'clock Saturday night and it was door duty one more time. Matty was perched on a stool by the front door, watching the parade of women pass under her flashlight. A white leather jacket, half unzipped to expose her bare chest, gleamed under the blue light by the door. Cool air tickled under the jacket where a cascade of tattooed stars shot across her chest. Her hair was no longer wild or waist-length; she'd cut it a few years before when it didn't matter any more. But she still wore Chanel No. 5. Babe had started her on that and said it suited her.

She'd been the manager at Babe's for the past five years. It was supposed to give Babe more free time, but she was still at the bar every night, running the poker game in the back room when she wasn't behind the bar. She'd moved the game out of the apartment when Faye moved in two years ago. The poker players didn't seem to mind. They even took up a collection to buy a table and set of chairs after they got tired of squatting on empty beer kegs.

The Radical Womyn's Center had closed in 1983; there just wasn't enough money or women to keep it going any longer. Sarama and Alice Wood, who were lovers by then, moved it to their apartment, where they tried to continue building their vision. They broke up in 1986 when Sarama started dating a peace activist and changed her name back to Lynette. She married him at the Oakland City Hall the day before they left for Nicaragua to pick coffee beans with a work brigade. No one knew what Alice thought of that—she'd accepted a job teaching history at a girl's boarding school in New England.

Matty herself had wandered through a series of lovers and passionate friends until she'd found A. J. in Los Angeles. They lived a life of quiet passion and patience, tending each other like flower gardens. But every Saturday night, Matty O'Donnell was exactly where she'd been for the past ten years.

On those rare nights and lonely nights when she bothered to think of such things, she still sometimes longed for the old days. The days when there was so much anger and so much love. A time of reckless bravery and celebration. The world had been theirs to conquer . . . and change. In a way, they'd done both. Not as much as they'd once dreamed, but changes all the same. Chris Williamson had sung of the changer and the changed, but who among them had thought they, too, would number among the changed? All around her were the shells of empty cocoons; which was hers? Did it even matter, or was it enough that she was one of the survivors who had finally known freedom?

As Babe had predicted all those years ago, Matty had seen the dream come full circle one night when she was sharing a campfire at the music festival. Stars spilled across the August sky into black emptiness. From the hollow of the night, she listened to a litany of hopes spill out in time to a softly hollow drumbeat. In the reaches of the fire's shadows, a woman named Velvet was dancing, whirling wildly to a rhythm caught in her head.

"It's like a river, Matty, and we're part of it." Star's words were spinning a familiar web. Matty turned to look at the woman behind the words. Her eyes sparkled even without the fire, her face flushed with the magic of dreams and anticipation. Matty smiled and turned back to watch Velvet dance in the firelight. "Women are growing and getting stronger and trying harder. We're moving right across this country, shit, the whole fucking world, and we're going to make it happen for the women. But first we have to give up—no that's too complacent a word—we have to throw off, destroy the evil of the patriarchy. We'll rebuild, move back to the land. Deny the patriarchy's power, break the shackles, set ourselves and every woman free. It's like building a whole new nation, a nation of women. Working together. Loving. And it'll be so beautiful, Matty."

Velvet's purple silk scarves shimmered in the moonlight as she danced half-naked under the stars. To Matty's eyes she was ancient and golden and brown and innocent, a beacon against time and change. Velvet twirled in time to a voiceless silent song while Star built castles on the night wind. Matty sat next to the fire, witness to the silent music and quiet magic. She had seen the dreams—conceived in bondage, born in hope—fly free. Basking in the warmth, she let the shared passion push away the ache of time passing.

Star's eyes burned angry against the night. Once, Matty would have joined the conversation, plotting the destruction of the patriarchy, but she wasn't sure how to do that anymore. *"Just remember whose backs this revolution of yours is built on,"* whispered Babe Daniels from what felt like a lifetime away. Matty turned to Star and pulled her close, wrapping her arms around her, tucking her head beneath her own.

Strange, now all Matty could remember of Star were those burning eyes and how she'd loved Velvet. And all she could remember of Velvet was shining skin and purple scarves that flashed like freedom in the firelight. It was the sisterhood she'd dreamed of gleaming like a beacon. Slowly, a smile warmed her face. That's how it was, she thought, moments frozen like dancers under a strobe light. She didn't have to wait—never had to, really—for the revolution, because it was made up of those moments. Isolated yet connected. And even if this one didn't last longer than that night, she had lived for a second in beauty and love. It wasn't all she'd dreamed of or wanted, but most times, it was enough.

The Scavenger Hunt

Bars, by their very Saturday-night nature, weren't Randi's sort of place. Too much sweat and confusion, laughter and music, tears and dramas all swirling, heaving, conspiring to pound out migraines that would hang on for days. Deadly mementos of bad judgment.

Randi was beyond it all, or thought she was. Late-night fantasies that only burst like dime-store balloons in the dust of day were for other women, those who still knew how to dream. And Randi knew dreams littered the floor at Babe's as surely as abandoned rubbish huddled in the gutter in front of the bar.

Fleeting fantasies, fragile as gauze, were best kept tucked away next to the vibrator, saved for lonely nights when solitary pleasure was the only kind around. Maybe for some, the bars offered hot sex, but never for her. Better to leave the bars and their promises of ecstasy to the true believers; Randi no longer chased floundering visions through futile fantasies.

Only the promise of cigarettes was enough to lure her into Babe's, which at least was safe; nobody there would stare at her leather jacket, her cropped hair, or worse yet, call her "sir."

So, Randi charged through lavender shadows that bathed the street in softness, sending out nightly promises of tempo-rary paradise, of secrets lurking just beyond the blazing purple neon sign that burned away the blackness. "Get in, get out, go home," she promised, pushing the door open and instinctively narrowing her eyes against the smoke-shrouded dimness. In one corner, shadowy webs of light illuminated the cigarette machine and the pay phone, where a tall blonde half-held the receiver to her ear, waiting, Randi assumed, for an answer to her call.

The blonde's bold eyes narrowed, then dropped to Randi's chest, circling, probing the depths of the black-leather vest that hung open over a T-shirt that stretched taut across full breasts. "Nice," the blonde muttered appreciatively, the eyes lingering shamelessly before beginning their slow ascent, tickling Randi's earlobes, licking at her mouth. Aqua eyes, shadowed in dark rainbows, rimmed in heavy lashes, finally locked, hard and even, in Randi's. This was the woman Randi had always dreamed of, standing before her, dressed in black satin and velvet. Long blond hair dipped perilously close to one eye before continuing an unencumbered journey across naked shoulders dusted with silver stars. Lace-mitted hands tipped with long red fingernails toyed with the phone cord. The woman's gaze never flinched. Feeling suddenly naked, exposed, Randi blushed; the woman smiled knowingly and turned back to the phone.

Unnerved, Randi quickly turned away, rummaging through her jeans to discover a button from her favorite flannel shirt, an empty cigarette pack, and twenty-three cents—eight of it in pennies. "Don't want that, do you?" she asked the cigarette machine, which winked an almost obscene reply when she crumpled the empty cigarette pack on its surface. Pulling a pair of bills free, Randi squeezed into an opening midway down the bar's long expanse of mahogany and mirrors, laughter and soft backs. Leaning into the cool hardness of the railing, she dangled the money across the bar. "Nothing attracts bartenders quicker than money waving in the breeze," she announced half to the woman at her left.

"It all depends on how much you're waving," a voice whispered from her right shoulder. Startled, Randi raised her eyes to the mirror and there, behind her own familiar reflection, was the woman from the phone. Just as the bartender's fingers plucked the bills free, long red-tipped fingers moved down Randi's shoulder, extending a pack of cigarettes: Randi's brand. But as she reached for the cigarettes, muttering, "Thanks," the fingers coiled around the gold-and-white package and tucked it into the soft-melting crevasse between a pair of delicately full breasts. The bartender jingled a handful of change into Randi's still-waiting palm, which automatically closed around the coins. Mesmerized, Randi was powerless to break her gaze from this woman whose hot breath kept tickling her earlobes. Luminous eyes shot into the mirror, then rebounded into Randi's soul. Randi's breath came short. Closing her eyes, Randi blinked hard, looked again. The vision stared back and smiled.

A lifetime might have passed, although the hands on the little clock imbedded in the belly of a mermaid who was permanently beached by the cash register hadn't moved at all. "That machine doesn't have what you want, but I do," the voice whispered, slipping in under the music, the noisy bar clatter. Randi turned to feel warm words brush past her ear. Shivers spilled down her back. "I drink Southern Comfort. On ice. With a piece of lime. Bring it over there." The vision pouted at her reflection, smiled brightly, then walked away—never looking back.

"Southern Comfort, on ice, with a piece of lime," Randi parroted. "And a bottle of Michelob, no glass." The looking glass exposed Randi's hungry eyes following the vision to a tiny table in a darkened corner where the woman watched and waited. Randi felt those eyes skimming her legs, defining her ass under wallet and keys, sliding across her shoulders, down to her breasts, until her cunt began to warm. All the while, delicate fingers tap-tapped the half-exposed pack of cigarettes. On any other woman, the actions would have been absentminded, innocent, nonchalant. But with this woman, every movement, every whisper was nothing less than a deliberate promise. A bright pink tongue determinedly licked lips that waited patiently for the smooth sweetness of Southern Comfort, of Randi.

The music, the noise, the crowd fell away until there was no one else in the bar, maybe in the world. "I've been waiting for you," the vision whispered when Randi finally reached the table. Tiny shadows, urged on by flickering candlelight, chased across the dark lady, as Randi had named her since their meeting by the phone. Randi began to speak, but something in this strange woman's eyes muted her. A black high-heel pump nudged the empty chair a little more open as Randi set the drink down. When the leg pulled back, a flash of naked thigh gleamed, a personal invitation.

Sliding onto the vinyl chair that wobbled from too many Saturday nights, Randi sat, as if there were no place else she would ever want to be again, as if there were no tomorrow, no yesterday. Tapping a cigarette free, the woman lit it, then extended it filter first toward Randi's mouth. "Better?" she asked. Randi nodded, almost afraid to breathe, to talk for fear the vision would fade into the smoke.

"These are yours." The dark lady pushed the cigarettes toward Randi. "And this, of course, is mine." She raised the glass and looked hard into Randi's dark eyes. "And that, of course, will be mine, too." The eyes forged a trail down the soft curve of Randi's chin, along her neck, across her chest, before settling where Randi's eager nipples stood on end, betraying her already prickling flesh. Randi wondered if her dark lady could see beneath the leather, the fabric, and was watching those shameless nipples harden. A piercing throb jarred Randi's belly, then slammed between her legs. She didn't want to control the sensation, couldn't even if she'd tried.

"How did you know about the cigarettes?" Randi asked finally, trying desperately to find something to say to this woman whose eyes kept rummaging under the T-shirt, tickling, licking, nuzzling the ever-hardening nipples. Finally, with a little sigh and a longing last look, the dark lady raised her eyes. "I notice things; it pays to notice things. I noticed you the second you stepped through the door." Randi could almost feel little demon tongues dancing over her burning skin, licking, sucking at her hidden secrets.

The dark lady smiled, very sweetly, very innocently, then the very tip of her tongue darted up across her lip. The effect wasn't wasted; Randi's heart exhaled, then plummeted to her cunt, where it lay pounding incessantly in time to her too-quick breathing.

"Actually, I'm on a bit of a scavenger hunt." A sparkling fingertip traced the edge of her glass. "That's why I'm dressed like this. I ordinarily wouldn't go out to a bar all alone on a Saturday night, dressed in satin and lace. But I was at a party and there was this scavenger hunt, and so here I am." Brightening, her eyes kissed every line, every detail on Randi's broad face.

"I don't understand." Randi was trying to ignore the throbbing between her legs, the tiny voices that kept prodding her to run back to reality, to the predictable safety that was her life, before being consumed by this smouldering fantasy that had remarkably become real.

"Everyone else had a partner for the scavenger hunt." The woman looked very innocent. Except a single finger kept circling and dipping into the cocktail glass. Except she kept bringing that finger to her lips, slowly licking off little droplets of Southern Comfort. The eyes never flinched. "There's a truly wonderful prize . . . for the one who comes with all the things she's supposed to. But I don't have a playmate—I mean teammate—so I have to do it all alone. And what if I lose? I don't like to lose." The full mouth pouted slightly, reminding Randi of a doll in a toy-store window.

"So you came here to find somebody to do it with?"

"Exactly. Want to play?"

"Oh, I couldn't really." Randi fidgeted in the chair, deciding to leave before the dream exploded in her face. For Randi, loving strangers, especially exotic ones, wasn't something that was likely to happen in real life. Better to go home, watch the late movie, and turn her dark lady into a full-blown fantasy, courtesy of the ever-faithful vibrator. "I've got things to do." Randi jingled her keys for emphasis.

"So do I." The dark lady exhaled in frustration, pursed her red lips, and then very patiently added, "That's why I asked." She smiled again; Randi's heart exploded. "You're really not interested in playing with me? It's a truly wonderful scavenger hunt. And we can party after it's over."

"I don't like parties much," Randi admitted, embarrassed.

"You'll like this one. Here, I'll even show you what I have so far . . . from the list, you know. I only need one more thing and then I'll win. You don't want me to lose, do you?" Randi shook her head.

"This is my list, pay attention." A naked pinup girl, frozen on a greeting card, pouted at Randi. "Cute, huh?" Randi nodded. "She reminds me of you"—the dark lady winked—"around the tits." Randi blushed, thankful for the bar's shadows. Watching the dark lady read, Randi imagined kissing those soft lips that moved with the words: "A feather fanny, to finger the leather, that unfingers the lace, that whips it all into shape, ties it up for a present, and . . ."

"And what?" Randi's curiosity peaked and she reached for the card, only to have it snapped back just out of reach and tucked away. "And . . . that's what I have so far." The dark lady ignored Randi's hungry fingers.

"What else is there?" Randi asked, suddenly very aware of the dark lady's foot rising up her leg, probing behind her knees, slipping between her thighs on a determined course to her throbbing, gushing cunt. The dark lady only smiled in reply, tossed off the last of the Southern Comfort, and extended her hand. "Come with me, we'll go get the rest." And Randi, hypnotized by her very essence, obediently let herself be led across the room, out the door, onto the street, all thoughts of leaving this woman as abandoned as the empty cocktail glass on the little table.

"My car's right here." The dark lady stood by a black sports car. "But I have a car here," Randi protested, "I mean over there." Leaning against Randi, the dark lady opened the passenger door, then trailed breasts and naked shoulders across Randi's back. "Which would you rather be in, that car or me?" A low groan answered for Randi, who sank into the car. "Good girl," the dark lady answered, slipping into the driver's seat, letting the skirt rise high and easy on her legs.

"The last thing will be at my place. We'll go there first and then party." Randi wasn't listening; instead, her ravenous fingers inched toward the naked shoulders only to have her errant hand caught midair. Soft red lips sucked each of the fingers, nuzzled Randi's hand, moved into the soft warmth of her neck, nibbling, licking. Finally, the dark lady kissed Randi hard and long as agile fingers rummaged inside the T-shirt, teasing, tormenting, until the nipples rose, pulsating, electrified.

So slowly Randi thought she would explode with desire, lace-covered hands moved to her waist, loosening, probing, exploring the coarse hair and soft skin just beyond the buttons. Finally, one long finger slipped into Randi's wet aching cunt, moving slowly back and forth, up and down almost in time to the music that crashed from the car stereo. Randi could think of nothing but fingers—greedy, hungry fingers—exploring her innermost secrets. Sliding further down in the seat, a low soft moan escaped as Randi raised her gushing cunt to devour the finger, which exited as deftly as it had come. Raising the finger first to Randi's lips for a moment, then to her own, the dark lady licked the dampness slowly, patiently, like a little girl seeking the very last traces of ice cream on a stick. "See, you

really are a very good girl, and I really do like good girls."
Randi felt her dark lady smiling.

"I don't even know your name." The words came soft, quiet
when Randi's power of speech finally returned. "Ah, but I know
yours." The dark lady was checking her eye shadow in the
rearview mirror. "That woman at the end of the bar told me.
Said you don't come to Babe's often, that you don't like the bars
much. Is that true?" As she turned from the mirror, night
shadows traced the dark lady's delicate features, and Randi
coveted every movement.

"I'm whoever you want me to be: Regina or Yvette or Ni-
colle or Natasha or Lydia. Do you like any of us?" Randi nodded, not daring to speak, fearing it would break the spell.
"Good, because I'm Lydia. Much better than Natasha, don't you
think? I was Natasha at the last scavenger hunt and I lost." A
tiny cloud darkened Lydia's eyes, prompted by the memory of
losing. But before pulling the car from the curb, a lacy hand
darted across the seat, took one of Randi's eager nipples and
turned it slowly while an anxious tongue sucked and licked at
her neck until the tiny hairs there shuddered erect. "Aren't
scavenger hunts fun?" Lydia demanded, sending the car into
the night.

Yet, each time Randi stretched nearer to Lydia, she was
nudged away. Instead, Lydia's hands stroked her own soft
thighs under lavender stockings caught by black lace garters.
Shimmers of streetlights sent strange shadows shooting up her
raised skirt. Randi's cunt pounded for want of Lydia; her fingers hungered for the naked shoulders. Mindless of the path
they followed, Randi imagined Lydia touching her, of Lydia
forgetting about the stupid scavenger hunt, the party, of Lydia
making time stand still. Finally, the car stopped by an eerie
Victorian mansion with a dozen mailboxes on the porch.

"Come with me." Lydia's first words since the drive began
jarred Randi back to reality. Without a backward glance, Lydia
slid out of the car, leaving Randi struggling to button her jeans.
The sound of Lydia's heels moving across the vine-covered
porch echoed faintly through the silence. Finally freeing herself from the car, afraid Lydia would vanish into the labyrin-
thine recesses of the house, Randi took the stairs two at a time,
hurled herself through the unlocked door, then charged ahead,
following the scent of Lydia's perfume, the sound of her heels.

"What kept you?" Lydia demanded when Randi reached

her, although only moments had passed. She was turning her key in the lock so slowly Randi could almost hear the tumblers move. "I don't like to be kept waiting."

"Lydia, I'm sorry." Breathless, Randi hung across the banister, gasping for breath, exhausted from her flight to the very top of the manor.

"You are a very bad girl. I'm very disappointed in you." Lydia never turned from the latch to face the agonizing Randi. "You really should be punished, you know?" The husky voice was modulated, as if she was discussing the weather on a perfectly clear day. "If I'm late, I'll never win the scavenger hunt." Sure that Lydia was about to send her away, Randi turned to the stairs, cursing herself for her stupidity: She'd walked into Babe's by accident, miraculously had been picked up by a fantasy, and now she'd blown it. "Don't worry," Lydia called after Randi's unspoken thoughts, "we still have time." And she laughed, the sound of wind chimes just before a storm.

Stepping into the darkened room, Lydia lit candles along her way before slipping into a black satin chair, rousing a sleeping black cat who growled in indignation. "Don't mind Miss Snooty Feline," Lydia said, draping a long leg across the chair's soft arm, studying Randi, pleased at her good fortune.

Glancing around the room, Randi's eyes lingered on the four-poster bed complete with gauzy curtains that shimmied in a soft September breeze. Illuminated by the candlelight was a gallery of nudes. In one, Lydia lounged by the sea, naked save for boots and a riding crop. A horse grazed in the background. "Somebody's idea of me." Lydia's voice followed Randi's hungry eyes.

Embarrassed, Randi turned too quickly from the painting and leaned against the wall, a miserable attempt at nonchalance, for she had realized immediately that except for the bed and the chair Lydia occupied, there was nowhere to sit. Self-conscious, she looked pleadingly toward Lydia, who was admiring her red fingernails. "There's champagne in the refrigerator and glasses in the cupboard. Get them." Lydia rearranged herself on the chair, apparently mindless of Randi's discomfort.

Once in the kitchen, her favorite part of every house, Randi hummed and puttered, her breathing finally normal at last. Finding towels and glasses, even a little mirrored tray, she selected a bottle of champagne from the half-dozen that kept company in the refrigerator with a brown head of lettuce and a dried-up half-loaf of bread. Trying to avoid the menacing eyes of the cat who watched from a cupboard sentry post, Randi opened the bottle, losing only traces of the foam. "Now that's talent," she observed, but the cat only closed her eyes in contempt, feigning sleep. Carrying the bottle and glasses on the little tray into the next room, Randi composed a symphony of small talk and wit, all for Lydia, who she imagined was settled in the satin chair, smoking, waiting for champagne. Randi had already decided to sit on the floor at Lydia's feet so she could caress Lydia's thighs, slide her fingers into that sweet pink cunt. She smiled in anticipation.

But the chair was empty. Lydia, instead, lay on the bed, a sequined mask hiding her eyes. The velvet top was gone, snow-white and pink breasts, which Lydia tickled with a feather fan, peeked over a black-lace corset. A forgotten cigarette fumed in a crystal ashtray. "Oh, you're back." The fan teased the pink nipples erect. "I was waiting for you, but you were late again, so I started without you. Too bad, it really was you I wanted." Randi's hands shook until she was sure tray, glasses, champagne, and confidence would all spill across the floor. "I'm sorry," she muttered miserably, ashamed that she had once again spoiled the moment.

"Stay there." Lydia's voice pierced the night as she slid off the bed. Taking the tray, Lydia filled the glasses, then began to peel away Randi's leather vest. "Such a bad girl, making me wait for you, making me want you, leaving me here all alone with nothing but my feather fanny. A bad girl who needs to be taught a lesson."

"Yes . . . I mean, no . . . I don't know." Randi stuttered, staring at the floor, then dragged her eyes to Lydia's commanding face. "That's my good girl," Lydia whispered, lowering her face to Randi's chest to nibble and suck on the fabric that encased nipples throbbing from want. "You like that, don't you?" Randi moaned; Lydia turned, looked slyly over her shoulder, and picked up a glass. "You may unfasten my skirt—carefully."

With shaking fingers, Randi tried to loosen the zipper, but the same fingers that could dance a carburetor back into shape had turned to wooden stumps. Her jeans, damp and coarse, rubbed against her burning cunt. Fingering the satin, the skirt finally fell open and Randi reached inside, only to have Lydia pull away. "No-no," she scolded, as if Randi was a naughty kitten into some new mischief, "not until I tell you." Lydia reached up, gently caressing the side of Randi's face before burying her lips in the soft waiting throat. Randi moaned, trembled, gasping for breath.

"Please, oh please, Lydia." Randi closed her eyes, begging, praying for Lydia's fingers, her tongue, wanting desperately to please her dark-lady fantasy.

"Just stay there, stand there." And Lydia slipped out of the skirt, exposing gleaming thighs against lavender stockings held high by their lacy garters. She smelled of roses, incense, champagne. Lydia stepped close to Randi, licking her neck, trailing her breasts across Randi's shirt. Lace-covered hands freed Randi from the T-shirt that clung mercilessly to her damp skin. Their nipples touched, hard, exploding, and Randi's legs trembled. Lydia then caressed Randi in earnest, teasing her magical tongue over each taut nipple until Randi arched her back, groaning. Still, Lydia's demanding tongue continued to torment the aching nipples, pulling them through insistent teeth before allowing them to all but escape again, then calling them back, harder each time. Curious fingers probed, explored, delighted the hidden niches of Randi's body. Tremors coursed through her veins.

Teasing and tempting, a thousand fingers seemed to circle and flutter in Randi's damp jeans as Lydia's insistent mouth forged ahead, following the beltline. Lydia pressed into Randi's back, licking, biting, until Randi felt her skin go hot then prickle as if she had been too long in the sun. Reaching back to caress Lydia, Randi's hungry fingers were guided across the corset up to petal-soft breasts, only to be brought back to reality by the snap of cold steel gripping her wrists.

Dancing in front of her prisoner, Lydia kissed Randi softly, silencing the moans. Toasting her own handiwork, Lydia's tongue caught droplets of champagne before moving the glass to Randi's nipples, which grew only harder from the chill. Persistent fingers slid down Randi's belly, unfastening the jeans' buttons, one by aching one. Sucking and biting the exposed skin, Lydia kept drawing Randi closer and closer to passion's brink. Randi groaned; the sound rose from deep in her cunt and spilled out her aching throat. "You must be very quiet. We don't want to wake the neighbors. And I have lots of neighbors, all very grouchy, very mean." Licking Randi's navel, the jeans slumped to the floor, and Lydia buried her face in the soft down of Randi's belly. The floor seemed to convulse and Randi's knees buckled in answer to the ultimate call of gravity, of passion.

Only then did Lydia lead Randi to the bed. Settling her captive on its edge, Lydia lay back against satin pillows. Shadows wrought by flickering candles illuminated Lydia's fingers, which piloted a waiting vibrator to her own cunt. All the time, Lydia's eyes burned into Randi's. Lydia pushed the buzzing vibrator between her legs until the tiny lace panties teased her clit. Arching her back a little, a low moan escaped, and Randi, mesmerized, moved closer, her own cunt dripping. Gartered thighs tensed from the vibrator's harsh demands. Randi leaned to Lydia, took a neglected nipple in her own eager mouth, and sucked. Electricity snapped from Lydia's flesh; stark passion exploded across the bed. Moving her head down along the lace corset, Randi nibbled until she reached Lydia's soft lace-covered mound, where the vibrator purred. Lydia's breath came hard and swift as she rose to Randi, hurtled ever higher by the vibrator, moaning, tensing, pushing against the gush of orgasm that threatened to consume them both.

Finally, Lydia switched off the vibrator and slipped free of Randi. "You really are a bad girl, aren't you?" She stroked Randi's hair, whispered against her temples. "I told you to stay there and here you are moving around, probably wanting to slip your fingers into my hot, juicy, throbbing cunt." Standing then, Lydia stepped out of the wet lace panties and angled her soft rounded ass toward Randi, smoothing each silky stocking.

Lydia's nipples brushed Randi's face. Dancing feathers fanned Randi's breasts; indignant goose bumps marched in cadence. "You like that, don't you?" Randi's eyes pleaded, begged for just one of the pink-tipped breasts that hovered out of her eager tongue's reach, for just one of the red-tipped fingers to dip into her anxious wetness. Inch by painful inch, a soft nipple moved toward Randi's eager mouth. Randi's cunt pounded out its own demands as Lydia's fingers guided hungry mouth to hard nipple. A silk scarf, the color of midnight, teased Randi's forehead, then grew taut across her temples. A determined finger circled lightly, stirring dampened secrets. Randi breathed only through gasps and moans. Fingers stroked her belly, tickled the soft mound that protected wet treasures.

Turning Randi on her belly, the fingers teased the ultimate depths of desire until the soft skin there trembled in anticipation. "You want me, don't you?" Lydia asked, although she needed no answer. Lydia's finger rimmed Randi's lips and when her tongue reached out, she tasted her own dampness there, smooth and cool. She sucked the finger—a kitten suckling from its mother for the first time. Lydia tickled her back, her buttocks, startling them with flicks and tremors, making them rise to the touch, then quiver there, waiting for more. Wanting Lydia to consume her, to quiet the aching throb that pounded relentlessly in her cunt, Randi trembled. Wetness gushed from her convulsing pussy. Hidden secrets exploded. Tremblings of release rippled through her throbbing body.

The feeling ravaged her, teased against her, slapped her exploding ass. Aching for more, her cunt tightened, her ass rose. She was nothing now but throbbing, pounding, demanding cunt, ravenous cunt, screaming for more. She wanted to come, moaning, pouring herself out across Lydia's bed, yet she wanted to wait, to prolong the passion. Randi buried her face deep into the pillow, savoring the scent of Lydia. Strong fingers moved against her clit; firm, persistent fingers kneaded the exploding wetness. Lydia knew Randi's body better than even Randi knew it.

In the distance, Randi heard the gentle hum of bumblebees, calling her to their hive on a summer afternoon. The hum moved closer, buzzing against her clit, along her ass, until she could no longer tell vibrations from fingers or tongue. As full and hot as she had ever been on a relentless August afternoon, she was only cunt, ass, tits, all aching and gushing, throbbing, beating, crying for more, for release, for ecstasy itself. Filled with the tingling, the pounding, Lydia relentlessly pushed her toward an abyss Randi had never known before.

Eagerly, Randi slipped into it and then fell jerking and trembling into the chasm, hurtling across time and space until the sky and ocean exploded into the universe.

Finally, she lay sweating, trembling at Lydia's touch, her very breath. Bumblebees silenced, her cunt was slowly emptied. Metal on metal tinkled, sounding very far away, freeing her wrists; her hands fell limp. Fingers tousled her hair and then moonlight crept across the bed. Drained, empty, void of movement, she lay quiet, her breath shallow. Sweet tears born of ultimate passion, consummate pleasure spilled into the pillow. Damp warmth caressed her skin and she smelled peppermint soap, felt warm towels against her back, her ass, her still-tingling cunt as Lydia washed and dried her gently, kissed her, pulled the covers up around Randi's shoulders.

Through sleep and passion-dimmed eyes, Randi watched Lydia undress: the stockings, the corset, the mask, all discarded on the satin chair. Watched her brush out her long hair, then move toward the bed, where she slipped in next to Randi, pulling her close, protecting her against the night.

"You really are a very good girl," Lydia mumbled, wrapping herself around Randi, stroking her hair, petting her to sleep.

"Can I ask you something?" Randi turned toward Lydia, as much afraid of the question as of the answer. Lydia kissed her hair, hugged her tighter. "What was the other thing you were supposed to get for the scavenger hunt?"

Lydia smiled. An almost silent, not-quite-breathless chuckle escaped. "You, my darling. Didn't you know?" The whisper stole into the night. "You were the scavenger hunt." And Randi slid into sleep, safe in Lydia's arms.

The Poolroom

Jake: Free-Falling

Jake smiled and the universe winked. Swift, smooth, her strong right arm moved and a white sun blasted a purple moon into a black hole. On nights like these she was magic: Merlin with the mythic scepter raised in triumph, watching it all unfold under mighty arms. Tonight the sun was a pawn and Jake the warrior queen, who ruled the table the way she never could rule life. That life wasn't more like pool was Jake's greatest regret. Pool was better than real life. Certainly easier, Jake thought, lining up her next shot.

"Pool's one of the few things in life that makes sense," Billy whispered against her mind. *"The stick connects with the cue ball that belts and kisses all her sisters. No surprises, no accidents, no regrets."* "Hush!" Jake muttered, leaning into the table. Billy chuckled and faded into a plume of smoke. Even if he never learned the physics of it, her Uncle Billy always knew the heart of it. Feeling the shot more than planning it, just as Billy had taught her, Jake felt the magic running down her arm through the stick and out onto the table. Pulling it together, making sense of the chaos, of the sometime ecstasy that churned through her, Jake watched the balls spin and scatter. White lightning energy shot like unleashed sunbeams through her fingers into Babe's poolroom and it warmed the handful of women who lounged against the walls, watching Jake, feeling the glow that made her special. And what they didn't know of Jake's life outside of Babe's, well, so much the better. A lot of secrets are left at barroom doors.

Except for a trio of women whose clumsy shots marked

them as killing time until the deejay came on at nine, the room was empty when Jake chalked her initials up on the board. Soon enough, the room would be full of serious players. It was still early when the three bored players threw up their hands in disgust and turned the table over to Bo, who grinned, waggled a frayed toothpick with her tongue, and roared, "Okay, let's shoot some pool!" It was five after nine when Jake stepped up for the break.

A lot of months had passed since Jake had held the table for a night, when only last call ended the game. Nights that sent her and the other stragglers into the dawn for eggs swimming in warm grease. Then tumbling into a strange bed with the latest in a long string of conquests. The women Jake pulled into the black light of dawn never paid for their own breakfast and they never slept in her bed—Jake's unwritten, unbroken rule. Until Tina. Sometimes Jake swore she could still hear Billy laughing about that. *"Let 'em in your bed and you let 'em in your life,"* Billy whispered in Jake's left ear, adding, *"Look what it got you."*

"I ain't doin' so bad," Jake answered. "Least I ain't dead."

"Says you," Billy mocked in an airless chuckle. Jake was used to her dead uncle's comments about her life. He talked to her more in death than he ever had in life. Although she never told anyone, Jake suspected that Billy had found his way to a big pool hall in the sky. Only there was one hell of a long wait for the tables and the john, which left him with a lot of eternal time on his hands. Some nights Billy offered advice on particularly tricky shots or uncommonly pretty women—they both liked green-eyed redheads in satin western shirts, although Jake was more partial to fringe. Lately, though, most of Billy's comments were on Jake's life with Tina, and tonight he'd been talking more than usual. Jake silenced him by blasting his whispers into infinity with the hard crack of the balls.

Shifting her weight a little, Jake smiled. She was playing well. Raising her eyes to meet Bo's at the next table, Jake moved the stick in a little salute, licked her lips, and turned her attention back to her own game. Facing Bo would come soon enough. Some things, she knew, couldn't be rushed. That was one of Billy's lessons, too. The table, the balls, the feel of the stick running smooth and hard between her strong stubby fingers—these were the things she understood. And she was the best, just like Billy.

Billy hadn't bothered with books, but he'd taught her all she'd ever needed to know to live in a world of pool halls and darkened bars. What she missed of Shakespeare and algebra, she made up for with a nearly innate knowledge of bar games and the people who played them. With Billy as coach and cheerleader, Jake learned life's lessons hard and fast: how to size up the marks; to keep a roll of nickels reinforced with strapping tape in your right-front pants pocket, just in case the mark's bigger than you are; ways of making a sawbuck stretch like a rubber band; how to hold the table, and when to give it up.

Squinting, Jake conjured Billy against the far wall, waiting, watching, offering encouragement and advice, a couple of Pepsis and a grin. Billy would've stuck out like a sore thumb at Babe's, but he sure would have liked it, Jake thought, taking careful aim, waiting for the inevitable crack and whoosh. A room full of pool-playing women would have made even Billy smile. The idea sent a fast raspy chuckle rattling across her parted lips.

Billy had always liked playing pool with his girls, as he called them. And Billy's girls included just about all the women he'd ever known. Jake never knew if he saw any of them outside the pool hall, though she sometimes imagined he did. *"All I taught you how to play was pool,"* Billy teased from the shadows. *"You picked up how to play with the women on your own."* Jake chuckled, remembering Billy and all those women. Welders from the shipyards, whose singed forearms were braced with hard muscles that would have been outlined with veins if they'd been men. Waitresses with honeycomb-colored hair piled high and cemented against strong winds and fast talkers by bottles of VO-5 hairspray, whose sharp eyes never missed a combination shot. Whores, who played barefoot, their four-inch patent-leather high heels abandoned under the pool table, their inch-long fire-engine-red fingernails tap-tapping out an impatient cadence against the table's edge as they studied their options. *"Pool ain't about men and women. It's about luck, a sure arm, and a sharp eye,"* Billy whispered across the years, winking and vanishing into the mists. As the balls skittered across the table, they pulled Jake back to other games, other tables, good times, and Billy.

A lot of years had passed since she'd last seen Billy, but it might have been yesterday when a thirteen-year-old Jake ran up the long stairs, wide as a tall man, that led to Jumbo Johnny's. Outside the cracked neon blinked P-O- -L, alternating blue and red. Billy was practicing shots in the far-back corner of the long room that was lined with a dozen tables. The faint smell of talcum and man-sweat and stale popcorn oozed through the air, joining the stench of stale cigars and cigarette ashes and cheap liquor that permeated the walls. Standing behind her uncle, Jake screwed up her face, practicing his studied look as he calculated the next shot.

Billy was the only father Jake had ever known and more mother than she could easily remember. The only tangible memory Jake carried of her parents was a yellowed wedding picture of Willow, a doe-eyed child bride in a lace dress, clutching the arm of Jackie, a boy whose face was shadowed by the Army cap he wore. Two months before she was born, Jackie was swallowed up by the war somewhere near the Mekong Delta. Years later, when history teachers had patiently explained the Vietnam War, Jake had listened intently, trying to sort out how a faceless, nameless battle in a country on the other side of the world had turned her life around. But there were no answers and Jake finally shed the questions like so many pairs of high heels left under the pool table.

Jake was five when her mother died a quiet bloody death from a self-inflicted abortion as she tried to rid herself of the ultimate evidence of a stolen weekend with the bartender at the country club where she worked in the kitchen. After Willow died, Billy refused to send Jake back to her grandmother on the reservation for fear of the social workers, who scattered the tribe's children into the arms of waiting white families; who believed life in the outside world was better; who thought their version of family was better than real family. Billy had run away from all that when he was fourteen; four years later, he'd found Willow, who was pregnant and a widow. She was seventeen. They called it freedom and neither Willow nor Billy dared look back. And neither would Jake. It was the silent promise Willow's ghost had extracted from Billy when she visited him on her final walk across the sands to the place where the horizon creeps into the mesa. Satisfied that her brother would raise her only child to know freedom and family, Willow had slipped into the purple and gold light of dawn, never to be seen again. That same morning, Billy, who lived by his promises as much as his wits, dressed his niece in blue jeans, a flannel shirt, and a baseball cap. Hand in hand, the pair of them vanished into the streets.

At first Jake changed schools more often than Billy changed the sheets. She was in fourth grade before most of the students realized she was a girl. It was another two years before Billy settled on Jumbo Johnny's as a home base and Jake took up residence in Wilma Higgins's class for slow learners at the Abraham Lincoln School five blocks away. A full two years older than most of the other sixth-graders, Jake's mind circled and soared outside the confines of the classroom where she was destined to spend the rest of her academic career.

Mrs. Higgins was a kind woman with a broad smile and a genuine love of children, even those she didn't understand. And she did her best to provide some glimpse of the outside world to her students, especially the ones like Jake, whose world began and ended in a twelve-block arena. At first, Wilma Higgins had struggled to find a way to reach the willful, bright, stubborn girl who approached school like a swimmer would an icy river. She'd seen such girls before, with eyes that questioned everything and asked nothing, eyes that reflected the world like mirrors. Eventually, Wilma Higgins would give up trying, just like all the others, and push Jake into the corner of her mind where it would be easy to forget about the girl. No one really expected it to be any other way, certainly not Jake or Billy, who only sent the girl to school because to do otherwise would bring the law or, worse, the social workers down on him. He and Jake had a pact: She would go to school until the law said she didn't have to, and she could stay with him.

"I got a *D* on my science test, Billy," Jake announced matter of factly when he finished his shot. The *D* was no surprise to her or anyone else; they were as common on her test papers as her name.

"Don't nobody care about that science stuff," Billy muttered, pulling his eyes back from the table to look at his niece.

"Miz Higgins says you got to sign it." Persistent, Jake shoved the crumpled test paper and a stubby pencil toward her uncle. Wilma Higgins knew with a teacher's myopic intuition that a signature on the girl's test paper would change nothing; it was simply school policy. Billy took the paper and pencil from his niece's outstretched hand; his face screwed in concentration as he carefully signed his name. The signature might have belonged to a child, so round and careful were the letters. "Miz

Higgins's gonna say I signed your name again," Jake grumbled, folding the test paper into her otherwise unopened science book.

"Piss on Miz Higgins," Billy mumbled, lighting the stub of cigarette that rested on his bottom lip and pushing a pair of crumpled bills toward the girl. "Go get yourself somethin' to eat." It was the signal that their conversation was ended until he'd taken care of the evening's business.

Making her way to the lunch counter at the front of the pool hall, Jake ignored the catcalls from the old men who gathered along the benches watching the real players at work. Maybe later one of the geezers'd spot her for a game. Leaning against the lunch counter, she narrowed her eyes and tossed her head back, a sneer crept across her face. She was Zorro. Clutching a rope, she swung fearlessly toward Abraham Lincoln School and crashed through the rear window of the assembly hall. Heads turned. Girls shrieked at the flying shards of glass. Her sword held the teachers, the principal, all of them at bay while the whole of the seventh grade fled into the blinding sun that blazed through the broken window. *"Thanks, Zorro,"* each one whispered reverently, making their escape. Raising her sword, she slashed a *Z* in the window shade, silently saluted Wilma Higgins, and dived through the window into the future.

Grinning, Jake stowed her fantasy and hauled herself onto a stool at the counter, where aging hot dogs spotted with sweat turned tiredly on a spit under a light bulb and stale peanuts lounged like Palm Springs matrons under a red-tinged glass dome. Jumbo Johnny was there waiting for her, his white starched shirt stretched taut across his huge frame, his dimpled fingers drumming the countertop. He'd told her once that he was really Minnesota Fats and for most of a year Jake had believed him, until Billy had set her straight. Since then, she'd been wary of Jumbo Johnny, but he was a good way to kill the afternoon. For nickels he'd spot anybody on the punch card and push an endless supply of hot dogs across the faded red enamel counter to pay up. Jake wondered absently if Jumbo Johnny knew anything about the solar system, her assignment for science class, but decided against asking. Across the room, between cigarette smoke and shots of warm Pepsi, Billy waited for the mark to sweat out his turn on the table. It was going to be a long night. Jake stretched up to send the abacus beads spinning along the wire over Jumbo Johnny's head, imagining it was the solar system.

Jake stayed with Billy until she was seventeen and he decided to go on the road for a while. And now Billy was five years gone across the mesa with Willow. A big yellow car—some said it was a Lincoln, others a Cadillac—ran him down outside an Oklahoma City pool hall. The cops called it an accident. Jake didn't really believe it but figured cops didn't worry much about dead Indians who made their living off other people's inflated egos in the back of pool halls when dawn was knocking hard. Only Jake could appreciate the irony of the yellow car: Billy'd lost more shots with that one-ball than any man in history. But accident or fate, Billy was dead, leaving her only his monogrammed pool stick in its genuine leather case, and all the dreams she could carry.

Jumbo Johnny's was gone now, too. Not six months after they'd buried Billy, Jumbo Johnny met the widow of an African missionary and got religion. They turned the pool hall into a mission for the wayward, where, for the price of "The Old Rugged Cross" and a forty-five-minute sermon delivered by the Reverend Mrs. Jumbo Johnny, haggard men and broken women could fill their bellies with thick soup, spongy white bread, and fatty meat.

A nest of ratty memories and a pool stick were all that remained of Jake's old life. Sometimes she imagined that one night when she was leaning over the table at Babe's she'd look up and Billy really would be there, cigarette curled deep into his lower lip, smoke tickling the side of his rugged handsome face, his black eyes grinning at her. *"It was some other old boy they found outside that Okie pool hall,"* he'd say, and linking arms, the pair of them would take off down the street into the night, just like old times. Sometimes dreams and promises are all life leaves, even for gamblers.

But growing up with Billy and Jumbo Johnny had given Jake a yearning for a regular life. From what she'd seen, the road didn't offer much, even to pool players. Lacking the skills for either the shipyards or the streets, Jake took a job in the kitchen at Mother's Garden, a restaurant and health-food store and one of the last holdouts from the days when feminism meant lesbian pride. Long before dawn, Jake was at the restaurant baking bread. Afternoons, she slept. Nights, she held court

at Babe's pool table. So it was when she met Tina, who sent her
life and heart spinning like an out-of-control cue ball.

Only now things weren't good with Tina, either. Tina's face
rose in Jake's mind, sending a black cloud across the night.
Jake scowled and blinked, trying to banish Tina back to the
suburbs where she was so damned happy, but the vision
wouldn't budge. It stood there, hands on hips, full lips pouting
and pursed, pale blue eyes flashing. Jake took a swig of Pepsi
and shook her head slightly, trying harder to dislodge Tina and
conjure up Billy. At least Billy was full of good times, right up
to the end. But more than that, Billy never asked Jake to be
anything more than she ever was—unlike Tina.

It wasn't that she didn't love Tina; it was more that Tina
loved her too much. Sometimes. No, all the time. Tina had
found Jake at Babe's pool table. They'd fallen in love over
Willie Nelson songs and fried eggs at 4:00 A.M., snuggled into
a booth at the Golden Lotus restaurant, a twenty-four-hour
diner full of late-night drunks, truck drivers, and neighborhood
insomniacs.

Through the fog and dust of that first morning, Tina had
spilled her life out on the table like a tormented child. As Jake
listened to the stories of love lost and pain won, it had become
impossible for her to turn away. "I want to take care of you,"
she'd whispered, and she'd meant it. Tina had smiled then, and
Jake had seen in her eyes a tender, fragile child who didn't
understand the pain of life, the unfairness of love. And that
night, for the first time, Jake had broken her unwritten rule:
She'd let Tina into her bed, her heart, even her life.

At the bar that next night, Jake's friends were eager to tell
all they knew about Tina. How her last lover, Castille, had
wallowed in an alcoholic stupor for years. How Tina would sit
at the bar watching Castille drink until last call, then lead
her—sometimes willingly, other times not—out to the parking
lot, where their arguments shattered the night. How Castille
would check herself into the hospital to try and dry out every
six months or so, and even stay, until Tina showed up a day or
two later to take her home. How Castille was prone to late-
night motorcycle accidents on lonely canyon roads—that some
believed weren't really accidents at all. How the last one, which
landed her in the hospital for nearly two months, had almost
killed Castille. And how the morning before she was supposed
to go home to Tina, Castille had called Matty to borrow two

hundred dollars. By noon Castille was on the plane home to Chicago. She'd told Matty it was the only way she could survive. The kindest among the women at Babe's said Castille was running away from the bars. But those whose sharp eyes were matched only by their razor tongues said it was Tina she was running from. Either way, Castille was only three weeks gone when Tina found Jake.

Listening politely, Jake had dismissed the stories as bar gossip. Tina had seemed too sweet and lost in those early days. Castille's drinking was legendary around the bars. She wasn't the first drunk to have a motorcycle accident, and she wouldn't be the last, Jake had reasoned. To her mind, Tina was well rid of the woman. Those were the words Jake had used to comfort Tina on nights when Castille's leaving had stalked her like a demon's breath. Jake had kissed away Tina's tears and confusion, losing her sight and her mind in the softness of Tina's belly and breasts. Wearing the taste and scent of Tina on her cheeks and tongue, Jake would stumble, still soft and sleepy and a half-hour late, to her bread-baking shift, shrugging off the snide looks and jokes of the women already dusted with white powder.

When Jake had first started dating the wan high school English teacher from the suburbs, Tina's jealousy was flattering. Night after night she would wrap herself into her new-found lover, hanging on so tightly that Jake was sure she'd suffocate. Every time she tried to squirm free, Tina's grip tightened until Jake finally lay still, caught so close their breath could have come from a single breast. The pity and the pain of it was that Jake had wanted it, once.

Those summer nights had stretched slow and easy in front of them. Tina had spent them perched like a proud parakeet on a bar stool by the pool table while Jake practiced and played. Tina always declined with a giggle, a smile, a quick kiss every time Jake offered her a stick. "Oh, honey, I can't play that game," she'd say, turning the innocent words into a loaded fantasy, until Jake's heart had plummeted to her belly and lay there pounding and throbbing; until Jake could feel the little hairs on the back of her neck prickle and shudder as if they were waiting for Tina's breath, her tongue. And Jake would cut the game short, grab Tina by the hand, pulling her off the stool and out the door. Tina the giggling, willing conspirator to their new love.

At first, Jake was happy, as happy as only a woman newly in love can be. And Tina, who had apparently forgotten about Castille, found her life unfolding like a long promise. It was perfectly natural, then, for Jake to give up her cramped studio apartment that looked out beyond iron bars onto a grubby courtyard and move into Tina's life.

Jake wasn't sure when it changed or how, only that it had, until she found herself faking happiness like a whore faking orgasm. Confusion and loneliness had settled across their life together like ocean fog that refused to lift, to burn off in the morning sun. On days when she dared to think about it, Jake could only shake her head, confused, hurt, angry at how effortlessly Tina's life was wrapped around her. Moving into the homogeneous town house had been Tina's idea. Tina was right, the daily commute to Mother's Garden was grueling; taking the job in the cafeteria at Tina's school was more sensible. And all the other high school teachers had unlisted phone numbers, and for good reason, Tina assured her, so Jake had gone along with that too, even though her friends always lost the number no matter how often she wrote it on Babe's bar napkins. Finally, the sensible hatchback replaced the aging crotchety Ford truck that had left Jake stranded once too often by the freeway entrance. The hatchback always started. The faceless cafeteria job paid better. And Jake didn't use phones much anyway.

Eventually, Jake put her old life away until finally the suburbs closed in, leaving her alone with Tina. Just as Tina had always dreamed, planned, plotted, Jake was all hers and nobody would ever take her away. Everything was going great; Tina said so, everyone said so. Even Jake knew she should be happier than she'd been in years. She had all the things she was supposed to want. Then why was she so miserable?

Roaring through the bar on a determined course to the table where Jake was chalking her cue, Pidge stopped short. Surprise registered on her broad handsome face. It had been three months since she'd seen Jake, but it might have been last week, so familiar was the sight of her best friend and one-time lover.

"So where you been?" Pidge demanded, slightly drunk and sunburned from a long week in the desert on the back of Lorna's new motorcycle. Squirming free of Jake's bear hug,

Pidge inhaled what was left of her beer, determined that Jake should appreciate the ripeness of her indignation at being abandoned for a schoolteacher who couldn't even shoot pool. "Still living out there in the beige wasteland with Our Miss Priss?" Pidge demanded, sucking in her cheeks until she looked slightly like a fish. It was her impression of Tina.

"It ain't like it's that far away," Jake offered, more as an apology than an explanation, deciding to ignore the bait about Tina. "You could come out. Tina'd like it."

Pidge chuckled at that, shaking her head slightly. Tina hated Pidge, just as she hated the city and everything else that had ever been a part of Jake before they'd met. It was no accident, Pidge thought, that when she went to live with Tina Jake had lost touch with her old life, old friends, everything that had ever been important to her. "Yeah, I figure I'd be about as welcome as old Faye over there. Maybe we could ride out together, give the schoolmarm a real thrill some Saturday afternoon."

Jake shot her old friend a black look. "She's not like that, really," Jake added, but her voice sounded like she didn't quite believe her words.

"Well, you never would listen to nothing nobody said about that woman," Pidge muttered. "So where's she at tonight? Off to the country club dance? Or'd you wise up and leave the bitch?" Jake shrugged miserably and turned away. So that's it, Pidge thought, Jake finally got the courage to walk out and now she doesn't know what to do. Pulling Jake close, Pidge whispered an obscene suggestion, winked, and laughed. Jake laughed, too, and pushed the butt end of Billy's custom cue toward Pidge, a genuine act of affection. Grinning, Pidge accepted the offer and moved to the table.

"How many nights you reckon we've shared this table?" Pidge suddenly asked, assessing the scatter of colored balls.

Jake shrugged. "Hundreds, maybe more." They laughed in the way of old friends, their thoughts turning back to that first night so many years ago when they'd marched into the bar wearing all the bravado and leather they could find, fake IDs in their wallets, and their hearts trembling in terror as much as anticipation. First their hearts stopped trembling, even for each other. They lost the bravado a couple of years later. Finally, the leather and a good laugh were all that remained of those first glorious days of celebration and discovery. Eventually Pidge and Jake moved to the intimacy that lies beyond passion. When one reached for the other across the night, it was as if she was reaching for a part of herself, the mirror of who she was and could be. Neither of them could change that or would even try. Pidge always suspected that was what Tina really hated about her.

Jake watched quietly, trying to sort out the events of the past four hours that had led her to Babe's pool table. It had all started with a wrong turn at the shopping mall; she was sure of that. Hodges, the school janitor, had told her about a short-cut that had turned instead into a nightmare where polite earth-tone houses on wide streets had led only to more houses and streets that turned into a labyrinth. Jake was a mouse she'd once seen in a maze. No matter which way the mouse ran, it never found its way out. As lost as she'd ever been in the tangle of suburban streets that stretched before her, Jake had suddenly known that there was no map that could ever help her find her way. Frozen in time, she no longer knew where home was or who it was. Maybe home was Tina; sometimes she thought so, even if it wasn't the town house that was identical to all the other houses on all the other neat streets where everyone was safe, even if it was only from themselves. That was Tina's kind of life; she understood it, even wanted it. But in that house with Tina, Jake was the little girl outside the darkened toy-store window. The feeling rocked her belly, all but knocking her breath loose. She wanted to run somewhere, anywhere, but her legs were turning to lead.

Finally, near tears, Jake had found her own street, the house she'd shared with Tina through these long last months. "They all look alike." She'd sobbed while Tina fumed, then laughed at the foolishness of it all.

"Now you know how I feel when I get lost in the city." Tina had chuckled. She was drunk. When Jake hadn't shown up to cook, Tina had decided to forgo the formalities of dinner and start with the afterdinner drinks—right after the before-dinner cocktails.

Jake's temper had risen until her face flushed red. "Don't you understand nothin'? I don't fucking belong here!" Sensing disaster, Tina had danced toward Jake, only stumbling a little as she attempted to lick and kiss the storm away. Any other night Jake might have pushed the anger, the fear to the back of her brain, giving herself up to the tinges of electricity that shot through her veins whenever Tina pulled her close. But this night felt different. She'd pushed Tina away.

"If I don't . . . get out . . . of here . . . I'm . . . gonna . . . die." Jake had stammered the words to life for the first time and was shocked at the sound. Uninvited tears had invaded her eyes. Ashen, she had tried to form words to meet her thoughts, sure that if she could just say it right, Tina would finally understand what was happening to her, to them.

But Tina hadn't been interested. Raising drunken eyes, she'd finally focused on her lover, who was babbling about leaving the suburbs, quitting her job, moving back to the city with all the filth that lived there. Jake's words were spilling out in a rush, washing around Tina, attempting to carry her along. The words were like a record played at the wrong speed, though, and Tina hadn't been able to sort out Jake's meaning.

"Don't be stupid," Tina had finally snapped, hoping that would silence Jake's suddenly intent and equally inept attempts at conversation, wishing Jake would just be quiet and watch television instead of trying to make her think. That was what she'd always liked about Jake, she didn't talk too much. But Jake had persisted, the sound swirling, the words jumbled.

"Well how many women need a damned map to find their way home from the grocery store?" Tina had finally demanded, her voice tinged with sarcasm, liquor, and hate.

The liquor bared the contempt in her voice. Nearly a year had passed since Jake had moved in, and she was still always getting lost. The logic and pattern of the suburbs escaped her. At first it had been cute, and Tina had been patient, drawing little maps to tape on the hatchback's dash. A big lavender heart marked their house, surrounded by a tangle of streets that were punctuated with notations for the school, the grocery store, the nearest shopping mall. The map was a necessity, a concession, a constant reminder of how to find home and Tina. But lately the map, Jake's seeming inability to learn even the simplest configuration of streets was an irritant, a burr, a seed that Jake was somehow using to mock her.

Tina had narrowed her eyes, studying Jake as if she were a moth on a laboratory pin. She was pleased with what she saw.

Should Jake ever think of escape, though she couldn't imagine
why she ever would, Tina was ready with the trump played in
their soft queen-sized waterbed. A child of shopping malls and
garden clubs, Tina understood the sheer bargaining power of
sex. That, the video cassette recorder, and the pool table in the
recreation room were the only entertainment Jake would ever
need; Tina was sure of it. Mostly it was true enough, for Jake
was a woman of habit as much as desire, and the sheer promise
of Tina's soft flesh was enough to keep her close—except for
nights when freedom called and Billy was whispering, cutting
through Tina's perfumed chains.

"Tina, please, listen to me." Jake had heard the pleading in
her voice and suddenly hated Tina for putting it there. All the
anger and hate that Jake had buried so carefully had welled up
in her throat, its bile choking her like acid. *"Don't never beg
nobody for nothin'; it'll only get you beat,"* Billy had chided.
Jake had fallen into sullen silence until the fuse to the dyna-
mite she'd kept secreted for so long ignited. The harder Jake
had tried to stop it, the stronger the fury grew, until her very
breath, every shadow of tone or thought or action had flared
into battle fires.

"You're supposed to be so fucking smart!" Jake had raged.
"Why can't you see that I want out!" Shaking off Tina's limply
offered smile, her outstretched hand, Jake had felt as if she was
fighting for her very soul. The rage was real and it triggered a
fear and a hatred so deeply ingrained in Tina that they both
had understood the only way to keep Jake was to destroy her—
or try.

"I'm sick of it . . . all of it . . . of this . . ." Jake had stammered,
her uncollected thoughts turning to an ugly red stain of sound.
At first, Jake hadn't been sure that what she heard was real.
But then Tina had started to laugh, at herself, at Jake, at the
two of them, at all they were and ever could be. Jake's stomach
churned in disgust at the sound.

"*You're* sick of it?" Tina had mocked, making her way toward Jake, who was visibly trembling. "Nobody could be as sick
of anything as I am of you." The words had come hard and cold,
turning Tina's face dark and ugly. Only inches from Jake, Tina
had stared for a long second and then laughed again. When
Jake's hand had shot out, knocking the highball glass to the
floor, it had been as much to silence Tina as to scare her.
Watching the brown liquid ooze a stain into the white shag

carpet, Tina had taken a deep breath and railed at Jake, her eyes narrow, gleaming, her voice shrill. She was the demon mother, conjuring all Jake's deepest, most secret fears, breathing life into them, setting them loose on her prey.

"So who asked you to stay?" she'd jeered. "Go back to that hole where I found you with the cockroaches in the kitchen and the garbage outside the window. That's where you belong. See if I care. There's a hundred more like you and I could have any one of them."

Her words had peeled back the skin on Jake's throat, exposing the throbbing jugular, then sunk in, hitting their mark, draining their victim. "I don't even know why I bother with you. You're not even a decent lay. The only thing you're good for is shooting pool in some bar with a bunch of other losers. You're nothing. You've always been nothing. Without me you'd crawl back into Babe's and rot there. Well, go ahead, do it! Nobody gives a shit about you, and you know it." Tina had straightened her shoulders then and stumbled from the room without looking back, leaving Jake motionless on the couch, her fingers curling around the reinforced role of pennies she still carried in her jeans—one of Billy's remaining legacies.

The anger had wrapped itself around Jake's fist. Coiled in her arm, tensing the muscles there. With one move, she could have pinned Tina against the floor, smashing her face into the carpet until the arrogance spilled out like blood. She could beat Tina, bruise her pale flesh until it turned dark and purple, but even that wouldn't stop the truth of what they were, what they'd let themselves become. Jake had wanted so desperately what Tina offered—a real life in a real house where wind-bells sent tinkling melodies to the moon while she wrapped a woman she loved close to her heart. Home. Was the price really so high, Jake wondered. Yes, she could beat the woman to silence, but not the words, or the memories, or the love. So she'd sat, hot tears of shame burning her eyes. They knew their roles too well: Jake was the snake, Tina the mongoose. Curses had welled in Jake's throat, caught there, and died.

Tina's sobs had shuddered against the night. Jake could go to the door, knock softly, comfort Tina just as she had all the times before. She might have, too, if only Tina hadn't made her beg, hadn't ripped away her pride, torn at her soul. Finally, the bedroom door had clicked slightly as Tina unlocked it, the signal for Jake to come and apologize. Jake had stood by the door for a long moment, listening to the tears, the desperation, willing Tina to walk out, to say she was sorry just once. Only there was no sound of movement beyond the door. Jake had trembled, waiting. The moment passed. Jake might have been a somnambulist, so slowly did she move toward the closet, taking down Billy's pool cue, where lately it had spent more time than not. Silently, she'd left the house, the fine line between love and hate melding strangely in her mind.

At the sound of the front door closing, Tina pulled herself off the bed and crept to the window. Half-blinded by tears, she heard more than saw Jake's car back out of the driveway. The worst of her fears was realized. She was left alone with demons of her own making that would stalk her into the dawn.

"Don't go," she whispered to the night. "Don't leave me . . . alone." The hatchback's tires spun slightly as Jake roared into the darkness leaving Tina's anguished face pressed against the cool glass. "I'm sorry. Oh, God! I'm so sorry," Tina moaned, her arms crossing around her full breasts as she rocked against the wall. "Why do they leave, why do they always leave me?" she asked the night. Only, the night made no reply.

"Six to the side," Pidge predicted, rousing Jake from her thoughts long enough to shrug at the improbable shot. On a good night, Pidge didn't miss Jake too much. Only when black winds bore down hard against her soul did Pidge marvel at the emptiness that haunted her core where Jake's laugh had been. The suburbs were probably a good place for schoolteachers and secretaries, Pidge reasoned, but not for her and probably not for Jake. She wondered absently how Jake even found her way around the strange landscape.

Jake seemed to be warming to the game, to the comfort of being on her own without Tina. It felt good. *"Freedom,"* Billy whispered, and Jake saw the flash of the eagle he'd had tattooed on his right forearm, the dead mate of the half-finished one she wore. Adding the red and yellow and green was somehow pointless after Billy was gone, so the bird remained only a blueprint of what might have been. Remembering Billy and the eagle—who trembled in flight when Billy moved his forearm—stoked Jake's belly. A broad smile exploded on her face. For that brief moment she glowed like diamonds in the sun.

A dozen feet away, a plump redhead with rosy freckled cheeks and full breasts caressed by a satin western shirt watched the players intently. Fingering a pool cue as if she was looking for something very special, the woman's green eyes inventoried Jake: the smile that showed off slightly crooked teeth; the wide-set black eyes that flashed like a falling star against a dark moon; the straight black hair that fell into her eyes. Sturdy legs in worn jeans she'd bought fifteen pounds ago and hadn't bothered to replace stretched taut across Jake's ass when she leaned into the table. Thick, powerful arms. A strange blue-green phoenix bird etched on the left. A red and gold snake curling into the right hand, so that when she made a fist, the snake's head trembled in fury and anticipation. The sheer power and promise of the snake caught Kris's breath hard against her throat.

For some, watching the players was better sport than actually playing. As the hard smoothness of the wood slid between their fingers like a whisper, the green-eyed woman followed their every practiced move. A novice at pool, she had come to see the players moving around the table like so many colorful balls. She liked the anonymous click-click of the balls, the good-natured hoots and jeers that followed the good players—and the bad. The warmth of the easy laughter and harmless poolroom jokes enfolded her like a blanket. The way the women touched each other so easily, as if they were comfortable in their skins, warmed her. Studying the players as closely as the players studied the table, the red-haired woman let her fingers memorize the feel of the slippery stick cupped in the fold of her right arm, let her mind fill with smooth velvet-wet skin moving under those fingers. She licked her lips absently, a move not lost on Pidge, who nudged Jake and nodded toward the woman by the wall. Jake smiled back, an open honest greeting that was accepted as an invitation.

Pidge was playing eagerly but badly. Long nights of whiskey and Lorna were showing. The game was going nowhere anyway, so Pidge decided to give it up and look for Lorna, who had promised to be at the bar by ten. It was almost ten-thirty. Signaling to Jake that the game was hers, Pidge widened her eyes in surprise when Jake shook her head no. The hungry eyes of the redhead in the corner kept following Jake, nudging feelings alive that she hadn't known in a long time. Jake wasn't sure she could be left alone with those eyes, which felt like a fist in her belly. Soon, maybe, but not just yet. Pidge's eyes skidded from Jake over to the wall. A cocky smile crossed Pidge's face. It had taken her years to cultivate and perfect that look. It was one she used to fell the hearts of the pretty hardened women she liked to carry on her arm. For an instant, Pidge's eyes locked with the green ones. Pidge liked the honesty, the simple hunger she saw there. Looking at Jake, she wondered if she saw it, too.

But Jake's attention appeared to be fixed on the game. Still, every time Jake looked up, those green eyes were there, watching, wanting, but willing to wait, too. Pidge smiled.

"What d'ya think about that," she muttered, nodding slightly toward the wall.

"Don't know her," Jake answered as her thumb rubbed chalk back and forth over the soft nub of the pool cue, then circled gently.

"Would you like to?" Pidge asked under her breath, winking. "Nine ball inna corner," she announced, willing the game over. Her eyes followed the long shimmering line of stick to the perfect white ball that waited for Jake's magic. A second later and it was ended.

"Pay up, Pidge," Jake demanded, her voice a little too light with laughter and triumph. "That'll be a fresh Pepsi and two big packages of them honey-coated peanuts." Jake didn't drink, everyone knew that, but Pidge never understood the Pepsi and peanuts. The floating peanuts always reminded Pidge of rabbit turds. And Jake's way of taking a swig of Pepsi, then catching the peanuts with her tongue and storing them in her cheeks like a chipmunk preparing for winter was disgusting. But Jake had been playing for Pepsi and peanuts, so the only honorable thing to do was pay up.

Shaking her head, Pidge picked her way through the crowd. Jake had told her once years ago that Billy had cured her of drinking when she was fifteen years old. He'd caught her in the alley behind Jumbo Johnny's with a stolen pint of Jack Daniels and Maybeth Conners, her best friend. Billy had sent Maybeth home and had dragged Jake by the collar into the liquor store downstairs from their apartment. Billy bought a six-pack of Pepsi and a fifth of Jack Daniels. Then he'd sat Jake down at their kitchen table and poured a glass of whiskey. When she'd drunk that, he poured another, and another, and another after that until the room spun wickedly and Jake had crawled to the bathroom to be sick. "I don't waste no time on drunks," he'd hissed. "You know what drunks are? They're pigeons, chumps. Which one are you—a pigeon or a chump?" It was a lesson Jake never forgot.

Wading into the cache of bodies pushed against the bar, Pidge could see Jake's reflection dimly in the mirror. Was she ignoring the self-conscious redhead who'd been watching their game and Jake so eagerly or just playing hard to get, Pidge wondered, a sly smile crinkling her round face. Jake knew a lot about pool but not much about women. "Sure hope this one's not a schoolteacher," Pidge muttered to herself, draping her arm across the back of the woman on the nearest bar stool.

"You ain't a schoolteacher, neither, are ya honey?" Pidge asked, leaning into the strange woman's neck, giving her a quick kiss and countering the anticipated indignant look with an exaggerated "Ex-cuse me!" and a laugh.

Leaning against the pool table, Jake was chalking her cue with deliberate care. The red-haired woman was watching her intently. Jake could feel the hungry eyes on her back, willing her to turn around, to look, just for a moment or maybe forever. All the while Jake's heart was straining against her skin, trembling, pounding in anticipation. No one had looked at her like that in a long time, certainly not Tina. Turning slowly back to the table, Jake assessed her opponent, Bo, a square dark woman whose arms were as hard as the set to her jaw. Her eyes grazed Bo's shoulder as Jake assessed the woman leaning into the wall.

Short red curls tumbled untamed around the woman's face, all but hiding her forehead. A collection of undisciplined freckles marched helter-skelter across her chest under the blue satin western shirt that was open just enough to show off the rise of her breasts. Jake inhaled slowly, savoring the feeling before she raised her gaze level with a pair of huge green eyes that smiled a shy secret, jolting Jake erect. *"Whoa, Mama!"* Billy whistled approvingly. Looking away quickly, Jake exhaled, then dared herself to look back at this woman. Green eyes again met Jake's gaze, then dropped shyly to study an invisible spot on the floor. Smiling, Jake nodded slightly and took the break. A lot of years had passed since she'd played as flamboyantly as she would that night under those beautiful, patient, watchful eyes that were sending her fantasies sliding free and easy.

Buying time while she decided what to do, Jake was glad she and Bo were going for two out of three. Nobody else wanted the table and Bo's game was like her body: careful, slow, deliberate, and hard to beat. Taking a swig of the lukewarm Pepsi, Jake's tongue was slightly disappointed to discover the peanuts were finally gone. The last game was close and a tiny fan club had grown up around each player. The green-eyed woman was in Jake's corner with Pidge, Lorna, and Bungie, who talked a better game of pool than she played. Two of Bo's buddies, their arms locked around the waists of their girlfriends, glowered in silence on the other side of the table. Jake's black eyes darted around the table, following the motion of the balls until the rainbow lay finally still. Rubbing the smooth sleekness of the pool cue across her cheek, Jake studied the table, evaluating each shot, every possibility and combination. Bo raised her left shoulder slightly, nodding toward the felt, a signal for Jake to stop grandstanding and get on with it.

In the mirror behind the pool table, the green-eyed woman was studying her own reflection. She liked to imagine herself as tough, hard, experienced, wise to the ways of women and bars and the world, even though she was none of those things. Looking like what she was, the part-owner of a small bookstore, irritated her. Just once she wanted the swagger, the hard edge that women like Pidge and Jake wore so easily. Moving slightly to the left so she could avoid her reflection, the woman turned her eyes back to Jake. Jake looked up, smiled, and winked. The green-eyed woman blushed at the wink, felt a cadence of goose bumps march across her breasts, rivaling the freckles there.

With an indignant yowl, Jake gave the game up to Bo. Familiar rivals, they'd meet again. Jake turned from the table, with a wide easy smile for Pidge and the green-eyed woman.

"Jake, this here's Kris," Pidge said, draping her arm loosely around the green-eyed woman's shoulder. "Kris, honey, this here's my good buddy Jake." Pidge was obviously pleased with herself. "And she ain't even a schoolteacher," she gloated in her best stage whisper. "Take care of each other, kids." Pidge winked and led Lorna off in the direction of the dance floor, chuckling.

Stolen Moments

By the time Jake conceded to Bo, it was nearly time for Luna's show. The poolroom emptied rapidly, except for Jake and Kris, who faced each other awkwardly. "So, you want to go see the show?" Jake finally asked. The words came slow and heavy. Kris shrugged. From the other side of the bar, they could hear the intro music begin: "Our Day Will Come," Luna's theme song.

"There's probably not any good seats left anyway," Jake offered, hoping Kris would stay here with her.

"Probably not," Kris agreed, running her fingers along the felt. "I've seen her show before."

Jake nodded. "You play much?" she asked, meaning pool.

"Hardly at all," Kris admitted. "But I could learn . . . if you'd teach me. You're very good. I was watching you."

"I know. You brought me luck," Jake lied, the kind of small lie new lovers tell. Jake nodded toward the table, then smiled and winked at Kris. "It's easier than it looks . . . mostly . . . so long as you're not serious. You're serious, then that's something else." She led Kris to the edge of the table. "You hold the stick like this." Jake positioned Kris, then stepped behind her, guiding her arms. Jake pulled the cue back. Kris's shoulders moved under Jake's breasts. "And this." She pushed the cue forward in a long smooth, sweep that brought Jake's mouth close to Kris's throat. She smells of flowers, Jake thought, her breath coming short.

In the next room, Luna was whirling across the stage, rainbow clouds of gossamer flying behind her as the music swelled like the wind before a summer storm.

Jake leaned more deeply into Kris, imagining the jeans, the satin shirt stripped away and Kris lying naked across the table. She has beautiful breasts, Jake thought, looking inside the blue satin shirt. She inhaled slowly, closing her eyes, feeling Kris breathing softly under her. With one slight move of her hand, Jake could slide her fingers inside the satin shirt, explore the treasures hidden there. With one slight breath, she could bury her face in the soft neck that was throbbing so innocently next to her hungry tongue. With one slight move . . .

Onstage, Luna moved her hand slightly across her shoulder and her costume fell away, leaving her covered only in spangles and baubles, her breasts shimmering.

"Like this?" Kris turned to look at Jake. She looked soft and sleepy, like a woman in love. Reaching full around Kris, Jake guided another shot, conscious more of her breasts buried warm and full in Kris's broad back. Bracing Kris's extended leg between her own, Jake led the arms, the hands, the stick through motions that were as familiar as breath itself. It had been more than a year since she'd held a woman other than Tina, and Jake's muscles and nerves were busy exploring, memorizing the feel of Kris's flesh. And Kris, her breath caught quick and uneasy in her throat, felt the flush of Jake's hot breath against her. Kris leaned back into the woman who held her, whose strong arms moved hers like a skilled puppeteer. Swaying back from the table, drunk with the feeling, the lights, the closeness, the magic, Kris and Jake found themselves moving to the music, locked in each other's arms.

Under the blue stage lights that made Luna's costume sparkle like an August country night full of stars, her fingers released the spangles, setting her perfect breasts free.

Closing her eyes, Jake buried her face in Kris's neck, smelling jasmine oil and soap. The background music from the stage whispered into the poolroom, which was silent except for soft murmurs and moans. Jake slowly unsnapped Kris's satin shirt, letting the air tickle the soft warm flesh that hid there. Cupping her breasts, one in each hand, Jake buried her face in them, opening her mouth slightly to inhale their perfume. Her tongue traced the pink nipples, delicate as camelias in the spring. Kris tangled her fingers in Jake's hair, pushing her face deeper into her, savoring the warmth, the tongue, insistent and rough as a kitten's. Jake tasted the salt dampness of sweat and flesh.

Luna ran her hands the length of her body, caressing her

own flesh, her head thrown back in mock ecstasy, her back arched in anticipation of a lover.

As Kris stepped closer into Jake, the bar fell away until they were swaying gently in a deep green forest. Her fingers fumbled with the buttons on Jake's shirt, then slid unafraid under the cloth to caress Jake's naked back. Jake's breasts kissed Kris's own puckering, anxious nipples. Their arms intertwined, bellies melding. Kris buried her face in Jake's hair, smelling peppermint soap and smoke. She moaned slightly, so softly that it might have been nothing more than a whisper or a sigh. And she offered her flesh, her heart, her very hunger to this woman whose confident tongue was sucking and lapping at her neck. The lights turned to spangles on the horizon, sparkling like bits of phosphorous on a pond.

Luna was in the audience, now, letting them tuck dollar bills, fives, and an occasional ten in the silvery costume that glittered as she moved from lap to lap, accepting kisses and adoration.

"I want you," Jake whispered, Kris's face cupped in her hands. Their eyes locked. Kris smiled. Jake kissed her—once, then again—marveling at the softness of her lips. Drawing Kris closer, Jake led her into a desert sun where they would dance naked on hot sand. Playing hide-and-seek like children, they would scamper and prance, chasing their own long shadows. The wind would cry, rustling against them. Kris would glow against the shining sand, her hair blazing like flame. They would tumble onto a bed of glowing embers, Jake pulling the flame closer, closer, until it burned them with passion and light. Her fingers would drown in the oasis protected by rings of fire. She would hold the light, touch the fire, protecting it even when the sun fell away, leaving the sand cold and gray beneath them. And then they would fly away like birds come together for a day or a season, each free to go her own way. Perhaps another day they would come together again as lovers. But always they would have the memory of the fire to warm them. Always.

Back onstage, Luna twirled and dipped, dancing like a woman possessed with passion and life. She was Terpsichore. She was freedom. She was passion and beauty unleashed. And the audience throbbed with want of her.

Kris breathed slowly, softly, as if she were trying to stop time. Clinging to Jake, her fingers roamed, touching, exploring the creases and dimples of flesh. Rolling a tender brown nipple between her thumb and forefinger, she probed Jake's open mouth with her tongue. Stopping only when their eyes met, she whispered, "I need you, more than I ever imagined." Jake moaned. Her strong determined fingers pushed deep inside Kris's jeans, moving slowly across her naked skin, exposing the passion rooted there, dancing in her wet cunt. The very thought of Jake's lips moving across her breasts, her belly, against her cunt made Kris sway, breathless. Her mind spun dreams and visions.

Jake's key would turn in the lock of Kris's door. In her left hand would be a bouquet of wildflowers stolen from a neat garden. Under her arm would be the Sunday paper, though it was only Saturday evening. Only, they would forget about the news, spreading each other out on the bed instead. Jake would shrug out of her clothes, a woman comfortable in her body. Kris would lean down and kiss her, gently at first, then harder, more insistent as Jake's fingers opened the robe, pushing it away, exposing soft freckled breasts tipped with rosebuds. Her cunt open, Kris would slide warm, wet, and open down Jake's leg, leaving traces of dampness on her tender flesh. It would feel like a mouth wide, soft, wet, hungry. She would ride the leg, her own fingers buried in Jake's cunt, which would smell of a secret sea. Night would fall away. Time would shudder and stop in the face of passion until there was neither time nor sense nor reason.

Luna, now wearing only a silver G-string, was slowing her dance. Tiny pearls of sweat slid like tears between her breasts.

Strains of "Our Day Will Come" began to swell and reach to the lovers in the poolroom. Luna's show was ending. The audience began to clap and cheer. In a few moments, they'd be streaming back to the dance floor, the bar, the game machines, the pool tables. Jake looked at Kris and grinned her crooked grin, stepping out of the embrace. She began closing the snaps on Kris's shirt, then buttoned her own, grinning self-consciously. Kris blushed, then smiled. "Thank you," she whispered.

"What for?" Jake asked, stuffing her shirt back in her jeans. She turned to look at Kris curiously. But she only shook her head. Jake kissed her quickly as Pidge roared back into the room.

"Ho-ho! What have we here?" She winked knowingly at Jake.

"I've been showing Kris how to shoot pool," Jake answered, trying to sound nonchalant.

"I can see that." Pidge laughed. "That's why the cues are over there and you're both over here." Her eyes twinkled. "I just come to tell you that we're gonna take off. Don't be a stranger." She punched Jake playfully. "And you, take care of my buddy, hear?" This last was directed at Kris, who blushed like a guilty child.

Holding hands, Kris and Jake leaned against the back wall, watching the last of the pool players. They shared secrets and whispers, giggling like teenagers. As if sensing their newfound passion, the women who eased past them smiled knowingly. Jake kissed Kris's eyelids. Kris's lips brushed Jake's knuckles. Standing so close, their breasts melted into one mass of flesh and flannel and satin, their cunts dampening against their jeans. Music throbbed through them until they seemed to beat with one heart.

"You could take me home with you," Kris whispered, hoping the music masked the terror in her voice. Jake only hugged her tighter, saying nothing. When Kris looked up, Jake's eyes had lost their smile.

"I have a lover," Jake confessed, averting her eyes, loosening her arms a little from Kris's waist. Kris nodded and looked at the floor, trying to hold back the tears, not sure why she felt like crying.

"I'm sorry," Jake offered finally, lifting Kris's chin so she could look into her eyes. Kris nodded again, then quickly brushed her lips across Jake's.

"I have a lover, too, sort of. At least I had one before this afternoon," Kris said. Jake nodded.

They moved onto the dance floor, but the mood had turned and their touch was lighter as their passion dimmed. They moved quickly and well, just as they might have in bed. They shook out their dreams like sheets against the wind, watching their fantasies blow free.

"We could go for breakfast," Jake offered once the music stopped, trying to capture the moment again, unwilling to let Kris go.

Kris started to smile in anticipation, then shook her head almost sadly. "I don't think so, but thanks for the possibilities."

Jake smiled then shrugged. "Well, just remember what I showed you. About pool, I mean."

The light returned to Kris's eyes, remembering Jake's strong hands, her muscled shoulders, her soft breasts, the glimmer of passion, of being wanted, desired. She wanted desperately to kiss Jake but instead reached out and squeezed her hand and smiled. "I'll remember," she said, letting Jake go, watching her make her way back to the pool table. "I'll always remember," Kris whispered as the door to Babe's closed behind her and she began the long walk home.

Kris: Lovers and Sometime Strangers

If anyone had bothered to ask, which was unlikely, Kris would have quickly explained that being at Babe's that Saturday night had been more by accident than intent. Of course, more living has been caused by accident than ever was by intent. Wasn't it only chance that had caused Sutra to stop over for a few days on her way back to Oregon? Hadn't everyone always said Jane had never really gotten over Sutra, even if she had lived with Kris for the past year? Certainly, no one had intended that the strange silence of lovemaking would rouse Kris from her nap and send her stumbling into the darkened living room that evening. It had all been an unfortunate, probably unavoidable, accident. An accident that had sent Jane raging into the lost night, and Sutra into the bathroom, where she'd done the logical thing: stuffed a towel under the door, lighted a pipeful of marijuana, filled the deep, footed tub with hot water, and watched her reflection fade from the mirror.

All these things had left Kris to prowl the bars, looking more for reasons and answers than for Jane. Any other night she would have been content to stay home, watching television or reading or sleeping. Sometimes she imagined she could gauge each year's passing by how much more she slept than the year before.

At seventeen, she had been the insomniac daughter, spending the night with F. Scott Fitzgerald and Zelda in her father's library. Of course, the insomnia—like the buoyant moods and bursts of creativity, which landed her a creative-writing scholarship—had all been fallout from the amphetamine prescription her mother's doctor had been too anxious to prescribe for the pudgy teenager Kris had been. When that prescription had run out, she just found another doctor. Then a cooperative pharmacist. Finally, an even more cooperative boy named Monkey who had an endless supply of black beauties and asked no questions. By then, she was a sophomore in college.

At twenty, Kris gave up the pills. Once too often, she'd started shouting at empty chairs and strangers. The pill-induced paranoia left quickly enough, but not before she was banished from her sorority house for behavior unbecoming a member of the sisterhood. Sometime after that, she'd started sleeping. It was as if she was trying to make up for all the years of sleep she'd lost. Of course, on those rare nights when she couldn't sleep, there was always the bottle of vodka tucked away behind her roommate's underwear drawer.

The next year Lavinia Wallraven had arrived. Lavinia was a crumbling, sodden playwright who'd spent more of her time cranking out Hollywood scripts than she ever did on Broadway. Still, Lavinia considered herself a playwright—maybe she thought the term had more class—waiting for fame. Apparently the university agreed. At any rate, her successes of a generation before still kept her in demand in college English departments. Kris was her senior assistant, taking dictation, polishing Lavinia's pair of elderly golden Oscars—that she'd never won a Tony was Lavinia's greatest regret—and developing a taste for older women and brandy. No one mentioned it when Kris started sleeping on Lavinia's office couch.

At twenty-one, with Lavinia only a blurred memory, Kris had taken her brand new diploma and Katheryn Mott, Yale's most promising literary gem, to New York for a last long stolen weekend. Kris was on her way to Hollywood, Katheryn to Paris. The weekend was extended to Monday, then Tuesday, as they clung to each other, afraid of the future. Then on a fateful Wednesday morning, Kris found herself alone in their hotel room. A note carefully penned in Katheryn's lavish script and written on the hotel stationary was tucked into the mirror: "Sometimes we do, as we must. Some things we do, as we must. I'll always miss you. Truly, Katheryn." Kris had shredded the note, flushed it, then crawled back into bed, cried herself to sleep, and stayed there for three days.

At the end of the third day, she cashed in her plane ticket for Hollywood, paid the hotel bill, and bought a fifth of Smirnoff, two boxes of crackers, a jar of peanut butter, and a Greyhound ticket to San Francisco. Three days later, she was home. She'd slept through most of the Midwest and all of the Rocky Mountains.

Sure that her life was over, Kristine Margaret Brooks used the small inheritance left by her grandmother to buy 28 percent of a Berkeley bookstore that specialized in children's fare and obscure poets. She was sleeping nine hours a night—far fewer than the hours she was working. The next year Katheryn's novel about sorority girls hit the best-seller list. By then, Kris was sleeping ten hours a night. On her twenty-fourth birthday, Kris watched a small man on a very tall ladder change the theater marquee: Katheryn's book had been made into a movie. Not long after that, Kris gave up vodka. She didn't need it any longer; she was sleeping twelve hours a day unassisted. Sleep didn't leave room to think about the loneliness that had settled around her like a too-heavy shawl woven of shreds of what might have been. It was as if she could no longer find anything worth staying awake for. And nobody seemed to notice. That thought, more than any other, was the one that left her choking on unshed tears.

Then Kris met Jane, who moved through life with the finesse and determination of a chainsaw, so unlike the other women Kris had known. She fell in love with the intensity that burned in Jane's black eyes. With the anger that raged beneath Jane's surface. With the passion that propelled her through life. Kris would spend hours listening to Jane talk—rant, really—about obscure causes and injustices. Sometimes as Jane talked, she cried.

Kris cared nothing about the politics. She wanted only to bathe warm and naked in the fiery pools of Jane's eyes. She wanted Jane the way she had wanted no woman since Katheryn. But Katheryn lived in Paris now with a well-placed, powerful husband who had helped her find fame. Jane was different, better somehow. She was solid and sensible, yet untamed—nothing at all like Katheryn. So, Kris crafted a seamless fantasy in which she and Jane were perfect lovers, hearts bursting, bellies throbbing with desire. Together they could do anything, be anything. They could change the world if that's what Jane wanted. They could explore the hidden dangerous parts of each other. Each could protect the other from herself.

Let the rest of the world see Jane as just another angry unrealistic zealot who chased losers and lost causes. Kris knew her better. Born to a broken promise of plenty, Jane had survived childhood rather than lived it, charged through adolescence, and exploded into adulthood. She'd discarded happily-ever-after at age five when her mother died and her activist father taught her the lesson she never forgot: If they can't touch you, they can't hurt you. She never let them touch her, even long after he was gone.

While Kris waited for life to be set to music, Jane sang of revolution. Both made promises they could never keep. Perhaps it was because Jane believed in everything and Kris believed in nothing that they found each other.

Seeing the pain frozen deep in her eyes, Kris pulled Jane into her love, wrapped it around her like a cloak. It started with long walks in the park, and carry-out espresso in tall Styrofoam cups, and thankless climbs to the top of the hill where Kris lived in the attic of a once-elegant mansion. On summer nights they would shed their shirts and follow the breeze out the garret window, resting their bare backs against the rough shingles of the roof, watching the stars kiss the city lights across the bay. There they forged a private world in the way of new lovers and those who would like to be.

But every time Kris reached for Jane with a lover's touch, she was rejected—softly, gently, carefully, but rejected nonetheless. "Did I do something wrong?" Kris asked one night. Jane shook her head. "Is it . . . another . . . woman?" Jane shrugged. "I won't play twenty questions with you," Kris finally managed. "What do you want?" The words rushed out like an angry breeze. Jane turned to look at her.

"I am celibate. I have been for more than a year," Jane answered slowly, adding, "I thought you knew."

Kris chewed at a hangnail, assessing her options. She could stop seeing Jane. She could continue seeing Jane in hopes that she'd eventually change her mind. Or she could ask Jane to move in with her, as she'd planned to do anyway, and maybe that would change her mind. Kris opted for the latter. So Kris found an overpriced third-floor Victorian flat in the city because Jane liked the city better than Berkeley. Kris provided the furniture, the dishes, the sheets and towels, all the art, and a spider plant. Jane brought her father's library, three file cabinets, a mimeograph machine, a portable typewriter, and a wok.

Kris promised herself that she could make Jane love her the way she loved Jane. Her heart had pounded when Jane agreed to share a bedroom—and a bed. But every night, Jane pulled the covers tightly around her and grunted a hasty good night before rolling over to her own side of the bed, leaving Kris alone with dashed hope and soured dreams. On rare nights, Kris would gingerly reach across the bed to gently touch Jane's shoulder. She could feel the muscles go tense, the skin nearly prickle. Embarrassed, Kris would pull her hand away. They never mentioned the incident the next morning.

"You don't love me," Kris had said once, hating the whine in her voice and the woman who heard it, who'd put it there.

"Of course I love you," Jane answered almost too quickly, as if she'd rehearsed the reply. "Why does it always come down to sex with you?"

Kris had looked away, ashamed. Jane was right, of course. *If she really loved you, she'd find you irresistible. She wasn't celibate with Sutra, you know,* whispered the demon voices of self-doubt. Tell me why you won't sleep with me, really? Kris wanted to ask—or scream—but never did. The answer was too dangerous. What if the truth was that Jane found her revolting at worst, tolerable at best. A pitiable beast, Kris would tell her reflection as the tears welled. Why can't she love me, she would ask the reflection, for she was so locked in her own fears that she could no longer see Jane. Until Jane no longer mattered.

Sutra, the aura and idea of her, frightened Kris more than the real woman ever could. It wasn't so much that Sutra was Jane's ex-lover, it was more the way Jane's face shone when talk turned to Sutra. Worldly, beautiful, determined, Sutra was an expatriate child of the American aristocracy. Sutra had spent her life trying to change the world. And in some small ways, she'd been successful. She was as wild and bright as a meteor. In her presence, Kris felt like a small ugly stone. And for three days now, Sutra had been sitting in their kitchen drinking tea, and lounging on the couch, and soaking in the bathtub in a cloud of smoke and steam—and making love with Jane . . . again.

If Kris was a rock in Sutra's presence, Jane was a child. When Sutra had arrived unannounced at their door that Wednesday night, Jane had danced through the kitchen unwrapping apologies and tea cakes, making small talk and special tea. They had kissed and held hands and laughed at private jokes. Kris had settled in the corner, confused by this side of Jane she'd never seen.

On her way back to Oregon from Nicaragua, Sutra had crouched barefoot on a chair by the kitchen table, carrying on a coded monologue that only Jane had understood. Jealousy had burned in Kris's belly when she saw how Jane's eyes coveted every movement of Sutra's sparse frame. Deep into the night, they had talked and argued about people and events that Kris had only seen mentioned in the most obscure of the revolutionary newspapers Jane brought home. And each time Kris had ventured a question, Jane had looked at her coldly, then turned her eyes to Sutra as if in a silent apology for Kris, for her ignorance. Sutra hadn't even noticed. She talked constantly, rarely looked up, never lost her place, seldom paused. Her ideas spilled out in one long uninterrupted breath. Tiring of the verbal portraits of pain and pride and revolution, Kris had muttered unheard excuses and went to bed. No one said good night.

Hours later, something—although she couldn't say what at the time—had awakened Kris. She checked the clock: 3:30 A.M. Jane hadn't come to bed, of that she was sure, yet her pillow was gone. With a shallow sigh, Kris rolled onto her back. Through the wall that separated the bedroom from the living room, she could hear the pulsating frantic sounds of lovemaking. Kris lay still, straining to hear every sound, every murmur. Tears spilled quietly from her eyes. Her breath shortened. Her chest heaved. The tears slid down her aching throat as her chest convulsed with silent spasms. She pretended to be asleep when Jane finally opened the door to the bedroom, slipped naked into the darkness, carrying her clothes. Was she smiling, Kris wondered, squeezing her eyes tight. She made no sound when Jane slid under the covers and arranged herself on the far edge of the bed. She lay awake and silent as Jane fell into the rhythm of sleep. Only the next day after Jane and Sutra had left to meet old friends for breakfast did Kris allow herself the luxury of real tears and sleep.

The pattern of the two days that followed was more of the same. Jane and Sutra were inseparable; Kris was the outsider. They were rarely at home, and when they were, the conversations were loud and erratic, and always about politics. When Sutra had asked about Kris's bookstore, Jane had looked embarrassed, saying, "It's mostly kid's stuff—nothing to see, really." And Kris had lowered her eyes, ashamed. "But children are the next wave of the revolution," Sutra had answered kindly, but she didn't mention the store again. When they'd made plans to see the Dance Brigade on Friday night, Kris had waited anxiously to be invited—she loved dancers, Jane knew that—but no invitation had come, so she'd fallen asleep in front of the television. The next morning, Kris had left early for work because Saturdays were her busiest days in the bookstore. Jane had been snoring softly as Kris slipped out of the bedroom and past the spare room where Sutra was meditating, naked, by a small oil lamp. She hadn't noticed Kris.

When Kris had climbed the long flight of stairs to the flat, afternoon was already falling away. It had been a good day at the bookstore; a popular children's author had given a reading, assisted by an elaborate puppet. The children had delighted at the author and her puppet, but more than that, at the way her eyes had shone with love when she talked to them. She made them feel important, Kris thought, the way Sutra makes Jane feel important. She had sobered at the thought. The apartment was empty, so Kris had slipped into bed, telling herself it really was from exhaustion.

The sound of the outside door had awakened her. The clock on the dresser registered late evening. Sutra and Jane must have been gone for hours, Kris thought. Long enough to resurrect a love affair or plan an escape. She conjured the image of them as lovers. Would Jane go to Oregon with Sutra? Or would Sutra come back to California? Kris sighed. How would it all end? Perhaps with a terse note, not unlike the one left by Katheryn, only with less finesse: "Gone to the revolution. Truly, Jane."

The bedroom door opened a crack and Kris quickly snapped her eyes shut. The door closed again. Kris tried to listen carefully to make out the conversation in the living room, but Jane and Sutra had turned on the stereo. Slipping from the bed, Kris moved closer to the wall. She looked around furtively as if to make sure there were no witnesses, then pressed her ear against the wall. Sutra was talking about the Nicaraguan villages where she'd worked as a midwife. "I need to spend some time in Oregon healing," she was saying, "then I'm going back to where I'm really needed." Sutra's voice washed warm and inviting. Kris could imagine Sutra crouched in a hut, comforting a woman about to give birth. No wonder everyone loves her, Kris thought, surprised at the uninvited image, the sudden unexpected warmth she felt for Sutra.

Just as she was lulling herself into the idea of getting to know Sutra better, Jane's voice pierced the wall. Excited? Angry? Pleading? Kris couldn't decide. "I need to go with you." The words chilled Kris, who tried to fight off the terror that was rising in her belly. Waves of nausea pushed through her. Straining to hear Sutra's answer, Kris couldn't sort words from the low hum of voices, then laughter, then silence for a long time. Kris felt as if someone had knocked the wind out of her. Her body ached as she fought for breath. Her head buzzed. Her eyes blurred. Then laughter came from the living room again.

Maybe *another* woman would have just walked into the room and joined them, but Kris wasn't another woman. A thousand ideas collided in her brain. She could pretend to stumble sleepily into the living room. Or slip out the back door and go—where? Or storm into the room, the outraged lover. Or stay where she was, listening, a thief of secret words. She pressed closer to the wall.

"But what about Kris?" Sutra asked, "Have you told her?"

Told me what? Kris wanted to bellow from the next room, but instead she held her breath, vainly trying to hear, and cursing Jane's whispers. If she was talking about the damned patriarchy or the revolution you could hear her two blocks away, Kris thought.

"What would you contribute?" Sutra asked, her voice rising, almost sharp. Again, Jane's answer was muffled. "You haven't changed at all," Sutra said. Her voice was mocking, almost snide. "I work alone, remember? Besides, you never could take the competition, if I recall." Now she sounded teasing.

Still, Jane's answer came back angry and miserable. "It would be different. I wouldn't mind . . . about the others."

Sutra's laugh rolled through the house. She laughed easily and well, as if life's twists genuinely amused her and she was long since beyond it all. "You still don't get it. You don't have the right to mind or not mind." Her voice was strained. "What I do is my business, not yours. If I want to love you tonight, I will. If I want to love somebody else tomorrow night, I will. It's my choice. You can say no about you but nothing about the rest of us. When are you ever going to learn?" Her voice was loud, almost angry. Obviously, they'd forgotten about Kris.

Jane muttered something that Kris couldn't make out and then Sutra's voice came back. Sharp words collided, unintelligible. Then silence. Kris strained to hear something, anything. Tiny sobs seeped through the wall. Overwhelmed by curiosity,

Kris dressed quickly and stepped into the living room, her face set bright and bubbly, meaningless banter mapped out in her brain like a day trip to the mountains.

"Well, hi . . ." she started and then gasped when she saw Jane's naked back kneeling by the couch where Sutra reclined, her blouse open, full breasts spilling out, her head thrown back, mouth open as sweet moans washed the room warm. Backing into the kitchen, Kris rocked against the cool enamel door of the refrigerator, trying to hold down the nausea that threatened. Kris fled through the back door and sat miserably on the top wooden step, picking at the peeling paint. Sure that if she could only keep her hands busy in routine common movements that everything would be all right again, that Jane wouldn't be making love to another woman in the next room. Sutra was moaning in earnest now, the sound shuddering across the night, ripping into Kris like a knife.

When the house had been silent for a long time, Kris let herself back in the kitchen and took down the teakettle. Long minutes dragged across the clock as the water steamed. By the time it was boiling hard, Sutra stepped into the kitchen, smiling, tying a red silk kimono at her waist. A large green and yellow dragon peered over her shoulder. "Up from your nap?" Sutra asked pleasantly. Rummaging through the boxes of tea, Sutra finally selected one, poured water into a cup, and perched on a chair, the way she had that first night. The kimono fell open, leaving her legs exposed. She folded the fabric into her lap, covering a shock of black pubic hair. The red silk made her skin look almost radiant, luminous. Kris looked at her closely. Sutra's body looked less firm, less supple than it had just minutes before. The dark circles under her eyes were real, just like the wrinkles that the overhead kitchen light exposed. Kris looked at each part of the woman before her as if she were a jigsaw puzzle, before putting the pieces together. She's just an ordinary woman, Kris thought, strangely moved by the revelation.

"Does it bother you?" Sutra asked, nodding toward the living room.

Kris shrugged, embarrassed, then turned away, pretending to busy herself with the ritual of tea. A strange silence blanketed the room. "Jane says you're a midwife," she finally managed, trying to blank the events of the last hour from her mind. Kris imagined she could feel Sutra nodding. "It must be rewarding, the work you do . . ." Kris began, her back still turned to the woman. In the next room they could hear Jane rummaging through drawers.

"It's what I do. I was in medicine for a while . . . a long time ago. Look, about Jane," she began again. Only, Kris turned and smiled brightly as if everything were perfectly normal.

"Jane's a great roommate," Kris said, surprised at the lightness of her voice. "Very busy, though. And I work a lot. And read. You know, for the bookstore. It really does take almost all my time. We're building up the poetry section. Lots of poetry, but not as much as I'd like. Children should be introduced to good poetry, don't you agree?" Kris sounded loud, animated. Suddenly, she pulled back the curtain and urgently looked out the window at nothing.

"I told Jane she should talk to you, but you know how young she is." Sutra lowered her eyes. Kris looked at her, surprised; Jane was only two years younger than Kris. "When she was with me, she always wanted to be taken care of." Sutra chuckled dryly. "That's why I was so happy when I met you. I can tell you're good for her. She's happy with you. She didn't tell me, but I can feel it. She needs somebody like you. By the way, how long have you been celibate?"

"Me? How long have *I*?" Kris exclaimed, looking at Sutra as if she was speaking in tongues. "Sutra, it's Jane who's celibate. At least that's what she's been telling me for the past year." Sutra choked slightly, her eyes widening. Then they both started to laugh.

Neither of them had seen Jane by the kitchen door, or maybe Sutra had; Kris didn't bother to ask. But they did hear her anger that shot her through the living room, down the stairs, out into the street. Kris turned, confused, and looked at Sutra, who was still laughing.

"I'll go look for her," Kris said with a finality that she didn't really feel. She didn't want to see Jane—certainly not at that moment, maybe never again. She'd been betrayed, lied to, used. And she didn't know then if she'd ever get over the empty feeling that gnawed at her. Sutra raised her teacup as if in a toast.

"Well, suit yourself," Sutra finally offered. "I don't know that I'd bother."

"But she's my lover," Kris answered automatically.

"A lover who tells you she's celibate and won't sleep with you but plans to run off with another woman? One that she's not so *celibate* with, I might add." Sutra looked at Kris closely. "I love Jane, don't question that. But I love a lot of women. She's just one of them. Janey will be all right, just give her a little time to sort things out on her own." Sutra smiled, then her eyes brightened. She bounded from the table and returned carrying a paper bag. "In all the excitement, I almost forgot. Jane and I were at the flea market this afternoon and found this. It's for your alter ego." Sutra pushed the bag toward Kris. Inside was a satin cowgirl shirt, blue with pearlized buttons. "Try it on!" Sutra insisted, letting out a low whistle as Kris closed the shirt over her bare breasts.

"It's very . . . nice," Kris managed, looking suspiciously at her reflection in the mirror.

"Nice! It's hot!" Sutra gushed, grinning. They laughed. "Jane should see you now," she said. Kris suddenly sobered. She'd forgotten about Jane.

"Look, Sutra, I need to go look for her. Make yourself at home."

"Oh, I always do." Sutra stretched, catlike, off the chair. "By the way, do you have any bubble bath?"

Kris widened her eyes in disbelief. "Bubble bath?" she echoed.

"I like to take a bath before traveling. I found a ride to Oregon; I'm leaving around midnight."

Is that how it would end? Sutra would take a bath and walk out of Jane's life, leaving Kris to pick up the pieces or try to. Then one day, on her way to another revolution, she'd just drop by? Suddenly images of Katheryn surged in front of Kris. Katheryn was being sued by a French actress for breach of promise. It seems she'd promised the actress a house but then changed her mind. Kris wondered if Katheryn had left a note for the actress like the one she'd left in that New York hotel room. Or did she dump European women with more finesse? Or did she just take a bubble bath and disappear?

Kris looked closely at Sutra. It was true, she was nothing like Katheryn and yet everything like Katheryn. And Jane was nothing like Kris and so very much like her. It was suddenly all so clear that Kris couldn't believe she hadn't seen it before. It was what Sutra was all about, what she'd seen in her, what she'd loved in Katheryn: how they were responsible for their own happiness. Kris checked her reflection in the mirror and smiled. Suddenly, it seemed very important to go out on the town. And if Jane found her way home, too, so much the better.

After Midnight

The Hallelujah Snake

"Give me a hallelujah, sister!" commanded the Reverend Peter Thomas, who beamed out in all his twelve-inch-high, black and white, horizontal-hold-gone-crazy glory. A greenish cast trembled around his ears where a halo might have hung on another man. "And praise the Lord! Sing hallelujah and ask God for forgiveness of YOUR wicked ways!" The voice, tinged with a tinny twang, bounced off the gray and white walls and soared to the couch, where it hovered, waiting for Maggie's reply.

"Hallelujah!" she shouted at the television, rising off the couch, her eyes narrowed to half-daggers, her fists clenched toward heaven.

"And speak His holy name!" The minister commanded, sweat beads gathering on his forehead and turning to tiny salt rivulets that sped through carefully pancaked wrinkles on their way to his chin, where they hung like tiny fluid diamonds.

"Hallelujah!" Maggie choked on the word. Dropping her arms, she knelt before the television until her face was only inches from the screen, so close she could see her own eyes reflected in the minister's. "You son of a bitch!"

Grumbling, she stumbled toward the door, pulling on her leather jacket, tucking her right hand carefully into the jacket pocket, then pulling the pocket zipper closed to hold the numb fingers in place. Passing the television, she raised her foot in a mock karate kick. "This is for you, old man!" she told the reverend. His face screwed tight in prayer, he swayed a little, his arms stretched heavenward, clutching a fat black Bible in both dimpled hands. With her good hand, Maggie propelled him back into the darkness.

Taking the stairs two at a time, her boots rattled out a sharp steady rhythm of machine-gun fire. Rat-a-tat, a-tat-tat-tat. Each round ripped through the minister's chest, his legs, his arms for all heaven—or hell—to see. By the time she hit the street, he was lying in the gutter, head blown open, brains spilling into the sewer grate, beady eyes burning lifelessly into the sun. She was careful not to step on him as she bounded against the light and headed across the eight blocks to Babe's, the sneer she saved for walking the night alone painted on her gaunt face.

Darkened store windows reflected a woman wound taut, striding across concrete and broken glass, piercing the darkness with features as sharp as the knife strapped to her belt. Under her breath she hummed a tuneless ditty, a bit of a church hymn put to a disco beat. But no matter what obscenities she inserted, "Sing hallelujah!" bounced through her brain. "Piss on it," she muttered, her mind still on the minister and his tiny eyes. Pig eyes. Or snake eyes? Trying to decide, she looked through the memories that were always lurking, waiting, crouched like a hungry animal on the dark side of her brain.

Last spring she'd read a newspaper article about him: how his life was paid for with prayers, faith, and no small number of love tokens from his followers who sat hungrily before their television sets waiting for Peter Thomas to perform a miracle. "Just put one hand on the Bible and the other on your TV," the reverend assured the stricken and afflicted, "and the spirit of the Lord will heal you." And the desperate, who had nowhere to turn, turned to him. And believed. And prayed. And sent him their worn pennies and crumpled dollars. And waited. One hand on the television, the other on Bibles with cracked leather covers that protect the precious names and dates of births, deaths, marriages from the light that threatens to suck away simple tributes to their being, just as it pales the ink that marks the great events of simple lives. Such Bibles always find their way to the laps of old women. Some, like Maggie's grandmother, carry one into death, the final entry unrecorded.

Shadows of Maggie's grandmother stalked the night. The old woman sitting alone on a threadbare couch in a living room ablaze with candlelight, watching and praying with the endless parade of television preachers. Singing hymns in a craggy voice. Waiting for salvation that never came. Doing without so the good reverend could buy another car for his fleet, add a tennis court to his estate.

The newspaper article had made Maggie ill. For most of a day she'd lain in her darkened room with cold compresses of vinegar and chamomile water across her aching brow. Even with her eyes closed tight against the day, the smell of vinegar and herbs soaking into her dreams, his face leered at her. Holding a bloodstained Bible high, he cried "Sing, hallelujah" while a nest of snakes shimmied and twitched in time to music from a choir of demons.

After the migraine passed, Maggie stumbled through the house like a stranger. She had become an animal, possessed, haunted, hunting, prowling the rain forest of memories. Every time she closed her eyes in sleep, he was there, holding out his fat dimpled hand, a coaxing smile painted too red on his lips. A young girl walked slowly toward him, taking a few steps, then hesitating, turning to look over her shoulder at Maggie, who was trying to call out a warning from her frozen throat. In the background, a choir was singing "Rock of Ages" louder and faster until the words ran together. As the girl reached the minister, he stopped smiling and held out a large black box and pushed back the lid. The girl looked inside; her eyes widened with anticipation, or fear; Maggie could no longer tell. "And the Lord saith: 'The weaned child shall put his hand on the poisonous serpent's den!' " cried the minister, taking the girl's right hand and shoving it into the box. Maggie screamed for the girl to run, to save herself, but the words were lost in the din of the choir and the minister who was shouting, " 'If ye suffer for righteousness sake, happy are ye!' "

The dream stalked her. Afraid to sleep, she would sit in front of the television watching him night after night, looking for some sign, some hint of remorse or even of memory in his round wrinkled face. Eventually she began dialing the Hotline to Heaven, the reverend's 800-number, where a smooth-voiced disciple would offer prayers and encourage a love gift to "help the good minister continue his holy mission." The reverend never answered the hotline himself.

"Let me talk to the reverend," Maggie muttered into the receiver night after night. "I gotta talk to the reverend. Just say it's Mary Magdalene. He'll talk to me." Only, the woman on the other end would never put her through.

"Let me pray for you, sister," the soothing voice coaxed from half a continent away. "Fall down on your knees and let's pray together and ask the Lord for His forgiveness."

"Bullshit," Maggie screeched into the phone. "Let me talk to the reverend, you stupid bitch!" At that, the velvet voice on the other end always turned icy, then with a quick "God bless you, sister," Maggie was left alone to wipe away the hot tears that refused to stay dried, even after all these years.

"Bastard!" she would scream at the silent telephone, until Gail came to lead her to bed. And there Maggie fought sleep and the dreams. Three, four, even a dozen times a day Maggie would dial the Hotline to Heaven number, until she knew it by heart. Each time the conversation was the same. No matter what she said, the faceless voices on the other end of the line never let her talk to the reverend. When they started asking her name, her address, where she was when she called, she began using the pay phone at Babe's. Only, Gail had pulled the late shift one night and overheard one of those calls, too.

"Babe don't like trouble," Gail had whispered. "Don't call there anymore, Maggie, it only gets everybody all upset, okay?" And Maggie had nodded, smiled her crooked smile, and kissed Gail lightly on the cheek.

But the calls didn't stop, only the locations changed. The drugstore. The gas station. Every phone Maggie passed beckoned: *"Call him. Call and be healed. Call and be saved."* And she did. Closing her eyes, her breath coming fast, the phone would ring once, twice. Then a soothing voice: "Welcome to the Hotline to Heaven. Shall we pray?"

In the sober light of day, Maggie knew Gail was right: Some things were better left dead. Like the fingers on her hand. Numb and quiet. And she would have left the minister alone, too, if she could. But some things refuse to be buried even when they're dead. The blood still flows through the memories. The dead fingers, worthless as starfish abandoned by the tide, still bleed when they meet the razor. Only the feeling leaves; the blood is still real, deep, blackening rivers of life streaming warm and sticky.

It had been like that when she was twelve and Johnny Bob Catlow paid her a dollar—a great deal of money to him—for the rare opportunity to stab her numb fingers with a long lethal hat pin. His eyes had widened in horror, then fascination as the blood spurted, red and clear, and ran down her hand. Maggie had felt no pain, only immense relief at having a whole dollar of her own.

Years later, when Ginny, her first lover, introduced Maggie to LSD, they'd searched for the inner soul of her hand, using a collection of art knives. The blood rose and oozed red across Maggie's strangely white skin. Through the haze she'd watched mesmerized, sure that if she could only find the right spot to slit, all the feeling in her hand would return. It never did. By the time she left art school and Ginny, each finger was lined with tiny white scars. Always, the sheer beauty of the hand, the blood, even the scars fascinated her.

It was her special secret fury, one that refused to die, refused to slip silently into the past. Sitting naked on the cold white-tiled bathroom floor, razor blade in one hand, Maggie carefully sliced the skin that covered each dead finger. " 'They sacrificed their sons and their daughters unto devils,' " she recited, the Bible verses spilling into the night. " 'And shed innocent blood, even the blood of their sons and of their daughters. And the land was polluted with blood.' "

Finally, when the hand dripped red, she lifted the numb fingers with her good hand and carefully guided them across her face, down her chest, across her breasts, down her belly, up each leg, reciting all the while: " 'Your hands are defiled with blood and your fingers with blood.' " At those times she believed she was a real artist again, not just a sign painter. Her body was palette, paint, brush, and canvas. Some nights she worked nearly until dawn creating her gory masterpiece. Other nights the work went quickly. When she was finished, she carefully examined her artistry in the full-length bathroom mirror she'd installed for just such showings.

The mirror reflected only horror: a bloodied, naked, half-mad woman stared out at her. " 'She discovered her nakedness; then my mind was alienated from her,' " Maggie told the mirror. Only it wasn't true because as much as she hated the goried monster the mirror reflected, Maggie still wanted her as much as she had ever wanted any lover. Staring at her reflection, she carefully critiqued each inch before lowering her body into the steaming bathtub. " 'The Lord with his sore and great and strong sword shall slay the dragon that is in the sea.' " Her blood turned the water a delicate pink.

One night when the blood-paint had flowed especially thick and the water was turning red, Maggie's grandmother called to her through the door: " 'Arise and be baptized and wash away thy sins.' " Confused, Maggie stepped out of the water and into the darkened hall that opened onto a blazing white light. Her grandmother, smiling, young again and so beautiful, stepped from the shadows and nodded toward the end of the light where the reverend was waiting, smiling, extending his dimpled hands.

"The Lord saith: 'Suffer the little children.' Are you ready to suffer for the Lord, Mary Magdalene?" he asked, his tiny eyes searching her face for any sin that might be etched on her brow. No one had called her Mary Magdalene in so many years she smiled without thinking and started to run toward him, but she then remembered she was naked and must stay hidden in the shadows. The reverend was no longer caught in his television-set chapel. He was real and if she would just walk down the hall toward the white light, she could be with him, too. She began to walk slowly, her fingers groping shadows that were filled with the hands and faces of people she'd known so long ago that she could no longer remember their names. The hands washed her, caressed her, dressed her. When she finally stepped into the room, she wore a white cotton pinafore. "And the Lord saith: 'In thy shirts is found the blood of the souls of the poor innocents! I have not found it by secret search, but upon these!' Say, hallelujah, my child," commanded the reverend, and Maggie automatically answered, "Hallelujah!"

He was so close she could feel the sweat fall from his face, drip onto the white dress, staining it red and bloody. Great droplets of blood fell to the floor until they formed a river of red, which turned into one snake and then a nest of them, which climbed her legs and wrapped themselves around her, choking back her voice, her very breath. While the minister's voice cried out, " 'I will send serpents among you which will not be charmed and they shall bite you, saith the Lord.' Praise His holy name! 'And the weaned child shall put his hand on the cockatrice's den.' Amen! 'Deliver this child from blood guiltiness, O God!' " A choir sang louder and faster until Maggie was covered with blood and trying to scream, only, no one could hear her, no one at all.

When Maggie awoke, a blaze of white light greeted her and she leaned back into the whiteness and smiled. It's over, she thought, raising her right arm, sure the hand would be there, whole, untouched, filled with feeling. In death the severed parts reunite with the body, finally I am redeemed. Instead, her eyes focused on a giant mitt of gauze and tape protecting the butchered hand, fingers, wrist. Gail slumped in a chair by the bed, her eyes asking, probing, until Maggie shook her head, turning her face to the wall. The disappointment was so deep it paralyzed her voice.

"He was there," she finally whispered, knowing Gail could never understand. "He came, and Grandma, too. You don't believe me, do you?" Gail exhaled, a long lowing sound that might have been the wail of a locomotive a mile gone, so soft and smooth it was. She looked out the window for a very long time, as if she were counting the leaves on the tree of heaven that grew there.

"No, Maggie," she finally answered, "I don't believe you."

The next day, the voice of the county psychiatrist kept rattling across the quiet of his desk, spitting out questions that threatened to expose Maggie's secret. Some things were better left unsaid, especially to strangers, she thought, listening to him try to probe her feelings the way a biologist tries to probe a dead amoeba. If the psychiatrist had been worth her fury, she might have hated him or cursed him, fought with him or attacked him. Instead, she looked at him with a curiosity usually reserved for rare and horrible insects. Why should any of it matter to this stranger who had never known her or the reverend? What difference could this man make at all?

"Do you have any recollection of what happened in the bathroom?" the psychiatrist probed. Prodded. Nudged. Inhaled. Waited.

Maggie nodded.

"And after?"

Maggie shook her head.

"But you told the nurses that the Reverend Peter Thomas came to see you. Have you ever imagined that he came to see you in the bathroom before, Maggie?"

She looked at him curiously; chewed lightly on her lower lip. So many answers swam across her brain. Which one did the insect-man-psychiatrist want? None of them would he believe. Finally, Maggie spoke: " 'Who can stand before his indignation? And who can abide in the fierceness of his anger? His fury is poured out like fire.' "

"That's from the Bible?" the psychiatrist asked. Maggie

nodded. "It's talking about God, Maggie, not the Reverend Peter Thomas. And you know Peter Thomas is not God, don't you?"

Maggie looked at the psychiatrist coldly, her eyes narrow, hostile. "The reverend is 'father of the fatherless.' Psalm 68, verse 5." Her eyes fell to the mound of gauze resting in her lap. "What could you possibly tell me about him . . . or me . . . that I don't already know?" she demanded, adding silently, And the rest of it isn't any of your business, Mister Insect Man.

That afternoon Maggie signed herself out of the hospital and went back to the nightmares born of the red ritual—the bloodletting—that hungered always for more. When the dreams came, she could share them with no one, not even Gail. Strangers, even lovers, couldn't know that as horrifying as the blood was to them, Maggie carried no fear of death in her belly, only hate that grew and transformed itself in her blood until it had to be let out. Little Mary Magdalene was dead and she'd left Maggie nothing but a blood liturgy of hate.

"This is eating you alive," Gail announced flatly after Maggie had gone home to the Victorian flat they shared. Gail had prepared carefully for Maggie's homecoming. Red roses and white daisies were on the mantle beneath a painting Maggie had once done of Big Sur. Maggie sat stiffly on the couch, like an anxious visitor. "Will you see a doctor?" The words came slowly, although Gail had rehearsed them for—how long?— days, weeks, months; she could only barely remember a time when she hadn't thought them.

Maggie shook her head. "No, because I'm not sick. And in answer to your next question, I won't see a shrink, either."

"Why not?"

For the first time since the hospital, Maggie looked deep into Gail's eyes. "Because this is between him and me, and only one of us can win."

"And it won't be you, will it?" Gail demanded, her voice rising, angry. Once she'd been so happy in this house with this woman that it had felt like forever, and now Maggie was willing to throw it all away for a television evangelist. "You think that damned phony Holy Roller would even give a fuck if you bled to death all over some damned bathroom floor? Well he doesn't care. Only I care. And either it stops or I leave."

Maggie glanced at Gail, who had shared her bed and her life but who knew her so little. Silently she walked to the closet, pulled down Gail's suitcase, set it on the floor, and left. The finality of the act frightened Gail. Later, Maggie would say that was when Gail finally understood the truth—that some people aren't worth loving or saving, so it's senseless to try. And Gail would say it was the night she finally knew that she would never be able to ever truly touch Maggie, no matter how intertwined they were deep into the February nights.

Now Maggie lived alone; she liked it better that way. There was no one to answer to. No one to lie to. No one to question why her worthless hand was bandaged and oozing red. No one to tell her to turn off the reverend, to forget, to remember, to live, to die. And when she wanted to see Gail, which was often, she could always be found behind the bar at Babe's.

The bar's neon winked as Maggie darted across the wide street, ignoring the traffic that swerved and buzzed past her, horns honking angry in the night. Shoving the bar door open with her shoulder, she fell into the cool warmth of voices and music that promised to drown out the reverend for another night. " 'Behold, this dreamer cometh!' " She laughed. "And say, hallelujah!" With a grandiose wave of her left hand she slid onto her favorite bar stool and winked at Gail, who only half-smiled. On the next stool, a stranger who had been deep in conversation with Gail looked up quizzically.

"I'm Kate Solomon." The stranger offered her right hand and a smile. Maggie ignored both.

"She's a photographer from New York. Here to take pictures of Babe and the place," Gail interjected, pushing a glass of club soda in front of Maggie.

A spark of recognition lit Maggie's face. Animated, she turned to the woman she'd ignored a moment earlier. "No shit! I've seen your stuff in *Rolling Stone,* right?" Maggie peered closely at Kate, her voice escalating in excitement. "And you shot the album covers for—hell, Gail, you know, that girl group that busted up a couple years ago. The one with the redhead lead singer. Sure, I know your stuff. You're good." Kate smiled, flattered. "I could've been a photographer. Once. Instead I became a sign painter." Maggie's voice suddenly soured.

"A sign painter who graduated—with honors—from the art institute," Gail prodded proudly. Maggie shot her a hard look.

"I still paint a little. In fact, I'm working on a new mural called 'The Garden of Eden.' Maybe Gail told you about it?"

Kate shook her head, but Maggie was eyeing Gail wickedly, her voice fogged in veiled knowing. "It's coming along nicely, dear, but I haven't worked on it in more than a week. Gail doesn't encourage my art, do you darling?" Her eyes belied the smile she wore.

"Stop it," Gail hissed. Maggie laughed and pulled her right hand from the coat pocket and gently laid it on the bar. The hand reminded Kate of a girl she'd known in grade school who was born with only one hand. The girl's parents had spent their savings on an artificial hand for their daughter—a present for eighth-grade graduation. The waxy lightly freckled hand, fingers eternally frozen in a graceful gesture, each slightly bent and separated, was beautiful and perfect. A tiny amethyst and gold band graced the ring finger. A matching bracelet hid the seam where the hand attached to the girl's wrist. The girl had worn it only that one night and never again. "It only looked real. But everybody still knew what it was," the girl had confided the next day.

Maggie's good hand carefully lifted its mate, turning it slowly side to side, raising then lowering each finger. "See, not so much as a Band-Aid. Go on, Gail, look." But the words were an empty dare that only marked time until the hate churned to the surface again. Until the snake demanded its quota of blood. Until Maggie gave in again. "I've been a very, very good girl," Maggie teased. "Now, how about a kiss?" Gail reached across the bar and lightly brushed her lips across Maggie's, then crinkled her nose.

"What's that look supposed to mean?" Maggie growled.

"What time did you start drinking?" Gail countered.

" 'I have eaten ashes like bread and mingled my drink with weeping,' " Maggie answered with a sneer. "Besides, who are you to pass judgment? 'Woe unto him'—or in your case, her— 'that giveth her neighbor drink, that puttest thy bottle to her.' " Maggie tapped Kate's empty beer bottle sharply and laughed, but the sound was hollow, pained.

"And you, are you here to covet thy neighbor's wife?" Maggie demanded, turning to Kate. "Well, don't mind me. I just dropped by to say hi or should it be bye?" Looking from one to the other, Maggie's eyes widened in mock horror.

"Shut up!" Gail barked. "You're a disgusting drunk. Look at yourself, Maggie."

And Maggie did look. Tiny eyes that belonged more to a pig

or perhaps a snake burned out of the mirror. She stared at the image until she imagined her tears were, instead, beads of sweat streaming down her face. A sudden shudder rocked her frail body, hard and fast. Just as suddenly, Gail was behind Maggie, hugging her, holding her close, trying to quiet the trembling. "Give it up, givit up, givitup," Gail crooned over and over, humming in a nonsense lullaby.

"Let go, Gail!" Maggie violently shook herself free.

"I'll walk you home, or get Matty to." Gail was already waving frantically toward the other end of the bar. "We'll talk about it. It'll be fine, you'll see." Fear iced her words, which came like a west wind rattling through barren winter branches.

"I am fine, and I'm not going anywhere except to the john," Maggie announced, raising her head high, almost proudly, Kate thought. "And forget Matty; she's already got a girl. No, darlin', I'm saving the last dance for you tonight." Cocking her head, Maggie winked and stepped into the crowd. For that moment, she was beyond the bar's clamor, Gail's hysteria. The fear was gone. Her eyes glinted. Her upper lip trembled in what Kate could only think was anticipation.

"I'll hold your place," Kate offered, but the defeat on Gail's face silenced her. A thousand questions stormed Kate. Gail's eyes froze on a spot across the room.

"She hurts herself." Gail finally answered the unspoken question. "A lot. Mostly when she's been drinking, but other times, too. I don't know how to make her stop and when I try, she only hates me more. It was killing us. I thought if I got out it wouldn't hurt so much, but it still does." Gail raised her eyes to Kate, looking for comfort or solace, maybe even for answers. Every word was bringing her closer to betraying Maggie's secret, but she didn't want to stop, not this time.

Gail closed her eyes, remembering. Maggie bloody. Maggie singing church hymns in pink bath water. Maggie painting an unearthly wilderness filled with demons and snakes and angels with wings reddened from her own blood. Maggie in bed reciting over and over, "And I shall dwell in the house of the damned forever and ever. Amen." Maggie denying any of it ever happened, even with her own blood under her fingernails. And then it starting all again. How could a stranger understand? "I can't," she whispered, shaking her head. Kate would think she was as mad as Maggie.

"She's a cutter," Kate surmised. "Why only on the one hand?" Gail's head shot up. Could this woman who had guessed what Maggie did perhaps understand why she did it—the secret Gail had been carrying like a dead child all these months?

"Because of what happened that made her hand like it is. A long time ago. Now it's as if she's losing her mind," Gail finally admitted in a quick whisper, wiping and rewiping the same wineglass until it glinted like crystal. "She can't sleep because the nightmares build up until she can't stand it. Then she cuts herself; she says she's letting the demons out. It's horrible, and it just gets worse. She almost died the last time. I found her in the bathtub. She was just lying there in water red from her own blood. I can't go through it again."

"Do you think she's crazy?" Kate asked, turning the picture over in her mind, the image sending a stark chill down her back.

"I don't know and she won't see a therapist," Gail confided. "When we first got together it was fine, then six months ago she turns into a religious fanatic. That's when she first saw him on TV—the Reverend Peter Thomas." Gail spat out the name as if it was a curse.

"Faith healer, Holy Roller, big spender with a shady past." Kate ticked off on her fingers. "Sure, I know who he is, a real modern-day Elmer Gantry."

"It was an accident she even saw him. We'd come in late and she was flipping through the channels, like you do, looking for something to watch at two in the morning. When I came in the room, she had this preacher on. Only, she wouldn't change the channel. It was weird. He'd go, 'Say, hallelujah!' and she'd shout, 'Hallelujah!' At first I thought she was kidding around, you know, drunk and being crazy." Her voice cracked. "Then she started staying up every night to watch him. Then the nightmares started. And the blood. It's as if she's possessed. She calls him on the phone—only he won't take the calls. I can't stop her, and when I try to talk to her, she says she's atoning for her sins and paying penance so her grandmother won't have to stay in hell."

"I don't understand." So many faces, so many stories, each one strange and beautiful crowded the last four months for Kate, and all of them scarred with life, like Maggie's hand. Secrets swirled through this bar—all the bars, really—like frantic bloodied angels. Kate thought of the women she'd met as special because they were survivors—but what about Maggie? Kate inhaled slowly and looked at Gail, her eyes urging the story to be completed.

"Maggie was raised really funny, on fire-and-brimstone religion." Gail's words spilled out in whispers, each one prodding the next along yet carried by their own current, like logs on a river. "Her dad, Claude Wiley, was a minister, one of those that preaches hellfire and damnation. I guess her mom couldn't take old Claude anymore, so one day she bundled up Maggie and ran off with the choir director. A couple of years later, when Maggie was four, her mom and the choir director were killed in a car accident. So Maggie ended up back with Claude, only, he'd really gone off the deep end by then. He'd lost his church and was just another traveling evangelist working the Bible Belt. Sometimes he had a tent; sometimes he just went from church to church. He made Maggie memorize six Bible verses a day. It was part of the act. He'd get her up in front of the audience and have them shout out stuff like Exodus 22:18, and she'd recite it. I gather it was a real crowd-pleaser. That's how they lived. She didn't go to school, they were on the road too much, so he taught her everything she knew. And all of it was based on the Bible—his version. Once in a great while, she had real schoolbooks, but if there was something in them Claude didn't like, he just tore it out. Well, that went on until her period started and the old man freaked. He found some verse in the Bible about shutting her away for seven days because she was 'unclean.' She was eleven years old; how could she be unclean? Anyway, he had her locked up in this little shed in back of the church he was working outside Rockwood, Tennessee. His people lived around there, I gather. A boy apparently heard Maggie crying and helped her escape. When her father found her hiding in the boy's barn, he had a fit."

To Kate, the image of a scared little girl that Gail was painting didn't fit with the hardened young woman who'd sat next to her only minutes before. Where had that child gone, Kate wondered; was she dead or only hiding, afraid of forgetting a Bible verse, fearful of being locked away, alone?

"Her dad kept saying she was the 'whore of the beast' and the 'seed of the adulterer.' He kept calling Maggie by her dead mother's name, and cursing her . . . and beating her. It went on all day. That night he made her put on this white dress that she always wore to the revivals and told her God would give her the chance to prove that she was pure. He kept saying she would come away as the bride of Christ or as Satan's harlot. When she went to the church, there was a black box on the altar right by where she stood to recite her Bible verses." Gail closed her eyes and her mouth puckered; she was trying very hard not to cry. Kate reached across the bar, touching her shoulder gently, urging her to continue. "He made her walk up the aisle to the front of the church while he told the congregation about her sins. When she got to him, he took down the box and grabbed her right arm . . . and he . . ." Gail sobbed, blinked hard, took a deep breath, and whispered, "He pushed her hand into a box of copperheads."

The bar sounds closed in around them, making Kate suddenly grateful for the din. More than a decade in the news business and she was still surprised by what humans were capable of doing to each other. When she looked up, Gail was no longer crying.

" 'And the flesh of your daughters shall ye eat.' " Kate mused.

Gail nodded. "Claude wasn't about to help her—it was the will of God, you see. Maggie would have died from the snakebites if her grandmother hadn't been there. Out of all those people there that night, his mother was the only one who'd cross the good reverend." Her voice dripped with hate and sarcasm. "Maybe she knew he was nuts. Maybe she was the only one in the room full of them that wasn't. Anyway, she half-carried, half-dragged Maggie out of the church and away from him. Claude was furious; he cursed them both as witches and prayed for God to kill them. Maggie's grandmother got the old country doctor from the next county to treat her, but he didn't know much and ended up butchering the nerves in her hand. These were ignorant hill people who wanted to believe in the devil, so when Maggie's old man told them the beast had marked Maggie's right hand, they believed it. In a way, they were right. Only they didn't connect that the beast was the reverend himself. Finally, Maggie and her grandmother had to leave Tennessee to get away from the rumors and harassment."

Tears like light rain had left Gail's face wet and shiny in the muted bar light. Kate suddenly wanted to pull her close, to wipe the tears, to make her laugh. How long had it been since she'd laughed, Kate wondered, before Gail's words nudged her back.

"They might have been okay, except the old granny got to be pretty cuckoo, too. It's as if she'd started to believe Maggie's father: that she really had sacrificed her own salvation by saving her granddaughter's life. She never went to a real church again, just sat home watching the TV preachers day and night. When she died, nobody came to her funeral but Maggie. Not even her own son."

"But Peter Thomas? What's he got to do with it?" Kate asked, hoping to put the puzzle together quickly and neatly.

"Peter Thomas is Claude Wiley." Gail inhaled sharply, then spat out the words: "He's her father!"

The revelation struck Kate's brain like a two-by-four. This was the kind of story journalists prayed for and panted after, and here it was—all for her—laid out like a gift. It could easily be as big as the holy wars, and Kate had the connections back East to make it happen. With Maggie's help, hell would look like a vacation paradise to the Reverend Peter Thomas when the press was through with him. Kate turned on the stool to scan the room for Maggie just as rumblings from the back hall rolled toward the bar in the shape of Matty.

"Gail, give me the john keys. Maggie's locked herself in the men's room." Matty's voice sounded like rubber bands ready to snap. Her eyes flashed angry; her fingers drummed against the bar. Gail's eyes widened as she reached under the bar for the keys. "Are you going or do I have to?" Matty demanded. Gail's hand shook as she handed over the keys.

"I can't." Gail's voice cracked. Matty stared at Gail, whose knuckles were whitening under her grip of the bar's edge. "I just . . . can't." Her eyes dropped to the floor, followed by tears. Matty nodded and started to turn away when Kate's hand shot out to stop her.

"I'll go with you. Maybe I can help," Kate said with more confidence than she felt. Matty shrugged and started toward the back of the bar. Picking their way through the crowd that milled in the hall outside the rest rooms, Matty sent those that she could back to the party. The rest would wait, some out of concern, most out of curiosity. From inside the men's room they could hear singing followed by lapses of silence, then more singing as Matty tried one key after the other.

"At least she's not dead," Kate offered.

"Yet," Matty answered. When a key turned, Matty's eyes connected with Kate's. "Are you ready?" she whispered. Kate nodded and Matty leaned into the door, opening it just enough for Kate to step through.

Slowly Maggie turned toward the door, to the light and the sound that opened and spilled into her shadowy cave sanctuary. Eyes so wide and vulnerable that they might belong to a child met Kate's. Her left hand still clutched the knife she always carried. Her right hand hung limply at her side. Blood snaked down Maggie's fingers leaving dark splotches on her jeans. Perfect droplets on the cement floor. Kate's eyes swept the tiny room: the white sink with spots and trails of blood; the gray metal stall; a pair of white urinals that strangely reminded her of sentries; the small mirror overhung by a single light fixture that cast long shadows on the gray floor. Maggie turned to look in the mirror, which reflected a frightened bleeding young woman, not the monster she'd seen so many times before. The choir had stopped singing.

Why? Kate's eyes roared, but her voice was cool, soothing as a night wind. "Give me the knife, Maggie. Please." Kate held out her hand, surprised that it didn't tremble.

Maggie didn't move her eyes from the mirror. She began to lower the blade to her right hand. Kate trembled, trying desperately to remember any snatch of biblical verse that she'd ever heard. Finally, she almost whispered, " 'Blessed are they which are persecuted for righteousness sake: for theirs is the kingdom of Heaven.' " Maggie turned from the mirror; Kate's gaze met eyes that belonged to a fox in a steel-jaw trap. "The knife, Maggie, give me the knife." After a long moment, the knife clattered to the floor, breaking the tip of its long blade. Maggie watched the knife fall. Then, with her left hand cradling the right like a broken baby, she offered it to Kate. Her face puckered and a deep sob rocked up from her belly.

"Please . . . help . . . me." The words rose from her soul, her very core, so deep were they. Her frail body swayed with the force of them. Like the moan of the dead, the sound rose in waves that would not, could not be stilled. "I'm . . . so . . . scared."

Kate gathered Maggie into her arms, touched her lips to each bloody finger, smoothed Maggie's hair, and smiled. A tiny smile replied. Maggie nodded. Later there would be time enough to talk about avenging the reverend's sins, to piece

Maggie back together, to finally put the snakes to rest after so many years. For now, though, it was over. Even if only for one more night.

And Kate carefully began to wash the blood away.

Mara: The Ascent of the Vampire

The Events of Tuesday Afternoon

There was nothing remarkable about Josephine Blodgett except the way she died.

She tended no dreams, asked no questions, made no demands. To a city of strangers, she was as easily forgettable as spent lust, and would have remained so, too, if she hadn't stepped into the shadows one September afternoon when the sun hung hot and steamy and low over Golden Gate Park. Stepped into the shadows where Mara was waiting. Waiting with the patience of time. Ancient, deep, and unforgiving. Waiting like the wind, for she was no more, no less than wind. Waiting without passion or shame. Waiting for the warm. For woman or man—it mattered little—who wanted what she could give. Who wanted her more than life itself. Who wanted her. Mara. A vampire of the highest order.

Perhaps if the carousel songs hadn't echoed against the breezeless afternoon, or the children's laughter hadn't evaporated like rain on scorched sand, or the heat of the day hadn't hung so long and heavy, or the shadows hadn't fallen so deep—none of it would have happened. Maybe if Josephine Blodgett had been another woman on another day, her chance meeting with Mara would have remained nothing more than a nodding embrace between strangers. But it didn't happen that way at all.

Nearly a week would pass before the city that had wrapped itself around Josephine Blodgett would know how she'd died. An eighteen-year-old version of the woman in the county morgue would stare out at the Monday-morning commuters from every newsstand on every corner in the city that Josephine Blodgett, Josey, had called home for six months. The picture would be smiling. The corpse, the morgue attendant would tell reporters later, was smiling; he was lying. The headline over the picture would scream NO SUSPECTS IN BIZARRE BEACH MURDER.

Picking up his morning paper, Phil Andrews, the man whose golden retriever Sammy had found the body the morning of the day before, would marvel for a moment at how the girl in the picture looked almost nothing like what he'd seen at the beach. Reaching for his coffee, he already would have forgotten how he puked into the sea foam before running the two miles back up the beach to phone the police. Later that morning, the police sergeant had told him that's what happens when saltwater and sun mix with death for too long. Four days, guessed the police photographer, who'd been nursing a hangover when the call had come in. The photographer hadn't puked into the sea. Guessing the time of death of his subjects was his hobby, he'd explained, gulping aspirin back at the station. Phil Andrews had cringed. Those pictures would end up in a file labeled "Blodgett, Josephine," with the yellow tag that designated homicides.

A young and ambitious detective and a pair of uniformed policemen would spend the rest of that Sunday sifting through the contents of room 243 of the Olympus Hotel. Home to Josey since she'd come to San Francisco, the room was as plain and unremarkable as on the day she'd moved in. Nothing changed. Nothing missing. The only thing added: a fuzzy fading picture of a woman who looked a little like Marilyn Monroe except for two dead, out-of-focus eyes staring from behind a plastic picture frame perched on the Formica-topped dresser.

It wouldn't take the police long to sort through what was left of Josephine Blodgett's twenty years of living. Three of the dresser's four drawers were empty. The top one held six pairs of white cotton underpants, the kind worn by little girls; four white cotton undershirts, the kind worn by old women; four pairs of white athletic socks rolled into fat balls; a high school diploma; and a phony passport that said she was twenty-three and a resident of San Diego who'd been to Denmark, Germany, and Switzerland, most recently returned three years before. Josephine Blodgett had never been outside California.

Babe Daniels would hear about Josey on the Sunday-night news. She would phone Matty, figuring it would be better if A. J. heard it from a friend first. "No! God, no," A. J. would moan, squeezing her eyes tight, tight as her fist that beat against the stove, splashing the coffee until it sputtered into the fire. That night, there would be a wine carafe next to Babe's cash register with a card taped to its side: "For Josey." By the next day the carafes would be in all the bars across the city, the bars Josey had known, the ones she had haunted as she looked for her mother. A pair of prostitutes who lived on the third floor of the hotel would take up a collection from the other tenants for "the kid," as they'd come to call her.

When it became obvious that nobody else was going to claim the body, Matty and A. J. would. It was the least they could do, Matty would say, writing the check for the mortician. She meant it was all anyone could do now for Josey Blodgett, who was once A. J.'s best friend.

At the simple memorial service the next weekend in the Oakland Rose Garden, the women there would cry, some of them, holding hands and comforting each other as best they could. In the back of the loosely assembled group, a stranger with dark eyes and wild black hair would stand silently listening to the eulogy. She would speak to no one and no one would speak to her. After the service, the crowd would buzz with questions, wondering through whispers and tears what had really happened there on that lonely stretch of beach. Only the stranger who faded like fog into the late afternoon would know how and one thing more: she would even know why.

When Josephine Blodgett was ten years old, she learned the world owes you nothing; that children can cry and nobody has to listen; that mothers don't have to love their children; that the children don't have to love anyone at all. It had all become clear one Saturday night when her mother shoved her into the bedroom closet, slammed the door, and turned the skeleton key in the lock. The key was long as a finger, with an open clover at one end and dull teeth at the other. Lily, Josephine's mother, wore it on a rubberband around her wrist when they were alone together. It wasn't the first time Lily Blodgett had locked her only child in a closet. It wasn't even the first time she'd left the apartment, shutting out the girl's tears. It was just the first time she didn't bother to come back.

As the night grew longer, Josey cleared a place for herself among Lily's sandals and high-heeled dancing shoes—discards with broken straps and heels. Picking up one of the shoes, a black-patent pump with very high heels and a rhinestone bow, Josey rubbed the place where the strap had broken. The closet smelled like her mother. White Shoulders. The men with whom Lily spent her nights and evenings, sometimes even her afternoons, brought her White Shoulders. It was Lily's trademark. And Lily Blodgett had very white shoulders, skin so pale the veins showed through, giving her a hauntingly fragile look that she tended with jars of bleaching cream. Josey had that same skin; as a woman she would grow into a dark-haired version of her mother, with the same unnerving beauty. Beauty that Lily had traded on and that her daughter never acknowledged.

Through the keyhole of the closet door, Josey could see a corner of the unmade bed illuminated by a small lamp in the shape of a pink ceramic ballerina. Josey loved that ballerina with her real lace skirt, her upraised arms holding the pink light bulb shaped like a flame. Sometimes when Lily was especially happy, she would let the girl play with the doll lamp. Sometimes didn't come very often, though. At the end of the bed was Lily's dressing table, a cheap plywood affair painted pink with a flowered skirt. The table top was covered with jars of Porcelana and bottles of White Shoulders. Josey sometimes imagined the bottles contained a magic potion left there by the good fairy who wore a lace dress just like the ballerina.

Lily's voice swirled through the quiet of Josey's thoughts. *"Mama's goin' out dancin' tonight, Josey, and don't she look fine? Just like a regular baby doll. Why you know, Mama could be the next Marilyn Monroe if she could just get to Hollywood. That's what they need there—a new Marilyn Monroe. Oh, and wouldn't Mama look just fine up there on that big silver screen? Now come over here and help Mama zip up her dress, honey. Josey! Get over here, dammit! Stop messing with my things. Now, that's better. Hand Mama that bottle of White Shoulders and be careful not to drop it. Mama surely does have white shoulders, don't you think, Josey-girl? David Dawson says he*

*never seen skin as white as mine. He's a rich man, Josey, real
rich. His daddy owns a couple of ranches or something. I play
my cards right and maybe he'll be your new daddy. How'd you
like a daddy, kid? Maybe even take me to Paris, France. Your
mama surely would like that. You gonna help fix it so Mama
can go to Paris, France? Be Mama's best little lover? Now, ain't
that fine! Don't that smell nice? Now, don't you answer the door
if anybody comes knockin' and Mama'll be home before you even
know she's been gone. 'Less I get lucky."*

David had stopped coming around, though. After David was
Milt, then Brian, Marco, and finally Carl. Josey had liked him
best. Carl had a few acres east of town where he kept three,
sometimes four horses. Whenever Lily took her to the ranch,
he'd saddle up an Appaloosa named Sparky and let Josey ride
as long as she liked. But then she and Lily stopped going there.
Josey sometimes imagined that she'd run into Carl some afternoon, maybe at the Buy & Save, and he'd say, "Josey! Sparky's
been missing you. Why don't you come on out this afternoon
and go riding?" Only it never happened.

Then there was a stretch of nobody. Just Lily being out a lot
at night and coming in real early. That was her shoe-breaking
period. She'd come up the walk, one foot barefoot, up on her
toes like the ballerina. Cursing as she tossed the broken shoe
into the back of the closet where there were a dozen others like
it. Lily never had the broken shoes fixed; she just went out and
bought another pair. Josey's favorites were the gold sandals
with the glittery heels. Lily said rich women in Hollywood even
wore shoes with real goldfish swimming in the heels. Josey was
glad they weren't rich; she'd worry about the fish too much.

Josey had started screaming that morning when she realized Lily wasn't coming back. She'd kept it up all Sunday afternoon. It was Sunday evening before Mrs. Thompson, who lived
on the first floor, called the police. "I don't want no trouble,"
she kept telling the policewoman who answered the call, "but
a body's got to be able to watch 'Sixty Minutes' in peace." The
policewoman's eyes widened as she scribbled something on her
pad. "This used to be a respectable building," Mrs. Thompson
confided, waving her arm toward the rambling house that had
been chopped into apartments years before. "But they don't
care what kind of trash they let in here no more. You wouldn't
believe what goes on in that apartment." Sounds of the rescue
were muffled in the yard where the policewoman had led Mrs.

Thompson, who was hoping there was a newspaper reporter among the clump of curiosity seekers who had gathered on the sidewalk. "And that poor little girl. What I could tell you," she announced loudly, sorry she hadn't thought to call the television station first. She cluck-clucked as the policeman who'd broken down the closet door carried Josey to the squad car. "I love children," she said, craning her neck to get a better look. Later she'd hear that little Josey Blodgett had screamed until her throat bled. "Might-a died, too, if it weren't for me," Mrs. Thompson told the neighbors, leaving out the part about "Sixty Minutes."

Even when she got her voice back, Josey rarely talked after that. It was if there was nothing left to say. There was no place else for her to go, so Josephine Blodgett became a ward of the state. And because she wouldn't talk or go to school or stop running away from the foster homes they put her in, she ended up in what the social workers called a group home and the children called jail. It was a place where children spin dreams until they can't be sorted out from reality.

That was where Josey met Alice Jean King, a streetwise baby butch who was two years older than Josey. A. J. was there because she'd stabbed her father with his own hunting knife. The old man didn't die, but that didn't stop A. J.'s mother from telling the court the girl was incorrigible. Or how she climbed out her bedroom window and spent most nights roaming the streets with "god knows what." Years later A. J. would recall that the streets had seemed safer.

Sometimes A. J. talked, but mostly she didn't. Sometimes Josey tried to talk, but mostly she couldn't. On those few times when she had anything to say, A. J. told Josey that Lily would have left no matter what—that it was just the way she was. Josey wasn't so sure. Maybe Mama was right, Josey wanted to say, but the words didn't seem to come. It was as if Lily was fogging her mind with memories.

"Josey, Mama's lined up a fine job for you. Nine years old is big enough to be helpin' out round here. And that nice Mister Riger from 'cross the way says he's lookin' for a girl just like you to come over and tidy up his place one night a week."

"Mama, please. I'm-a scared of him. Nights when you're gone he comes over and looks in the window, just watchin' me, and playin' with his old thing. I seen him, I know it's him, his old beard just a shinin' there in the moonlight."

"Now, don't you stand there shakin' your head 'no' at me, Miss Priss! He pays ten dollars. Ten dollars is a fine lot of money to have just for pickin' up after some old geezer and washin' up a few dishes."

"Mama, he's a vampire, just like I seen on the TV, with yellow teeth and everything. Mama, stop laughin' at me. Mister Riger's gonna get me one-a these nights, you'll see, then you'll be sorry!"

"Don't you lie to me, you ungrateful brat! You don't deserve a decent Mama. I give up everything for you and this is the thanks I get? Serve you right if I was to just take off one day and never come back. You're drivin' me to it. Is that what you want? To drive your own lovin' Mama off?"

"No, Mama! Don't leave me, please Mama, I take it back. Mama, I'm sorry! Mama, please!"

"I told Mister Riger you'd be over there tomorrow night and that's where you're going to be. Now you go get that ten dollars. Be nice to him and maybe he'll make it twenty. Now, let Mama see you smile. There, that's my girl. Now rub Mama's feet, that's right. Oh, you got the touch, Josey. Make Mama feel good. That's right, honey."

Sometimes late at night in the group home, Josey and A. J. would lie awake listening to the soft gasps and whimpers that the pillows couldn't muffle. So many tears shed under the cover of night. But she didn't cry and neither did A. J., so when the social workers looked at them, they saw the hardened eyes of women who'd already seen too much to be children ever again. Twice they'd tried to separate the girls, saying they were a bad example for the others. But inevitably Josey stopped talking and A. J. started running away, so it was easier to leave them together. Besides, A. J. was due to graduate soon. The problem would resolve itself.

Once for a few months when she was fifteen, Josey had imagined she was in love with A. J., but they were better friends than lovers. In a way it was a good thing, because on A. J.'s eighteenth birthday she moved out of the group home. Josey tried writing a few times but couldn't think of anything much to say. Once she'd even cut school and taken the Greyhound to Los Angeles, where A. J. was living in an apartment with three other women, but it wasn't the same. Josey could have taken the next bus back; she would have, too, if A. J. hadn't said she'd seen a woman who looked remarkably like the picture of Lily Blodgett. "I saw her three, maybe four times. She's waiting tables at a diner by where I work. Seein' her made me think of you . . . how you always had that picture of your ma out on a desk or something. Wherever you were." A. J. laughed. Josey laughed, too.

"Take me there," she found herself saying. "Please, A. J., I want to see . . . if it's her."

"Sure. You don't think she's Lily, though, do you?"

Josey shrugged, looked at the ground, and fell silent.

The next day they'd gone to see the waitress at the diner, who looked nothing at all like Lily. That woman was a good three inches taller, big-boned, but with an exceptionally tiny waist. Bright blond hair was piled high in a tangle of bows and curls. Still, it was enough to plant the idea. Lily was out there, somewhere, and Josey could find her—if she looked hard enough.

In her junior year, Josey transferred to the technical high school to study auto mechanics and discovered it was easier to cut classes there than at the regular high school. So she started spending one or two days a week haunting the bars and diners where graying men and lost women spent their days. It seemed as good a place as any to start looking for Lily. Josey was following a ghost along a cold and crumbling trail, mostly down. That trail took her into back-street bars with their bottomless stock of drunks and rivers of cheap wine. It made her look into the night faces of the women waiting at bus stops and behind counters. Looking, until they'd scream with their eyes for her to stop, to leave them and their secrets alone. On her eighteenth birthday, Josey walked out of the group home for good with fifty dollars and a fake passport in her back pocket, a high school diploma in her backpack. She was on her way to L.A.

Lily had always wanted to be a movie star, so Josey went to Hollywood. But if Lily was there, Josey couldn't find her. Then a drunken sailor said he'd seen her waiting tables at a topless joint in San Diego. Josey caught a bus south. Eventually, still following rumors of Lily, she moved on to San Francisco, to another rented room with pale painted walls and orange shag carpeting and window shades that couldn't shut out the night that kept calling. By day she worked in garages, catching naps after work and before dawn. So it was when Mara found her.

The day was clear, hot, and sunny. Josey was stretched full length on the park bench that stood just beyond the shadows. The sun was soaking her black T-shirt and jeans hot. She was glad work was over. The afternoon had weighed heavy inside Mel's Foreign Specialties, where she was one of four mechanics who specialized in putting small expensive cars back together. It was the third job she'd had in two years.

Josey's black eyes were closed against the sun. She had her father's eyes, although she'd never known him, and his wavy hair that shone blue-black. It was a startling contrast against the pale, almost luminous complexion she'd inherited from Lily. Her mouth pouted full and naturally red. She was a beautiful woman who had no use for beauty.

As Mara drew nearer, she could feel it: the churning, the emptiness, the rage of need that glowed from the warm. Josey. Mara studied the young woman carefully: tall, although not unusually so. But thin, Josey was so thin her ribs prodded the T-shirt, which was covered loosely with a blue mechanic's shirt with the sleeves ripped out and MEL'S stitched in red thread over the breast pocket where Josey kept a roll of peppermints. Her bony hands had the telltale grease stains of a mechanic. They were folded across the Walkman on her chest. The city's vintage rock 'n' roll station churned into her brain from the earphones. Occasionally her thumb adjusted the volume, up.

In a few hours, Josey planned to be back on the streets again—looking. For her. For Lily. The wallet in her back pocket held a frayed fuzzy Polaroid snapshot of a woman in a white sundress, pouting and posing for the man behind the camera. And it was always for the man behind the camera, Josey thought, shifting a little on the park bench. Every night that she could stand it, Josey would push that picture into the hand of anyone who would look, who might have some glimmer of recognition in their eyes. Once or twice she'd seen it, that flash of knowing. It was always enough to send her wherever the bartender or the waitress or the clerk at the all-night doughnut shop said the woman who looked like Lily might have gone. On nights when she couldn't stand the empty eyes of the strangers any longer, she'd go to Babe's or Pinkie's or any of the other bars where the eyes were friendly with promise.

Lying there, Josey turned over again in her mind—for the millionth time it seemed—what it would be like to finally find Lily. Would she be happy? Or just happy that the search was over? And what about Lily? What would she do? Or what if she never found her? What then? She considered moving off the bench and hopping a bus back to the hotel. Or jogging through the park, savoring the cool shadows of the trees, their leaves hanging heavy like sleepy eyes. She could always stop for a ride on the antique carousel's lion. It was cool there in the carousel building. Sometimes the dyke who ran the controls let Josey have an extra ride for free. She was thinking of all these things when the dream stole up on her, seducing her, pulling her down. Always down.

Two minutes to midnight. The witching hour come at last. Be witching, be coming. Nonsense rhymes and rhythms keep on dancing out over a full moon, tripping over the lady there who's brushing out long fine moon-madness maiden hair. Fallen angel, down and drunk, stumbles into the mouth of the big old man who's been laughing down on humanity for—how long now—longer than any of us'll ever know, that's for damned sure. Longer than anybody, 'cept for the scientists who live up on the hill lookin' out into the eyes of heaven itself, even cares.

They say magic's to be had on a night like this, when a bloated moon hangs low and heavy, threatening to dump out all her promises and prayers on the unbelievers, making them the true believers after all.

They say in the dungeons of the madhouses, a hundred years or more ago, the women locked in the snake pits would turn and charm the snakes, teaching them to howl at the moon that peeked in through open bars . . . on a night like this.

They say, even now, the oceans turn and open wide to suck in the moon's precious crystals, tickling the very core of sunken Atlantis, on a night like this. And the ones that are truly blest see visions swirling on the night air. And demons dancing with fairies on the moonflowers. Blessed are the mad, for theirs is the kingdom of the void.

Black water swirls cones of death, sucking, dragging the unwitting traveler into dungeons beneath the sea itself. Another captive held for death herself. Wait. Grope. Learn its passages by touch. Too deep, too black, too unforgiving. The ocean has swallowed the moon. Wait. Grope. Seawater etches the virgin pores, blackening them. No choice, no chance at all.

They say the sow nurses her piglets grudgingly, that only the strongest survive the senseless attacks of a mother who wallows

on top of fragile pink piglet bodies, crushing them beneath her
mass of muck and flesh. And if the least stirrings of hunger
tremble in the sow's belly, she feasts on her own, taking them,
still alive and screaming into her strong jaws, crushing tender
bones, chewing warm flesh until new blood runs rich and black
down the sow's jowls, staining the dirt beneath her feet. And
she, grunting in glutted satisfaction, ignores their squeals, their
screams . . . on a night like this.

The light rips the blackness wide. The moon has opened the
tides, once again. Snakes howl with madwomen on craggy cliffs
that overlook the sea. Their cant shatters the night; it's the
muffled sound of a child crying somewhere very far away.

The sun had escaped behind a grove of trees, leaving Josey cold
and trembling as much from the dream as the shadows. But it
was the scream that had awakened her. She looked around
quickly, alarmed. Had she heard it—or only dreamed it? She
couldn't tell, only that it had sounded like hell itself howling.
A woman was sitting quietly on the bench opposite, watching
Josey closely from behind dark glasses. Smiling. Eyes hidden
by green plastic lenses surrounded by white plastic frames.
Narrow. Winged, like they used to wear in the fifties but popular again. Wisps of pale blond hair curled around her white
chiffon scarf, which was tied over her head and knotted around
her throat. Her white sundress moved softly under the fingers
of afternoon breezes. Bare-legged, she was wearing gold high-
heeled sandals that crisscrossed over long narrow feet with toes
tipped in red polish. The red matched her fingernails. She was
holding a cigarette, smoke pluming out of the corners of her
mouth, but she didn't inhale.

Josey could smell the smoke and ocean and perfume that
teased against her memories. The woman smiled. Josey smiled
back. The woman nodded in the way of familiar strangers.
Josey tried to place her. One of the women who brought their
broken fantasy machines to Mel's, perhaps? Or who just lived
in the neighborhood and had passed Josey at the bus stop? Or
maybe Josey had simply dreamed her into reality there on that
park bench, although that seemed unlikely. Anyway, what did
it matter? She was beautiful and the afternoon was warm, and
for the first time in a very long time, Josey was aware of being
lonely. And it made her afraid.

That was how it started. Simple. Easy. They went for hamburgers and coffee. Real coffee, not instant with hot tap water like Josey was used to making in her bathroom. The woman said her name was Yvonne Delacroix, although she didn't look French. She said she'd been "in films." Foreign, mostly. Very limited, one might even say exclusive, releases at select art theaters in this country. She'd planned to go back to Hollywood, but there was a small . . . legal . . . problem. Then she got sick, very sick, so she went to Acapulco . . . to an elegant resort that catered to . . . artists, and those who appreciated them.

She'd once seen a man run down by an out-of-control bus, right in front of her, just outside her hotel. The image had haunted her for weeks—months—even now it was difficult to eat rare meat, the red juices running. So like blood. The man's blood . . . there in the street. She had gone to find a bucket and a broom to wash the blood away.

Josey hung on every word, watching Yvonne's painted red lips. "So, tell me about yourself," Yvonne finally asked, gingerly biting into her hamburger. A bit of red juice escaped from the corner of her mouth. She caught it with a napkin, sniffed the napkin, and chewed stiffly, as if she didn't want the food to touch her lips.

Josey shrugged. There was nothing to tell, really. What was she supposed to say? "When I was a kid, my mama loved me so much she locked me in a closet and forgot to come back, so I was raised in a group home with a bunch of girls who were beaten by their mothers and raped by their fathers?" Or maybe Yvonne would like to hear how the other girls called Josey "Lucky"—a nickname she despised—because the worst that happened to her was getting locked in a closet? Or maybe she could try to explain why even now sleeping in a room with the doors closed still gives her the shakes, so she'd taken to drinking instant coffee and walking the streets, thinking maybe there's some real daylight out there somewhere?

Or maybe Yvonne would like to hear how the home had turned Josey out the day of her eighteenth birthday. Armed her with a high school diploma that affirmed she knew the capitals of all fifty states—she didn't—and how to balance a checkbook, even though she'd never seen more than ten dollars in her pocket at one time, Josey had free-fallen into the world. What the high school diploma didn't tell was her gift for automobile engines. Better than any of the boys in her classes, Josey seemed able to almost breathe life into what anyone else would have dismissed as hopeless. "Guess it's just something I come by natural," she'd stammer, her eyes memorizing the lines in her boots, whenever anyone wondered about her talent.

The truth was very nearly that simple, but there was no way Josey would ever know that her father had been a small-town stock-car driver who'd spent most of his twenty-two years dreaming of driving the Daytona 500. She'd never know that the 1957 Chevy with the big orange No. 51 painted on the side was where she'd been conceived. Or how a fifteen-year-old runaway, her belly already swelling with Josephine, had sat in the dust by the stock-car track all one Saturday night. How Lily had sat there until there was no one and nothing left but the dust and the moon, waiting for No. 51 to roar through the gate and take her into the new life he'd promised they'd find beyond the dirt and dust of the back roads.

Josey would never know that, anymore than she would ever know how three years later No. 51 had spun out of control like a flaming top across a Texas speedway, frying the boy inside until his own mother couldn't recognize him. No one bothered to tell Lily, because no one knew about her. She read about it later in the *Bakersfield Californian.*

Eight years later, Lily Blodgett locked her bedroom closet door, tossed the apartment keys on her unmade bed, picked up her pink paisley suitcase, and walked the three blocks to the Bakersfield bus station, where she bought a one-way ticket to Hollywood. A few weeks later, she met a man who promised to make her a star. That was the only promise he didn't break. By the time her career ended, Lily Blodgett had changed her name, adopted an accent she thought sounded French, and starred in twenty-seven films, all of them X-rated, most of them made in Mexico. She was finally a star, and A. J. was right— Lily never bothered to look back.

"Do you like the beach, Josey?" Yvonne was examining her lovely face in the mirror of a mother-of-pearl-encrusted compact. "I love the beach, especially at sunset, how the sun tumbles into the ocean. When I was in Acapulco, I used to sit at my window every day and watch the sunset. We used to say if you listened hard enough you could hear it sizzle when it hit the waves. But it was a lie. It never really sizzles, only in your mind." She was staring at Josey, the sunglasses gone, her eyes pale blue and sparkling under the fluorescent light fixtures of the hamburger joint.

Josey shook her head. Any other evening, with any other woman, she would have gone to the beach, but Lily was heavy on her mind. "My mother. She's not well. I need to go to her," she stammered, staring at Yvonne's hands—one holding the compact mirror, the other stroking on layers of red lipstick over and over. The hamburger lay cold and forgotten on her plate.

"I know a beach where no one goes until the weekend, and even then only when its very, very hot," Yvonne was saying. "It's beautiful there, almost like a world you've always known existed but have never really seen before. Please come, let me take you there . . . to my secret place." She closed the compact and took Josey's hand, waving off her protests. "I have a car. We could make it to the beach and go for a walk even before the sun sizzles." She was smiling, charming, beguiling, and not an easy woman to deny.

Josey looked at her watch. It was already past six. She shook her head. "I'm sorry. I already have plans. I'm going out."

Yvonne looked at Josey closely, suspicion clouded her voice. "But you just said your mother was ill. That you were going to see her."

"I did. I mean I hope to." Josey felt Yvonne's eyes burning against her, probing. Josey inhaled sharply. Yvonne's eyes didn't flinch. "I'm . . . I'm looking . . . for her." Josey fumbled over the words, trying to make them sound believable. Yvonne's eyes shone like pale stars. "I'm looking for my mother. She got sick, like amnesia, and I have to find her. I followed her here from Los Angeles." The words spilled out before Josey could stop them. "Maybe you've seen her," she finally ended, reaching for Lily's picture.

Yvonne accepted the picture, glanced at it, then laid it on the green Formica between them. "Why do you want to find her?" Yvonne asked, leaning forward across the table, her hands clasped in front of her.

Josey gasped. No one had ever asked her that before; it had always seemed so clear, so understood. "Because she's my mother. I gotta find her. She's my mom. She's all I've got."

Yvonne regarded her hands carefully, the litter on the table between them, the grain of the coarse paper napkins, the fine skin that covered the girl's fingers. She raised her eyes to Josey's face, studying her. "We all can't be mothers." Her voice was soft, no louder than a whisper. Blotting her lips with a folded paper napkin, she never let her eyes leave Josey's. Challenging eyes. Daring. "If she wanted to see you, she probably would have looked you up by now. Or did you never consider that?"

Josey bit deep into her trembling lip, held her breath, squeezed her eyes tightly against the tears that threatened. Why was Yvonne being so mean? Why couldn't she just understand what it was always to be looking . . . looking. And waiting for something you don't even know if you can have.

"Why are you crying?" Yvonne asked in the same voice, a voice that was not kind nor comforting, just probing, pricking like needles.

Not wanting to look at Yvonne, wanting only to escape, Josey felt Lily roar out of her memories. *"Why don't you cry, crybaby?"* taunted Lily, her voice laughing, cruel. *"Go on, crybaby. Cry because Mama's going out."* Lily was laughing then, her red wet lips stretched wide leaving lipstick stains on her teeth. Josey blinked hard and looked at Yvonne.

Yvonne laid the napkin on the table between them, a perfect red lip print on white paper. Josey looked at the lip print floating on the napkin. Another lip print on a piece of white toilet paper. Floating there in the toilet, forgotten by Lily, who was standing at the bathroom sink, her satin slip drawn tight across her behind. While the red lip print floated. Floated. Josey shuddered at the memory.

Reaching across the table, Yvonne took Josey's hand. "Now I'd like to go for that walk on the beach we were talking about." Her hand was cool, smooth, but surprisingly strong. They walked hand in hand down the street to the new sea-green Mercedes sports convertible that waited by the curb.

If anyone had bothered to check—as the police would when they found the Mercedes parked near the beach the following Sunday—the serial number would have come up on the list of stolen vehicles at the Oakland Police Department. It had most recently belonged, in a way, to Leroy Jenks, who had made his living supplying happy rocks to anyone with a ten-dollar bill. He'd rented it from a Hertz agency and had promptly forgotten to take it back. She had acquired it the night before, not long after the drug dealer had spotted her standing in the shadows of a flashing neon. He'd thought she was very beautiful, very stoned, and very rich. Her skin had glowed like fine mahogany under the full-length silver-fox coat that she wore open over a very short red dress with spangles.

She had smiled, open and daring, inviting Leroy to come closer into the night. She was every woman he had ever wanted, and he had wanted many more than he'd ever had. But more than want, he needed this one, this glimmer of icy wealth. She was the girl from the big white house on the corner, whose mama chased him off her front porch with a broom when he was ten. She was the woman he'd watched from his bedroom window that looked down across the apartment building air shaft. Leroy had watched her all through his twelfth summer. Watched her loosen her blouse, unhook her bra, unfasten her skirt as she looked out her open window, as her man lay naked and hard on her bed. All summer, he'd watched—and then one day, she was gone. She was the woman his brother Ajax had worn on his arm like a trophy for a year—her breasts heavy, her legs long—until she left him for a man with a golden Cadillac and an endless trail of cocaine. And this one was rich— whether it was her money or her man's didn't matter to Leroy Jenks—which made her so much finer than all those other women.

She had looked at him and smiled and made Leroy Jenks want her, need her more than anything he had ever wanted in his life. "Do you want me?" she had whispered, although she'd already guessed the answer. And when he came to her, she had taken him hard and swift, giving him all that he had ever wanted, all that he was willing to die for. His final submission. When his body had turned up facedown in a deserted warehouse in East Oakland, the police charged it off to the drug wars. The condition of the corpse, they decided, was some sort of warning to usurping drug dealers. They were wrong.

"You drive," Yvonne said, tossing Josey the keys and dropping into the seat on the passenger side. "I must admit, I'm not much of a driver. I haven't been at it very long."

"You rent a car like this and you just learned to drive?" Josey asked. She'd seen the license plate that identified the car as a rental. Settling behind the wheel, running her fingers across the leather upholstery, readjusting the mirrors, she listened to the magnificent engine purr. Josey had never met anyone over seventeen who didn't know how to drive. She guessed Yvonne to be about thirty-five, maybe a little older. What a waste of car, she thought to herself.

"The car is nothing, just something I picked up. I like the color. It reminds me of the sea," Yvonne said, as if she were answering Josey's thoughts. "Where I was . . . before . . . it wasn't important."

"Manhattan," Josey said.

"What?"

"Did you just get in from New York? I mean, I know it's a rental and I figure you're from Manhattan because that's about the only place you can live in this country and get away with not driving."

"Yes, of course," Yvonne said smiling, "Manhattan."

As Josey drove, Yvonne loosened the scarf, letting her hair fly free in the evening breeze. They crossed the Golden Gate Bridge just as the sun was beginning to kiss the waves. Yvonne turned to Josey and smiled. When she reached to push the cigarette lighter in, her hand brushed Josey's thigh. Josey trembled; Yvonne smiled and leaned closer. "Beautiful," she said.

"You mean the sunset?" Josey answered, although she sensed Yvonne's meaning.

"No, you. You are beautiful, you do know that, don't you?"

Josey blushed; no one had ever told her that before. Yvonne placed her hand on Josey's leg and pressed lightly. Josey covered the hand with her own, following the winding road to the sea. She wanted Yvonne. Wanted her as she could remember wanting no other woman before her. Wanted. Wanting. Yvonne smiled as if she knew.

The ocean was tinged with colors from a tangerine sky by the time they reached the beach. Yvonne had shed her shoes and was walking barefoot, her scarf draped loosely across her shoulders. The chiffon billowed like a cloud from the sea breeze. Josey had laced her shoes together and draped them over her right shoulder. Those shoes were what would lead Phil Andrews to Josey's body. Sammy would come dragging them up the beach and Phil would unlace them to play fetch for a while. They'd move along, Phil throwing first one shoe, then the other as Sammy retrieved. The sun would be rising pink and steady. The sand would still be hard and wet from the tide. Finally, the dog would disappear behind a pair of boulders and clumps of sea grass. Phil Andrews would call Sammy for a while, then go to investigate, dropping the shoes there in the sand by the big rock that still lay a hundred yards ahead of Josey and Yvonne.

"I love the sea. Movie stars, the real ones, all have houses at Malibu. I've been to a few parties there. It's more beautiful than anything you can imagine. Marilyn Monroe probably had a house there. She was beautiful; she belonged there by the sea," Yvonne was saying as they walked, their shoulders touching. Josey was basking in the warmth of her smile.

"You know what they need in Hollywood, Josey? A new Marilyn Monroe," Yvonne was saying as they walked. Josey looked at Yvonne closely. She was even more beautiful than she'd seemed in the restaurant. The light, Josey decided. She wanted to kiss her—started to, in fact—when Yvonne danced ahead on the sand, twirling and dipping like a leaf. She was laughing and talking all at once. But the sea was loud; it stole her words, so that Josey heard only snatches of whole sentences.

"Marilyn . . . I could . . . new star" was all Josey heard. She chuckled. Yvonne might look a little like the dead movie star, but with the light pink and pale it was difficult to say whether or not it was real or just the magic of the moment. Why would anyone want to be Marilyn Monroe? So sad, too sad an ending for a goddess, Josey decided. Except Lily. That had always been Lily's dream. The thought caught Josey unaware. She shook her head, watching Yvonne dancing on the sand, twirling, bowing, carrying those gold sandals in her hand. Suddenly Yvonne whirled around, bent forward, and with her hands on her knees, pursed her lips, blowing kisses to imaginary fans. "What d'ya think, Josey-girl? Should I be the next Marilyn Monroe?" Yvonne was laughing wildly.

Josey started to laugh, too, then froze. There in the twilight, Yvonne looked so much like Lily. Lily studying her reflection in the mirror. Pursing her still-girlishly full lips. Blowing kisses. Winking seductively. *"Come on, Josey-girl, come and dance with Mama."* Lily, wrapped only in a white bath towel, strutting across the bedroom floor, then letting the towel drop, exposing her perfect full breasts, then laughing. Laughing at what, Josey never knew. Just laughing. Josey closed her eyes, trying to block out the vision. "Don't!" she heard herself scream. "Don't laugh at me!"

And then Yvonne was next to her, pulling Josey close, warming her, drying her tears, quieting her. "I would never laugh at you," she whispered as they started walking again. Josey shook her head again to clear it. What had she been thinking of? This woman wasn't Lily, she was Yvonne. Yvonne Delacroix. She had a rented Mercedes and lived in Manhattan and was in San Francisco on vacation—or business—she never really said which. She was rich and beautiful and experienced, and she would let Josey make love to her if she wanted to. And at that moment, Josey wanted that very much. The last light was fast fading and they seemed to be walking quickly into the night; the ocean roared next to them.

"What would you say to your mother if you found her?" Yvonne finally asked. They had walked for what seemed miles. The road where the Mercedes was parked was no longer visible. The beach was deserted, as if no one had been there in a long time. Yvonne was holding Josey's hand, their backs resting against the boulders. The sea was angry and loud. Fog had settled cold and gray across the night. Yvonne kissed her. Josey shivered. Yvonne asked the same question again.

Again, Josey didn't answer. Instead, she suggested, "Maybe we should be getting back." Josey was rubbing her arms briskly with her hands.

"Stay just a little while with me. You want to stay with me, don't you?" Yvonne asked, wrapping herself around Josey's back, her breath warm, comforting against her throat. Josey settled deep into the warmth. "You love your mother, don't you, Josey?" she asked, her arms tightening a little. "Even after all she did, you still love her."

Josey nodded. "I used to think I didn't. That if she ever came back, I'd kill her, toss her gizzard to the lizards." She chuckled. "But now I just want to know why. No, I don't even need to know that anymore. I just want to see her one more time. That's all. Just once more. She never even told me she loved me. Not ever. Nobody ever loved me. But I love her. I do."

"Shhh," Yvonne crooned, her voice soothing as a love song. She was holding Josey tightly, feeling her chest rise and fall with each breath, feeling the warm. Wanting. Needing. The warm. The very force of the transmutation was beginning to tug at the sinew in her bones. Soon it would be complete. Soon. "Mamas always love their baby girls. You know that, don't you?" Josey shook her head. "If your mama were here, I know just what she would say. She'd tell you it wasn't like you thought, that she never left you. You were playing in the closet. Don't you remember? How you loved to play in there. How the scent of White Shoulders hung there. And the door . . . locked.

That's all. It was a terrible accident. Maybe she couldn't open it herself, so she ran to get help. Ran and ran, calling, crying, but no one would come. She only lost her way. For a very long time. Lost. She couldn't come back, no matter how hard she tried. They wouldn't let her. That's what she would tell you. And you would believe your mama, wouldn't you, Josey-girl? You always believed your mama." Yvonne's voice was husky, pleading. Tears hung in the words that brushed against Josey's throat.

Josey's brow furrowed. She didn't remember telling Yvonne about the closet, but she must have. She struggled free and stood up, brushing the sand from her jeans. She didn't want to talk about Lily anymore, didn't want to hear what she might have said. She didn't want to be near Yvonne; she was too much like Lily, after all. "Look, Yvonne, I've really got to go. You can drive me or I'll hitch, but I've got to go."

Yvonne stretched her legs out on the sand. The dusk was as heavy as shadows across her face. She was smiling, but Josey couldn't see it, so thin was the light. "Fine," she said. "I never planned to be with you so long anyway. But Josey, find your own way back. I can't waste time on crybabies."

"Why don't you cry, crybaby?" called Lily through the fog. Josey started walking, but the sand was deep and her progress was slowed by the incoming tide that kept licking at her feet. In the distance she could hear Lily laughing. "Shut up, Mama!" she screamed. "I don't want you anymore." And she started to cry then, because it was a lie and because it would never happen. She wanted Lily, but she would never find her, no matter where she looked, no matter how hard she tried. Lily was gone and Josey was alone; all that she had left was Yvonne. How could I have been such a fool? Josey thought, going back to where Yvonne was still reclining on the sand, letting the sea wash across her feet and ankles.

The transmutation was almost complete; soon Josey would see it, would know but would never understand. "I can tell you what happened to Lily after she locked you in that closet." The voice was soft but uncaring, cold as the sea. "You were right about her going to Hollywood, only she didn't stay there long. She ended up in Mexico with a Hollywood producer, at least that's what he called himself. He produced what are politely called specialty films. Very special films for men with very special appetites. He made Lily a star. It's what she wanted—

what she'd always wanted—and she didn't care how it happened. She spent most of her time in resorts frequented by rich foreigners visiting Acapulco. Rich men with exotic appetites and the money to satisfy them. In those circles, in those places, in those times, she was famous, coveted, a prize to be won or bought, depending on the circumstances. By then Lily Blodgett had changed everything about herself. No one knew she'd ever had a daughter, and eventually even she forgot about it. She learned Spanish but acquired a French accent. She thought it went better with her new name, Yvonne Delacroix. So now you know."

"Mama?" Josey sank to her knees, trying to see through the heavy dusk. "You're my mother?"

"No, I'm not your mother. I'm Yvonne Delacroix. I just told you, she doesn't have a daughter. Now get out of here."

"Please, Mama." Josey's head was buzzing. She felt dizzy. She'd just found what she'd been looking for all these years. She couldn't just go. It wasn't supposed to be like that. "Don't send me away, Mama. Please." Josey was begging; tears burned her eyes, her throat. She struggled for breath. "Please, Mama, I've been looking for you for such a long time. Mama, please." And then Josey's mother opened her arms.

She was crooning the words Josey had waited half her life to hear. Feeling warm and sleepy there in her mother's arms, Josey listened to the lullaby of words. "Mama wanted to take you away with her; you know that now, don't you, Josey-girl? But she couldn't. Mexico wouldn't have been any kind of life for a girl like you. And you did want Mama to be a star, didn't you? If she'd come back for you, they would've locked her away. Nobody would've believed you getting locked in that closet was an accident. They never would've understood about us, Josey. But Mama never meant to leave you. And now that we've found each other, we can be together always. You'd like that, wouldn't you, Josey, to be with Mama always?" Lily's voice was all around Josey: the same tinny laughter, the same hardened accent like cream going bad, unpleasant now, but once so sweet.

"I would've come with you, Mama," Josey whispered, fighting for the words. "I wouldn't have cared. I could've taken care of you. You always needed me to take care of you. You said nobody could take care of you the way I could. Don't you remember, Mama? I waited such a long time. I looked and I looked but I couldn't find my mama anywhere." Tears stormed down her cheeks. Josey tried to turn, to look at the woman who was holding her, rocking her, but her eyes were heavy lidded, impossible to focus. She could only make out the blond hair, the white dress. Her face had gone fuzzy into the night. The dress fluttered like wings around them, lifting in billows, then falling limp. Salt stung her eyes. Josey wailed, low at first, then louder, louder still until the sound seemed to pour out of her into the night. Arms tightened around her. Strong arms, strong hands. Hands stronger than any she'd ever known held her firm.

Josey struggled, then relaxed. Let her lungs fill with the cold night, with the salt air. She could feel her breath hot against the damp cold. Visions of Lily flashed in front of her. She was trying to find warmth in the arms that held her, but there was only fog and the cold and the crashing of the sea.

"Remember how you used to rub Mama's feet?" The words pierced the night. "Remember how you loved Mama better than anyone in the world? Remember, Josey-girl? Rub Mama's feet now, honey." The hands that held her guided Josey's fingers toward long slender feet, bare now, still damp from the sea and dusted with sand. Dancer's feet, with red toenails. Dancer's feet for a woman who never danced. Josey touched the skin, hesitating, brushing the sand away. "Go on," whispered the wind, "make Mama feel good." Josey cupped one foot in her hands. She was crying. And as she bent over the foot, the ankle, the scent of White Shoulders rose up to greet her.

"Oh, Mama," she whispered.

"Shhh," the voice cooed, rocking the girl slowly back and forth in her arms. "You're with Mama now and nobody's ever going to take you away again. Hush, Josey-girl, hush my little lover."

"I love you, Mama," Josey whispered, tears streaking her face, falling onto the woman's white skirt, her fine long-boned feet, Josey's hands. "Oh, Mama." Josey sobbed as the hands gripped her tightly by her thin shoulders, guided her upright, brought her face-to-face with the woman in the Polaroid snapshot. Josey felt the warmth of her mother's breath on her skin as she bent to kiss her. Josey turned and looked into the eyes that burned pale as stars under the full moon that was hanging heavy and ripe on the horizon. And in that moment, she knew. "Mama, please" was the last thing she said.

And then, it was over. Taking no longer than a second. Mara inhaled the warm, pulling it into her, deep, through her, hard.

The ocean roared. Mara howled in ecstasy as the warm pounded into her. Beat through her. Churned like river rapids unrelenting. Filling her. Glutting her with its sweet heat until she swelled with it, tender and moist. She moaned from the weight of it, the terrible exhilaration that threatened to explode, to break through her skin. She rode with it. Panting. Gasping. Clawing at her own skin that burned and raged at the invasion. Breathless, she crawled to the water's edge and lapped at the foam, letting her tongue drip with the coolness of the sea. Weak. She rolled back into the damp sand as the waves washed gentle around her, over her. She lay silent for a long, long time, feeling the sand warm then grow hot beneath her, burning into her core, to the heart of her very being.

Much later, as the night chill fell across the sand, she arose. The exhilaration was spent. She licked her lips like a cat, seeking the last traces of pleasure. Found nothing. She retreated from the reaches of the sea where she had found such comfort, known such pleasure. The salt of it made her pores ache. The transmutation was beginning. Time, so little time. She crept back up the beach, feeling the sand give way a little and a little less with each step. She had to escape the sea. If she was there at the time of the change, it would surely claim her. She could feel the warm propel her toward the distant lights on the cliffs. There she could wait. Wait like the wind. Like the sea. Ancient, deep, and unforgiving.

Last Call

Three A.M. and the rage of the city is spent to the silence of the robbers and the damned. Silence cutting clean and deep as a blade. Leaking quiet: spilled blood and tears. It was to this silence Mara finally came. Quiet as a shadow, she crept through the streets, following the scent of the warm. She moved quickly, then slowly. A page from someone's newspaper scurrying through the gutter, a breeze catching a flag unaware. Moving. Waiting. Moving again. Deep and old. And unforgiving.

It was the warm that brought her finally to the alley beneath Babe's bar windows. The warm that spilled out through the grating, wafting perfume on the night air. The warm that made her lips part, her tongue tentatively touch the roof of her mouth, move to the back of her teeth, then moisten her lips. Dry. Tasting of salt. Cold. Hungering for the warm, for the taste, the very ecstasy of the warm.

Night winds scuttling dust demons past the alley stirred a cache of trash, shooting it out of the gutter, across the sidewalk to brick and battered buildings where it clung, rattling out an eerie rhapsody. Mara shivered slightly and pressed closer into the patch of brick wall beneath the open window, breathing deeply. Cold mortar scratched her cheek as she hugged the wall, lifting her face to the space just below the window, as if the very scent of the warm could fill her, would satiate her need, her want. The night hung dark and restless, a full moon casting about for figures to shadow. Finding none in the alley, it moved on.

In the street, deep lavender shadows cast by the big purple neon sign burned cold and silent against the dust-gray city sky, turning bits of newspaper, shattered half-pint whiskey bottles, the shards of somebody's violated Hefty bag into fragile works of art. Filled with life from the night wind, soft colored shadows playing against it, the trash trembled, almost breathing, shuddering against the dawn when it will be, once again, only the castoffs of living.

The hot white of headlights shot down the alley, exposing nothing. Shadows streaked into the dark. Mara's black eyes burned like coals against the intrusion that flashed against the wall opposite where she was, still as night itself. As quick as they'd come, the lights were gone, save for the pale yellow glow at the far end of the alley as the car's left-front door opened. Mara sensed the woman before she saw her: big, full, but hungry, too. A woman of large appetites. A woman used to sampling many things. A woman used to wanting so much more.

Danni stepped into the alley, closed the car's door carefully, and leaned against the front fender, puffing on a pipe that she occasionally held to a flame. The heady scent of smoke and the warm filled the night. Mara moved slowly, quiet as whispers toward the woman, toward the warm. Sensing the moving shadows, Danni peered into the alley's black depths. Her eyes burned from the smoke, watered against the chill air. An empty vodka bottle rattled, then exploded on the concrete with a hollow pop. Danni's stomach knotted, her right hand trembled, the lighter's flame suspended over the wooden pipe. A yellow tomcat yowled and darted down the alley, his tail bushed in fright. Danni laughed as the cat sped past her and vanished down the street.

She checked her watch. Almost an hour until last call. An hour left to find someone to warm the night, or what was left of it. Wasn't that why she'd brought the Elvis car instead of taking it back to the garage and picking up her Honda? A sensible machine, but tonight she wanted more—she wanted glamour and fantasies come true. That was why she hadn't taken the limo back to the garage, hadn't changed out of the black jodhpurs and the red velvet jacket. Why she'd unbuttoned the top four buttons of the ruffled shirt. Why she was at Babe's an hour before last call.

Most of her day had been spent showing a trio of sisters from Des Moines, Iowa, the wonders of San Francisco.

"We're with the Women of the Moose," Laura had announced, crawling into the depths of the car's interior. She'd reminded Danni of her mother's youngest sister, a woman who had devoted her life to raising sons and chickens.

"This was Loretta's idea. She's our travel agent back home," Irene had explained. She was a nervous version of Laura, who clutched her patent-leather handbag close to her bosom.

"Loretta said you have complementary champagne, is that true?" Elmira had asked, her hands trembling as she'd tried to light a cigarette. She'd laughed nervously when Danni smoothly extended a flame to her waiting Marlboro.

"Can't you wait until lunch?" Laura had demanded, prodding her youngest sister with the dog-eared tour-guide book she would use like a Bible the rest of the day. Laura had slammed the limo's door shut before Danni had a chance to close it. "Time is money," she'd announced, pushing the list of attractions she'd compiled through the privacy window at Danni. First on the list was a driving tour of Golden Gate Park. "Let's hit the road."

Danni had added a few stops that Laura's list overlooked. She'd even settled them on the Hyde Street cable car and was, at least to Laura's amazement, waiting for them at the end of the line. "I told you she'd pick us up," Irene had hissed at Laura, who'd shushed her. At that, Danni had laughed out loud. The sisters could have been her own aunts: simple, direct, suspicious, demanding, but sweet, too. Like the way they'd invited her to eat lunch with them at Fisherman's Wharf and were genuinely disappointed when Danni had declined. In truth, Danni was famished, but for something unnamed, something that had nagged at the edge of her mind for a very long time.

She'd been spinning the fantasy for—well, for as long as she wanted to remember. It kept her sane while she worked, invaded her dreams while she slept. A hunger without a name or a face, but a hunger just the same. She imagined it was a woman but couldn't even be certain of that, for what woman could fill a need this deep, could warm an emptiness so great?

So as she drove the sisters through the city, Danni's hunger began to build a fantasy: A woman, soft and warm, who laughed easily, whose eyes shone when she smiled. Beautiful in the classic sense, perhaps, but more than beautiful in the way she moved when she danced. A woman full of herself, bright with life, and daring. A woman whose hunger could meet, could match Danni's own. A wild adventuresome amazon of a woman who, if she'd known great sorrow, wasn't bowed by it. A woman who knew not to take life's mysteries too seriously. That was the dream that kept Danni company while she drove the Des Moines sisters through the city, who licked at her lips, tasted her honey while she slept.

But even if she didn't find her fantasy tonight, Danni had no intention of waking up alone. It would be late by the time she arrived at the bar, the crowd thinned to the stragglers and the hopeful. The woman would be there, Danni thought. Beautiful and hungry. Alone, but not lonely. Danni would buy her a drink; just one for the road; there was a bottle of champagne on ice in the car's bar. They'd drive. Maybe to the beach. Maybe into the hills to watch the sun rise. Only from the backseat, they wouldn't see the coming of the day, and it wouldn't matter at all. Danni smiled; even Elvis Presley would be proud of the plans she had for his car.

Of three limos owned by Star-Struck Limousines, the Elvis car was Danni's favorite. She and A. J. had been business partners for almost two years. Danni had put up the money her father had left her when he'd died, supplemented by a loan that was supposed to be spent on business school. She'd dropped out after the first semester. A. J. had talked Matty into borrowing her share from Babe Daniels, who was very loud for a silent partner. They'd started the business with two cars: a classic white Rolls-Royce from the 1930s that had been owned by Veronica Lake and a pink Caddy with matching leather interior that had belonged to Jayne Mansfield. The Elvis car had turned up at a car auction; Danni had closed her eyes and, hoping she wasn't crazy, topped the last bid.

The car was a white 1971 Cadillac limousine that Elvis Presley had owned but never used. It was a bargain because its rhinestone-studded white velvet upholstery had been ripped out and sold off by the square inch after Elvis died. A man named Reggie had acquired the car in payment of a gambling debt from one of Elvis's body guards. Reggie had big plans for the fortune the upholstery was supposed to generate, only there wasn't that much demand for velvet by the square inch. So Reggie had hauled what was left of the limo to the car auction.

Having a limo service featuring cars once owned by dead movie stars had originally been A. J.'s plan to get rich or, at the very least, famous. So far they were neither, but the cars amused Danni, in a macabre sort of way. In extravagant moments she imagined a fleet of cars that played a part in a few of the black moments in history—like the car that carried Bobby Kennedy to his fateful meeting with Sirhan Sirhan; or the fabled limo that snaked through the back roads of America with a drug-wracked John Lennon crumpled inside; or the one Marilyn Monroe rode home in after the studio fired her. So far, though, they'd had to settle with their modest fleet, and the Veronica Lake car wasn't even running at the moment. A. J.'s buddy Josey had spent most every Sunday for the last four months in the garage working on it. If anyone could get it running again, it would be Josey, A. J. said, but it hadn't happened yet. So Danni concentrated on making the Elvis car a success: More people wanted that car anyway.

It was Danni's idea to etch two different views of Elvis's profile on the privacy glass. She liked to tell clients that she was chauffeuring Elvis through eternity while he sang to himself. Mostly they thought it was funny, too, but once in a while a real Elvis fan would glare at the blasphemy. Danni had even programmed the stereo system with nine hours of uninterrupted Elvis songs. No repeats. With seasonal and inspirational music on request.

The Elvis car was so popular that Danni wanted another

like it, but A. J. had talked her into Jayne Mansfield. Danni suspected A. J. had a crush on the blond bombshell who'd lost her head on a deserted Nevada highway. A. J. said, "Don't be silly, it's strictly business." Besides, there were no Elvis cars on the market when Veronica Lake gave up the ghost, and Jayne Mansfield was a bargain. Business was good, especially in the spring and summer, when weekends were booked up months in advance for weddings and proms. At other times, they were part of convention packages offered by travel agents, which was how Danni had ended up with three Women of the Moose from Des Moines, Iowa.

That evening the sisters had been joined by their husbands—men with big rough hands who looked uncomfortable in their stiff white shirts and green silk ties with moose heads on them. They'd finally decided to call it a night after a trip to Twin Peaks to see the lights of the city spill out beneath them. As each of the sisters stepped into the glow of the Hyatt's marquee, Danni handed her a single red rose—an extra service paid for by the husbands. "Why, isn't she the sweetest thing?" they asked each other as they disappeared into the hotel. Danni had pocketed the tip the husbands had awkwardly collected. Small for San Francisco but generous by Iowa standards, she'd reasoned, rolling down the windows and cranking up the all-night rock station. At least they didn't puke on the upholstery, like the kids on prom night. She pulled into the night, on her way to the bar, to her dream. And to Mara, who was waiting there in the shadows.

Danni haunted the bars mostly after midnight, saying she was too busy to go any other time. The truth was that she was tired of them, of the games and the crush of the crowd that surged in waves across the floor like fitful dreams. Once they had offered excitement, but that had faded with each year passing. In her hard-drinking days, she'd gone there to drink and to fight, to find a release for the rage that burned in her gut. Those were the days when Babe, her face purple with anger, had banned Danni from the bar "for life." She'd relented, of course; she always did. But by then Danni had met Tinder and life had settled into a quiet routine. She'd loved Tinder: at first too much, and then not enough, but never just enough or just right. Finally Danni moved into the garage, where she kept a cot and her driving clothes, and a change of jeans and underwear. After Tinder moved to Phoenix, Danni went back to the apartment that they'd called home in happier days. Once while she was cleaning a closet, she'd found a forgotten T-shirt that Tinder had left behind. Danni slept with it curled in a ball under her chin until it stopped smelling like the woman she'd loved, once.

Had she felt the hunger, the emptiness, even with Tinder? It was a question she asked herself too often lately, and there was no answer. So she prowled the night as if she was hunting a dream only half-remembered, stalking something, even if she didn't know what she was hunting any longer. Sometimes it reminded her of how the men with their deer rifles would sit still as air in the trees, almost afraid to breathe, waiting for their prey to pass by, unaware. Some nights she was the deer; most nights, she was the hunter.

Rapping the empty pipe against her palm, Danni straightened and headed toward the bar, unaware of the force that sensed her every movement from the depths of the alley. Mara waited until the transmutation was complete, until she could pull Danni's fantasy on like a robe. The alley was empty before she stepped from the shadows and toward the bar door, following the heady scent of Danni, of the warm. The door whooshed gentle behind her. Narrowing her dark eyes against the blue smoke and odor of whiskey and beer, she made a slow survey of the room. Everywhere was the scent of the warm. Mara closed her eyes, letting the scent fill her, the hunger rise from her belly that was already churning with want. The warm was everywhere: along the stretch of the bar, swaying on the dance floor, moving around the pool table, huddled at tiny tables. She leaned into a space of cool wall and smiled.

Already most of the crowd had called it a night, gone for breakfast, headed home. Only the hopeful late-night hangers-on were still going through the Saturday-night shuffle. Behind the bar, Matty was doing a tired two-step to the mumbled drink orders, which always move in slow motion after midnight. Responding to a secret cue, a trio of women rose from a table and pushed past Mara into the blackness beyond the door. A couple who had been necking in one of the far corners for the past half-hour emerged from the shadows to share a beer and a bar stool. One balanced on the other's knee, their arms entangled around each other's waists, breasts touching, fingers entwined. Mara approached the bar with tentative steps and claimed an empty stool in a cluster of empty stools. She ordered a drink and turned to watch the dancers who were seducing themselves in the mirrors where blue and red lights flashed to loud and relentless music. Danni emerged from the hall by the rest rooms and paused, her eyes drifting across the dance floor, past the tables of would-be lovers, down the row of women at the bar. Her eyes settled on the woman who was sitting alone. Waiting. Watching. She caught Danni's eye and smiled, then lowered her gaze as she turned back to the dancers.

The woman was a brunette with curly hair that grazed her shoulders, a compact well-muscled woman whose tanned skin seemed to make her white vest and shorts glow in the bar's pale light. Drawing closer, Danni saw the vest and shorts were white leather decorated with fluted etched silver buttons centered with tiny chunks of turquoise, the color of the woman's eyes. Fringe from the short vest tickled her bare midriff. Beaded leather ribbons meant to close the vest hung loose. She wore no jewelry except for a beaded leather thong tied loosely around one wrist. Occasionally, she fingered the beads, almost nervously, turning them, rolling them against her wrist. If she was aware Danni was watching, she didn't raise her eyes in acknowledgment or greeting. Instead, she sat there motionless except for how she turned those blue and silver beads.

Snagging the stool next to the woman, Danni leaned her back against the bar and stretched out her legs. The brunette turned to her, a quick but smooth motion that left one pouting pink nipple trembling perilously close to exposure. She smiled then and stretched, the vest opening across her bare chest, her long neck arching, her hair fully caressing her shoulders. She kicked off the red high heels she'd been wearing, leaving them under the bar stool. She crossed her bare legs, pointed her toes in the way of a dancer. Her arms were hard but smooth and tanned, like those belonging to a woman who works outdoors. Danni's eyes widened, astonished, but then continued to sweep along her neck, across her collarbone, down to where the vest could only try to cover the warm mounds of breasts from view. But her eyes lingered too long. The brunette abruptly lowered her arms, then slipped from her stool, moving across the room to dance with herself in the flashing mirrors, watching Danni all the while. Extending her arms like a young bird unsure of its own strength, she twirled with the music, her dark hair floating above her shoulders, then wrapping across her face. The little vest teased the emancipated nipples that stood flushed and erect from the sudden attention. And Danni watched, the private dancer's secret audience waiting for curtain call.

Danni motioned for Matty, who was deep in conversation with a woman at the far end of the bar. "Who *is* that?" she asked when Matty set a draft next to Danni's elbow. From the way the brunette was dressed, the way she moved, Danni assumed she was one of Luna's dancers.

"Never saw her before five minutes ago. I figured she was with you," Matty grumbled, plucking the twenty from Danni's outstretched fingers.

"I wish," Danni said, exhaling a long low sigh. "So where's the Dragon Lady and her faithful dog Toto?"

"You know Babe's never here this late unless she's got a damned good reason, and Gail and some woman photographer who's here to photograph Babe took Maggie to the hospital. You missed all the excitement."

"So Dracula's daughter's still hanging around? I thought Gail got rid of her."

Matty shrugged. "She tries. But there's not much she can do about it, you know?"

Danni nodded, turning her attention back to the woman in the mirror. "Long end to a long day," she muttered, smiling at the brunette, little traces of lust filtering across the floor. Tense images of light and motion twisted and swirled against the mirror, moving in time to the music, seducing Danni with subtleness and cunning. Flame tongues licked the darkness. The mirror was catching the dancer in a hundred different poses. Her arms extended, she moved her hips slowly, swaying, thrusting, bumps and grinds against the driving beat. None of the other dancers noticed her; the women at the bar had eyes only for each other. Only Danni's eyes were riveted into the mirror, following the woman there. By tilting her head a little to the right and squinting ever so slightly, the woman in the mirror became a circle of dancers cavorting on shooting stars, whirling, swirling, swaying, gyrating on a thousand gold lights that teased at Danni's senses, threatening to catapult them all out of the bar and into a waiting universe of promise and passion.

Something about the brunette was familiar—maybe just the way she moved her head as she swayed to the music, or the defiant lift of her chin when her gaze leveled on Danni. But something familiar, all the same. The sisters, the reefer she'd smoked in the alley, the music, even the pale blue magic of the brunette's dance were intertwining like a tapestry on a loom in Danni's brain. The music had fallen out of synch, a little too slow, dragging, then speeding up without warning. It was like a movie: Danni was the audience; the brunette was the star. Only, it was all to crazy rhythms, as if the little hole in the record had somehow gotten too big and the record was moving back and forth, making not-quite-warped, not-quite-right music. She tried to turn away from the image in the mirror and realized her body had suddenly grown heavy, too heavy. The bar had turned to slow motion. Except for the brunette in the mirror.

Throwing her head and shoulders back, she bent low, her back arched, her beautiful breasts fully exposed. With one hand extended to the floor, the dancer lowered her shoulders to the parquet of the floor. She extended first her right leg, then the left, her toes pointed, her eyes never leaving Danni's. She was alone on the dance floor now, and yet it seemed nobody but Danni was watching. Then she sprang erect again, quick as a cat. Her fingers caressed her own flesh, patient and un-ashamed, challenging any lover to be better than those hands. Danni trembled, suddenly aware that she'd been holding her breath for a very long time. She exhaled, feeling as if the rush of air were being pulled from her. The dancer fell in and out of focus, like the music. Throbbing. Pulsating.

She hadn't felt that way since . . . well, in a long time. That feeling of naked passion surged through her breasts, across her belly, into her cunt, then spilled down her legs. It was like that the first time she'd ever kissed a woman. Although in seventh grade, Robin Lee Gaye wasn't really anybody's idea of a woman. Robin Lee had brought a bottle of 7-Up that was half vodka—she'd poured the 7-Up on her mother's prize azalea and was relieved for months after that the plant hadn't died. They'd sat on a garbage can in the alley behind the YWCA the night of the Spring Swing. None of the boys ever asked either of them to dance. And the girls always outnumbered the boys three to one at such affairs, which meant the unpopular girls danced with each other. That spring, Danni and Robin Lee were both unpopular.

In the shelter of those dances, held in the same room where they took ballet lessons on Tuesday afternoons, Danni Ford first felt the electric shock of breasts touching almost unaware. Then, as she and Robin Lee shared the 7-Up bottle, they'd touched no longer by accident. Danni sometimes could still feel the stiff lacy ruffles on Robin Lee's bra. She'd touched many women since then but never with such innocent tenderness and fear. Funny, she hadn't thought about Robin Lee in years. They didn't have much in common anymore: Robin Lee was still waiting tables at the restaurant she and her husband opened along the highway in the same town where they'd grown up. The last time Danni had seen her, they'd stumbled over things to say, in the way of old friends who time has turned into strangers. Danni didn't bother stopping by the café anymore, even when she was driving back to the city after visiting her mother. A parking lot was where the YWCA had been.

"Thirty minutes to last call!" announced Matty, jarring Danni back to the bar. The music stopped and the dancer stood motionless. Her skin was damp from a fine mist of perspiration. She glowed under the blue and red lights. Her hair was wet, matting in ringlets. Each breath came hard. Wiping her forearm across her dripping forehead, she smiled full and open at Danni, who mock-applauded. The dancer started across the floor to where Danni was waiting. The music had started again, but she didn't seem to notice, or maybe to care.

"You were wonderful," Danni offered hoarsely. She wanted this woman, this wild untethered creature of the night. Wanted to pull close her fire, to drown in her, to be consumed by her.

The brunette nodded; her eyes burned against Danni. *Everything. In me. Me. Mara. For . . . me.* Danni heard a guttural voice throbbing in her brain, though no words were spoken. Danni tried to break the woman's gaze, which was boring into her core. Her brain was pulsating, hot, fever-flushed. Danni closed her eyes and saw the sea rolling, crashing, until her lips could taste the cold salt mist rising. Rising. *Take me!* the voice cried, soaring until it became nothing more audible than a gull's cry.

And Danni nodded, taking Mara's arm, guiding her into the waiting night.

Mara curled on the seat next to Danni, her head resting warm in Danni's lap. Danni's right hand played in the damp ringlets as she drove, following the winding highway to the sea. Up. To where the stars seemed to connect with the limo's headlights. Then down. The Elvis car snaked along the sea cliffs, through groves of eucalyptus, on its way to the ocean while dawn began to tickle the edge of the hills. Finally, Danni turned onto a narrow road that led to a strip of beach. It was a popular spot for tourists, but it would be hours before any tourist would come here.

Careful not to disturb Mara, Danni opened the driver's door and listened to the sea roar. Mara stirred. Kissing her awake, Danni's hand moved easily under Mara's vest. Mara raised her lips to Danni's, her tongue roaming. She breathed then, inhaling the warm, wrapping her arms around Danni, pulling her down. Mara's smooth skin turned to goose bumps under Danni's touch. She tasted of salt, like the sea air.

"Come with me," Danni said, taking Mara's hand as she stepped out of the car and into the night. The sand prickled against Mara's bare feet; she had forgotten her shoes at the bar. She breathed deeply, tasting the sea on the night wind. Danni unlocked the back door of the limo, turned to Mara, and smiled. *Want me.* The words howled on the wind. Gulls called, beckoning the dawn. Danni opened the door for Mara, who eagerly slid inside. Mara smiled, feeling the warm close around her.

"A cave," she whispered. "A white cave." Her voice was throaty, heavy with an accent Danni couldn't place. A beautiful voice that sounded like thunder very far away. And then Mara touched her.

Hands that fluttered like an angry hummingbird moved across Danni's chest, over nipples that rose hard and puckered to Mara's lips. Gathering both breasts in her hands, Mara buried her face between them, murmuring words of love, of ecstasy in a language Danni didn't understand. Sucking. Inhaling. Stroking the angry nipple with her tongue, rough like a kitten's. Turning from one to the other, until Danni was sure the rest of her body had somehow fallen away. She looked down at Mara, who raised her eyes in what looked almost like love. "Do you want me?" she asked, and Danni moaned softly, letting Mara fill the emptiness she'd carried for so long.

Then Danni pulled her up until Mara lay next to her, hard nipples touching, flesh warming flesh. Burying her head in Mara's neck, Danni licked and nibbled the soft salty flesh there. A few inches below her earlobe, Danni felt the telltale smoothness of a wide scar—two, maybe three inches long—and Mara squirmed, protesting. Danni's lips moved on—to the hollow of her neck, down her chest, to the gentle rise of breasts, surprisingly cool. Cupping one in each hand, feeling the flesh move under her fingers. Kneading like a kitten as Mara moaned softly with each touch.

They helped each other out of their clothes, shivering a bit, as much from embarrassment as from cold. Mara was beautiful in the pale light that was beginning to filter across them. Her arms stretched out to Danni, who came to her. Mara kissed her deeply, then let her tongue trail along Danni's jaw and down her throat. Her tongue paused over the skin that covered the powerful jugular. Mara felt the warm moving under her lips. Close. So close. Danni moaned and the tongue moved on, Mara's hands already exploring the fine down of Danni's legs. Fingers warmed by the tangle of damp hair. Sliding her fingers into the damp, Mara separated the layers of pink flesh and brought her face close, inhaling the warm. Pressing her cheek against Danni's open cunt, Mara lapped patiently at her clit, played with it, tongued it until Danni arched her back, waves of greedy passion slamming into her chest. She frantically massaged her nipples with one hand, the other knotted around one of Mara's breasts.

Moving then, Mara lowered herself along Danni, whose own tongue bored into Mara's own open cunt. She tasted the sea there, deep and salty, heavy with the damp of life. No longer could they tell flesh from flesh. They had become a growling, yowling tangle of lust. Howling as the day crested the ridge, they came in a final rushing roar.

They rested, motionless, feeling the dawn. Mara was the first to stir, the worsening hunger was ripping at her belly, like an angry anxious beast. Waiting. She studied the woman naked there beside her. The hunger was beginning to burn the back of her throat. Pulling herself up on the seat, Danni opened her arms and smiled, motioning Mara closer. She looked at Danni closely. "So beautiful," Danni whispered, slipping her arms around Mara's flesh, still slick with sweat, but cool. Mara lay there, feeling the warm, trying to push down the hunger just a little more. Her fingers played in the ringlets of dark hair that curled out from between Danni's closed legs. Then, when she could bear it no longer, she turned to Danni and buried her face in the soft neck, her mouth at the place where the warm surged, so close, too close.

"Do you want me?" she whispered for the second time that night.

"Sure," Danni shrugged, smiling a little, only half-awake.

Mara's breath came more quickly then. She had been so sure of this one. Had given her all she had wanted. Wanted, but perhaps not needed. Mara turned her head a little as if she was listening very hard for voices on the wind. "But do you really *want* me?" The words filled the car like a sudden summer storm.

Danni smiled, then frowned. *Want her?* Did she mean want her the way Danni sometimes still wanted Tinder late at night when she was alone? Or the way she sometimes wanted a stranger whose walk reminded her a little of a woman she'd loved once? *Want her?* She turned the phrase over, examining it carefully. The woman was a one-night stand—an exciting one to be sure, but a casual fling all the same. Did she want more? Is that what she meant? Finally, Danni looked at Mara closely. "I don't understand," she said.

"I know," Mara answered, sounding very sad as she moved her head under Danni's chin. "I know."

Dawn was coloring their stretch of beach in brazen blues when Mara freed herself from Danni's arms, careful not to disturb the sleeper. The hunger was raging in earnest now. Weak and trembling, she pulled herself up in the seat. Cold, so cold, she felt as if the sea were running through her veins. The warm beside her mumbled, then turned a little in sleep. Mara's eyes glowed. Close. So close. And so wrong. She shuddered. The hunger rose in her throat, making her gag with want of the warm. If only this one had understood, had wanted her—no, needed her—enough. If only this one had known herself what it was she truly hungered for. Mara sighed. It wasn't often she was deceived by the warm who thought they wanted her, but only wanted themselves instead. And she could not take without giving, and they could not take without needing. Without wanting. Such was the way with the forces of nature. And Mara was nothing but that.

Her hand was on the door when she saw the bracelet, still knotted to her wrist. Almost as an afterthought, she untied the beaded leather thong, and draped it gingerly over Danni's hand, careful not to disturb her. Then shielding her eyes with her hands, preparing for the dawn, Mara crouched by the door. Only for a moment. The hunger pulled against her, weakening her, then thrusting her into the day. Mara walked into the sea without looking back. She left no footprints in the sand.

And when Danni finally awoke, she was alone.

The Last Dance

Berenice Abbott was, as such things are measured, an exceptional cat. Not because she was an especially shrewd mouser, for she had never caught anything more fearsome than a crippled beetle. Not even for an exceptional climbing prowess—her few feeble attempts had more often left her trembling in embarrassment and fear on the low branches of the youngest elms. She'd produced no remarkable numbers of brave kits—only Kitten, a sweet but simple daughter whose precarious beginnings had left her with few gifts of reason for even the most basic of things that a cat must know.

No, Berenice Abbott had none of the qualities her kind considered remarkable, any more than she had the ability to look back across her past lives, retracing each step through each moment to the Court of Bast, the cat queen. Even in her deepest, most dreamlike state, she could only think back one or two lifetimes. Yet, Berenice Abbott knew she was truly exceptional because, unlike others, she could mend broken hearts. It was her special gift, one she used for women who belonged together but were separated by words, deeds, pride.

No one, not even Berenice Abbott, could say when or how she first developed her gift. But all who heard of it agreed that she was, indeed, an extraordinary cat, a cat worthy of a place in the Court of Bast, where all cats go at the end of their journey. Perhaps not as food-bringer, or far-seer, or great mother, or oracle, or tale-sayer, even, but as matchmaker to those who share cat lives. And in that, Berenice Abbott took great pride.

So it was with her special gift that she'd come to rest in Babe Daniels's office one Saturday night. Of course, Berenice Abbott had no way of knowing how her gift would be needed when Kate Solomon tucked her away in the small cluttered room with its stacks of yellowing newspapers piled in boxes, an oversized oak desk littered with unanswered mail and empty glasses, and a sagging couch.

"Hang tight, Miss Meow," Kate had instructed as she deposited Berenice Abbott on the couch, which smelled of dust and stale perfume, and quickly closed the door behind her. Miss Meow was what Kate sometimes called her when she was about to do something she was sure Berenice Abbott wouldn't like. Kate had roused her from a late-night nap in the van, and carried Berenice Abbott into the bar through the back door, down a darkened hall, past a dozen hands that reached out to stroke her soft white fur. The cat had been too sleepy to respond with more than a low involuntary purr. And then Kate was gone, leaving Berenice Abbott to continue her nap or begin her grooming ritual, whichever suited her fancy.

Her eyes, yellow as a summer sun, quickly surveyed her surroundings: nothing unusual, here. Her pink nose and white whiskers worked against the air. No cat nor even dog lived in this place, she decided. And it was no wonder. Smoke hung blue in the air. Woman music and laughter blasted against the quiet of the night. Stomping feet shook the floor. Woman talk and wails echoed through the walls and under the door. It was enough to fray the nerves of even the most remarkable and adventuresome cat. But Berenice Abbott was not a cat whose fur was easily ruffled, so she stretched, pawed the night, and began addressing a bit of dust on her tail. She was, she reminded herself, an adaptable cat, a necessary trait since not the least of her daily duties was watching after Kate.

There weren't many of her kind who would have undertaken such a task. Most cats she'd met were more content to stay at home, stalking catnip mice and beetles, perhaps an occasional sparrow. But such cats rarely left their own neighborhoods. Of course, she'd heard of cats who roamed the countryside, living wild and dangerous lives, but even they only occasionally ventured beyond the hunting grounds of their birth. Very few cats would do as she had done.

Together, she and Kate had bounced across three thousand miles of country, Eleanor Roosevelt's engine purring as loud and unhurried as Berenice Abbott herself. Sometimes Kate sang; other times she spun long fantasy tales for Berenice Abbott about owls and pussycats who went to sea, and of another white cat who lived in a castle in France. Berenice Abbott listened politely. She never once reminded Kate that only the most foolhardy of cats would ever put to sea with an owl, who could never be trusted not to turn a fearsome yellow eye on his hapless companion once his gullet rattled with hunger. The tale of the white cat was much better. Berenice Abbott was enchanted with Kate's descriptions of that fortunate feline's castle, which was staffed by all manner of truly clever cats. Cats who played music for other cats who danced. Cats who spent their time preparing mice and rats that were served up on silver trays at cat banquets. Berenice Abbott thought it must surely be the French Court of Bast, who in her thousand star lives could have certainly reigned there or anywhere else at all.

Kate had reveled in the stories, embellishing on them, adding a new twist as the miles fell into months. Berenice Abbott eventually became bored, though, and settled down to watch the countryside fly past Eleanor Roosevelt's windows. At night they often camped under trees and stars that peeked into the deep woods, which were filled with strange and awful songs of wild birds and crickets. Sounds that stirred something deep and primal in her belly. Other times they shared houses and rooms with strangers. And their dogs, who growled and shook and scratched and brazenly sniffed, as dogs do. And their cats, who warned her away from their food and shared a bit of catnip, as cats do.

Berenice Abbott always assured her kind hostesses that at home she had her own willow basket with a soft cedar pillow, an endless supply of catnip-stuffed pink and yellow mice, and her daughter-companion Kitten. As they flicked their tails— sometimes in disbelief, sometimes in admiration—she would explain how she was traveling by choice and duty, not necessity.

No one had gathered her into a box and loaded her into the van as she knew humans sometimes did to her kind. Instead, she had haunted the van, finding secret spots and hiding places that later would come in handy. She'd even stocked it with a few necessary provisions for their trip: a bent Ping-Pong ball that she'd discovered in a tall clump of weeds; a tiny government-issue-green toy soldier, just the right size for batting the length of the van; a bit of pink yarn. Chris had been the first to notice Berenice Abbott's interest in the van, but she hadn't mentioned it to Kate until it was almost time to leave. Woman and cat had made a pact: if Kate was determined to go without human companionship—and she would let no woman, not even Chris go along—then it was up to one of the cats. After all, Kate would need someone to curl warm and soft next to her, purring and kneading away the fright of lonely nights. Kitten was far too innocent and inexperienced in the ways of the world. That left only Berenice Abbott.

Chris had carefully broached the idea. "Maybe you'd like some company," she'd said after they'd made love for the second time that evening. The closer the time drew to Kate's leaving, the less they talked, the more they touched. It was as if they were trying to memorize the sense and essence of each other. Johnny Carson was on the television with a green and yellow parrot who was supposed to recite nursery rhymes; so far it hadn't uttered a word.

"Not again," Kate had grumbled at Chris's words, rolling over on her back and glaring at the television. The bird flapped its wings twice and squawked. Still no nursery rhymes. She'd thought Chris was resigned to the trip; at least they hadn't argued about it for nearly a week.

"I think you should take Berenice Abbott," Chris pressed. She was propped on one elbow, watching the television light send kaleidoscope shadows across Kate's skin. Kate dropped her arm over her eyes. The woman who owned the parrot was singing to it, still hopeful that it would do something, anything.

"You know the cat likes the van. She's down there playing in it whenever you've got it open. Other people travel with cats, why not you?" The parrot cocked its green head, looked square into the camera, and winked. Berenice Abbott winked back. The parrot smirked. She wasn't surprised—birds were unpredictable; no one knows that better than a cat. At the sound of her name, Berenice Abbott—who was never called Bernie or even just Berenice—twitched her ears as if to hear better, although she was between them on the bed and had missed not a word. Kitten was curled into her belly, dreaming kitten dreams, although she was well into her third summer.

"Cats don't travel well," Kate mumbled from under her

arm, although Berenice Abbott heard a hint of promise in her voice. "Besides, she'd go crazy without Kitten."

Kitten was a replica of her mother save for her black whiskers and a black tip on the very end of her white tail. She was the result of Berenice Abbott's starcrossed encounter with a worldly black and white tom named Percy. They'd met when Chris and Kate had rented a small house in Ithaca the summer of 1985, while Chris took postgraduate courses at Cornell. Percy had spent his days lounging in the cat-mint patch in back of the house. Berenice Abbott had immediately seen that he was a thoughtful stalwart fellow who wore spectacular black whiskers and carried a truly magnificent tail, tipped in white that matched his boots and belly. His home was across the street with a poet and her woman lover, who played duets. Evening breezes carried their music across the neighborhood gardens where Berenice Abbott and Percy hunted and courted and sometimes played.

Late that summer, Berenice Abbott had retreated into Kate's darkroom, where she produced four blind, deaf, and mewing balls of black and white kitten fur. But only Kitten had survived. Her three sisters had died, one by one, and were buried with Berenice Abbott's silent tears and Chris and Kate's sobs near the edge of that cat-mint garden. Afraid that the last kitten would die, too, for she seemed as sick as the others, Chris and Kate had put off naming her until Kitten was finally the only name she would ever know. Even Berenice Abbott had forgotten it wasn't much of a real name at all.

It was true, she had missed Kitten on this trip. Still, the traveling had worked out better than any of them had imagined. Berenice Abbott was a real trooper, as Kate readily announced to anyone, especially strangers, who had stay-at-home cats. Berenice Abbott rarely complained, and had only gotten lost once, when she'd followed the scent of rodent too far into the woods. She'd stayed in hotels with large mirrors and feather pillows nearly as soft as the one she'd left behind. She'd strolled the length of fishing piers, where men with thick deep voices tossed her fish heads and livers. She'd listened to the mountain birds' songs. She'd watched western sunsets blaze into the blue desert night. Strange fingers had ruffled her fur when Kate invited them into the van, or when she and Kate slept in houses with foreign scents and unexplored hiding places.

"She's a remarkable cat," Kate would say, and the strangers would nod, thinking she meant Berenice Abbott's soft white fur or her long shining whiskers, which turned down just a little. The strangers readily listened to Kate's stories of the cat's special gift as a matchmaker.

Berenice Abbott had brought Kate and Chris back together in 1983. Kate had departed in a flurry of rage and tears, taking only her cameras and a few boxes of clothes, books, and memories—leaving Berenice Abbott and Chris to build a new life. The apartment had been quiet and cold as dread for the first few weeks, then Anne and her surly Doberman, Sal, had moved in. Anne and Chris couldn't get enough of each other, which left Sal to his own amusements: following Berenice Abbott from room to room; stealing her food, even when it was on the kitchen counter; poking his head into her wicker basket as she slept and chuckling his doggy chuckle when she awoke to the stench of hot dog breath against her whiskers. Finally, after an especially terrifying afternoon, Berenice Abbott had retreated to the top shelf of the linen closet; there she had wailed, inconsolable, for Kate and her lost life. That was when Chris had decided Berenice Abbott would be happier with Kate.

But Kate's new apartment was tiny and cluttered with the boxes she hadn't bothered to unpack. Berenice Abbott had yowled at the indignity of sleeping on a lumpy sofa bed and a foam pillow. And she had only one used-up catnip mouse instead of the dozen she'd kept tucked away in convenient spots at home. It was no help to remember that Sal had mauled most of the mice until they were gummy and torn. Kate was rarely in the apartment. Even when she was, her breath smelled of whiskey and cigarettes, and she snored loudly, sprawled half-naked across the sofa bed, oblivious to Berenice Abbott's overtures of concern. So Berenice Abbott was reduced to spending lonely days and evenings hunting the legions of roaches and beetles. She hunted so well and waited so long that eventually Kate's was the only apartment on the block without even one roach inhabitant.

Eventually Berenice Abbott decided that if her fate was left to the pair of errant lovers, she would never get to go home. She considered her options and devised a plan. She pawed through the boxes that were as dusty by then as the cheap furniture. She was looking for something. Something of Chris's. Something important enough, maybe even valuable enough that

Kate would have to call and Chris would have to come. After all, more than two months had passed since the breakup, time enough to nurse hurt pride and bandage broken hearts. Eventually she found what she was looking for: a sparkling blue sapphire ear clip, one of Chris's favorites, one Kate had given her. It lay overlooked in the corner of a box. Kate's leaving had been so sudden and angry that she'd dumped whole drawers into the boxes, mixing her things and Chris's—although Berenice Abbott hardly saw any difference in the endless pairs of socks and underwear and jeans and T-shirts that Kate would pull from one or another of the boxes, rummaging through the mess until something suitable surfaced. And so it was that Berenice Abbott had the bait.

After finding the ear clip, she'd batted it around the dingy apartment for most of a day before Kate noticed and finally bent to retrieve it. Berenice Abbott had been relieved, for she'd long since tired of playing with the sparkling bauble. Kate had raged for a while, then cried for a while, wetting Berenice Abbott's fur with her tears. Then, she'd called Chris.

Chris had arrived before Kate had a chance to gather up the clothes that were piled in heaps on the few chairs and tables in the place, even before she could stow the half-empty cartons of take-out chow mein in the trash, long before she was able to fold up the rumpled unmade sofa bed. Kate had seemed surprised to see Chris standing at the door alone, sad and unhurried. Berenice Abbott had carefully sniffed Chris's pant leg. She wore no scent of Anne or her dog. Chris and Kate had stood, formal and unbending in their pride, such was the pain of their parting. So cold were their voices, they might have been strangers passing in the subway, but hungry and lonely and wanting each other, too. Berenice Abbott could hear all those things, feel the want trying to reach across the pain, and decided her time had come.

Berenice Abbott raced to the tiny kitchen and jumped onto the drainboard by the sink, being careful to knock over the garbage in her flight and then to send a pair of juice glasses, still half-full, crashing to the floor. She yowled loudly, once, then again. The women ran to her rescue. They stopped short by the sink, laughing at Berenice Abbott, her paws soaked with orange juice. Chris reached for the cat, her eyes brushing past Kate, then pausing. Her breath caught short. "Chrissy . . ." Kate began, and Chris had turned, looking into Kate's eyes.

They had smiled and laughed, washing Berenice Abbott's paws, cleaning up the mess.

Later the three of them sat on the sofa bed—there was nowhere else to sit—while late-night jazz played on the radio. Chris and Kate were drinking beer and trying to talk. Eight inches and pride separated them. Berenice Abbott was curled between them, her eyes closed more in thought than sleep. Her head rested on Kate's thigh, her back against Chris's leg. First Kate would stroke her, then Chris would. Taking turns, they were careful not to touch each other. It went on like that for a long time. No one had bothered to turn on the lights, so the room was lit only by the streetlamp outside the window. Berenice Abbott, tired of the waiting, had stretched and curled across Chris's lap, so that when Kate turned to pet her, the women's hands touched. Then Kate's hand had moved as she stroked the cat's fur, continuing up Chris's leg. She didn't pull away or even mumble in protest. Chris didn't go home that night; Kate didn't come home the next. By the end of the week, Berenice Abbott was napping on Chris's feather pillow again. Kate and Chris told everyone it was the cat who'd brought them back together. Hearing the tale, nearly everyone agreed that Berenice Abbott was, indeed, an exceptional cat.

Berenice Abbott was thinking of all these things when a stranger's footsteps stopped in front of Babe's office door. She turned toward the sound, her eyes wide as the door opened. There stood a shadowy hulk of a woman, planted square in the doorway, blocking Berenice Abbott's only escape. Berenice Abbott arched her back and bushed her tail, preparing for battle. And so it was when Babe Daniels flicked on the overhead light that her office was filled with a loud "hh-aahhsst."

"What the?" boomed the woman, blinking, as if Berenice Abbott, who was standing square in the center of her desk, wasn't real. Berenice Abbott spit again; then, as if rethinking the situation, lowered her back, unfurled her tail, and meowed a loud plaintive greeting. "Well, I'll be damned," said the woman, slamming the door with her foot. Woman and cat regarded each other for a long moment. "So whose little lost pussy are you?" Babe asked, starting toward Berenice Abbott, who shot off the desk, across the pile of newspapers, and under the sagging sofa. The woman laughed, a great joyous whoop-whooping sound that bounced through the tiny room. Berenice

Abbott saw nothing amusing but had long ago stopped trying to sort out the ways of women. Babe lowered herself into the chair behind the desk and patted her lap invitingly, asking "kitty-kitty-kitty?" The lap looked warm and wide. With a loud mew that ended in her most refined purr, Berenice Abbott hopped into Babe Daniels's lap.

"Well, you look fat and sassy enough. You're somebody's pussy, that's for sure." Babe was tickling Berenice Abbott under her chin. "So tell me, cat, did Matty unlock the door for you, or are you a cat burglar?" The woman chuckled and Berenice Abbott flicked her tail indignantly. The woman reached for the telephone, her fingers rum-drumming against the desktop, then abruptly dropped the receiver. Setting Berenice Abbott gingerly on the floor, Babe Daniels pulled herself up with a loud yawning stretch. "I'm gonna go get us a nightcap, cat. I drink bourbon. Oh, cream you say? Well, straight up or on the rocks?" She chuckled. Berenice Abbott started amiably toward the door, only to have Babe nudge her away. "Don't worry, I'll be back. Not often I find a little pussy in my office." Babe chortled as she closed the door.

It was ten minutes to last call and Babe Daniels was tired. She wasn't even sure why she'd come back to the bar at all instead of going home. Except that it was easier. Here, nobody asked questions or expected anything more from her than a paycheck. She told herself that, even if it wasn't true. At home, Sharon didn't ask questions, either, and it had been a long time since she'd needed any of Babe's money. *Or anything else from you,* the late-night demons chuckled. Once, Tara had needed her, but now even she was all grown-up. "Left me for another woman," Babe would tease her daughter. In a way, it was true; Tara had Luna and a future. Even without Luna, Tara would be an important woman one day, a woman who would make a difference in people's lives. *Not like her old mom,* the demons reminded her. Babe let the late-night blues follow her to the bar. At least this is mine, she reminded herself, pushing down the demons before they could ask who needed Babe Daniels, even here.

As the boss approached, Matty raised her eyebrows, surprised. It was a rare Saturday night when Babe was here so late. "Sneaking in the back way to check up on us, I see." Matty greeted Babe with a grin and a glass of bourbon and water. She put the glass and a few sugar cubes on a paper napkin in front of Babe's favorite stool.

"Comes with being the boss. You get your own parking space, a set of keys, the whole shebang." Even Babe was surprised at the way her voice growled. Another night it might have been a joke, but tonight her mood was dark and unbending. "Thought I'd stop by for a nightcap and catch up on some paperwork," she lied. "Good thing I did, too; somebody left me a little pussy in my office." This time she laughed, a loud snort that ended as abruptly as it had begun.

Matty's eyes widened. She'd forgotten about Berenice Abbott. Kate had asked if the cat could stay there before she and Gail took Maggie to the emergency room—and that was at least two hours ago. "That's Kate's cat—Berenice something. I'm sorry, Babe. With all the excitement, I forgot about her."

"What excitement's that?" Babe asked, dropping the sugar cubes on the bourbon and rattling the ice a little. She tested the drink and closed her eyes, just for a moment, then picked up the third sugar cube, shaking it absently in her hand like a die over the glass.

"Maggie was here—again. This time she locked herself in the men's john. Kate and Gail took her to the emergency room. Kate actually got her to come out. I figured they'd be back by now." Matty kept adding words, hoping they would somehow defuse Babe, who had banned Maggie from the bar more than once.

"It's Saturday night; they've no doubt got wackos out the ass down at County General. So we do 'em a favor and send 'em one more." Babe exhaled slowly, leaning against the wall. "What do I have to do to keep her out of here? I can't fire Gail. I don't even mind Maggie, really, except when she's—you know." Babe held an imaginary razor blade and sliced it through the air above her hand. Matty nodded.

"Well, you better plan on slipping Crystal an extra fifty bucks when she comes in to clean; the men's room is a fright, and I haven't had the time to get back there—and you don't have the stomach." Babe nodded, lighting a Lucky.

"So what time did all this happen?" Babe blew a perfect smoke ring, looked at it, then sliced through it with her index finger. She'd gone to pick Roxie up at nine-thirty and they'd left right after the show. *You ought to be here, then you'd know these things,* a demon whispered. Babe scowled.

"A couple of hours ago. I don't know exactly. It wasn't one of Gail's best nights, I do know that." Matty stretched and smiled. She reminded Babe a little of a cat. "Some woman came by fairly early, and Gail fell for her—hard, I'd say. But you know Gail's bad luck with women—and this one had a lover who showed up with her other girlfriend. A real soap opera. And poor Gail ends up with nothing but this glove—and, of course, Maggie. With her luck, the woman who lost the glove will either never come back for it or show up on Gail's night off." Matty smiled and placed Sadie's leather glove by the cash register.

"Maybe no luck's better'n bad luck," Babe observed, turning to watch a lone couple swaying on the dance floor. Her mind turned to Roxie—and to Tara, who had cornered Babe in her office before Luna's show. *"How can you do this to my mother?"* kept echoing in Babe's mind. Dammit, why did Luna have to tell Tara about Roxie? *Damn you, for making a fool of yourself,* the demons hissed. Tara had been too hurt and angry to listen to anything Babe had to say, so she'd said nothing that really mattered. Tara still had all the arrogance and indignation of youth on her side; Babe knew that probably better than anyone, even Sharon. And to Babe's mind, Roxie had nothing to do with Tara or Sharon. She was just . . . what? Babe turned the question over carefully. What was Roxie? *Roxie is gone, that's what she is. She said she doesn't need you. She's on her way to Las Vegas, and even if she isn't, she would have left you soon enough anyway. It was just a matter of time,* whispered the demons.

"Kate was saying she thinks she got some good shots of the pool players. Jake was in tonight; she went up against Bo—and lost. She must not get in much practice out there in Walnut Creek. Other than that, it was a quiet night. And you were so worried about the Fool showing up in your cards." Matty's voice was light. "See, nothing to worry about after all. I keep telling you, it's all coincidence, anyway." She was teasing.

Babe smiled, but it felt stiff. *Tell her what your daughter thinks of you,* jeered the demons. *Tell her why you're afraid to go home. Tell her that Roxie thinks you're not a good time. That's the real reason she's leaving, isn't it? Isn't it?* Babe shook her head, trying to clear it.

"Since we haven't heard from Gail and Kate, do you suppose that means Maggie's going to be okay?" Matty asked.

Babe shrugged. Maggie was just one more added to a long line of the lost, scared, and lonely who came to the bar looking for something better. They never really found it, but they kept coming back and back and back until it was hard to tell them apart any longer. When one was gone, there was always one more to take her place. And Babe couldn't think about them any longer.

"You think cats can drink out of old-fashioned glasses?" Babe finally asked, remembering her promise of cream to Berenice Abbott. Matty nodded, although she didn't know much about cats. "Why don't you take that one in my office some cream and then hit the road. I'll close up, kid." Babe winked and slid off the bar stool. She hadn't called Matty "kid" in a long time. Stepping behind the bar, she flipped on the overhead lights and announced loudly, "Goodnight, ladies. If you ain't found it by now, it ain't here. So you might as well give it up and go to breakfast."

Campy was the last of a group of good-natured but grumbling stragglers to shuffle through the door and onto the sidewalk, where they dawdled, calling out good nights and loudly discussing where to go for pancakes. The tide jostled past Kate, who was picking her way toward the door before Babe locked it.

"The bar's closed, Kate!" Campy announced, surfacing from a knot of women. "We're going out for breakfast, wanna come?" Her round face was beaming. A pale fragile woman wearing cut-off overalls and a crew cut had her fingers looped through Campy's belt. "This is Jenny."

"Jeany," the woman corrected. They were both more than a little drunk.

Kate laughed and shook her head. "Some other time, Campy. I left something in Babe's office for safekeeping."

"It'll be okay till tomorrow," Campy urged, still beaming. She very much wanted to show Kate off to her new friend.

"Not tonight, really. Maybe some other time," Kate said, moving away.

Campy shrugged. "Suit yourself," she called, disappearing into the night with Jeany in tow.

"Well, well. Missed your little lost pussy, did you?" Babe greeted Kate when she stepped up to the bar. Kate blinked. In the glare of the fluorescent lights, the bar looked a little like Babe, herself: tired, frayed, ordinary. The magic was gone, and

Kate found herself wishing it back. "She's in the office with Matty. By the way, how's Maggie?"

"The doctors say her hand'll be okay. Otherwise, who can say? She's scared. I think she needs somebody." Kate sighed. "But then we all do, right?" Babe nodded. "Anyway, I told Maggie I'd stay with her for a few days. She needs a friend and it doesn't seem like she's got a whole lot of those left."

Babe nodded. Kate was stalling and Babe didn't know why. "You want a Coke or something?" she finally asked, pushing a glass toward Kate before she had the chance to answer. Babe dropped a pair of red cherries on top of the ice and with a flourish added a twist of orange to the edge. "I used to do this for Tara when she was a kid. Now she drinks Mexican beer from a bottle. Still snitches my cherries and fruit slices, though."

Kate laughed. "Babe, I've got a problem."

"I only listen to problems up to last call," Babe answered, still grinning.

"Okay, then, not a problem, a situation. How's that?" Babe shrugged and nodded. "Maggie's allergic to cats and Gail's got a cat-eating dog. And Berenice Abbott—the little lost pussy, I think you called her—can't stay alone in the van." Babe grinned; the glasses she was washing clack-clacked in the sink. "So do you think Matty could put her up for a few days? She's no bother. She mostly sleeps, and I've got food and her stuff. She really is a nice cat," Kate ended feebly. She'd never learned to ask a favor well.

Babe laughed and Kate looked hurt. "Oh, don't look at me like that," Babe teased. "If you knew about Matty, you'd understand. She and A. J. have got more dogs than the SPCA. That cat'd think she was in hell. Tell you what I'll do, though; you go get her stuff and I'll take her out to the house with me. We haven't had a cat since . . . well, in a long time. Sharon'll get a kick out of it. And Berenice Whoosit'll have almost a half acre of rosebushes to fertilize."

"Berenice Abbott," Kate replied, smiling. Babe nodded.

"Can't say as I ever met a cat with a last name before."

"She's named for a famous photographer, the kind I always wanted to be—and might have been . . . if things had worked out the way I planned." Kate was silent for a long moment, and then smiled almost sadly. "I guess you wouldn't know about that."

"About photographers, no. About the tricks life plays on you? On that, I'm an expert, honey." Babe smiled kindly. "And you know what I learned? There ain't no other options, so just roll with it for the ride, no matter how long it lasts and wherever it takes you. Now hit the road; you got a friend who needs you."

Kate nodded and started to leave, paused, and turned back to Babe. "You're sure, I mean about Berenice Abbott? About her staying?"

"Sure I'm sure. I offered, didn't I? Now go kiss your pussy good-night and let me close up." Babe turned to the cash register. "And go out the back way; I don't want nobody thinking I'm running an afterhours club."

When she was finally alone in the bar, Babe Daniels drained the last of the bourbon and walked toward her office, where Berenice Abbott was waiting, licking droplets of cream from her chin. "Well, it's you an' me, cat," Babe announced, tucking Berenice Abbott under her arm and carrying her back to the couches by the big-screen television in the main room. "You up for a little Bogey and the *Maltese Falcon* on the 'Late Late Show'? Don't worry, if we've missed some of it, I'll fill you in. I probably seen it a dozen times," she told the cat, who purred in reply.

The bar was dark when the Mustang's headlights shot across the gravel parking lot, catching the bumper sticker on Babe's orange Toyota: The Personal is Political. Tara had given it to Babe after they'd come back from the national March on Washington the year before. They'd marched arm in arm with lesbian mothers from all across the country. Babe had made friends, fallen in love two or three times a day, and come back bubbling with stories that had entertained Sharon for weeks.

There were some stories Babe didn't tell, even to Sharon. "You should've seen Ma," Tara had confided days later when she and Sharon were alone in the rose garden. "There was this woman from the District—way younger than me—and she had a baby and this little boy. He was too little to keep up, and she ended up trying to carry the baby and him. She was all alone; you could sort of tell. It was so hard for her; you could see it in her face. And then Babe's over there putting that little kid on her shoulders. She carried him for the whole march. For hours.

And she never put him down and she never complained. I always thought she had a bad back."

"She does," Sharon had answered, turning to look at her daughter closely. "She does."

Sharon parked next to the Toyota and doused the lights. She sat for a long time in the dark and quiet trying to decide what to do. Morning was close and she suddenly was embarrassed to be sitting alone in a parking lot behind a bar. Waiting. "Waiting, the passion of the lonely" echoed through her mind. It was a line from a poem she'd written years ago, not long before she'd met Babe. Funny how lines from the past manage to intrude, she mused. Funny, too, how that one line was the only thing she could remember about the poem. She lit a cigarette. She told herself she was gathering courage. The courage to get out of the car and unlock the back door of the bar. The courage to go inside and find—what? She could leave and Babe would never even know she'd been here. Go back home to her bed, no, their bed, and wait. But she felt as if she'd been waiting for eternity. Or find an all-night diner and have breakfast, read the early edition of the Sunday paper. Let Babe wonder where she was for a change. If Babe came home. No, when Babe came home.

Sharon imagined Babe pulling into their driveway. Would she wonder where the Mustang was? Would she even notice? Sharon couldn't remember if she'd closed the garage door and it suddenly seemed very important. Babe would turn her key in the lock, slip off her shoes without bothering to unlace them. No wonder they fall apart, Sharon thought. Padding in her stocking feet, Babe would go to the kitchen for a glass of milk, then to the bathroom, then she would open the bedroom door. For the first time, she would notice how dark, how truly quiet, how cold the house was, and how empty. It had been so cold there lately, even in the heat of the day. The kind of cold that can only come on the heels of love. Lost. Dying. Was it? Did it even matter? Sharon didn't know. She'd never had to think of it before.

And what would Babe do? Would she slip into her bed, no, their bed, and try to sleep, listening to the clock tick, a relentless reminder of time sifting too slowly? Six o'clock. Do you know where your lover is? Would she run through the house looking for Sharon? Into the rose garden, calling her name?

Tears streaming? It was unlikely. Babe Daniels was, after all, no Stanley Kowalski.

More likely, she'd get up, drink bourbon, and wait. Spread the tarot cards and wait. Make coffee and wait. And then, when Sharon finally pulled into the driveway, she'd dart for the bedroom and pretend to be asleep. As if the bourbon and the cards and the hot coffee still on the stove wouldn't give her away. "Couldn't sleep?" she would ask gruffly, pretending to rub the sleep from her eyes. And Sharon would shrug and shower and make breakfast and go into the garden, waiting for the words from Babe that wouldn't come.

Is that how it ends? In a series of seconds that can't be identified, so that you can never say with any sense of assurance: "Yes, that is the moment when my lover started to leave me. That is when the ending began." Or was it ending for them? Maybe it had only changed, leaving them unaware. Had they spent so many years having their lives revolve around Tara, then the bar, then Sharon's books that they hadn't even noticed change? Was that possible? Surely, this wasn't the first time they had felt pulled apart, like a jigsaw puzzle waiting to be pieced together again. Or was it? Sharon had to know, and the only one who could tell her was Babe.

Her key still fit easily in the lock. Somehow, she'd imagined it wouldn't, she'd used it so rarely over the years. The bar was so much Babe's that Sharon rarely went there alone anymore. In the early years, though, it had been different. She had often slipped downstairs after hours to help Babe close up. Then they would walk upstairs, holding hands, wishing for morning not to come so quickly. Those times seemed special now, and lost somehow. They didn't come often—no, ever—anymore.

Babe had never understood why Sharon avoided the bar after they moved. At first, she had charged it off to work and Tara, or maybe it was just too far to come. Whatever it was, Sharon would never say. "Sharon's a busy woman," Babe would always answer, if anyone ever asked. And that was true, especially in the early years when she and Arlan and Charles were just starting out. But it ran more deeply than that: The bar was a part of the Babe Daniels that Sharon didn't really know. Sometimes she still felt as if she was living with a stranger, even after all their years together.

The hallway was dim, lit only by the EXIT sign that glowed over the door. In the main room Sharon could hear the sounds of the "Late Late Show," an orchestra warning of impending doom, then Humphrey Bogart's voice. She found Babe there stretched out on the couch by the big-screen television, sleeping. *The Maltese Falcon* was on the screen. Sharon stood quietly for a moment. What had she expected: Babe to be orchestrating an orgy in the middle of the dance floor? A poker game with Babe losing her watch or her car or anything else she could put a marker on—which she'd done often enough in the old days? Or just what she'd found—Babe asleep in the bosom of her lover, her bar?

Berenice Abbott was the first to sense the woman in the shadows, although Babe stirred on the edge of dreams. The stranger padded softly through the darkness, hesitated, then moved closer. Berenice Abbott's whiskers twitched, her tail flicked, and she vanished under the couch where Babe was sleeping. The cat's nose worked. The woman smelled of roses and musk and Babe. The mingling of woman smells, each distinct but blended, too, like fine perfume. Even now, so many months and miles since she and Kate had been with Chris, Berenice Abbott could still sometimes catch her essence on Kate.

Babe opened her eyes and smiled as if she'd been waiting for Sharon, who was late but always expected. She looked soft and sleepy, but not the way she did after making love in the afternoon. It was more how she'd always looked when she'd carried the little girl Tara to bed long after she'd fallen asleep in front of the television. *"I love you, Ma,"* Tara whispered across the years. *"I love you, too, snooks,"* Sharon heard Babe answer in her dreams. Snooks. They hadn't called Tara that in years; Sharon couldn't even remember how it had started or why they'd stopped. Sharon smiled back.

"Couldn't sleep," she mumbled as Babe pulled herself up on the couch, making room for her love, her lover, sister, family, and friend. Babe automatically reached for the highball glass with its traces of too-sweet watered-down bourbon. A few shards of ice died under the warmth of her tongue.

"I'm glad" was all she said. They sat quietly for what seemed a long time, watching Humphrey Bogart play a deadly game.

"Babe . . ." Sharon finally began, then stumbled, forgetting all the speeches she'd so carefully rehearsed. Babe raised her eyebrows expectantly. "It's not true . . . what I said . . . about not being able to sleep." Babe looked at Sharon closely. "I woke up and you were gone . . . and . . . for the first time I was afraid, really afraid. You were gone." She was fighting back tears that caught in her throat, washing away her words, leaving the pain.

"Not gone, just not home," Babe answered slowly. She leaned her head back against the couch, her eyes closed, her throat exposed. I could kill her, Sharon suddenly thought. No one would ever suspect me. I could do it and she'd never be able to hurt me again. Sharon shuddered as if trying to shake off the unspoken curse. As if she'd heard the thought, Babe opened her eyes and added the word *yet.* She was tired. Tired of bars at dawn. Maybe even more tired of still finding herself in them. She closed her eyes again and leaned her head back in a silent dare.

"No. Gone." Sharon's words were stronger now; she had beaten back the tears. "It felt like maybe you weren't coming back this time. Ever. Or if not tonight, then sometime you wouldn't. I haven't felt like this since you used to leave me in that ratty cabin on Stinson Beach. And I don't like how it feels."

Babe was silent for a long moment, peeling back the years like the skin of a grape, looking at the soft tangle of webbed memories still moist and sweet inside. She sighed, a soft, almost imperceptible sound. "You remember Tommy Agres?" Babe asked finally without looking at Sharon or waiting for the automatic nod she knew would come. "You remember how he used to call me kid? I can't remember any other man ever calling me that. Maybe they knew better." She chuckled dryly. "Tommy always had that cigarette hanging out of his mouth and it would sort of balance on his bottom lip while he talked. I never could figure out how he managed that. Anyway, he'd say to me: 'Kid, when I bought this place I was the hottest piece of shit in it. Now I ain't shit. And I'm only hot on a really good night. This, *however,* ain't one of 'em.' You remember that? Well, Sharon, it's been one of those nights. What can I say?"

"I'm sorry you had a bad night," Sharon finally said, although she didn't really mean it and they were long beyond idle conversation.

"I should've listened to the cards. They told me. The Fool showed up . . . twice," she added pointedly. "So I should've known."

"Babe, who is she?" Sharon asked, surprising even herself. She hadn't planned to ask. Had promised herself she never would ask. Over the years she'd imagined that the women who caught Babe's attention were like shiny balloons—lovely fancies, short-lived for the real world of the bar and the house and raising a child. Sharon had seen one or two of them, always by accident, on those rare occasions when she'd dropped by the bar unexpected, unannounced. She'd known who they were from the way Babe leaned a little too close on the bar stool, her arm draped protectively around the waist of one or perhaps the shoulder of another. Sharon had seen Babe's eyes gleaming with anticipation as the newest conquest crossed the floor. Babe's women were the real reason Sharon had stopped coming to the bar, although she'd never admitted it to Babe, and only rarely to herself. So it had been easier to come to the bar only when she was expected, because on those nights Babe was always there, hovering protectively over Sharon, showing her off, just like in the old days when they'd lived upstairs. "I won the prettiest girl to ever come out in Kansas City," Babe would boast on those nights. And everyone would laugh and believe it was true, even Babe, especially Babe.

Babe straightened her back, surprised at the stiffness that always crept into her bones after midnight. She looked at Sharon for a long moment, lit a cigarette, and blew a smoke ring. "Does it really matter? She's gone."

Sharon considered this and shook her head. No, the name didn't matter, any more than the face or the way she walked or what perfume she wore. None of it mattered, really. "Are you sorry?" Sharon asked. It was suddenly very important that she know.

Babe snorted. "You know me, Winston, no expectations, no regrets. You're the one who always wanted happily ever after. My one and only dreamgirl who never could stop dreaming." Sarcasm chilled her voice.

"Did you love her?"

"No," Babe whispered hoarsely, shaking her head sadly. "No, Sharon, I didn't love her."

"But you loved some of them, didn't you?" Sharon pressed, prodding, trying to find the point that would prick this flatness that had settled over Babe's face, trying to make her bleed, scream, do anything but sit there as quietly frozen as Humphrey Bogart's Maltese falcon.

"Yes, Sharon, I loved some of them. Sometimes. But never like I loved you . . . love you. Now, do you want a drink?" Babe suddenly asked, standing up and heading toward the bar, a signal the conversation was over, unless Sharon wanted to fight and it was far too late even for that.

Sharon shook her head, new tears welling against her eyes. "I should go," she said, stirring on the couch but taking too long, waiting for some word, some sign from Babe, but too proud to ask.

Berenice Abbott, who had been watching the scene from beneath one of the little tables nearby, followed Babe to the bar, sniffing at her heels, sensing her despair. Not for the love of Roxie, certainly. It was more for the loss of herself. At Sharon's words, Babe's steps slowed, her shoulders slumped just a little. If Sharon had looked, she would have seen, but she didn't look. She only sat locked in her own thoughts.

"Stay," Babe whispered on the breath of a sigh, her back still turned to the woman she'd loved for so many years. Whether Sharon willed it, or heard it, or only wished that she had, neither of them could ever say. But she didn't leave, and she couldn't stop the tears that spilled as quiet and untended as rain. Babe painted a smile on her face and ruffled Berenice Abbott's fur.

"I got somebody here for you to meet, Winston," she called, too brightly, too loudly across the room. Her voice bounced like glass ball through the emptiness. "This here's my newest buddy, Berenice Abbott. Only cat I ever met with a last name." Sharon raised her eyes inquisitively to the bar, where Berenice Abbott was investigating her shadow. Sharon smiled. Babe started back across the room with Berenice Abbott riding on her shoulder. She was carrying a pair of wineglasses and a bottle.

"Ms. Berenice Abbott, meet Sharon Winston, mistress of the Daniels-Winston manor and keeper of the famous Winston rose garden, which it will be your duty to visit at least once or twice during your stay." Babe laughed as the cat hopped from Babe's shoulder onto the couch. In a stage whisper Babe confided, "Better be nice to her; this woman does the grocery shopping and she *knows* where they keep the salmon." Sharon and Berenice Abbott exchanged glances. "Berenice was needing a place to hang her—well, whatever a cat hangs in place of a hat—for a few days, so I volunteered your rose garden as a cat box."

Sharon chuckled. It had been a long time since there'd been a cat in the bar or the house. Not since Humpty, the great yellow tom. Babe had found him stranded on the high wall in the parking lot. They were still living over the bar, and Humpty would spend his days sleeping in the bar and his evenings in the apartment with Tara. Babe had always called him her watch cat: "I work, he watches." Humpty had retired when they moved to the house on Archer Lane. There he became king of the cul-de-sac. He was buried in a place of honor under a Queen Elizabeth rose in the middle of Sharon's garden.

"I was going to call you—about the cat—but it was late when I told Kate she could stay with us. You'll like Kate. She's a photographer from New York, and she and this cat have been living out of a van all summer. Kate says she's photographing the lesbian nation for a book." Babe shook her head and chuckled. "Me in a book on the lesbian nation. Remember when I was a pawn of the patriarchy?"

Sharon laughed a little as Berenice Abbott nibbled at her fingers. "No, Babe, *I* was the pawn of the patriarchy. You were the sexist oppressor of women." Babe screwed up her face and shrugged at the memory.

"Well, whatever. So what do you think? Should we offer my old buddy here a place to stay?"

"Of course," answered Sharon. "I think she likes me." Berenice Abbott had climbed into Sharon's lap.

"She's got good taste," Babe said, smiling. "She likes me, too. She thinks I'm cute, dontcha cat?" She winked at Berenice Abbott, who winked back.

Berenice Abbott nuzzled her head under Sharon's strong soft hands, which smelled of rosewater and glycerin. The hands ruffled the cat's fur until Berenice Abbott purred loudly and narrowed her eyes in pleasure. Sharon's touch reminded Berenice Abbott of how Kate touched her when the world was pressing up against her, when the loneliness was almost too much to bear, even when other women were around. Berenice Abbott had let Kate wet her fur with tears on those nights. She peered into Sharon's face; it was still damp with tears.

Silence fell across them like snow. Babe turned her attention back to the television and Humphrey Bogart. Want grew between them and dissolved against the wall of pride they'd built. Berenice Abbott looked across the distance that separated the two—no more than a yard—and marveled at how the smallest gaps were the hardest to breach.

Finally, Babe broke the silence. "You remember how old Humpty used to dance?"

Sharon laughed at the memory of the yellow tom chasing the chips of pink and blue and gold light that the mirror ball sent across the dance floor. Long after the bar was closed on nights not so different from this, Sharon would come down to help Babe close, Humpty at her heels. Then, before they went upstairs, Babe would sometimes turn on the mirror ball for Humpty's dance.

"Do you dance, Ms. Abbott?" Sharon asked the cat on her lap. Berenice Abbott had no idea what they were talking about but let herself be carried to the edge of the dance floor while Babe turned on the mirror ball and the music. And then the floor came alive with bits of colored lights racing and chasing each other. Berenice Abbott's whiskers twitched in delight. Better than beetles or even snowflakes, the colors scuttled and skidded. She found herself following first a blue one, then a pink, then yellow, her paws never quite quick enough to stop them, but so delightful to pursue.

At the edge of the dance floor, Babe and Sharon stood, laughing and urging her on, until their shoulders brushed. Then their fingers entwined. Finally, their lips touched, softly at first, then longer as if each was tasting the other's want for the first time. Berenice Abbott continued with her game as Babe took Sharon's hand and led her to the dance floor. Wrapping her arms around her love, her lover, sister, family, and friend, they moved to the slow beat of the music. Even when the music stopped, they continued to hold each other.

Sharon's tears were gone. The questions remained, but she didn't have to answer them tonight. Sharon buried her head against Babe's shoulder, letting the warmth of a familiar landscape wrap itself around her. And Berenice Abbott danced, safe in the knowledge that she was truly a remarkable cat after all.

Epilogue

It is dawn now. Traces of light begin to color the concrete, to tame the shadows. The purple neon sign grows cold, its promises muted in the hard light of day. Once again, Babe's is only one more bar on another run-down city street. Rubbish trembles in the gutter. Bits of broken bottles that shone like a pirate's lost treasure the night before, crumble underfoot, waiting for the scoop and swoosh of the street sweeper.

A bum rattles himself free from the doorway of an abandoned haberdashery and stumbles past the bar, stopping for a moment to browse through the garbage cans that line the alley. In another form, another life, he might have been a matron pinching tomatoes in the supermarket produce section, his fingers are that practiced, that meticulous. He drains the last droplets from a half-dozen abandoned whiskey and vodka bottles before stumbling on down the street to Park's Café, where a brown mongrel sniffs and growls, protecting its early-morning find.

The street lies silent. Sleepy cars pause at the traffic lights flashing out red and yellow warnings. An orange truck jerks to a stop by a yellow hatchback. The truck door opens and a pair of women, bleary eyed, still dressed for a party, climb into the morning. They wave good morning, good-bye as the truck bounces down the street. Holding hands, they stand by the little yellow car, kissing, laughing, looking for keys. And then they, too, are gone, leaving the street to the drunk, the mongrel, to the pair of alley cats that roam the doorways and porches and vacant lots.

Soon the light of day will set the street to life in earnest, the Sunday parade of the pious and the pitiful, the righteous and the rejected, the little pieces of humanity that are the fabric of this street where Babe's sits, waiting. Waiting for dusk. Waiting for the time to crank up the magic machine again.

Then, as the darkness settles, the street will change to Babe's domain once again. The purple neon script will blaze away the night terrors. In a street awash with fragile temporary beauty, women will answer the unspoken call, one, two, three, until they number a hundred and more. Crowded up against the bar, they'll forget and remember the good times.